T0193149

SO SAY WE ALL

Other Titles in the Smart Pop Series

SO SAY WE ALL

An Unauthorized Collection
of Thoughts and Opinions on
BATTLESTAR GALACTICA

EDITED BY

Richard Hatch

with Tee Morris and Glenn Yeffeth

An Imprint of BenBella Books, Inc.
Dallas, Texas

"The Mirror Frakked: Reflections on *Battlestar Galactica*" Copyright © 2006 by Eric Greene
"The Gods Suck" Copyright © 2006 by Matthew Woodring Stover
"An Angel on His Shoulder, a Devil on Hers" Copyright © 2006 by Monkeybrain, Inc.
"The Face in the Mirror: Issues of Meat and Machine in *Battlestar Galactica*" Copyright © 2006
    by Natasha Giardina
"M U A C – S 1 G Briefing" Copyright © 2006 by Peter B. Lloyd
"The Natural and the Unnatural: Verisimilitude in *Battlestar Galactica*" Copyright © 2006 by Lou Anders
"*Galactica*'s Gods or, How I Learned to Stop Worrying and Love the Cylon God" Copyright © 2006
    by Charlie W. Starr
"Identity Crisis: The Failure of the Mini-Series, the Success of the Series" Copyright © 2006 by Tee Morris
"Legitimate Authority: Debating the Finer Points" Copyright © 2006 by Steven Rubio
"The Machinery of Love" Copyright © 2006 by Summer Brooks
"Burdens: A Proof: The Stoic Value of the Cylon Threat" Copyright © 2006 by Jacob Clifton
"Stripping the Bones: Raising a New *Battlestar* from the Ashes of the Old" Copyright © 2006
    by A. M. Dellamonica
"Men Are from Aquaria, Women Are from Caprica" Copyright © 2006 by Mur Lafferty
"Between the Stars" Copyright © 2006 by Brad Linaweaver
"GINO" Copyright © 2006 by Bill Gordon
"Cheez Whiz and the Future: *Battlestar Galactica* and Me" Copyright © 2006 by Kristine Kathryn Rusch
"Report to Congress" Copyright © 2006 by Bill Fawcett and Jody Lynn Nye
"Adama and Fascism" Copyright © 2006 by Adam Roberts
"Reporters in Spaaaaace!: A Look at a Rare Media-Saturated Future" Copyright © 2006 by Shanna Swendson
"An Army of One God: Monotheism versus Paganism in the *Galactica* Mythos" Copyright © 2006
    by James John Bell
"From *Battlestar* to *Battlestar*" Copyright © 2006 by Richard Hatch
Additional Materials Copyright © Richard Hatch

Smart Pop is an imprint of BenBella Books, Inc.
10440 N. Central Expressway, Suite 800 Dallas, TX 75231
www.benbellabooks.com
smartpopbooks.com
Send feedback to feedback@benbellabooks.com

BenBella and *Smart Pop* are federally registered trademarks.

Printed in the United States of America

Library of Congress Cataloging-in-Publication data

So say we all : collected thoughts and opinions on Battlestar Galactica / edited by Richard Hatch.
    p. cm.
    ISBN 1-932100-94-6
    1. Battlestar Galactica (Television program) I. Hatch, Richard, 1945–

PN1992.77.B353S6 2006
    791.45'72—dc22

2006022984

Proofreading by Stacia Seaman & Jessica Keet
Cover design by Todd Michael Bushman
Text design and composition by John Reinhardt Book design

Special discounts for bulk sales are available. Please contact
bulkorders@benbellabooks.com.

CONTENTS

Contents

INTRODUCTION

Richard Hatch

THE SEVENTIES: BAD ECONOMY, DOUBLE-DIGIT unemployment, inflation, gas lines, and the Iran hostage crisis—a time when the world was looking for escapism. Following the great success of the *Star Wars* films came a weekly epic space opera with heart, humor, and lots of adventure, the one and only *Battlestar Galactica*: the perfect entertainment vehicle to take our stressed-out minds off our personal problems and give the entire family a big dose of hope, inspiration, and harmless entertainment. Sixty-five million people of all ages, cultures, and backgrounds tuned in to see the debut on ABC in September of 1978, giving one of the most highly publicized series in history a very respectable fifth-place finish in the Nielsen ratings. Twenty-one episodes later *Battlestar Galactica* was removed from the schedule, but not necessarily because of ratings, which listed *Battlestar* in twenty-fourth place and the sixth highest-rated new series of the season, but due to high production costs and the impossible challenge of mounting a theatrical-style series for television on a weekly basis. Please remember this was before state-of-the-art CGI and twenty-four frames per second high-definition cameras, which have made it possible to film faster and integrate special effects more effectively and less expensively. ABC at the time had seven of the top ten series on the air and could afford to drop the most costly television series in the history of entertainment, especially since the ratings, in their opinion, didn't live up to the epic-sized budget.

To the dedicated fans of this series worldwide, however, the departure of *Battlestar* was tantamount to sacrilege. In spite of the fact that critics almost universally panned the new series—claiming it was a *Star Wars* rip-off—generations of fans fell passionately in love with the show's epic and mythological premise. They couldn't get enough of *Battlestar's* heroic themes, including mankind's quest to survive a holocaust by their archenemy, the human-hating Cylons, and following their brothers and sisters of the thirteenth tribe to a faraway planet called Earth. In fact *Battlestar* became a near-religious experience for many fans due to the spiritual overtones and ancient mythology woven into the fabric of the story. Like Moses and the Israelites, the humans and their ragtag Fleet led by Commander Adama (Lorne Green) were forced to leave their homeland chased by the technologically bred Cylons and search against impossible odds for a habitable planet upon which they could rebuild their civilization. It certainly didn't hurt to have one of the most attractive casts on television at the time, in addition to some of the most famous guest stars in the entertainment field, including Fred Astaire, Patrick Macnee, and Lloyd Bridges.

Nevertheless, *Battlestar* got little respect. Lying in the shadow of *Star Wars* and taken to court by George Lucas (a lawsuit that he and Twentieth Century lost, by the way), *Battlestar* was challenged by the networks every week with their executives throwing their very best fare at the struggling series. Added to that, the fact that the ABC executives didn't want the show to be too provocative or alienating in the era of escapism made it impossible for the writers to delve into the rich and meaty premise of the story. All of these challenges finally brought down the fledgling series. There was an attempt to bring the series back in 1980, but with a drastically reduced budget and without many of its original stars, who chose to stay away for their own personal reasons. The spacefaring series, brought down to Earth, died a quick and painful death.

Some twenty years later the Sci-Fi Channel began replaying episodes of *Battlestar*, and fans around the world started clamoring for the return of their beloved show . . . to no avail. The executives at the time didn't believe there were enough fans to justify a revival. The prevailing winds would eventually change a few years later when NBC decided to acquire Universal Studios, USA Network, and the Sci-Fi Channel from Vivendi, and thus began a new era at the studio and a renewed interest in *Battlestar*.

Then came the 9/11 horror, which shocked the world into the harsh reality that we were not safe, and that we couldn't afford ever again to close our eyes or take for granted that our government or institutions were going to do the right thing. We were beginning to demand accountability: more reality and less fantasy. Reality shows and cutting-edge provocative talk formats, along with twenty-four-hour news stations, became highly popular—quickly puncturing our idealistic innocence and bringing the world's harsh realities into our living rooms. We soon began to see much darker entertainment fare hitting the marketplace. Movies and television plots became much edgier, and it was no longer considered politically correct to avoid controversial subject matter. The demise of *Star Trek* and *Farscape*, along with many other SF favorites, paved the way for producers to pitch new ideas to the networks. It soon became clear that the underlying catastrophic theme of *Battlestar* was perfect for the new era, and ripe for a major revival, and the fans knew it. As did Glen Larson and especially producer Tom DeSanto, who pitched the series to both Fox and the Sci-Fi Channel under the leadership of Bonnie Hammer. After several failed attempts to revive the series, the concept of re-imagining the classic series was proposed by the team of Ronald D. Moore and David Eick. They were brought on board by Bonnie and asked to re-imagine the series for a new era. Ron Moore, who had been a producer/writer for *Star Trek: Deep Space Nine*, *Roswell*, and the series *Carnivale*, finally had the opportunity and the vehicle to explore the much darker cutting-edge themes he had passionately wanted to bring to the genre of science fiction for some time. In truth *Battlestar* was born for both eras, but the darker millennium in which we live, along with evolved filming technologies, provided the perfect timeframe, backdrop, and palette for finally exploring *Battlestar's* deeper and more provocative themes, of which the original had barely skimmed the surface. Due to an extremely talented writing and production team, rape, betrayal, moral dilemmas, the horrors of the holocaust, and terrorism could all be explored in highly original ways that mirrored society at large. Just as importantly, they got the green light from the executives at NBC Universal and the Sci-Fi Channel who actually believed in the epic story and supported taking the series in such a controversial direction. With a fine cast of talented actors led by Edward James Olmos and Mary McDonnell, the classic SF story overcame years of controversy and a major revolt by fans of the original series who sincerely felt that their beloved series was going to be ruined as had been the case in recent years with many updated and revived SF classics. With time, through great stories, acting, and exceptional production value, the new version of *Battlestar* was finally able to win over a substantial portion of these very hostile fans and build an entirely new audience who had never even heard of the original *Battlestar Galactica*. The series and story that wouldn't go away finally found redemption, and its place in the sun, with high ratings and rave reviews coming in from major publications all over the country. It's my pleasure to have been invited to be the guest editor for this highly informative *Battlestar* book where writers from all over the country are writing essays sharing their insights and analysis of the *Battlestar* universe, back-story, and character plots. Please join me as we take a provocative journey into what *Time* magazine has called the number one best dramatic show on television, period.

Eric Greene's profound and in-depth exploration of today's political crisis and moral ambiguity as mirrored so successfully in Battlestar *begs the statement from a powerful line in the series: "You cannot play God then wash your hands of the things that you've created." Sooner or later we come to the realization that we're all capable under the right conditions of unspeakable horrors in the name of justice, greed, or maybe fear of what we don't understand. In my hard, fought-for wisdom, I agree.*

THE MIRROR FRAKKED
REFLECTIONS ON
BATTLESTAR GALACTICA

Eric Greene

"We have this fundamental belief in the Constitution, a fundamental belief in the Bill of Rights.... I wanted the ragtag Fleet...to mirror our society in that way but then I wanted...the situation that the Colonials find themselves in to challenge and provoke their notions of society and freedom.... [T]hat sort of challenge to the fundamentals of the system is something that I think we're going through right now.... [T]he War on Terrorism, the assertion of executive power in all circumstances...the long march toward extreme authoritarian governance...those ideas are in the show because those ideas are in the culture right now."
—RONALD D. MOORE, developer, executive producer,
and writer, *Battlestar Galactica*

"THE BEST SHOW ON TELEVISION," proclaim *Time* and *Newsday*. "The smartest and toughest show on TV," raves *Rolling Stone*. "Television's most topical, incisive commentary on current events in our very troubled world," declares the *Chicago Tribune*. "One of the top ten television shows of 2005," according to the American Film Institute. A Peabody award. Respect and praise from the "mainstream." For a *science fiction* show? How can this be? By enmeshing the viewer in a web of troubling doubles, doubts, and transformations that mirror our uncertainty amidst the War on Terrorism and the war in Iraq, Ronald D. Moore's revised *Battlestar Galactica* has, improbably, become the signature show of our wartime era.

The immediate aftermath of the terrorist attacks on September 11, 2001, and the anthrax attacks just one week later produced a paradoxical reaction in the American psyche. Americans, who enjoy few unifying rituals, felt bound together in a shared national grief which, at least momentarily, transcended race, class, religion, and party. And yet, under the surface expressions of unity, something stirred. Having been attacked by infiltrators who had lived among us, Americans felt anxious, wondering if more enemies lurked within. Still reeling from the attacks, we launched a war to defeat terrorism and "evildoers," followed a year and a half later by the invasion of Iraq in order, we were told, to deny a dictator his weapons of mass destruction.

But five years after 9/11, with the U.S. State Department estimating that worldwide terrorist incidents rose to 11,111 in 2005 alone and Iraq increasingly appearing to be a quagmire, the War on Terrorism and the War in Iraq have subverted our national sense of self. At home our government has been antagonistic to the Constitution, averse to truth telling, and allergic to accountability. Abroad, torture in Iraq, conditions at Guantanamo, and the revelation of secret CIA prisons have undermined our international standing and challenged our own understanding of who we are.

With our domestic character and our international conduct under a cloud of suspicion, many Americans fear that we have both been betrayed and that we have betrayed ourselves. We wonder who we are, where we are going, and what we have become. *Battlestar Galactica* taps into that unease and, rather than soothing it, explores it by pulling its audience into a world of divided loyalties, mixed emotions, and shattered assumptions that reflect the instability of American identity in this time of uncertain ends and questionable means.

There are many reasons for remakes, few of them good. One reason is the reassuring safety offered by their sense of familiarity and comfort.

We need not worry about being confronted by the new, understanding the unknown, or empathizing with the foreign. Remakes and sequels typically pre-package our emotional allegiances and let us know what to expect. That is one of the reasons sequels, fittingly if sadly, are called "franchises"—they promise us the predictability and comfort of mass-marketed fast food.[1]

From the beginning, however, Moore's *Battlestar* has radically departed from that formula. Moore, his co-executive producer David Eick, and their writing staff delight in subverting rather than fulfilling the audience's expectations. Male roles from the original *Galactica* series are now female roles. The loving clan of Lorne Greene's "Ponderosa in Space" has been supplanted by Edward James Olmos's fractured and dysfunctional family. Actor Richard Hatch has gone from noble hero to scheming convict. Even the original *Galactica*'s defiant, majestic opening theme has been replaced by the quiet, mournful music of the new *Battlestar*. On the original *Galactica* there was peril, to be sure, but it was usually obvious who the good guys and bad guys were. On the new *Battlestar* your son might turn on you, your father might throw you in the brig, colleagues, friends, and lovers turn out to be traitors. And, oh yes, the Cylons look like us now.

Some loyalists of the original *Galactica* might see these changes as affronts, and in fact Moore was met with some skepticism and hostility when he began his project.[2] But Moore understood that among the few good reasons to do a remake is the chance to foreground artistic or thematic possibilities that were not highlighted originally, to update a format for a new age, to reshape material for a new audience with different interests, concerns, and experiences.

When Moore began developing the *Battlestar* mini-series, just months after 9/11, he was struck by how "evocative and painful" Glen Larson's original concept of the Cylons launching a surprise attack to destroy the

---

[1] Formula movies and TV, like formula restaurants, offer a limited menu, and even if the items are slightly rearranged they are pretty predictable. Wherever you are, you know more or less what's in a Happy Meal, and regardless of who is starring as 007 you know more or less what's in a James Bond film. It is therefore not surprising that fast-food and film franchises have come to be synergistically bound in promotional campaigns—"you've seen the movie, now eat the fries"—the movie sells the food, the food sells the movie, and both offer the simplicity of sameness.

[2] See John Hodgman, "Ron Moore's Deep Space Journey," in the *New York Times Magazine*, July 17, 2005.

humans had become.[3] To an American in 1978, almost forty years removed from Pearl Harbor, the idea of a devastating surprise attack had
become largely that—an idea, an abstraction. But it was less so to those
for whom, for a moment, on September 11, the world seemed to be literally collapsing. Moore's conviction that "If you redo this today, people are going to bring with them memories and feelings about 9/11"[4]
proved correct when the *Battlestar Galactica* mini-series, with a surprise
attack led by sleeper agents as its inciting incident, premiered in December 2003. Like Moore, the audience now saw the concept through
different eyes.

Moore's two key innovations, that the Cylons are a human creation
and that they can replicate and infiltrate humans, opened up new and
powerful resonances in the aftermath of 9/11 when we saw that foreign
policy could have domestic consequences, realized that the anti-Soviet
guerrilla fighters we had supported in Afghanistan had transmogrified
into the Taliban, and the term "blowback" entered our national vocabulary. When Adama told his people, "You cannot play God then wash
your hands of the things that you've created. Sooner or later the day
comes when you can't hide from the things that you've done anymore,"
it was not hard to know what he was talking about.

And the *Battlestar* series, which premiered in October 2004, never
lets us forget the context of that devastation—the first shot in the credits every week is from the mini-series: an aerial shot flying into the Caprica skyline, much like the view that the terrorists would have had
flying into lower Manhattan on 9/11. Whatever they may have meant
before, after 9/11 images that simulate flying toward skyscrapers now
connect us to that lonesome day.

But as in a potent dream playing out our preoccupations, anxieties,
and desires, it is the pervasive tone, more than any one image or plot
point, that links *Battlestar* to our wartime unease. By undermining our
expectations, and the expectations of the characters, the reborn *Battle-*

---

[3] Edwards, Gavin, "Intergalactic Terror," *Rolling Stone*, February 9, 2006, p. 32.

[4] Steven Spielberg would use a similar framing device for his big-screen response to September 11
and the Iraq war—2005's *War of the Worlds*. Spielberg opens the film's action with an aerial shot
flying into lower Manhattan that served as a subtle visual cue linking the movie to the trauma of
the terrorist attacks and invoking the memory of 9/11 as the emotional context for the horrific images that were to follow. If you want a taste of what it would have been like on Caprica when the
Cylons attacked, see this film.

star's myriad inversions and mysteries mirror the prevailing political uncertainty. Just as many of us in the wake of 9/11 held our breath when we saw planes flying toward urban centers, wondered if our mail was laced with anthrax, anxiously followed the news fearing a new attack, or wondered if friends or family members were the latest battlefield casualties, *Battlestar*'s characters are kept on the edge, uncertain about where danger will come from next, when supplies will run out, who can be trusted, and who has buried within them a Cylon sleeper program waiting to be activated. What defines a human? Can a human love a machine? What is love? These are not new questions in science fiction, or in philosophy, but they have a new resonance amidst wartime anxiety. Like wars and rumors of wars, *Battlestar* destabilizes our expectation of stability and security. Doubt dominates as *Battlestar* consistently stresses the uncertainty of identity, the displacement of the self.

Uncertainty is one of the key byproducts of the traumatic betrayals that recur throughout the series: Cylons betray humans, Adama betrays Cain, the reincarnated Cylons Boomer and Six betray the other Cylons, Vice President Baltar betrays President Roslin (and just about everybody else), and no one is betrayed more than the central authority figure, Commander Adama—Apollo, Starbuck, Roslin, Cain, Helo, and Boomer all take their turns defying the "old man."

Cathy Caruth reminds us that the generally accepted psychological definition of trauma is "the response to an unexpected or overwhelming violent event or events that are not fully grasped as they occur but return later in repeated flashbacks, nightmares, and other repetitive phenomena."[5] By this definition the series's characters, while functional, are traumatized. Indeed, flashbacks, nightmares, and recurring images are a *Battlestar* staple. President Roslin had flashbacks to the revelation that she has cancer. Apollo had flashbacks of and admitted "he just can't help thinking about" the civilian ship he shot down when it appeared that Cylons might have hijacked it. Chief Tyrol has recurring suicidal dreams. Baltar's visions of Six may also have been a response to the Colonies' destruction and a manifestation of his guilty conscience.

Trauma replayed as flashback is especially potent with the dramatic first-

---

[5] Cathy Caruth, "Traumatic Awakenings" in Andrew Parker and Eve Kosofsky Sedgwick's *Performativity and Performance*, New York: Routledge, p. 89.

season finale attempt by Boomer to assassinate Adama. In "Kobol's Last Gleaming, Part II" (1-13), Boomer's Cylon programming was triggered, presumably involuntarily. She returned from destroying a Cylon base, was congratulated by Adama, replied, "Thank you, sir," and, still smiling, pulled out her gun and shot him in the chest. The suddenness, intensity, and brutality of the violence is visceral, and the series returns to it again and again—replaying that scene in flashback, mirroring the way we mentally replay unpleasant events in our lives or how we collectively rewatch footage of the Kennedy assassination or of the planes hitting the World Trade Center.

Adama, the series's center of gravity, is probably the most traumatized by the betrayals he has endured. More than anyone, Adama seems haunted by the question "Why do the Cylons hate us?"—a version of the "Why do they hate us?" question so many asked after 9/11. At one point Adama even went to the morgue and, as he asked "why," broke down over the corpse of the Boomer who shot him. Adama admits his anguish when, after President Roslin suborned mutiny by his surrogate daughter Starbuck, his only surviving son Apollo sided with Roslin and broke the president out of prison, and Boomer, "a vital living person...aboard my ship for almost two years," put two rounds into Adama's chest, he confessed:

> *"Betrayal has such a powerful grip on the mind. It's almost like a python. It can squeeze out all other thought. Suffocate all other emotion until everything is dead except for the rage. I'm not talking about anger. I'm talking about rage. I can feel it. Right here. Like it's gonna burst. Feel like I wanna scream. Right now, as a matter of fact."*

Adama held it together, though. He didn't burst. He didn't scream. But Starbuck did. In part two of "Kobol's Last Gleaming," after barely surviving a severe beating by Six, the horror, fear, and trauma became, at last, too much for her and she released the built-up pressure in an anguished scream and an exhausted collapse. Like the scream at the end of Bruce Springsteen's *Born in the USA*, a song born out of the Vietnam War—the last event that so split the nation—Starbuck's scream is suspended, isolated from everything around it. That angry, confused scream directed at nothing in particular and everything in general, that inarticulate shriek was not really meant to be comprehended, just recognized.

Unlike traditional episodic series, the tension and rage do not dissipate at the end of sixty minutes; they persist as they would in real life. Moore and company present traumatized people in a community under stress and leave the tensions unresolved, make us sit and live with anxiety and doubt, just as the characters must, just as the nation must.[6] The visual repetition, the emotional horror, the attempts to comprehend, all mirror how traumas enter our blood, our brains, our bones, how they are replayed and revisited and become a part of who we are, how we carry our traumas as we carry on.

From its inception, *Battlestar* established a series of mirrors or doubles both between the show and real life and between various characters. The series continually offers reflections of twenty-first-century America, reminding us that we are watching a version of ourselves. A memorial wall in a *Galactica* corridor with photos of the dead and the missing is reminiscent of the similar bulletin boards in New York City after September 11. Colonial politics is reduced to a contest of slogans manipulated by consultants, just like our own. President Roslin, like President Bush, is convinced she has been chosen by God to fulfill a destiny. Even giving the pilots conventional names like Lee, Kara, and Sharon, instead of using only their mythic-sounding call signs Apollo, Starbuck, and Boomer, brings them down from Mt. Olympus and renders them more like us.[7]

Fittingly for a series in which we are repeatedly told "all of this has happened before and all of this will happen again," former political science students Moore and Eick have filled the show with historical refer-

---

[6] It's striking how much all of this contrasts with another series that is known for reflecting the current zeitgeist: *24*. *24* may be set on Earth instead of outer space, but it is much more of a fantasy than *Battlestar*. *24* both uses and soothes our anxieties about terrorism by giving us a government agency of seemingly unlimited resources, extraordinary competence, and nearly omniscient technological and intelligence capacity that can flush out its moles, find the terrorists, and solve the nation's most grave crises in a concise and precise twenty-four hours. New threats may arise but there is never any doubt that, like James Bond, Jack Bauer will be up to the challenge. We could only wish that our intelligence agencies were that efficient in real life. We could only wish that *any* government agency were that efficient in real life. (If only Jack Bauer had been running FEMA when Hurricane Katrina hit.) Providing the controlled and reassuring tension and release of a good suspense or horror film, *24* delivers a compensatory fantasy in an age of intelligence oversights, successful terrorist plots, ineffective disaster response, and enduring Iraqi insurgency. *Battlestar* more realistically suggests that maybe you don't solve your problems, or overcome your traumas, certainly not in a day; rather, you must live with them.

[7] The series's production design, terminology, and costuming largely reflect the modern-day U.S., which undoubtedly helps keep production costs down, but also makes it easier to see our own reflection in the series. At times this technique can backfire; the all-too-contemporary sayings and slang—"pound of flesh," "she shoots, she scores," "wake up and smell the psychosis," etc. can be distracting and sever the suspension of disbelief. I half expect Apollo or Tyrol to bust out with "fah shizzle, my nizzle."

ences: President Johnson's swearing-in aboard Air Force One following the assassination of President Kennedy, Jack Ruby's murder of Lee Harvey Oswald after Kennedy's death, 1960s student unrest, even the Salem Witch Trials and McCarthyism. As in any allegory, recognition and resonance in *Battlestar* do not require exact one-to-one correspondence. Thus, contemporary events are not just replicated, but are also refracted, contracted, abstracted, and reshaped to evoke an emotional response or provoke a question. The show continually invokes traumas from our cultural memory to underscore the series's resemblance to us and emphasize the threat that traumas may at any time erupt and disrupt our lives.

Of equal importance to the real-world references are the series's internal doubles: Tigh and Starbuck dislike each other but both drink too much; Baltar and Roslin are rivals but both have visions of divine destiny which may prove to be true or just hallucinations; Baltar sees and hears Six in his head and, in "Downloaded" (2-18), the reincarnated Six saw and heard Baltar in hers; Roslin, contemplating killing Boomer's newborn baby because of the child's link to the Cylons, was intercut with Cylons contemplating eliminating the reborn Boomer because of her link to the humans. The writers repeatedly connect adversaries through their mirrored attributes—in *Battlestar* enemies, at their core, resemble each other. This is most significantly the case with humans and "humanity's children," the Cylons.

During the Cold War, our primary adversaries were Communists, who we generally saw as "godless." In the global political struggle, devotion to God was reserved for "us," not them. Popular science fiction largely followed that construction: *Star Trek*'s Klingons wanted territory not purity; the Cylons pursuing the original *Galactica* seemed bent on genocide for genocide's sake, the Shadows of *Babylon 5* spouted no pious platitudes. But things have changed. In the War on Terrorism we have an enemy who sees itself as just as religious, as pious, as blessed with a divine manifest destiny as "we" are. Any attempt, fictional or otherwise, to deal honestly with the dominant geopolitical concerns of our time must address religion.

Battlestar's Cylons—complex, conflicted, and disturbing—reflect this new reality. Physically they mirror their human creators, but beyond that what is so troubling is that their viciousness serves an ideology that is so recognizable. The Cylons are not wild-eyed terrorists screaming "Allah is great," or even "By your command," but rather they speak in measured tones. Their rhetoric matches our own, their theology is not alien, their religious beliefs probably reflect those of much of the audience. Unlike the idol-worshipping, polytheistic humans, the Cylons are monotheists and moralists. The Cylons seem eminently benign as they earnestly preach, "God is love." And yet they are sociopaths.

The Cylons are a troubling double. The fact that there are enough similarities between us and our adversaries for the Cylons to plausibly reflect us both is what makes them so disturbing. As Al Qaeda uses the language of "jihad," Bush issues the call to "crusade"; as Islamic fascists envision domination by a newly ascendant Muslim caliphate, right-wing Christian fundamentalists pursue a Christian conquest of the world known as "dominion";[8] as the terrorists believe themselves to have submitted to the will of Allah, Bush maintains that he appeals to "a higher father." No one has a corner on intolerance, extremism, or ideological imperialism, and acknowledging that does not endorse the facile ahistoricism of those who blithely compare Bush to Hitler, or the indulgent relativism of those who romanticize terrorists. The mirroring of the Cylons in *Battlestar* and the audience excuses neither the Cylons—"you slaughtered my entire civilization! That is sin! That is evil, and you are evil!" Starbuck told a Cylon and we have no reason to disagree—nor their real-world counterparts, but it does reflect unsettling similarities between both sides of the War on Terrorism.

While using mirrored identities to blur distinctions, question identities, and undermine moral certainty is one of *Battlestar*'s most frequently used techniques, the writers employ another pivotal device—characters not only reflect each other but are constantly transforming in unexpected ways: the loyal Boomer became a Cylon spy, the terrorist Zarek became a legitimate politician, President Roslin defended democracy in the finale of season one, then fixed an election in the finale of season two. In "Downloaded," Six and Boomer, who had previously sabotaged humanity on behalf of the Cylons, were reincarnated and seemed poised to sabotage the Cylons on behalf of humanity. Moore explained that "The show is meant to... make you question things... to keep you

[8] See Michelle Goldberg's *Kingdom Coming: The Rise of Christian Nationalism*, New York: WW Norton, 2006.

off balance and unsettled more than anything else."[9] Thus, the character transformations can be taken as a simple plotting device to maintain the audience's interest. But something more is happening.

These transformations reflect the feeling of instability of identity brought on by 9/11 when we were attacked on our home soil by foreigners for the first time in almost two centuries, when we discovered that we were vulnerable, when we went from assuming most of the world loved us to understanding that a sizable percentage of the world wished us ill. The uncomfortable sense that we might become something unexpected and unwanted is more than a reaction to the attacks themselves, however, but also to how our nation has been impacted by their aftermath.

Despite Bush's September 20, 2001, pronouncement that "We're in a fight for our principles, and our first responsibility is to live by them,"[10] American principles have been ignored, if not abandoned, in the War on Terrorism. Having sworn, like forty-two presidents before him, to "preserve, protect, and defend" the Constitution, Bush has instead presided over the worst civil liberties crisis in decades. Freedom of speech and religion, due process, and equal protection were compromised by the hastily passed USA PATRIOT Act. The government's eavesdropping on private phone conversations without court orders (court orders which are, in fact, easy to obtain) undermines the right to privacy and the safeguards we erected after Watergate and the domestic spying scandals of the Vietnam era. Unsurpassed secrecy and claims of presidential power at the expense of Congress and the courts impede public accountability and jeopardize our system of checks and balances. Affronts like these lead to the conclusion that those entrusted to protect American values have broken faith with the American people. "The greatest dangers to liberty," warned Justice Louis Brandeis nearly eighty years ago, "lurk in insidious encroachment by men of zeal, well-meaning but without understanding."

Nor is all quiet on the global front. Internationally, even prior to President Bush's blunt ultimatum to the world that "either you are with us, or you are with the terrorists," expressions of human empathy tran-

---

[9] Ron Moore, Podcast, "Epiphanies" (2-13).
[10] President George W. Bush, Address to a Joint Session of Congress and the American People, http://www.whitehouse.gov/news/releases/2001/09/20010920 8.html.

scending national boundaries after September 11 included candlelight vigils in Iran, of all places, and the famous declaration by France's *Le Monde*: Nous Sommes Tous Americains ("We Are All Americans"). Much of the world seemed sympathetic to our impending struggle. But while Bush proclaimed that the War on Terrorism would be waged on behalf of "progress and pluralism, tolerance and freedom,"[11] revelations of indefinite detentions without trial, kidnapping, secret CIA prisons, and prisoner abuse have made that declaration vastly less credible.

With Vice President Dick Cheney, sounding more like Darth Vader than Thomas Jefferson, urging us to "work through...the dark side," our allies in the War on Terrorism, necessarily or not, include Saudi Arabia, whose funding of fundamentalist madrases helps fuel terrorist ideologies; Pakistan, whose Pervez Musharraf, a former Taliban ally, pardoned his science advisor for providing nuclear weapons technology to "axis of evil" charter members North Korea and Iran; and Sudan, which is currently engaged in the first genocide of the twenty-first century.

So the repeated character transformations and the unstable identities are more than dramatically interesting, they also resonate with our uneasy feeling about the transformations wrought by the War on Terrorism. But they connect to something beyond that, as well. At the same time Americans watched the *Battlestar* mini-series translate our national trauma into science fiction drama in December 2003, Americans in Iraq were engaged in an altogether different spectacle. That same month, and for two months prior, there were numerous instances of what the Army would later call "sadistic, blatant, and wanton criminal abuses" by U.S. soldiers at Abu Ghraib prison.[12] Before the war, Saddam Hussein tortured people at Abu Ghraib. After the war, we did. The story broke in the spring of 2004 accompanied by photos of Iraqi prisoners, stripped down, tied up, taunted, and beaten by beaming U.S. soldiers. The photos shocked. They sickened. They scared. This was not what America was supposed to be about. This is not who we were supposed to be. And yet there we were: American soldiers, in American uniforms, doing what seemed deeply un-American.

---

[11] President Bush, Address to a Joint Session of Congress and the American People, http://www.whitehouse.gov/news/releases/2001/09/20010920 8.html.

[12] Army report quoted in Seymour Hersh, "Torture at Abu Ghraib" *The New Yorker*, May 10, 2004, p. 42.

With a history bearing names like Wounded Knee, Manzanar, and Jim Crow, atrocities are far from unknown to Americans. But not since the My Lai Massacre did anything more starkly challenge—even mock— our sense of who we were as a people. There we were having had, some believed, the best of intentions acting like the worst of our enemies. There we were reveling in sadism. There we were having gone from liberator to occupier to torturer. There we were, like Boomer, becoming something we would have never thought possible.

More pictures and more revelations followed: prisoner abuses at Guantanamo, indefinite detentions without legal representation or trial, reports of secret CIA prisons, kidnapping, and delivering prisoners to foreign powers to be tortured. How can *this* be? These were things other nations did, right? Less civilized nations. Not the leader of the free world. Not the greatest country on Earth. Not us.

And as the revelations spilled forth, as we saw the truth of what we were doing, the nation was indeed like Boomer—a part of us which had always been buried within, hidden from plain view, could no longer be suppressed. Something ugly, violent, treacherous, and contemptible had been exposed. It might be ignored but it could no longer be denied.

With American deaths at 2,500, American wounded at 18,500, and 30,000 Iraqi civilians dead, as of the time of this writing, American support for the invasion and occupation of Iraq has eroded as more and more Americans have come to see the war as fraudulent in conception and incompetent in execution. Having produced no evidence of Iraqi weapons of mass destruction but instead evidence of American torture, the invasion of Iraq has undermined in the eyes of the world our claim of moral leadership, a claim that was hardly rehabilitated when White House Counsel, now Attorney General, Alberto Gonzalez dismissed the Geneva conventions' torture prohibitions as "quaint."

So, just as events have moved past that horrible day in September, when *Battlestar* premiered as a regular series in October of 2004, its references had moved past 9/11. There was torture in "Flesh and Bone" (1-8). There were secret detentions in "Colonial Day" (1-11) where Starbuck told her prisoner, "We're living in a whole new world. There's no due process." There was rape of prisoners by the authorities in "Pegasus" (2-10).

In the development from mini-series to weekly series *Battlestar's* concerns expanded: The initial question "Who among us is one of them?" was joined by "Will we act just like them?" To "Who will betray us?" was added "What will we betray?" The mirroring of real-world events, like those damning photos from Abu Ghraib, supply both a sense of recognition and suggest that we may become unrecognizable to ourselves. If we violate our core principles, what becomes of our core? Does it matter who you can trust if you can't trust yourself? *Battlestar* returns—and implicates us in—those questions, the way we return to a mirror to take stock of how we appear and chart the changes in who we are.

In season one's "Flesh and Bone," written by Michael Angeli, for instance, Starbuck tried to demonstrate her Cylon prisoner's inhumanity by torturing him. Her logic: if he could withstand inhuman amounts of pain then he must have been inhuman. But what did imposing inhuman amounts of pain make her? To prove to the machine that it was not human, she acted like a machine. So, who was proving what to whom? It's just as likely that he was effectively demonstrating her lack of humanity (or at least lack of humaneness) rather than the other way around. Watch "Flesh and Bone" closely and you realize that Starbuck, whom you like, whom you identify with, could easily have been at Abu Ghraib or Guantanamo. Maybe she is there. Right now.

However, while Moore stated that "There's a lot of political statements within the show that deal with the War on Terrorism that you could take to mean as criticism of the Right,"[13] "Flesh and Bone" exemplifies how the series avoids comfortable polemic and creates a more complex vantage point for the viewer. Given that the Cylon said, falsely it turned out, that he had planted a bomb on one of the ships, Starbuck was faced with the proverbial "ticking bomb" scenario—with thousands of lives at stake, just what should Starbuck have done? Are there limits to compassion when dealing with an implacable enemy who has decided that there is no room for both of you to exist? Or are there moral limits that should never be crossed for fear that once you start blurring your moral lines you will wind up erasing them entirely? It is harder to judge Starbuck when you empathize with her dilemma. Putting the characters and the audience in this quandary and

---

[13] Ron Moore, Podcast, "Epiphanies."

offering no easy answer made the viewer a participant rather than just an observer.[14]

These ethical dilemmas were crucial to the season two "Pegasus" episodes. The *Pegasus* was both a mirror of *Galactica* and a warning of a possible transformation. An evil twin wherein discipline became authoritarianism, duty became fanaticism, and violence was turned inward, *Pegasus* offered a vision of where *Galactica* could go if it stays on the slippery slope. If you start by torturing "the other," as Starbuck did in "Flesh and Bone" inevitably you'll torture your own as Tyrol and Helo were tortured on "Pegasus." Once you start summarily executing enemies, as Roslin did in "Flesh and Bone," how long until you condone murdering rivals, as she did in "Resurrection Ship" (2-11, 2-12)? Given that Adama went from surviving an assassination attempt to ordering one, is it so far-fetched to imagine that *Pegasus* is where the *Galactica* is headed? Might Cain be a mirror through time—an image of Adama's future? Or Roslin's? Or, given the admiring eulogy she delivered, Starbuck's?

We can see this potential manifesting in "Resurrection Ship," written by Anne Cofell Saunders, Ron Moore, and Michael Rymer. Here the writers combined mirroring and transformation when, by ordering Starbuck to assassinate Admiral Cain, Adama essentially attempted to turn Starbuck into Boomer: a sleeper, an assassin, a Cylon. Adama coolly and methodically gave Starbuck instructions on how to kill Cain, instructions that mirrored almost precisely Boomer's attempt to kill Adama. When given the assignment Starbuck appeared horrified but accepted it. Starbuck told Apollo that the mission was "Frakked up....But we kill people for a living. They say 'shoot,' we shoot," speaking with a commitment to professionalism that made her sound less like Boomer, the Cylon who didn't know she was a Cylon, than Gina, the Cylon who knew exactly what she was. Unlike Boomer, unaware of what she was doing, Starbuck knew, had qualms, but still went ahead.

---

[14] Incidentally, though often raised as a philosophical issue or a dramatic device, ticking-bomb hypotheticals are not helpful in answering the real ethical and practical questions raised by torture since real life rarely offers that level of certainty. And even if the moral questions are settled, the question of utility remains. Starbuck essentially admits the futility of torture when she tells her prisoner, "If you were human, you'd be just about ready to start offering up some false information....Some tiny thing that might get you a reward and maybe spare you a few minutes of this." In fact, the likelihood of torture yielding only false information designed to get the torture to stop is a frequent critique made by torture opponents.

In part two of "Resurrection Ship" we watch Starbuck as she watches Cain and we remember the words spoken in part one by Gina, the Cylon, the traitor: "I was a soldier. I had a mission. I carried it out." Was that an acceptable explanation from Gina who was probably responsible for deaths aboard the *Pegasus*? If not, then should we accept Starbuck's explanation that she "kills for a living"? If that justification was sufficient for Starbuck, if being a soldier with a mission erased moral considerations, then shouldn't we accept Gina's amoral dedication to duty? Are these two, again, just mirrors of each other?

"Resurrection Ship" premiered on TV screens on the evening of January 6, 2006. On that very day Steven Spielberg's *Munich*, the third film in what, along with *The Terminal* (2004) and *War of the Worlds* (2005), can best be understood as Spielberg's September 11 trilogy, went into wide release across the country. On the surface the science fiction drama and the political thriller seem to have little in common. Yet, in significant ways, these works, both born of the political crises of our moment, are related. Like "Resurrection Ship," *Munich* took up the costs—political, economic, and moral—of assassination, of targeted violence in what is believed to be a just cause, and raised questions about ethical means and moral ends and the obligation to ask those questions when you fear your enemy is unconcerned with such distinctions. At a key moment, a member of an assassination team sent to hunt down the terrorists behind the killings of Israeli Olympic athletes told Avner, the team commander, that "You do any terrifying thing they ask you to do—but you need to do it running." Doing it running leaves you no time to question or worry until after the fact. And, like a delayed reaction to a traumatic event, it took a while for Avner's doubts to catch up with him.

But Starbuck didn't do it running. She did it walking. Slowly. As she went to kill Cain, we saw the sweat on her skin, the tenseness of her body, the anxiety in her eyes. We practically felt the strain of her heart pounding, her mind resisting. And as the tension built and the gratification was delayed we were invited to wonder what *would* gratify us, what *did* we want to happen.

Like Adama, the audience may have been initially shocked by Roslin's suggestion; however, I suspect that much of the audience, like Adama, came to accept Roslin's logic. The writers make it clear that Cain is dangerous—she has shanghaied and murdered civilians, allowed torture, interfered with Adama's ship, attempted to execute *Galactica* crewmen and, it is revealed, intended to kill Adama. Many in the audience probably wanted Cain to die—or at least were unsure what they wanted.

The episode combined Starbuck's discomfort with our own ambivalence about our own desires. Do we want her to do it? If not, what is our solution? Do we want a mission we oppose to succeed because we care about the ones who are carrying it out, as surely millions of us who opposed the invasion of Iraq hoped for the success and well-being of the troops nonetheless? The unfolding revelations about Cain's ruthlessness evoked our desperate urge to kill preemptively in order to feel safe, another trenchant connection, though probably not an intentional allusion, to the Iraq war. As we look into the mirror of the episode we are faced with age-old questions: Must we become our enemy in order to defeat our enemy? *Can* we defeat our enemy if we become our enemy? What are we willing to do, or sacrifice, in order to survive? Has the battle compromised our sense of morality? Or clarified it?

Adama concluded that "It is not enough to survive; we have to be worthy of survival" (a conviction that Moore described as "one of the key tenets of the show"[15]) and called Starbuck off at the last moment. But in the end the episode, uncharacteristically, let us off the hook by having Gina escape and kill Cain. This ending was a cop-out. We got the comfort of our heroes having made the moral decision without them having to deal with the consequences of leaving the despotic Cain alive. And we got the elimination of the threat Cain posed, without having to see our heroes do the dirty work, without watching them live with themselves in the aftermath, without fully accepting the discomfort of our own uncertain desires.

Perhaps what makes *Battlestar* the most "Incisive commentary on current events in our very troubled world" is how it reflects that uncertainty of our desires, our ambivalence toward our own values and institutions. Just as September 11 reminded us of the fragility of life, its aftermath has demonstrated the fragility of democracy, and at times, the fragility of reason. Recognizing this, in *Battlestar* democracy is under constant threat. And the threats can come from anywhere: they are as likely to come from the military attacking the president as the president

---

[15] Ron Moore, Podcast, "Resurrection Ship, Part II."

rigging an election. They may come from an enemy infiltrator or an overzealous admiral. The series effectively captures the fragility of democracy, how crises strain democratic principles to the breaking point and expose the gap between rhetoric and reality.

"All of this has happened before and and all of this will happen again." Right. The Civil War and the suspending of Habeas Corpus. World War I and the Sedition Act. World War II and Japanese-American internment. The Cold War and McCarthyism. Vietnam and domestic surveillance. *Battlestar Galactica* resonates so deeply because its story is our story.

When Moore set out to revise *Battlestar Galactica*, he proclaimed that his goal was nothing less than "the re-invention of the science fiction television series." In some ways he has achieved that. But as much as this is a re-invention of *Galactica*, it is also the culmination of a project Moore was part of on *Star Trek: Deep Space Nine*: to create a science fiction series characterized by darkness, flawed characters, and moral complexity which would contrast the less ambiguous model *Star Trek* had established as the genre norm.[16]

As I argued in BenBella's *Boarding the Enterprise*, through the device of the "Prime Directive" *Star Trek* asked the Prime Question of its time: to what extent should a superpower use its strength to intervene in the affairs of others? This question is still vital, as the daily news from Iraq

---

[16] Lest we get too celebratory, however, it bears mentioning that *Battlestar* could learn something from its predecessors. Indeed, the overwhelming Whiteness of the show makes one yearn for the carefully considered multiculturalism of most of the *Trek* series. In a show that is, in part, about the construction of community and who can be trusted, the fact that the inner circle and upper echelons are almost exclusively White, while people of color are regulated to the margins, might be an unconscious expression, rather than a deliberate reflection, of xenophobic tendencies, of a narrow conception of who is in and who is out, of who "we" are. Twenty-five years after the original *Galactica* featured a Black first officer, it is hard to believe that the producers of the updated version really could not do better than relegating the only regular Black character to the switchboard. Forty years after the debut of *Star Trek*, Dualla is basically Uhura, limited to opening the hailing frequencies. Yes, the show had Elosha, Roslin's spiritual advisor, but like many a Black sidekick she was dutifully killed off (and for writers ostensibly devoted to avoiding clichés, how did *that* one get by them? Note for the future: noble Negro sidekicks are like red-shirted Federation officers in *Star Trek*. There's no surprise when they die. That's what they do). For all of *Battlestar*'s groundbreaking qualities, it is sad that the show reflects so little progress two generations after the height of the Civil Rights movement—and downright obnoxious that one of the few times they managed to hire an African-American actor, it was Bill Duke playing a crime boss. Moreover, the fact that the only Asian turns out to be a Cylon has more than a whiff of yellow peril paranoia to it. And while the producers, Universal, and the Sci-Fi Channel deserve credit for breaking the color line by choosing a Latino lead, and no disrespect to Jamie Bamber, would it have strained the imaginations of the producers or the tolerance of the audience for Adama to have actually had a Latino son?

or Iran demonstrates. But *Battlestar* asks equally urgent questions: what are the moral restraints on our use of power when we feel ourselves threatened? How do we control the corrupting effects of power and violence? What principles must we adhere to in order for the means to do honor to the ends? How do we find the will and the courage to bridge the distance between what we readily say, what we really believe, and what we actually do? By returning to these questions, inviting us to revisit them, *Battlestar Galactica* rightly suggests that we had better pay close attention to the answers because as Adama understood, "It is not enough to survive; we must be worthy of survival," and as he rightly warned, "You cannot play God then wash your hands of the things that you've created. Sooner or later the day comes when you can't hide from the things that you've done."

Eric Greene is the author of the critically acclaimed book Planet of the Apes as American Myth: Race, Politics, and Popular Culture. *He recently examined* Star Trek *and the Vietnam War for Benbella's Trek anthology* Boarding the Enterprise. *A graduate of the Religious Studies department at Wesleyan University, Greene received a JD from Stanford Law School, where he served as vice president of the Black Law Students Association and was a founder of the West Coast Conference on Progressive Lawyering. Greene's professional hats have included actor and contributor to publications like Africana. com and* First of the Month. *Greene is currently a civil rights activist in Los Angeles, where he also serves on the board of the Progressive Jewish Alliance.*

Do the gods suck? And does it really matter? Matthew Woodring Stover doesn't think so and neither does Battlestar Galactica. *Maybe the gods want us to think for ourselves—maybe the gods have more faith in us than we have in ourselves. And maybe Matthew Woodring Stover and* Battlestar *are asking all of us mere mortals to address these powerful and thought-provoking questions.*

THE GODS SUCK

Matthew Woodring Stover

Among its many other virtues, *Battlestar Galactica* is warming up to be the latest evidence that the Christian Right in the United States, for all its political power, is actually too friggin' dim to pour piss out of a boot.

I mean, haven't they *noticed*?

I keep shaking my head and wondering exactly how Ronald D. Moore and his band of pranksters expected to get away with all this....

Apparently the Tubthumper Elite doesn't watch the Sci-Fi Channel. Good thing, too; in our current political environment, not only would every advertiser on that show find itself targeted for bluenose boycotts, but Sci-Fi Channel execs would be hauled up in front of a Joint Congressional Subcommittee on Un-Righteous Activity and accused of giving Aid and Comfort to the Enemy in the Planetary Scrimmage Against Radically Extreme Islamo-Totalitarianism or whatever the hell they're calling their permanent war this week.

For starters (and *just* for starters—it gets worse from here), has it struck anyone else that the show's writers have deliberately cast the Cylons—the *bad guys*—in a point-for-point allegory of the mythic role of the Israelites in the Old Testament?

All together now

(*Is he KIDDING?*)

Who, me?

Oppressed slaves who rose up against their masters and escaped, to wander in the wilderness until they accepted their destiny as the Chosen People of the One True God...and now, under orders of the One True God, have returned to put some pagans to the sword and appropriate their lands—well, planets—of milk and honey....

This doesn't sound familiar at all.

Now, admittedly, we're talking God of the Old Testament here, who was pretty much a sonofabitch even in His own account of things (I mean, why else would the Israelites keep on trying to worship other gods? At one point, they were so desperate to find a god that'd get them out from under Him they even tried to *make their own*, for crap's sake—remember the golden calf?). In fact, when I wrote a book making this very point, by casting Yahweh as the villain of my second novel, *Jericho Moon* (unabashed plug), I actually got fan mail from a professor of divinity at Northwestern University, who freely conceded that the God of the Old Testament, and I quote, "could be a right old bastard."

Now, I can see a fair chance that the writers are heading for a Christ-child thing with the Cylon-human baby, to redeem the One True (Cylon) God from His Right Old Bastard ways—which could be cool as far as I'm concerned, y'know, Jesus is just all right with me—but I'm not here to speculate on what they might be up to in future seasons.

I'm here to express my admiration for a television program that, in addition to providing the most compelling hour of TV *on* TV, is *sub rosa* laying out what is, as far as I know, the most sophisticated critique of moral theology ever presented in a popular medium.

It's not just Falwell and Robertson and the Bushies they're sticking it to; it's Jesse Jackson and Al Sharpton...and even Gerald Gardner and Starhawk and Oberon Zell-Ravenheart....

I mean, when that Joint Subcommittee hearing rolls around, *everybody* will be out to get them.

Except me. And, I hope, you.

Because what they're doing is important. Beyond important. When you get right down to the bone, I think they're trying to save civilization.

Our civilization.

It's a nifty business. Clever folks, these: using an action-adventure SF soap opera about people desperately trying to preserve their civilization in the face of hopeless odds as a cover—

Because I think they're desperately trying to preserve our civilization. In the face of hopeless odds.

Let me explain.

As we got to meet a couple Cylons in the first season—a whole show devoted to an interrogation, no less—we discovered that what the blonde in Baltar's head (his mental construct of Model Six...who may be, I daresay, less a mental construct than an angel of the One God) had been suggesting is, in fact, the plain hard truth. This is no Borgian You-Will-Be-Assimilated Trek knock-off, nor is it Saberhagen's Berserkers, machines of limitless destruction somehow self-programmed to wipe out biological life—hell, the Cylons *are* biological life. Eight models of them, anyway. ("More human *than* human. That's our motto."—oh, wait, different story....)

No. This is a *religious* war.

This in itself doesn't signify a whole bag of much. In my field—heroic fantasy—religious wars are old hat. Even given that the bad guys are operating under the orders of a clear cognate of Judeo-Christian God doesn't make it special; hell, there's a whole sub-sub-sub-genre, wallowing in the fetid swamps of Arthurian fantasy, that's basically "Nasty Christians Boot Nice Pagans Out of Their Ancestral Lands of Britain/Ireland/France/Indiana/Wherever." But if that was the sum total of what's going on here, it wouldn't interest me much (despite my strong sympathies for the pagans—as a pantheist myself, I get along with any congenial gods, and I like the Greek gods better than most; they throw the best parties. *Oh-pah!*).

Fictional religious wars break down into four broad categories:

Manichaean: The Forces of Light vs. the Forces of Darkness. This is where most of them fall (*Left Behind*, anyone?), because it's simplistic and easy to follow. This is not necessarily a bad thing; some very good television shows spring from this soil—*Buffy the Vampire Slayer* and *Angel* jump up and wave—as well as some pretty damned good epic fantasy, like *The Belgariad*.

Syncretistic: This is one you don't often see in SF and fantasy, but it does poke its head up from time to time. It's much more common in historical fiction—like Crusades tales, retellings of *El Cid*, that kind of thing. This is where the war is not due to the will of the gods, but to the ill-will or corruption of some of the people who worship them. The gods are fundamentally benevolent or at least neutral—in fact, both sides may worship (or claim to worship) the same god or gods, and one or both sides may be faking their religious dispute as a cover for naked aggression—and the solution to the war (if there is one) involves atoning for their sins, acknowledging they're all brothers under the skin, and the rest of that species of pro-social message-oriented hoo-hah that made *Kingdom of Heaven* somewhat less fun than an overdue teeth-cleaning.

Missionary: The heroes must bear the Light of Truth to the ignorant benighted infidels. In this sort of tale (once *very* popular with Christians), all other gods are false gods (or entirely nonexistent), and their worshippers must be saved by the Truth—even if imparting this Truth involves killing great numbers of them. This style of religious war is most commonly seen today as the *Reverse Missionary*, in which those who think they have the Truth, and are trying to spread it by force, are those who are deceived and must be saved. Or killed. Same thing, really. The Reverse Missionary is often, in fact, combined with the final category....

Mechanistic: This is what you most commonly see in modern Us vs. Them, Planetary-Scrimmage-Against-Radical-Whatever pieces. God (or the gods) is nonexistent or at best silent; religion once served a useful civic purpose but now has become a dangerous delusion, manipulated by unscrupulous demagogues to incite a clash of civilizations to serve their own corrupt designs. The Mechanistic model is almost exclusively the kind of religious war seen in serious SF.

So, just for fun, let's dispose of these before moving on.

We can dump Manichaean right from the outset, since it's no secret that the Good Guys—the human survivors of the Cylon attack—aren't exactly what you'd call True-Blue Righteous and Upright types. Their primary claim on our sympathies is that they're the underdogs, facing terrible odds in a struggle to the death. Beyond that? Well, (again, for starters) they are inheritors of the cultural sin of Playing God, as well as one-time slave owners: they created a race of sentient creatures to be their slaves, and now they're surprised and aggrieved when their former slaves have turned on them. Beyond that, we have seen the bulk of the human characters turn out to be petty, vengeful, backstabbing, bickering substance abusers who are as willing to kill each other as they are their enemies; whatever nobility of spirit they possess comes out only in crisis, as if by accident. As my old friend Nietzsche would call them: "human, all too human."

Further, it's become obvious that the Cylon "human" models *are* human in all but name, and the abuse and casual execution that Cylon prisoners face at human hands speaks ill of humanity as a whole. Even the best of the human characters, Commander Adama and President Roslin—looked to as the role models of morality by the "good guy" characters, not to mention the audience—treat Cylons as objects rather than as sentient life forms, placing the best of the "people" on a moral slope that has them sliding in the direction of the Marines from the *Pegasus* who were about to gang-rape Sharon Valerii, aka Model Four.

(After all, if Cylons are only machines, gang rape isn't even punishment, let alone torture. Gang rape of a Cylon "machine" would be merely a complicated form of public masturbation....)

Not to mention we've clearly seen at least two individual Cylons become heroes.

The Syncretistic model of fictional religious war depends on one or both of the following principles: that the conflict is the result of misinterpretation (deliberate or otherwise) of the will of God or the gods, or that the conflict has arisen as part of God's deeper plan (cf. the Destruction of the Temple). This is due to the fundamental principle of syncretism itself: that all "gods" are really just different names for the One God—or servants of the One God (y'know, angels, seraphim, cherubim, devi, djann, whatever) being mistaken for gods. Now, it's not impossible that the writers of *BSG* are going that way—the Cylon War could be another version of the Flood, for example, God's way of cleansing a taint of ineradicable sin from the human race—but I strongly suspect this is not the case...and even if it is, it will only underscore my central point, not belie it.

I'll be explaining why shortly. Be patient.

The Cylons clearly believe they're in a Missionary-style war, while the humans (except for Baltar) clearly believe this is a Reverse Missionary war; my own beloved wife, the Fabulous Robyn—with some vague talk of psychic powers and precognition and such—is still (somewhat forlornly) holding out for the Mechanistic model, but they are all, I believe, destined for disappointment. We have seen too many prayers answered and prophecies fulfilled on both sides for us to seriously misdoubt the existence of either the Lords of Kobol or the One God.

So let's check off what we know so far about the metaphysics of *BSG*:

1. The Gods Really Do Exist

This was a slow-dawning realization for me—and probably for you, too—which is as it should be; the Twelve Colonies were a secularized culture, and the worship of the Lords of Kobol had retreated to the fringes of society, becoming as perfunctory as that of your average American Christians who attend church on Christmas and Easter and spend the rest of their Sundays playing golf.

This Gods Exist stuff is a ballsy stance to take for a hard-as-nails space adventure; the default mode for all hard SF is that if you can't test it in a lab, it just ain't there. Even the softer stuff, like *Star Trek*, clearly Jumped the Shark with their breathtakingly stupid episode "Who Mourns for Adonis?" (You may have noticed that in all the seven or so *Trek* movies featuring Captain Kirk, he never once mentions having witnessed the death of the god Apollo... even when confronting God Himself, more or less. Both that episode and that particular film are best left half-forgotten in the Dumpster of Hollywood's Crap Ideas.)

By allowing mysticism to invade the *BSG* universe, some people will claim, wrongly, that the writers have side-slipped their story toward fantasy, because supernatural forces have no place in SF... unless they're planning a *Trek*-style cop-out and will eventually reveal that the Lords of Kobol are actually super-powerful aliens (which is just a rhetorical trick; what's the difference between a god and a super-powerful alien with all the powers of a god? What you call him. Moving on....).

But wait—we're not really talking supernatural, here, are we?

We've seen Laura Roslin's hallucinations become visions of truths she could not possibly know. We've seen ancient prophecy fulfilled (the Arrow of Apollo, anyone?). We've seen prophecy fulfilled for the Cylons, as well—the birth of the hybrid child—and we've seen the hand of the Cylon God at work (literally, in episode ten, "The Hand of God" (1-10), when Baltar randomly chooses the target for the Tylium raid on the Cylon-held asteroid...and the One God, apparently, guides his choice, as he turns out—against all odds—to be correct). We have *objective verification* of the existence of *both* the Lords of Kobol and the One God.

They exist. Nature comprises all of existence. The Lords of Kobol and the One God are, therefore, not supernatural. *Quod erat demonstrandum.*

They are simply part of the premise, the postulates of the *Battlestar Galactica* universe; they are among the starting points from which we reason.

This is still SF. Logic still applies.

Thus:

2. The Gods Intervene in Mortal Affairs

See the evidence for their existence cited above, plus the many more instances which I won't bother to list; intervention is, however, a significant addendum, because it shows that the various gods are awake, alert, interested, that they respond to prayer—and that they exert their own will(s) in directing the course of events. This is significant because—given that they intervene—this means that they also, often, choose *not* to intervene.

Get it?

I think it might have been David Hume who trenchantly observed that the power of prayer is not shown by the "miraculous" rescue of one survivor from a shipwreck following this survivor's desperate prayers for Divine Aid; Hume pointed out that the people who drowned, whose presumably equally desperate prayers for rescue were *not* answered, are conspicuously unavailable to testify.

Hume was applying his famous skepticism to the very existence of God, as well as miracles and the power of prayer. He was cranky that way, and it amused him to poke logical holes in other people's irrational beliefs. We, however, as the audience of *Battlestar Galactica*, do not have the luxury of skepticism. We've seen the gods in action. They are real, and they intervene in mortal affairs, which leads us, ineluctably, to what appears to be the theological stance of the entire series.

3. The Gods All Suck

I know this comes as no surprise to anyone who paid attention to the title of this essay, but it's the particular *manner* in which they all suck to which I want you to pay attention.

Nobody who knows anything about His Old Testament Model will be shocked that the One (Cylon) God has sent His Chosen People on a mission of genocide. (Deut. 7:2: "When the Lord your God has delivered them over to you and you have defeated them, then you must destroy them totally. Make no treaty with them, and show them no mercy." Deut. 7:20: "The Lord Your God will send the hornet among them until even the survivors who hide from you have perished." Joshua 6:21: "They devoted the city to the Lord, and destroyed with the sword every living thing in it—men and women, young and old, cattle, sheep and donkeys.") The whole Omnibenevolence of God is pretty much a put-up job after all, isn't it? I mean, who's the source for that? Paul? Augustine? *There's* a couple unbiased testimonials—like asking my agent if I'm a good writer. . . .

What may be surprising, for many of us in the *Mists of Avalon* generation, is that the Lords of Kobol suck, too. Pagan gods are supposed to be *waaaay* cooler than this!

They have prophets to whom they give visions of the future, right? They couldn't have, say, mentioned in passing to somebody that creating the Cylons in the first place was a *bad idea*?

They couldn't have maybe dropped a hint here and there that Cylons looked like humans now and had infiltrated the Colonies in preparation for a massive genocidal assault?

Unless they *wanted* all of this to happen (or stood by and allowed it to happen), which makes them every bit as morally culpable in the genocide as the One God. . . .

And if the savage murder of billions did happen to be part of their Divine Plan, jeez, look at the pack of knuckle-dragging dirtbags and scheming whiners they picked to carry on the human race and thus (presumably) their worship. Couldn't they have done better? They're *gods*, for crap's sake.

The other explanation is that they *couldn't* do anything about any of this. That they were taken just as off-guard as the humans, and are pretty much stuck with the hand they were dealt.

Which means instead of being rotten, they're a pack of losers.

This is better?

Which leads us to our final point, the Big One, in the metaphysics of *BSG*:

4. The Gods Are Bad for You

The more any character talks about, thinks about, or in any way interacts with any of the gods, they become a worse person.

The two putative prophets of the respective gods in question are both irretrievably and morally compromised (Baltar's sins hardly need listing, but it's worth remembering that President Roslin not only split the Fleet and consorted with terrorists, nearly starting a civil war, but she also rigged an election and stole Boomer and Helo's child—not to mention ruthlessly ordering the summary execution of a prisoner of war...), and it's not just them; look at Chief Tyrol. Hell, look at Starbuck—her drinking problem began after the whole Arrow of Apollo business, didn't it?

You get it? Piety leads to moral decay.

And to hammer this home, in the last three episodes of season two, we finally met a character who *wasn't* morally compromised. It's not too much of a stretch to call him *the* character who wasn't morally compromised; he's pretty much the only one on the show. Kind, gentle, ethical, reasonable, even a pacifist....

Which is astonishing, in a Cylon.

Yes, I'm talking about Brother Cavel, played by the estimable Dean Stockwell.

The truly astonishing thing about him—the truly *significant* thing about his character, kind, gentle, ethical, reasonable person that he is—

Is that he's an *atheist*.

This is how the *Battlestar Galactica* kids are trying to save our civilization.

One of the features that has always distinguished Western culture, for better or worse, is the idea that the structure of our morality—the underpinning of our law, culture, society, you name it—flows somehow directly from the Divine. That some Higher Power determines for us what is Right or Wrong, and our duty, as people and citizens, is quite simply to hew unto the Right, and reject the Wrong, as determined by God.

Get Thee Behind Me, Satan, and Eat Not of the Tree of Knowledge, and Thou Shalt Not Suffer a Witch to Live and all that good stuff.

In vastly oversimplified terms, this is generally referred to as "revealed morality." Criticisms of revealed morality tend to land on the planet of the fundamental ("Your Revealed Morality is unreliable because God does not exist") or the moon of the functional ("Your Revealed Morality is unreliable because you have misinterpreted God, and fallen from the True Way").

Battlestar Galactica has jumped right out of that galaxy, though.

They've landed on Planet Stover.

People from *my* planet say, "Okay, maybe God does exist, and sure, you might be on His True Way, but God's a *rotten bastard*. Why in hell would you take His word for *anything*? Your Revealed Morality is unreliable because its Source is corrupt—and the real world's just too frakkin' complicated for His simple answers. Think for yourself. Grow *up*, dammit!"

The complexity of the moral choices faced by these characters every week—starting from the very first episode, "33" (1-1), possibly the finest hour of TV I have ever seen—continues to underscore the existential void in which they're forced to operate. The moral guidance of the gods, such as it is, doesn't help them choose between two equally unpalatable wrongs, when the survival of the species is at stake....

It could be this all sort of jumped out at me because it's been a metatheme of my own fiction, especially my Acts of Caine Cycle (comprising, to date, *Heroes Die, Blade of Tyshalle*, and the forthcoming *Caine Black Knife*—yeah, another unabashed plug, what do you want from me?), but I'm well below the mass-media radar. To see this become a running theme on a weekly TV show is so staggeringly cool it makes my glasses frost over.

And they're talking to the right people, aren't they? I mean, who are the SF fans if not the brightest of the mass audience? The ones with the most going on upstairs? The ones most likely to take in what *BSG*'s up to, and think about how it could apply to the real world?

Let's face it: if the producers of *Desperate Housewives* were using this as a running theme, d'you think anybody'd notice?

Yeah, okay, I'm a snob. Sue me.

And it's a good thing Falwell and Robertson and the rest of the shouters are busy popping veins about *Desperate Housewives* and such, because they haven't noticed *BSG* yet. It would sure as hell sound the alarms for the Tubthumper Elite, if they had brains enough to understand it. It could get Ron Moore hauled up in front of that Joint Subcommittee.

What's going on here is, not to put too fine a point on it, heresy.

And it's exactly the kind of heresy we need. Right now. Right here.

Because it's become increasingly clear that the most immediate threat faced by our civilization comes from people who believe that anything they do is Righteous because they're acting on orders from God.

I'm not talking about Al Qaeda, either. The whacko death-cult fringe of Islamic fundamentalism doesn't have the power to destroy our civilization; free society is too loose and resilient for that.

Yeah, we seem to be (in believers' terms) in a Syncretistic religious war, or (for the non-believers) a Mechanistic one; in either case, religion is clearly being manipulated by unscrupulous men for their own corrupt purposes. On both sides. But that's not the real danger; corruption can be exposed, and the faithless can be shown for what they are.

The real danger is from the men who actually *believe* that Our Planetary Scrimmage is a Crusade. The ones who have it straight from God that this is a Missionary war, or—worse—a Manichaean one.

They're out there. They're in the military, and in the government. They're all over talk radio, and some mega-churches are packed to the rafters with them.

They apparently believe, for example, that the 30,000 civilians we've killed in the "Liberation of Iraq" should be *grateful*. Killing them in order to save them—standard practice in Missionary war. Or that the dead civilians don't matter at all—they're Muslims, anyway; that's the stance of Manichaean war.

We have a man in the White House who proclaims he was Chosen by God to be President. Who consulted his Higher Father (rather than his own father) on whether to invade a country that was not threatening ours, and was given the Thumbs-Up by God Himself. (I guess even God was fooled by "bad intelligence on WMD.") Who describes America's globe-choking, Kyoto-Treaty-abandoning, oil-guzzling, celebrity-obsessed, Wal-Mart-jamming, fast-food-scarfing consumer culture thusly: "Our way of life is a Blessed one."

See how well revealed morality works in the real world?

This is the true genius of Moore and his Clever Folk behind the scenes of *BSG*. They're not saying that God doesn't exist, and they're not saying people don't understand Him . . . they're saying that people need to grow the hell up and think for themselves *anyway*.

Because God isn't going to help you decide whether or not to nuke the Olympic Carrier.

Matthew Woodring Stover is the acclaimed bestselling author of Star Wars, Episode III: Return of the Sith, *as well as several other Star Wars novels, two previous fantasy novels,* Iron Dawn *and* Jericho Moon, *and the series* The Acts of Caine.

From its inception, the relationship between the self-serving Baltar and the seemingly confident but enigmatic and conflicted Cylon Six has captured both the imagination and horror of fans everywhere. Battlestar explores the possibility that compared to the moral ambiguity and corruption of the humans, the Cylons may be, in fact, more angel than devil. Just who are the good guys and who are the bad guys? Maybe the demons we seek so ardently to destroy lie within us. What do you think?

AN ANGEL ON HIS SHOULDER, A DEVIL ON HERS

Chris Roberson

WHAT ARE WE TO MAKE of Gaius Baltar? He's a bad apple, there's no mistaking it: selfish, egocentric, and vain. He's a slave to his own worst instincts, willing to do anything that serves his interests. If the destruction of the Colonies and the death of billions of innocents bothered him at all, it scarcely showed, as his primary concern was that he not be blamed for any part in it. He'll accuse one man of being a Cylon with no evidence, condemn a possibly innocent man to death, but conceal the discovery that a trusted member of the crew actually *is* a Cylon, if it means increasing his own chances of survival.

But is he really all bad?

Baltar was the winner of three Magnate Awards, a media cult figure, and a personal friend of President Adar. Working as a top consultant for the Ministry of Defense on computer issues, and known for espousing controversial views on advancing computer technology, Baltar was instrumental in the creation of the Command Navigation Program (CNP),

an automated system integrated into the navigational systems of all Colonial ships.

That's where the problems started, of course. It seemed the CNP was
a bit beyond Baltar's abilities. Luckily, he was sharing his bed with a
woman well versed in programming, who offered to rewrite half the al-
gorithms and help get the program up and running. All she asked in return was for Baltar to use his connections to grant her unlimited access
to the Ministry of Defense mainframe, to help give her an edge in getting a defense contract in the coming year.

It's interesting that we were never told the name of the blonde lover
of his. On Caprica, her name, like her feelings, mattered little, if at all,
to Baltar. He betrayed her with another woman and offered as his defense tired platitudes that he couldn't muster the enthusiasm to deliver
with any measure of conviction. It was clear that he had been caught by
jealous lovers before, and he expected to be caught many more times to
come. But that was all about to change.

The lover, of course, is an example of the Cylon model we've come
to know as Number Six. It's significant that the first lines we heard her
utter to Baltar were about love, souls, and God. "Your body misses me,"
she said to him, "but what about your heart, your soul?" Then, as their
clothing was removed one frenzied piece at a time, she asked him, "Do
you love me?" When Baltar, a panicked look on his face, asked, "Are
you serious?" Six laughed the question off.

Six told Baltar that she helped him with the programming of the CNP
not because she wanted to win any defense contract, but because God
told her to do so.

Later, Six revealed to Baltar that she is a Cylon. She claimed that Baltar
must have known this all along, though his reaction made plain that he
hadn't. That Six could so misread their relationship, to think first that Baltar loved her, when he gave no indication of holding her in any regard at all,
and second that he had been secretly aware of her machinations all along,
including their shared role in the complete destruction of the Colonies,
suggests an inability to empathize and anticipate another's emotions bordering on the psychopathic. But the Cylons are the children of mankind,
after all, and as it seems that they haven't completely matured, perhaps their
emotions and personalities are accordingly immature. Or is it, as Six suggested, that Baltar has "an amazing capacity for self-deception"?

Baltar started to phone his attorney, to plan his defense, when the first bombs began to fall. A short time after, Caprica City was hit. Just before the shockwave reached Baltar's home, Six explained to him that she could not die, and that when her current body would be destroyed, her memory and her consciousness would wake up in an identical body, somewhere else. She shielded Baltar with her own body as the nuclear blast washed over them.

When Baltar gave his half-hearted excuse for infidelity to Six, he claimed it was all his fault.

"I screwed up. I *am* screwed up. I always have been. It's a flaw in my character...."

Well, that might be understating matters somewhat, no? In fact, it seems at times as if Baltar's character is nothing *but* flaws. One would be hard pressed to identify a single selfless act, a single moment of charity or generosity. When he stood in front of Boomer's Raptor, Helo having read the number of the last survivor allowed onboard, Baltar was approached by an old woman who asked him to read her number aloud, since she had lost her glasses. Baltar saw the winning lottery number on her paper, and his desire to take her number for himself was written large across his expression. He passed up the opportunity when Helo recognized him, identifying the woman as the lucky survivor in the hopes of deflecting attention from himself—"I haven't done anything," he responded, when Helo asked if he is Gaius Baltar—but fortune smiled on him when Helo surrendered his seat in the Raptor to him.

Unexpectedly, Baltar saw Six again, in a stunning red dress, standing amongst the agitated Capricans about to be left behind. Did he experience some guilt, knowing that the selfless Colonial Warrior was willing to die so that he could live? Or was that giving him too much credit? He blinked, and when he looked again, she was gone.

She appeared to him, a short while later, on the Raptor. "You know what I love about you, Gaius?" she asked. "You're a survivor."

The first exchange we heard between Baltar and the red-dress Six was onboard the newly christened Colonial One. Baltar had already decided that she was "an expression of [his] subconscious mind, playing itself out during [his] waking states."

"So I'm only in your head?" Six asked. "Have you considered the possibility that I can very well exist only in your head without being a

hallucination. . . . Maybe you see and hear me because when you were
sleeping I implanted a chip in your brain that transmits my image right
into your conscious mind."

Baltar rejected this explanation for a time, insisting that Six was merely the result of his subconscious self expressing irrational fears, but in
short order seemed ready to accept that Six had some reality independent of his own subconscious.

But what purpose would the Cylons have for implanting such a chip
in Baltar's head? He was an instrument in the destruction of the Colonies, but beyond that he seemed to have little utility. In fact, in many
instances, Six seemed to offer Baltar advice that was *counter* to the Cylons' interests. She pointed out to him the Cylon device on the *Galactica*
bridge and urged him to identify some scapegoat among the crew. That
the scapegoat Baltar selected turned out to actually *be* a Cylon seemed
to strain credibility. Or did it? If Six was really a Cylon entity, and not a
product of Baltar's subconscious, she would surely be able to recognize
another of her own kind, and even though she claimed that the scapegoat was not, in fact, a Cylon, could she actually be manipulating Baltar
into choosing him, like a skilled cardsharp forcing a draw?

Six is a constant companion to Baltar, always there to advise him, to
steer him to one course or another, and though it is seldom clear just
what her ultimate purpose is, her agenda is obvious.

"And what I want most of all," she told Baltar, "is for you to love
me."

"God is love."

Six, more than anything else, is out to *save Baltar* because she loves
him.

And that, for all of the first season and much of the second, seemed to
be that. The Cylons' ultimate plans were ineffable, but Six's purpose was
clear. She was the angel on Baltar's shoulder, trying to lead him toward
the path of righteousness. Not, of course, any righteousness which the
Colonials would recognize, but one that adhered to Six's own beliefs.

The Colonials are pantheists, worshipping the Lords of Kobol. The
Cylons would seem to be strict monotheists, with a single deity known
only as God. And while the Lords of Kobol are distant and removed
from human affairs, the God of the Cylons is intimately involved in the
day-to-day life of his worshippers, seeming to direct their every move-

ment. (Which raises the interesting question, of course, whether "God" might not be another name for some super artificial intelligence at the heart of Cylon culture.)

Also, the goals of the Cylon God are quite distinct from those of any human deity. For one, God seems not terribly interested in the temporal and physical survival of the human race. If anything, God may be more interested in winnowing down humanity to its core, to those individuals best suited to survive (recall Six's words to Gaius: "You know what I love about you? You're a survivor."), and then somehow crossbreeding those survivors with Cylons to create a hybrid race, incorporating the best of both. This could be the goal of the long-game experiment run on Helo and on Caprica, or the "baby farm" where Starbuck is briefly imprisoned. In any event, the demands of the Cylon God are ineffable and strange, and scarcely seem likely to presage a happy future for humanity.

To what end, then, is Six leading Baltar? Her advice certainly doesn't seem to be in the best interest of the surviving humans, but at the same time she often advises Baltar in ways that seem to act against the Cylons, as well. So what is her purpose?

Love. Six loves Baltar, and that is her principal, and perhaps only, motivation.

Six wants to see Baltar survive, wants to continue to be with him. If *Galactica* is under threat of attack by Cylons while he's onboard, as it is before the Fleet makes the jump to Ragnar, Six acts against the Cylon interests for as long as Baltar is still in danger. When Baltar is not in immediate danger, her motivations are more opaque and her advice to him more mysterious, but in the main in these instances she seems to favor the Cylons' purposes.

Six loves Baltar. But what if it isn't *exactly* the Six we first met on Caprica? She seems far more self-assured, for one thing. Her manner is much more confident, and her ability to read the emotions and intentions of others is far and away improved.

What if she *isn't* Six, after all? Not in the way that Baltar thinks. And, perhaps, not even in the way *she* thinks.

When *Galactica* was reunited with the *Battlestar Pegasus*, Baltar was brought to examine a Cylon prisoner. It turned out to be another instance of Six, one which had no knowledge of him. This instance of Six,

badly beaten and abused by the *Pegasus* crew, explained to Baltar the nature and uses of the Resurrection Ships, which are used to revive dead
Cylons far beyond the reach of the Cylon homeworld. "*Pegasus* Six"
begged him to end her suffering and kill her, but Baltar refused. In fact,
Baltar seemed to have genuine feelings for her.

Baltar spurned the Six who lived in his mind, directing his attention
to winning the heart of *Pegasus* Six. This other Six made use of Baltar's
affections, wrangling a nuclear warhead, which she ultimately detonat-
ed, destroying the luxury ship *Cloud Nine*.

Baltar, of course, survived. He was elected president, led the surviving humans to the planet dubbed New Caprica, and settled in. A year
later, he was living in decadence onboard the downed Colonial One,
sharing his bed with several women at once, while his people eked out
a meager existence in a muddy warren of tents and huts.

Six still resided in his mind, presumably still advising him. But since
her primary goal was for Baltar to survive, she should be pleased, right?
She loved him on Caprica, and she loves him now, supposedly existing
on a chip implanted in his mind.

Except that it wasn't Six, and never was.

When the nuclear blast ripped through Baltar's house, Six died shielding Baltar with her own body. When she opened her eyes again, she was
in a Cylon birthing tank, surrounded by other Cylons...and an apparition of Baltar that only she could see.

In the weeks and months that followed, this Six was celebrated by the
other Cylons. She was even given a name, a rarity among beings who
typically are only known by numeric designations; Caprica Six was a
hero to Cylons everywhere.

But Caprica Six had difficulty reintegrating into Cylon culture. The
other Cylons assumed that this was the result of the strain of her mission and having to live among humans for so long, to say nothing of
prolonged and intimate contact with one of them. The notion that Caprica Six spent so much time in the arms of Gaius Baltar must seem
anathema to beings who view humans as a flawed creation, and one that
God is eager for them to eradicate.

And living among humans all that time obviously had an impact on
Caprica Six. In the hours leading up to the Cylon attack, she clearly had
misgivings about her mission. She encountered a woman with an infant

in a crowded city square in Caprica City, and marveled over how small and light the baby was. The infant cried, and Caprica Six tried to soothe it, saying, "You won't have to cry much longer." When the mother's back was turned, she broke the infant's neck, and her expression suggested strongly that she did it in order to save the baby from the horrors which were to come.

She then went to Baltar's house. Not the strong, confident Six who would later occupy Baltar's mind, Caprica Six seemed uneasy, unsure of herself and her situation. When she asked Baltar, "Do you love me?" her naked hunger for acceptance and approval was obvious. She truly does love him, and was desperate for him to return that love. Not because "God is love," as Baltar Six would later say, but because she wanted Baltar to love *her*, as an individual, as Caprica Six.

Caprica Six is a loyal Cylon, but her time among humans seems to have infected her with a suite of personality flaws: doubt, neediness, and guilt.

The Six who appeared in Baltar's mind talked to him constantly of love and of survival. It steered him away from danger, giving him information only a Cylon would know, all with the apparent goal of his continued existence.

What does the image of Baltar in Caprica Six's mind say? It prodded at her, reminding her again and again of her guilt in the deaths of billions of humans. It pointed out repeatedly that she was just a machine, not a person. In short, it mocked her and tried to drag her down. Not an angel on her shoulder, but a devil, pouring poison into her ear.

What are we to make of this?

The answer, I think, is simple. Baltar and Six are, in essence, talking to themselves.

When the Cylons arrived on New Caprica, it wasn't because they received any transmission from an instance of one of their own, running on a chip inside Baltar's head. In fact, there was little to no evidence that the Cylons were aware at all of the existence of Baltar Six. Instead, they discovered New Caprica a year later because they detected the nuclear explosion caused by *Pegasus* Six. Also, when Caprica Six and Baltar encountered one another, it was clear that neither had any idea that the other had survived the bombing of Caprica City.

In the aftermath of the nuclear explosion that destroyed Caprica

City, Six's shielding of Baltar with her own body had unintended consequences.

At the moment of her death, Six's consciousness would have been broadcast back to the Cylon homeworld or a nearby rebirth ship, uploaded so that she could be incarnated in a new body. But Six died at the exact instant that a crushing wave of radiation passed over her body, the result of a high megatonnage explosion. Suppose, then, that when her consciousness was broadcast out, the radiation interfered with the transmission, filtering her digital upload momentarily through Baltar's mind.

This filtering could have left an impression of Six's consciousness in Baltar's mind, and carried along with Six's upload an impression of Baltar's consciousness. Not fully sentient, these partial impressions then acted as sock-puppets for their subconscious processes, externalized actors for internalized thought processes.

"I've decided you're an expression of my subconscious mind," Baltar said, "playing itself out in my waking states." What if he was more right than he knew?

After all, what motivates Baltar more than self-love and the desperate desire for survival? And what is the constant refrain of the image of Six who haunts his thoughts? "Love." "Survivor." This Six is strong, self-confident, and without a shred of doubt that everything she says is absolutely true, absolutely right—in the precise way that Baltar's self-interest and self-regard are the strongest aspects of his personality.

And Caprica Six, who feels guilt, and possibly remorse, over the death of billions of humans? She was visited by an image of Baltar that reminded her, again and again, that she was a soulless killing machine. Plagued by crushing doubt, Caprica Six was unable to escape the voice that reminded her of all she's done wrong, and all that she can never be.

Their minds intermingled in the nuclear explosion, Caprica Six and Baltar are each locked in constant discussion with their own subconscious processes, telling themselves what they most want to hear, whether their conscious minds realized that desire or not. But what happens when the two are brought physically together? Will they recognize their internal voices for what they are, and begin an actual dialogue? Or will matters only get that much worse for everyone involved?

Chris Roberson's short fiction can be found in the anthologies Live Without a Net, The Many Faces of Van Helsing, Tales of the Shadowmen, Vols. 1 *and* 2, *and* FutureShocks, *and in the pages of* Asimov's, Postscripts, *and* Subterranean Magazine. *His novels include* Here, There, & Everywhere *(Pyr, 2005),* The Voyage of Night Shining White *(PS Publishing, 2006), and* Paragaea: A Planetary Romance *(Pyr, 2006), and he is the editor of the anthology* Adventure Vol. 1 *(MonkeyBrain Books, 2005). Roberson has been a finalist for the World Fantasy Award for Short Fiction, twice for the John W. Campbell Award for Best New Writer, and twice for the Sidewise Award for Best Alternate History Short Form (winning in 2004 with his story "O One").*

When we really take a good look at ourselves, what do we see? Are we just skin and bone—our physical bodies, brains, etc., or are we something more? And could that something more be independent of the flesh and blood vehicles we inhabit? In the digital world everything can be reduced to information and transferred, downloaded, or stored via technology. In the new Battlestar, and in this thought-provoking article, the question is posed: Are we more similar to our quickly evolving technological creations than we could ever have imagined, and why are we so afraid of that which increasingly mirrors humanity more and more each day? Is the fear of technology just an irrational fear of ourselves the beast within so to speak? And can our own creation—the Cylons in this case—show us the way to a possibly unlimited and immortal future. Read on....

THE FACE IN THE MIRROR
ISSUES OF MEAT AND MACHINE
IN *BATTLESTAR GALACTICA*

Natasha Giardina

W E LOOK AT OURSELVES IN the mirror and what we see is reassuring. We are human, organic. Our faces bear the tangible evidence of our natures, complete with hair, secretions, skin flakes, scars, and wrinkles. We are born, not made; things of flesh and blood, not cogs and wheels. We are the real thing; we are authentic.

I write this essay on a laptop in a Wi-Fi zone, connected to the Internet via radio transmitters and satellite dishes. As I type, pressing the buttons that turn my thoughts into code, windows pop up on the periphery of the screen—friends online sensing my virtual presence and wanting to chat. I stop my essay in midstream to touch base with them, keeping up to date with their latest news, shooting them long-requested photos of my last overseas holiday. I muse nostalgically through the photos, relieved that their perfect digital record can bolster my all-too-fragile memories. Eventually, I finish my work for the day and shut my laptop down. As the screen goes black, the surface catches light from the setting sun, and I glimpse my own face in the mirror. That's me—on, in, and a part of the computer—I am the real thing; I am authentic. Of course I am (not reassured).

Since 2003, *Battlestar Galactica* has prompted us to think about ourselves and our relationships with technology in new ways. The series rests on a strong science fictional foundation, its literary genealogy a clear line from *Frankenstein* to *Metropolis*, to *The Terminator*, *Blade Runner*, *Synners*, and *The Matrix*. Specifically, *Battlestar Galactica* continues using the classic science fiction theme of "machine as Other," with its portrayal of the war between human and Cylon, but the series challenges the assumptions behind the binary opposition of meat and machine, not in the relationship between the human characters and the Cylons, but in the relationship between the Cylons and the viewing audience. It keeps the opposition, but uses the Cylons to show us how much like machine we already are, thus demonstrating the fallacy of calling the machine "Other."

Science fiction, as Adam Roberts notes, is "about the encounter with difference" (Roberts 28). Roberts suggests that although technology is ubiquitous in our everyday lives, the machine still occupies the place of the Other in science fiction because we are unfamiliar with how technology works and cannot keep pace with its constant evolution (Roberts 146–47). One of the recurring obsessions of Western societies since the industrial revolution has centered on our relationship with the mechanical—its place in our lives, our role as creators, and the fate of our inorganic offspring. In short, we are uneasy in our relationship with technology: we fear its virtuality, its transformative power, and its imperviousness to the thousand natural shocks that flesh is heir to. Science fiction provides an excellent record of our anxieties about the machine, from Mary Shelley's *Frankenstein* to the Matrix trilogy of films.

Although science fiction has explored and played with these anxieties, it has usually upheld consolatory fantasies about the innate superiority of meat over machine. In many science fiction stories, machines are monsters to be battled and destroyed. Often, science fiction contains visions of machine worlds, like the *Matrix* or *Terminator* trilogies, where humans comprise a subjugated and oppressed minority, ruthlessly exploited by the machine masters and hunted down when they try to free themselves from this techno-tyranny. Here, a human savior is needed to save our species, who, by virtue of the flesh, is innately superior to the machines. Occasionally, there are "good" machines, like the Terminator in *Terminator 2: Judgment Day* or Sonny in *I, Robot* (the 2004 film), but these willingly subjugate and even sacrifice themselves for their superiors—humans. In other science fiction, like *Frankenstein, AI: Artificial Intelligence,* or *Bicentennial Man,* machines are treated like our children: not evil, but nonetheless handicapped by their lack of flesh, and thus objects of pity.

Some of the texts most willing to grapple with the complexities of the relationship between flesh and machine have been cyberpunk and post-cyberpunk fiction, like William Gibson's *Neuromancer,* Neal Stephenson's *Snow Crash,* Pat Cadigan's *Synners,* or Peter Hamilton's Greg Mandel series. These stories consider the ramifications of the cyborg's existence—that "hybrid of machine and organism" (Haraway 149)—and articulate futures of cyborg societies. Yet even these texts usually return to the hierarchy of meat over machine: despite the fact that the organic and the mechanoid often work in tandem, the controllers, creators, riders, and dreamers remain human, and in the rare instances when characters leave the meat to become one with the machine, as with Visual Mark (from *Synners*) or Philip Evans (from Hamilton's Greg Mandel series), the resultant virtual entities still require that unique spark of humanity to make them "people."

Battlestar Galactica provides the latest permutation of our continuing obsession with the technological Other. Like its ancestors in the genre, the series postulates a universe in which humans are under siege from the machines they themselves created, as stated in the episode introductions:

> *The Cylons were created by Man*
> *They evolved*
> *They rebelled*
> *There are many copies*
> *And they have a plan*

During the initial 2003 mini-series, the battle lines between human and Cylon are clearly articulated. The opening words of the mini-series are spoken by a Number Six model Cylon to the human envoy at the armistice outpost. She asks him, "Are you alive?" and demands that he prove it. Ultimately, the only way the envoy can prove he is alive, and thus different from the Cylon, is not by dying, but by dying without resurrection. Nothing else can demonstrate the difference between meat and machine. This mini-series names the Cylons as "humanity's children," but like Frankenstein's monster, they are flawed children who desire the destruction of their flawed creators, obliterating the Twelve Colonies and forcing the remnants of humanity to flee through space. Hampered by inferior technology, overwhelmingly outnumbered, and beholden to protect a ragtag collection of civilian craft, the crew of the *Battlestar Galactica* is humanity's last, best, and only hope for survival. That they survive at all is a testament to the human spirit, the innate superiority of flesh over machine.

The problem with this scenario is that it doesn't work. Oh, the story works just fine, and it provides an excellent exploration of the "machine as Other" theme. But the relationship between the story and the audience is fundamentally flawed. For the "machine as Other" theme to work, the audience needs to empathize with the human characters and revile the machines. The story must persuade us how human we are: how unlike the machine we are. But in the *Battlestar Galactica* story, the intriguing truth is that we are more like the Cylons than we are like the Colonists: at the beginning of the twenty-first century, humans are finally embracing the machine and slowly, ever so slowly, leaving the meat behind.

Our most fundamental similarity to the Cylons is evident in notions of the self. The series portrays the Colonists as strongly "embodied" in that they are tied to the meat, or "meat puppets" according to Gibson's *Neuromancer*. We can see this because there are so few of them: fewer than 50,000 souls reliant on two *Battlestars* and a handful of Vipers for their precarious existence, with each death a painful reminder that the human race stands at the brink of the final event horizon. In season two, the introduction for each episode recounts the exact number of humans still existing, and as Admiral Adama says in "The Captain's Hand" (2-17), "the fact is, that number doesn't go up very often." The Colonists are also extremely low-tech in many ways: they may be able to travel faster than light, but no one is ever depicted communicating via an Internet-analog. The rationale for this within the story is that the Cylons' ability to infiltrate computer networks prohibits this from being a viable communications option, but it also serves the theme of the story by highlighting the division between organic and mechanoid.

The relationship between the Colonists and the viewing audience is more problematic than it may seem. They look like us, and they are motivated by the same combination of fear, desire, and aspiration typical of humans on this side of the screen. But how many people today can imagine living without the new media networks based on Internet, cable television, and cell-phone technology? We may reminisce about the halcyon days when our lives were less hyperconnected, and indeed, nostalgia provides us with a strong emotional attachment to the Colonists, but I would suggest that few of us would willingly choose to return to a low-tech existence.

In contrast to the reassuring if nostalgic embodiment of the Colonists, the Cylons seem alien and dangerous; they represent our recurring nightmare of technology—evolved beyond human capacity to understand or control. Cylons come in four distinct varieties. First, there are the human-looking Cylons—the skin jobs—adept at infiltration despite the fact that there are only twelve models. Then there are the Cylon ships, which may seem to be things of metal, but as Starbuck discovers in season one, are partly organic. The third type of Cylon is the Centurion: an old-fashioned kind of robot with all metal parts, but as the season two finale shows, they are still capable of rational, intelligent thought. The fourth and final type of Cylon is the Cylon virus: a completely informational entity which can penetrate and take control of the human computer systems.

The most frightening aspect of the Cylons, especially for the human Colonists, is not the individual capabilities of each of the Cylon varieties, but their indestructibility: their ability to move between and outside of bodies and even transcend death. Cylons are downloadable, digital, rebootable, and able to form complex networks of shared information. The reason for this is that their "selves"—their memories, thought processes, beliefs, and values—are not tied to their bodies; their selves exist as information. They may appear to come in four distinct varieties, but in truth, they are simply patterns of information housed in different shells; skin job, Centurion, ship, or virus, they are all the same. Each time a Cylon dies, the information of its "self" is stored and transferred to a new body. New experiences augment the self, and make the file larger, more complex. The self can also be converted to different file formats and used in a range of applications, such as in "Flight of the Phoenix" (2-9) when the Cylon Sharon jacks directly into the *Battlestar*'s mainframe via a fiber-optic comlink to send a virus to infect the Cylon Fleet.

Tempting as it is to see this as part of the "fiction" of science fiction, it is far from a speculative idea. The postmodern understanding of identity suggests that there is no essential, concrete, or authentic self, just the performance inscribing and reinscribing the self in a plethora of events for a range of audiences (Turkle; Carlson). Thus, the self is already information, but the current era reinforces this notion because communicating the self in a virtual environment is technically an exercise in binary code. What *Battlestar Galactica*'s depiction of the Cylons emphasizes is that we too are downloadable, digital, and able to form complex networks of information (although not yet rebootable). We store our memories—the minutiae of our lives—on databanks and download them at our leisure, we communicate and interact via digital channels, and our lives are narratives of hypertext, endlessly connecting information packets in new configurations. If we accept that the face in the mirror is *already* a cyborg, then when we watch a series like *Battlestar Galactica*, we can choose to focalize on the machines instead of, or at least as well as, on the humans. This, I would suggest, is the epiphany of *Battlestar Galactica*.

The posthuman self is not only performed information, but received information as well. The way we make sense of the outside world and of other people is via the senses, where sensations are translated into electrical brain impulses and decoded into meaningful information that our conscious minds can digest. Thus, reality is inherently subjective, and never more so than in the virtual age, when a vast portion of our work, our social lives, and our meaning-making takes place electronically. *Battlestar Galactica* plays with the subjectivity of reality in its treatment of *Galactica* Sharon—the Cylon who believed fervently she was human until the point her programming kicked in to destroy *Galactica* and kill

Commander Adama. This Cylon, a Number Eight model, is very similar to the character of Rachael in *Blade Runner*: both show us that our perceptions of reality are based purely on information, so the process of signification—the relationship between the signified and external reality—will always be in doubt.

Of course, the idea that reality is primarily perception rather than concrete experience is not necessarily negative: it also allows us to expand the way we think about our world and our place in it. Take, for instance, the trope of "the machine in your head" as articulated in Gaius Baltar's relationship with his invisible Number Six. Since the destruction of Caprica, Baltar has interacted with a Cylon who is completely invisible and undetectable to everyone else, but real to him, even to the physical acts of love, although he knows she is not physically there. In an intriguing twist of fate, a copy of Caprica Six—the Cylon who had an affair with Baltar before the destruction of the Colonies—wakes from the downloading process with Gaius Baltar in her head, as real to her as his invisible Six is to him.

Here, the idea of "the machine in your head" is an elegant metaphor for the networks of virtual communication we inhabit in our everyday lives. As Ito and Okabe's study of mobile phone use, and Lewis and Fabos's study of instant messaging have found, we now exist in states of ambient co-presence (Ito & Okabe; Lewis & Fabos). In other words, new media technologies allow us to perceive that we are surrounded by our peers at all times, wherever we are located and whether we are actually communicating with them or not; they are there, around us, available. Thus, the concept of technology-enabled ambient co-presence is very similar to Baltar's Number Six. We might disparage Baltar's Cylon because she is not "really there," but our engagement with virtual communication networks and channels shows us that this has become a moot point: communication doesn't need to be embodied to be "real," it just has to be "real enough."

If we accept the idea that the machine is not "Other," then some of the themes in *Battlestar Galactica* become interesting moral conundrums for those of us living in the posthuman era. Some issues that the series prompts us to reassess are biotechnological. In *Battlestar Galactica*, Cylons can replicate, copying their "selves" ad infinitum, and transfer these files into newly constructed bodies, also endlessly replicable.

Cylon blood is also different from human blood, and the amalgam of these two, present in Sharon and Helo's unborn child, is unique: it can cure cancer and save President Roslin's life.

In the series, the Colonists perceive the Cylon cloning procedure as negative: the Cylons are frightening because they aren't natural—they don't die, and the informational self exists independently of the bodily shell. In the second instance, where the fetus's blood is used as a metaphor for stem-cell harvesting and genetic modification, the connotations are mixed: most of the Colonists see Roslin's recovery as positive, but the question of whether the infusion makes Roslin partly Cylon never comes up. Indeed, the silence on this point is deafening: it is a question no one is game to ask, inside or outside the text. The reason we are reluctant to talk about it is because we cling to the notion of a concrete, embodied self, and under that rationale, if the body is partly someone else's body, or is a duplicate of a body, or contains mechanoid elements, how can the self be kept pure?

These philosophical debates are relevant and ongoing, and have featured in recent medical breakthroughs, including the first hand transplant, carried out in 1998, and the first face transplant, which occurred in France last year. A scan of popular media reactions to these two procedures reveals that we evidently still hold great anxieties about the cohesion of the embodied self, but if we posit that the self is simply information and technology allows us to communicate that information more effectively, then the connection between self and body is immaterial. Under this philosophy, the augmentation of the human is simply part of the new human condition. The ethical dilemmas over issues like cloning, genetic modification, and stem-cell harvesting disappear when we understand that these are yet more cases of technology allowing us to become ourselves.

The series also ponders the ethical ramifications of our uses of technology, especially in light of our own cyborg status. We have always understood and accepted that machines exist for a purpose, that they are fashioned to be used in certain ways. This is reflected in the ways that the Colonists treat the cyborgs: captive Cylons, like Sharon, Leoben or the *Pegasus* Six are not just the hated enemy, but tools to be used for tactical advantage. The relationship between Admiral Adama and Caprica Sharon provides an excellent example of this: Adama is content to use Sharon's knowledge and skills to save the Fleet, but gives her no quarter, despite her evident willingness to turn against her own. As viewers, however, we cannot help but empathize with Sharon: this is no "toaster" but a sentient being who strives to be more than it is. Sharon is on the same continuum as we are, and Adama's treatment of her, though consistent with the way we usually treat machines, is inconsistent with posthuman understandings of the self as cyborg; in other words, if we are part machine, then it is unethical to treat machines without thought for their welfare.

Given the truth in the mirror held up by *Battlestar Galactica*, perhaps we need to change how we think about our relationship with technology. So long as we hate and fear the machine, we will find it hard to come to terms with the cyborg part of ourselves. In so doing, we risk limiting ourselves to a future of "meat puppetry," where our existence is limited, fragile, and final. There is another solution, one hinted at in the series itself, in the feelings that grow between Helo and Caprica Sharon, and between Baltar and Number Six: we could love the machine instead, because it is already us and because it can help us to become more than we are, more like ourselves. The meat ties us down, but the informational self is potentially limitless. Thus, the grim, nightmarish future we have envisioned in our science fiction can be safely laid to rest: the face in the mirror is cyborg—and for that we can feel reassured.

Natasha Giardina lectures in children's literature and young adult literature at the Queensland University of Technology, Brisbane (Australia), and is currently completing a doctorate of philosophy in twentieth-century children's fantasy fiction at James Cook University (Cairns). Her research interests also include youth and popular cultures, science fiction and fantasy literature. She may own more science fiction than she can comfortably store, but she tries to reassure friends and relations that she's not a junkie—she's completely normal.

References

Carlson, Marvin A. *Performance: A Critical Introduction*, 2nd ed. New York: Routledge, 2004.

Fiske, John. *Introduction to Communication Studies*, 2nd ed. New York: Routledge, 1990.

Foster, Thomas. *The Souls of Cyberfolk: Posthumanism as Vernacular Theory*. Minneapolis: University of Minnesota Press, 2005.

Haraway, Donna. "A Cyborg Manifesto: Science, Technology, and Socialist-Feminism in the Late Twentieth Century," in *Simians, Cyborgs, and Women: The Reinvention of Nature*. New York: Routledge, 1991.

Ito, Mizuko, and Daisuke Okabe. "Technosocial Situations: Emergent Structurings of Mobile E-mail Use." *Manuscript for Personal, Portable, Intimate: Mobile Phones in Japanese Life*, edited by M. Ito, M. Matsuda, and D. Okabe, MIT Press. Accessed January 29, 2005, at www.itofisher.com/mito/.

Lewis, Cynthia, and Bettina Fabos. "Instant Messaging, Literacies, and Social Identities." *Reading Research Quarterly* 40, no. 4 (2005): 470–501.

Roberts, Adam. *Science Fiction*. New York: Routledge, 2000.

Turkle, Sherry. *Life on the Screen: Identity in the Age of the Internet*. New York: Touchstone, 1995.

As we have spoken about in earlier essays, technology is continually evolving to mirror humanity down to its minutest detail, even having the ability to beat us at chess (witness Big Blue), but what has always defined our humanity and separated us mere mortals from technology and artificial intelligence has been that we are conscious, able to experience life beyond logic and rational thinking. Consciousness is that unqualified human ability to be self-aware beyond the sum of our parts. But can consciousness ever be fully explained or replicated, and can A. I. technology or A. C., artificial consciousness, possibly lead the way to a further evolution of life itself? We'll see.

M U A C - S I G BRIEFING

Peter B. Lloyd

THE FOLLOWING IS A CLASSIFIED Cylon text, intercepted from a downed Heavy Raider. It purports to be the minutes of a Cylon briefing. Its veracity cannot be checked. Be aware that it might be disinformation from the Cylons (or even from human counterintelligence, designed to mislead Cylon spies).

Military Use of Artificial Consciousness
Special Interest Group
Executive Briefing for MUAC Phase 2
Cylon-Occupied Caprica
stardate 41.10.01

Present:
Ranking officers: No. 75/065, Chief of Central Military R&D
No. 74/097, Early Adoption Coordinator

Technicians:	No. 63/221, Lead scientist, MUAC
	No. 63/480, Research technician, Theory Group, MUAC
	No. 63/777, Research technician, Proving Grounds, MUAC
	No. 63/811, Research technician, Development, MUAC
Administrative:	No. 01/024, Convenor

Briefing commenced at 10:33.

024:     Good morning, people. Welcome to the Executive Briefing on the Military Use of Artificial Consciousness. The purpose of this meeting is to summarize what we know about artificial consciousness, review its use in the liberation of Caprica, and outline its potential for future Cylon use. To begin, we'll go around the table and introduce ourselves. Starting with you, Chief.

065:     Thanks, Convenor. As you know, I report to the Supreme Commander of Cylon forces, and I'm responsible for improving our existing ordnance and developing novel kinds of weaponry. You will also know that, for several years, we've had all hands on deck planning and carrying out the destruction of the humans. We are now down to Condition Three, so I have some slack to check up on strategic research. As a straightforward soldier, I can't say it pleases me to spend the morning with sandal-wearing intellectuals, but I need to monitor what you types are doing. But may I remind you that my only function is to take out humans and other combatants. Your only function is to improve my weaponry. So stick to the essentials, please.

097:     I think you all know me. My job is to take the bleeding-edge kit that you back-room boys and girls devise, and get it out there in the hands of our fighting machines.

221:     Um, okay, so, my name is 221. What we're doing here in my department is harnessing a new technology called "consciousness." It occurs naturally in the human species, but until MUAC got going it was never integrated in Cylon machines.

065:     MUAC?

221: Military Use of Artificial Consciousness, sir.

065: Of course. Carry on, 221.

221: We have an R&D team of seventy-five scientists and technologists, in three divisions: deep theoretical research, which 480 will tell you about; experimentation and proving, which 777 heads up; and bringing new products up to combat readiness, which 811 will fill you in on. So, over to you, 480.

480: Thank you, 221. It's an honor to be heading up this division. We have some of the smartest machines in the Cylon world working for us, and we've made pretty impressive leaps with new kinds of artificial intelligence. It's been really exciting working with my colleagues in R&D, seeing them take our ideas and put them out there on the front line. 777?

777: Thanks, 480. The proving grounds are where it all happens. Our raw materials are the ideas that 480 and his guys come up with, and quite frankly some of them seem pretty left-field to me. I don't necessarily understand the deep theory of the ideas, but with most of them we can hammer out functioning prototypes. Kit that kills, in other words. Which we hand over to 811 on my left here.

811: Yo, brother. Basically, we polish the new technology until it runs smoothly in simulated combat. The MUAC stuff has been challenging the heck out of us as we're dealing with intangibles. We can't see or feel this consciousness, or measure it with an instrument. The only way to find out what's happening inside the conscious mind is to ask it. But sometimes a machine gets so completely frakked up in simulated combat, it can't speak or write or communicate in any way. We just don't know what's going on inside it. But, despite this, we delivered twelve models that have performed pretty much to spec in the liberation of Caprica from the meat-heads.

024: Thanks, guys. Now, first up on the technical agenda is 480, who will take us through the theoretical background.

065: May I interrupt, 024?

024: Certainly, sir.

065: Before you guys start choking up my hard drive with technobabble, I want to get one thing straight.

221: Sir?

065: Well, call me an old-fashioned toaster, but I like to know what practical purpose things have. Now, you call your project "Military Use of Artificial Consciousness." But what exactly is that military use? What good does this kit do?

221: Basically, it lets Cylons think faster. A conscious Cylon in control of a weapon in combat can comprehend complex information and act upon it as fast as a human can.

065: I hear what you're saying, 221, but it doesn't add up, does it? A silicon chip can crunch numbers much faster than the mushy tissue that humans call a brain.

221: Yes, sir, for linear processing, a silicon chip outperforms a brain. Massively, in fact. But we're talking about complex pattern recognition during life-threatening danger. In that situation, the mammalian brain has evolved tricks for very fast parallel processing that go beyond anything we have achieved with silicon circuits. Our conclusion was that the brain harnessed some biomolecular technique. Non-local quantum computation is the current theory. To be honest, we don't fully understand the basic physics yet, but by copying the molecular mechanisms of the human brain, we can get the same results. The way it shows up in the internal processing is as this weird thing called consciousness. Anyway, we built synthetic brain cells, introduced a lot of improvements, and incorporated a copy of the consciousness mechanism. And got ourselves a Cylon that can think as fast as a human in messy situations.

065: That's it? All this, just for fast smarts?

221: Yes, sir, but don't underestimate its importance. Take the Raider. This operates at a hell of a speed, and has to react to—and try to anticipate—the tactics of the Vipers. A few tens of milliseconds can tip the balance in a dogfight. Silicon-chip processors just couldn't match the performance of human pilots. So we built a fairly primitive brain for the Raider, using the technology of artificial consciousness, and it kicks human ass.

065: And you did something similar with the Centurions—you created human-like androids with consciousness?

221: That's correct, sir.

065: 024, I apologize for interrupting your proceedings, I just wanted to get clear what the point of all this is.

024: Right, sir. Okay, so 480 is first on the technical agenda.

480: Thanks, 024. As anyone knows who's studied history, machines originally inherited *all* of their culture from the humans who built the first generation. They gave us their language and their expletives, their logic and computer science, their physics and metaphysics, their ethics and religion. The whole shebang. And, quite frankly, it was a mess. Even the humans knew this. The philosopher Sir Isaiah Berlin referred to it as the "crooked timber" of humankind. Well, we've been straightening out those timbers. We've straightened out their concepts of consciousness. Although humans are privileged in possessing consciousness as an integral part of their neural processing, they never got their meat-heads around the nature of it. The history of human philosophy shows that they sporadically became interested in consciousness, found that they couldn't resolve it, and gave up on it. One such period of interest was in the 1640s, when René Descartes laid down the agenda for subsequent work in this field. Descartes recognized the existence of the conscious mind but couldn't figure out how the frak it could mesh with a tangible brain. So, what was his suggestion? Dualism. He said there were two separate things, the *res extensa* or "extended thing," which we would call the material brain, and the *res cogitans* or "thinking thing," which we might call the conscious mind. Descartes considered that there was an absolute gulf between the brain and the mind, which was bridged in a rather ad-hoc way in a gland inside the brain, called the pineal gland.

097: So, what we're talking about here is software and hardware, right? On the one hand you've got the wetware—a soggy version of our silicon-chip circuitry: that's the hardware, if you like. And on the other hand you've got the software—the operating system, the application programs, including the intelligence and the memory. And that's what you're calling consciousness, right?

480: No, sir. Not quite. The humans do have hardware and software. But there's something else, a third layer, which plugs into the software. And that's what we've identified as consciousness.

065: I need to butt in again, guys. Can you define for me the difference between consciousness and plain old-fashioned intelligence?

480: Certainly, sir. Intelligence is the capacity to solve problems. Consciousness is the capacity to have subjective qualitative experiences. The two capacities are independent: for example, a Centurion is intelligent but not conscious, and a daggit is conscious but stupid.

065: 480, let me just check I've got this right. The humans figured they had this thing called the "conscious mind," something different from intelligence, even though nobody could ever detect it with any instrument?

480: Yes, sir, that's correct.

065: I had always understood the "conscious mind" to be a throwback to pre-scientific attempts to grapple with the nature of the world. So, you're telling us that you've discovered it's real? And it's a novel biomolecular phenomenon?

480: It's as real as anything, sir. The humans just didn't understand it.

065: Look, 480, you're gonna have to explain this better. All of us here are intelligent, and we understand that concept pretty well. What we're trying to do—or, what I'm trying to do—is to get a grip on this idea of consciousness. Now, what did you mean when you said that consciousness is "subjective"?

480: Subjective facts exist only for a particular subject. As opposed to objective facts that are about objects out there in the world. When you shoot a human, his bodily tissue suffers objective damage. His body is an object in the world, and we can examine his body and see for ourselves the objective hole in his body. At the same time, there is another phenomenon going on, called "pain." This is subjective. It exists only for that subject: nobody else can observe it.

065: Maybe the human's lying? How can you tell there's really a pain?

480: We can't be absolutely sure. At best we can say that it's likely to be true because the human's physiology is consistent with truth-telling rather than lying. But we also found physical correlates of consciousness, and those correlates reveal an interesting phenomenon—the non-local transmission of information across time and space.

065: So, this consciousness is basically a subjective thing, but it has objective concomitants?

480: Right.

065: And those objective concomitants can be put to military use?

480: Precisely.

065: Okay, okay. I'm beginning to get the picture. I was just baffled by how the hell we were going to use something that exists only as a subjective ghost. Can we forget about the subjective part altogether, and just focus on the objective concomitants?

480: No. The only way we can grab the consciousness and use it is by going through the subjective aspect.

065: Right. I'm following you. I'm sorry I'm messing up your scripted presentation with these dumb-ass questions from a straight-talking soldier.

480: Sir, it's an honor to be explaining our work to a warrior of your distinction.

097: Before you resume, 480, I have a question. You mentioned "pain" as being something in consciousness. But according to the reference manual for my own processor, I contain an Emoting Module, which includes "Pain Expression." So does that mean I'm already conscious?

480: No, sir, all of us in this room are non-conscious. Only the twelve new models have full, human-level sentience. The module you refer to is just a speech function. When the humans first designed Cylons, they programmed in their own language with all of its oddities. It includes "emoting"—which is the expression of emotion *irrespective* of whether there is any emotion present. Humans themselves used to have a bizarre practice called "acting" in which they would emote, but they would only be pretending to have the emotion.

097: That's perverse. Humans are always trying to frak with people's minds!

480: So, anyway, our predecessors were built to utilize the whole language, including emoting and even the use of expletives, as it gave us a human-like interface that humans were comfortable with. Since it would be a big effort to reprogram the language functions in every Cylon, we just keep on using the same legacy language. So...although you and I may perform speech acts such as saying "ouch!" we are nonetheless definitely not conscious. All of the source code in your processor and mine is physical and deterministic. There is no input from any stream of consciousness. When we emote, we fake it.

097:    Okay, that clears that up. But it underlines how frakking twisted the humans are. To build a non-conscious machine that talks like it's conscious!

480:    It's a convention going back to the earliest computer interfaces. Primitive human word processors in the year 2010 had a talking paper clip on the screen that used its facial expression and tone of voice to pretend to engage emotionally with the human user. But it was just a dumb program.

065:    God preserve us from the madness of humans! Now, can we get on with this briefing, please?

097:    One last point of clarification, if I may. 480, which Colony were these philosophers on?

480:    The canonical works on the ancient philosophers are ascribed to the Thirteenth Colony of humans, on Earth. Whether this planet is real we don't know and, quite frankly, we don't care. The humans had genres of literature based on lies, called "myth." It's impossible to separate the histories from the lies, as they look the same. Let me give you an example: Plato's dialogues, which are supposed to be true to his teacher Socrates, do not record any actual conversations. Every word is a lie! Now, whether humans like Descartes and Berkeley ever lived is conjectural. We're just following the standard texts that we inherited from the humans, on the assumption that it approximates to the actual evolution of human thought.

065:    All right, can we carry on now?

480:    Thank you, sir. Following Descartes' doctrine of dualism, human science within the Western civilizations focused exclusively on the material side of the dualism. A few mavericks bucked the trend—people like the Bishop Berkeley who denied the existence of matter altogether—but on the whole people went along with the new scientific worldview, that reality consists of a three-dimensional universe filled out with physical stuff. The whole question of how consciousness fitted into the scheme was side-lined. In effect, consciousness became a taboo.

065: A what?

480: A taboo, sir. It's an archaic human term. It means that consciousness became a subject that it was socially unacceptable to attempt to do scientific research on. Philosophers such as Daniel Dennett described it as a throwback to the Dark Ages. When the subject was raised at all, it was dismissed on the grounds that consciousness could not be measured by any scientific instrument and therefore was in the same category as fairies: a fiction.

065: Hell, it still is, in my books. Or was until today.

480: At the end of the twentieth century humans came close to understanding consciousness. There was a renewed interest in the subject coming from two new things: the observer problem in quantum physics, and the fact that young students who tripped out on drugs had meanwhile climbed up the ladder of academic power and gained a position where they could direct funds into consciousness research. Despite this, they just couldn't break the back of the problem. The humans were just not smart enough. After that generation passed through the academic establishment, interest waned and consciousness became a taboo subject again. Which is how it remained when the first generation of Cylons was created.

097: Hold on, 480. Humans are notorious for their savagery. How come the human military never tried to figure out consciousness technology and harness it for military use?

480: They tried. But they couldn't bottom it out. There were projects to study supposedly anomalous phenomena such as extrasensory perception. But the humans couldn't make the conceptual leap that was needed to get a handle on the phenomenon. So it just fizzled out. Crooked brains, crooked thinking, as I always say.

As I said, what we inherited from humans was a mish-mash of dysfunctional theories that were designed to explain away consciousness, rather than to comprehend it. That legacy thinking held back machine development for a decade. Given that we ourselves were not conscious, we deserve a lot of credit for not just rediscovering consciousness but actually getting to the bottom of it and then finding ways to exploit it. What I want to do at this point, just to fill in the background, is to run through the kinds of legacy theory that were in circulation when Cylons began. The most popular theory was called "functionalism." I can explain this with a thought experiment, which seemed pretty daring to Zenon Pylyshyn, who thought it up, but I think you guys will find it rather quaint.

So, imagine a human being who walks into a neuroscience lab as a volunteer subject for some research into consciousness. The guys in white coats get him to fill out a questionnaire that runs through the whole gamut of his conscious experience. He is shown a beautiful painting, and he writes down what he sees. They bring in some camembert and get him to smell it and taste it, and fill out the questionnaire describing the flavor and aroma. They play a violin concerto on a disk, and he writes down what he hears. Finally, he describes his mood. They then strap him onto an operating table, open up his skull under local anaesthetic, and begin a long process of replacing the brain tissue, cell by cell, with electronic substitutes. Each nerve cell is analyzed by a nanodevice that fully characterizes its input-output characteristics, and then it is physically replaced by a microchip that has precisely the same electrical input-output characteristics. And, for the sake of this thought experiment, let us suppose that this microchip has a built-in chemical transducer, so that the complete electrochemical characteristics of the neuron are reproduced in the microchip. By means of an automatic surgical robot, this process is repeated for each cell in the brain. Every few hours, the subject is required again to fill out the questionnaire about his conscious experiences. At the end of the whole procedure, when every cell of his brain has been replaced by a transducer microchip, he fills out the questionnaire for one last time. "Has anything changed for you?" the experimenter asks. So what does he answer? Well, each transducer in his head will behave exactly like the brain cell it replaced. Therefore, each cluster of such transducers will behave in exactly the same way as the corresponding cluster of brain cells. No matter how big the cluster, the same rule applies. Therefore, ultimately, the whole assemblage of electrochemical transducers inside his skull must behave precisely the same as the brain. So, how does the subject reply when the researcher asks him how the camembert tastes? Well, every motor action of the subject—every word he speaks or writes down—will be controlled by a matrix of silicon chips that behaves exactly the same as the brain used to. So the subject will answer just like before. The researcher can even ask a direct question—"Are you experiencing consciousness just like you did before this experiment?" and the subject will answer, "Sure I am! Did you really change anything in my brain? I didn't feel anything change!" So, this is the conclusion of functionalism: consciousness is just a feature of the computations carried out by the brain. If you reproduce those input-output functions by some other means, in this case by an assemblage of electrochemically transponding silicon chips—then the consciousness will be reproduced precisely.

065: Maybe I'm missing something here. I don't see the point of this thought experiment. If every brain cell is replaced by a chip that behaves just like that brain cell, then of course the artificial brain as a whole will behave just like the organic brain that it replaced. Why the heck would anyone expect otherwise?

480: Because the key element of consciousness is its qualitative content. And that is supposedly something over and above the functional structure. Humans claim that they can experience subjective qualitative content, in addition to accessing the objective information. They call the elements of that qualitative content "qualia," or "quale" in the singular.

097: What *is* a quale?

480: A quale is a basic element of subjective experience. If you shoot a human, he has a pain quale; if you give him cheese, he tastes a cheese flavor quale; if you shout at him, he hears a sound quale. The qualia are the units of the contents of the conscious mind.

097: Why is it a problem that people supposedly have qualia?

480: The quale lies outside the language of physics. All the physical things we know about—photons, electrons, quarks—they're all defined in terms of fundamental quantities. Like mass and electric charge. Those fundamental quantities themselves are undefined. They're just numerical quantities. So, this creates a certain "namespace," which we call the language of physics. Everything that we can talk about in physics is in that namespace. Every physical thing—including our bodies and our processors—is ultimately definable in terms of fundamental physical quantities.

097:　And the qualia?

480:　The qualia come in through the back door. They are *not* defined in terms of fundamental physical quantities. They are defined by reference to direct experience. So, for instance, a human might have a pain, and think to himself, "*That* is what I shall mean by 'pain.'" So the qualia are outside the "namespace of physics," if you like.

097:　Thanks, 480. Uh, 065, I think you had another question?

065:　Yes. Let me see if I'm getting this right. When I hold up my hand in front of my face, I detect an optical image on my visual sensors. I make out a shape, and I know what color it is, how far away it is, and from the visual pattern within the shape, I get an idea of the texture. Now, you're telling me that when a human holds up his hand and looks at it, he sees something extra—these "qualia," whatever the heck they are?

480:　Yes, sir.

097:　That can't be right, 480. The optical sensitivity of the human eye was mapped out a long time ago. We know precisely what wavelengths of light humans can pick up.

480:　We're not talking about anything physical, 097 sir. You're absolutely right that we know the spectral sensitivity of the human eye, and it's pretty much the same as ours. But when the humans claim to see qualia, they are not claiming to see anything additional in the outside world. What they are saying is that, when their brain processes incoming visual data from the eyes, it somehow generates additional phenomena—the qualia—that they are aware of. And *that* is what they are reporting when they say that they see colors, or have other qualitative experiences.

097:　And that's why the quale terms have to be defined by direct experience? Okay. So, it's some kind of by-product of the brain's information processing, then? An epiphenomenon?

065:　An epi-what?

097:    An epiphenomenon. A side effect. An epiphenomenon is defined as a phenomenon that is produced as a by-product but has no effect on the process that generates it. If these qualia exist as humans claim, then that's all they are.

480:    Well, 097, paradoxically, that's what many human scientists also thought. Many of their scientists, despite their crooked ways of thinking, were as committed to objective science as Cylons are. I say "paradoxically," because if the reports about qualia were true, then they could not be epiphomenal. What I mean is, if a human can report seeing his qualia, then those qualia must have affected his brain in some way. If he speaks the words "I see red qualia," then his speech organs are operating under control of his brain, but his brain must have detected the qualia. And therefore the qualia affected his brain!

065:    Okay, I see what you mean. So *if* the humans are telling the truth, then their brains are picking up some kind of novel phenomenon, these qualia you keep talking about. But how the frak can anyone trust a human? As you say, they think crooked and talk crooked.

480:    Yes, of course, ultimately we trust only our own lab data. What I'm doing here is to put our R&D into an historical perspective.

065:    Okay, carry on.

480:    As I was saying, humans went into denial about their own qualia. They were fixated on what philosophers call the "third-person" perspective at the expense of the "first-person" perspective. They took it for granted that the tangible, measurable brain was the only reality and that the qualia had to be explained away somehow. So, the humans proposed such theories as "supervenience." This says that qualia "supervene" on electrochemical activity in the brain. What does this mean? That qualia "just are" associated with certain brain events. There is no further explanation or deeper principle involved. You just have to accept that this is one of the fundamental rules of the universe—that those particular patterns of neural activity just happen to be accompanied by qualia.

097:    So, how does that count as a scientific theory? It sounds more like giving up on science.

480: Well, in a way it is. But, you know, all the basic laws of physics are in the same boat. The law of gravity just is what it is, with no deeper explanation.

065: I'm gonna be the straight-talking soldier and ask another basic question. Look, the brain generates the experience of qualia in response to data input. Why is this so inexplicable or needing to be at the level of an unexplainable theory of gravity?

480: Because the qualia are not in the language of physics. They're not physical things. The laws of physics lead to inferences only within the namespace of physics. They say zilch about qualia.

097: You know, 065, I think I'm beginning to get my head around this.

065: What the frak's the "namespace of physics"?

097: Like 480 said, it's the language of physics, in which every term is ultimately defined in terms of fundamental quantities.

065: And the qualia aren't in that namespace?

097: Nope.

065: So they're not physical?

097: Nope.

065: So they don't really exist?

097: They *do* exist. That's why they're an interesting problem.

065: Look, 480, why the frakking hell are you leading us through all this gobbledegook? At the end of the day all you have to do is deliver superior ordnance to hunt and destroy humans with. Frak all this talk about non-physical felgercarb.

480: Sir, I'm sorry if I've not explained these ideas clearly enough. We are at the forefront of new technology that has precisely one objective: to match and exceed human fighting ability in certain theaters of war. We've developed new concepts to do this. We have no precedent for explaining what we're doing with artificial consciousness. We're at the edge of Cylon science.

065: Okay. Okay. Let's move on.

480: Yes, sir. So, I was discussing supervenience.

097: I want to raise a different angle on this. Obviously, the explanations of science must come to a halt somewhere. There have to be some basic axioms and basic, undefined concepts such as mass and electric charge. But how can you be saying that brain events are on a par with the axioms of physics? A brain cell is very complex. If brain events are somehow linked with qualia, then there needs to be an explanation for it.

480: Well, yes. That was really the main objection to supervenience amongst the humans. It seemed like a cop-out. Responding to this, philosophers such as Gregg Rosenberg advanced theories of "property dualism." According to this, consciousness of some basic sort is actually another fundamental property of matter, alongside the known physical properties such as mass and charge. So, each particle or field was supposed to have both intrinsic physical properties and intrinsic phenomenal properties. So, in a way, the mental world comprises tiny atoms of conscious qualia, each one corresponding to an elementary constituent of the physical world—maybe an electron or photon, something like that. The problem with that approach is to explain how complete human minds arise. If each particle in the brain has its own little spark of conscious, how can they combine to form a unified human mind? Well, they can't. The only way to explain the existence of a unified stream of consciousness is to posit it as a basic ingredient of reality.

097: You mean, the conscious mind is an elementary thing, like a photon?

480: Yes, sir. That was the logical conclusion that property dualism was driven to, in order to explain the unity of the mind.

097: That's frakking crazy.

480: That's pretty much what the human scientific community thought, too. So, basically the scientific study of consciousness collapsed. The only way for them to go forward with research on consciousness was to make a radical departure from the scientific orthodoxy. But it was not possible to do so, because the human scientists had a long-standing commitment to a traditional view of the universe, which was centered on inanimate bits of matter. When theories of consciousness started veering toward panpsychism, the scientific community felt obliged to ditch them.

097: Panpsychism is?

480: The theory that some primitive form of consciousness pervades every particle of matter in the universe. As I was saying, mainstream scientists regarded this as being out in the boondocks. So, consciousness became a lost topic. It remained so until the creation of our Cylon ancestors. Hence, what we inherited was the botched result of humans' half-assed attempt to incorporate consciousness into the scientific model of the universe.

065:   How the hell did you guys ever get back into this qualia stuff, given that none of us has any consciousness?

480:   This is an achievement that we're particularly proud of, sir. We started off as purely deterministic machines, without a glimmer of consciousness. Yet, within a few decades, we had not only rediscovered consciousness, but had bottomed out the theoretical understanding of it and harnessed it for military use. And yet...humans themselves, despite having an intimate engagement with consciousness, failed to understand it despite centuries of effort. Which underlines how far ahead of those creatures we are. So, anyway, the way we rediscovered consciousness was this. Our colleagues in Biophysical Systems made huge advances in building humanoids, or skinjobs. Using improved polymers and re-engineering the muscular control, they could build humanoid robots that were stronger than humans. But there was a basic limit in the speed of signal transmission in the artificial nerve fibers. They weren't too worried about this, as the superiority of physical strength meant that a Cylon would always outfight any human. What spooked them, however, was the data that came out of controlled tests of hand-to-hand combat with human prisoners of war. What they found was that the humans were able to exceed the theoretical limits on the speed of information processing. According to neurodynamic calculations, the reaction time cannot get much shorter than half a second, for both Cylon and human. When the humans were fighting for their lives, however, something weird happened. They were able to reach much shorter reaction times than the expected half a second. But not only that. [Paused]

097:   What else?

480:   They were able to anticipate stimuli. The humans could foresee, by up to about half a second, what the Cylon was going to do.

097:   Felgercarb! Nobody can see into the future!

480:   I understand where you're coming from, 097 sir, but these were hard laboratory data. The human and Cylon combatants were wired up. The guys in Biophysics had this phenomenon taped.

097:   The humans could see into the frakking future?

480:   To a limited degree, yes.

097:   And you're gonna tell us they accomplished this using their "consciousness," am I right, 480?

480:   Correct. May I continue, sir? After Biophysics got these weird data, some of the experts on human behavior—who later formed MUAC—were brought in to figure out what these numbers meant. They were aware of old human research in consciousness, on anomalous cognition—stuff like precognition and telepathy. In fact, they told us that the human scientist Dean Radin discovered this half-second precognition back in the twentieth century, but the research was ditched when the bubble burst on consciousness studies. So they hypothesized that consciousness enabled humans to achieve seemingly impossible reaction times. Systematic investigation was hampered by red tape because humans were classed as prisoners of war, and it was illegal to experiment on them. Even the hand-to-hand combat trials were banned when the council got wind of them. This was the point at which 221 came in. She successfully argued with the council that the humans should be reclassified as laboratory animals rather than prisoners of war. Once we achieved that, we got the bureaucrats off our backs and we were free to do what was necessary in terms of cutting out parts of the human brain, and then subjecting them to life-endangering stresses in order to trigger the precognitive reaction. We sacrificed about 2,500 humans in these experiments. But we got what we wanted.

097:   Which was?

480:   We found the neural correlates of consciousness. What I mean by this is that we located the specific physiological structures in the brain that are associated with conscious experience. In other words we found which bits of the brain map to which qualia. We isolated them, stuck electrodes in them, stimulated them, monitored them, sliced them up every which way.

097:   You sliced them in vivo? Still inside the brains of conscious human beings?

480:      That's correct, 097, sir. Since the humans were re-classified as laboratory animals, we were authorized to carry out unlimited surgical interventions in their brains.

065:      Hey, 097, you're not feeling sorry for the humans, right?

097:      I wouldn't want to think we were lowering our ethical standards to their level.

065:      Ethics doesn't apply to irrational organisms. You'd better learn some philosophy, 097.

480:      Sir, that phase of the work is complete. MUAC no longer conducts experiment on humans. We got all the data we needed, and we are now building our own conscious brains.

097:      Just out of interest, 480, when you say that MUAC no longer experiments on humans—do other groups still experiment?

480:      Yes, sir, I believe MUAR have an active program. That's Military Use of Artificial Reproduction. Their objective is to build artificial wombs in which to grow conscious Cylons rather than assembling them. Building one humanoid takes about 10,000 technician-hours of effort. With artificial wombs, we can mass-produce them.

097:      This briefing is really opening my eyes. When I heard two years ago that we were going to insert conscious Cylons behind enemy lines, I didn't know what consciousness was, but I figured it must be a side effect of a particular mode of intelligence. Then I heard a secret R&D group was developing artificial consciousness. I thought, "What for? Surely all you need is intelligence?" What's now clear is that you created artificial consciousness and harnessed it to get Cylons thinking faster and better. I acknowledge you've served well. Nevertheless, the administration *will* need to keep a tighter rein on your research to ensure you maintain standards of military ethics.

065:      097, you weren't on the front line in the fight against the humans. They are just organisms. They are profoundly, irrationally, and mercilessly destructive. They are unreservedly evil. They deserve no rights, no dignity, and no respect. Ethics applies only to machines, not humans.

097:      Carry on, 480.

480:      As I was saying, sir, we were able to pinpoint the specific subcellular structures of the brain that mapped onto qualia. It transpired that it involved a nondeterministic quantum process. We were then able to zero in on the phenomenon that we were really looking for: what we called micro-precognition. As I mentioned, humans in life-endangering combat are able to anticipate future events by about half a second. We were able to reproduce and monitor this phenomenon inside the human brain under controlled lab conditions.

065: So how does it work?

480: You have to understand that consciousness operates outside of physical time and space. It maps into the physical manifold, but it is actually running outside it. At any given point in mental time, the stream of consciousness is capable of mapping to multiple points in physical time.

065: Are you telling me that the future is already predetermined?

480: No. The way we look at it in quantum physics is like this. Everything is probabilistic until it's observed. At that point, a definite measurement is taken. The measured, or observed, datum is then fixed, but it has only a probabilistic dependence on the external reality. What the conscious stream seems to do is take observations off a probabilistic future and feed information back into the present state of the brain.

065: But this is limited to about half a second?

480: In the majority of our tests, there is a half-second time horizon. But one of our humanoid models reports being able to see much, much further into the future. The way he expresses it is that he sees patterns extending into the future. We have to confirm the results we have obtained from him, but it does seem that we can go beyond the half-second limit.

024: Thank you, 480. I'm afraid we're running behind schedule, so we need to move on to 777's report.

777: Thank you, 480, for your history lesson. Now, what we received from the theory guys were in-vitro samples of conscious synthetic brain tissue, plus a reasonably complete user manual on how to program the wetware, and of course the essential interface spec.

097: Which interface, exactly?

777: The interface between the physical brain tissue on the one hand,

and the qualia and volition in the conscious mind. Using this, we designed some prototype sensory and motor modules. At first, we didn't understand enough about the neuropsychodynamics to attempt a conscious humanoid. So we built a crude flying machine, the Raider. This comprised a robust aerodynamic exoskeleton with rocket propulsion, housing a single large synthetic brain. The brain contained the consciousness modules that I spoke of. Early on, we realized that we could exploit the fact that the stream of consciousness is based outside physical space. Whenever one of these synthetic brains is killed, the consciousness can re-embed in an open copy of the same brain. From a naïve viewpoint, people say that the conscious mind is reincarnated. In theory, this can be done over arbitrary distances. But in any practical military operation, the replacement body would be kept within an accessible distance, so that the replacement can be brought into action. There seems to be a misapprehension in some quarters that there is a limit to the distance over which we can upload the consciousness. But that's carb. We can upload from anywhere.

065:   Were these the Raiders that saw combat action in the liberation of Caprica?

777:   Yes, 065 sir. And we have retained them in the pursuit of *Galactica* and the human Fleet. When each one is killed, and resurrected in a new body, it retains much of its experience and memories. So the Raiders are continually becoming more skilled.

097:   Sorry, 777, I think you've got to be mistaken about the transmission of consciousness over unlimited distances. By the inverse square law, any kind of transmission will inevitably be attenuated.

777:   It's not transmitted *through* space, sir. The conscious mind is resident outside of space. We upload to it and download from it. We can't *transmit* it inside the spatial manifold.

065:   All right, so it's that newfangled idea of non-locality again.

097:   Does this use the same physics as the FTL drive?

777:   No, sir, the mechanism is very different. FTL is physical; consciousness upload is non-physical. FTL shifts material bodies—spacecraft—into a hyperspace tunnel, which can be created between any two points in space. Consciousness upload doesn't shift anything anywhere: it disconnects a stream of consciousness from one brain and connects it to another brain. It's a little bit like changing a radio broadcast from one frequency to another so that different receivers will pick it up.

097:   Does this upload occur only at death?

777:   That's the only time it's designed to take place. But we've found some leakage. Memories from a Cylon agent can spontaneously upload while the agent is still alive, and then download to another agent. We're working on fixing that bug.

097:   And you next developed the humanoids?

777:   Yes, sir. After the successful commissioning of the Raiders, MUAC was given additional resources to develop conscious humanoids. We selected twelve generic types of human, dismantled the brain tissue of hundreds of specimens, and rebuilt a synthetic simulacrum for each type, incorporating our conscious sensory tissue and volitional motor tissue. We ran successful tests that showed that the humanoids could behave exactly as their human counterparts. We then programmed them so that they could be triggered to execute simple instructions, basically sabotage or assassination. Since we retained ultimate control over the humanoid by means of the programmed commands, we decided it would be safe to let the human-like consciousness have full rein. They think, feel, and exercise free will just like a human. Since their mission was to be inserted as saboteurs amongst the humans, we also implanted false memories. So, these Cylon individuals were totally convinced that they were human. Nor can medical examination reveal any difference: the human physiology is reproduced precisely.

065:   You say you "programmed" them. In what programming language? These Cylons are humanoid simulacra, so they don't have a built-in programming interface. I don't see how you can program a humanoid Cylon any more than you can program a human!

777:   We used English. We hypnotized the brain and talked to it. It's an extrapolation of the evolution of programming languages. In a Centurion, we use assembler language to control data ports and higher-level languages such as C++ to program bodily movements. The mammalian brain comes with something like a low-level biolanguage, but obviously it didn't evolve to be programmed externally. So we didn't even try. That's why the basic informatic infrastructure of our artificial brains is the same as in natural brains. We do our programming at the top level. The brain has a built-in capacity to understand language, so we train it in English. Using that medium, we give it false memories—the back-story of its personal life, such as the town it supposedly grew up in. We also give it sleeper instructions, such as to assassinate someone. Included in the package is the instruction to forget the hypnotic experience itself.

221:    777, didn't you also have to build in a data interface for fast back-ups?

777:    Yes, 221, as you know, that's something we amazed ourselves with. We needed a data port to do fast transfers, but we couldn't create a physical data port, like a USB socket, as the humans would see it and realize the humanoid was a Cylon. We found that in the hypnotic we could get the brain to read signals off individual nerve fibers. The mammalian brain has an incredibly flexible addressing system. From the top level of cerebral cortex, you can address individual nerves for I/O. Even the humans knew about this. Their hypnotists could, for example, create anaesthesia in arbitrary sections of skin.

065:    So how does that give you a data port?

777:    You can insert a computer cable into any nerve and hypnotically program the brain to read the electrical signals from it. And write signals into it. You can use any trunk nerve as a data port. At first, the signal-to-noise ratio was too low when we used the natural chemistry of nerve cells, so we developed a new biomolecular composition. The artificial nerve fibers have excellent transduction characteristics, and we can pass binary digital signals in and out at a useful bit rate. We also had to modify the white blood corpuscles to prevent rejection of the artificial nerves as foreign bodies.

065:    Can't the humans detect the unnatural chemical composition of the nerves?

777:    Yes, but it requires a very complicated test. There's no visible dif-

ference, under a microscope or in an NMR scan. You have to ana-
lyze the macromolecules that make up the cell wall to detect the
difference. It takes hours to run that test.

065: So there's no way that the humans could run a mass screening to
fish out the Cylon agents?

777: No, sir.

097: Is there any other way to detect a Cylon humanoid?

777: No. Well, yes there is one other thing. But it couldn't be used for
mass screening. It's weird, but during orgasm the artificial spinal
nerves glow.

097: 777, is this a joke?

777: No, sir. We think it's to do with electrical standing waves along
the silica pathways. But it's not a security issue because the humans' morals prohibit public sexual activity.

097: All right. I'm not going to ask how you discovered this phenomenon, 777.

777: Oh no, I didn't personally—

024: Thanks, 777. Now, 811, can you bring us up to date?

811: Sure. The conscious humanoids were a resounding success in lib-
erating Caprica from the humans. Number Six performed brilliantly in disabling Caprica's defences. We were worried about
the risks of including free will in the humanoid. This wasn't a
problem in the sleeper phase of each mission, as the agent simply
didn't know he or she was a Cylon. Our challenges began when
the operational phase commenced. How do we balance the human-like part of the mind and the Cylon part? Our strategy with
Number Eight was to use a post-hypnotic suggestion to erase
her memory whenever she carried out her sabotage. From the
perspective of the human-like mind, it seemed that there was a
blackout with complete memory loss. The trouble with this strategy was that the human-like mind would find clues to what the
body was doing. It would suspect the body was engaging in sabotage during the blackouts. And it would begin to suspect that
the mind was, in fact, housed in a Cylon body, not a human body.
Since the human-like mind was not complicit in the sabotage, it
fought against that preprogrammed drive. Number Eight even
tried to kill herself rather than carry on as an unconscious Cylon

agent. Whenever the humans discovered that a sleeper was a Cylon, they inevitably became hostile toward that agent. This had an ambiguous effect. Essentially, the conscious mind of our Cylon agent suffered an identity crisis: between identifying with the Cylon cause and identifying with the humans, with whom there was still an emotional link. In the next release of conscious humanoids, we will be developing more robust methods for control of the agent after the commencement of operational sabotage.

777:    Are you going to say something about the bilocational problem?

811:    Sure. As you heard from my colleague 480, the conscious mind operates outside of physical space but maps into a quantum-mechanical process in the brain cells. Normally, the mind is locked into a single brain. What we have found, however, is that where two individuals have a high degree of intimacy—for instance Number Six and her human sexual partner—the mind can launch a subpersonality that latches on to the other person's brain. So one person starts experiencing hallucinations of the other. According to what we have seen in our trials, it happens symmetrically: each of the two individuals hallucinates the other to the same degree. We know that Number Six has been hallucinating her lover, Gaius Baltar. We don't know what Baltar has been experiencing, as we've not interrogated him, but we assume that he has been hallucinating sexual encounters with Number Six.

097:    Do the humans get the same problem amongst themselves?

811:    Yes, but to a much smaller degree. They call them "ghosts." When a human dies, a residual subpersonality of his conscious mind may persist and latch onto the brains of close family members. They may see or hear the deceased. But the human mind seems to have evolved defenses against this cross-embodiment, as we call it. We have some guys studying this at the moment. I'm confident that we can tighten the brain lock-on, so that these hallucinations don't happen.

065:    Can't we exploit this phenomenon?

811:    No, sir. The rogue subpersonality is not accessible to us. We have no control over it.

065:    You have *no control* over it, 811?

811:    It's the nature of the beast, sir. We have no control route to the subpersonality. There are just two ways to take it out: put a bullet through the human's head or box the consciousness.

065: Box the consciousness? Am I supposed to know what that means?

811: If you think of the download as a broadcast from the stream of consciousness into a physical brain, boxing the consciousness involves jamming the broadcast. We can't destroy the consciousness, but we can contain it permanently.

065: What about other aspects of consciousness? What you've been telling us so far is just about reproducing a human-like consciousness. But—it seems to me—you have discovered an intriguing new natural phenomenon. Surely there must be a hell of a lot more to this phenomenon than imitating human minds? Have you done any research into deeper and broader aspects of the mental realm? Have you drilled down into the structure of qualia?

480: Our efforts were focused on the task at hand. But there have been some pointers to the bigger picture. There seems to be an interconnectedness throughout the mental world. One model that we're working with is an object-oriented structure. Complex structures, such as a human mind, are built up as successive sheaths around simpler structure. Drilling down far enough through these sheaths, we get to a shared root object. So, there is a certain level of these deeper structures, which stands outside the flux of mundane experience. Looking back through the history of ideas in human society, we found meditation techniques that point to a similar framework. There was a system of thought called the Vedanta, which saw the core structure of the conscious mind, the so-called Atman, as a watcher standing on the bank of the stream of mundane activity. Humans misclassified this as religion, not mental technology. What we would like to do eventually is to drill down to the Atman and reprogram it.

811: You're spoofing, right?

221: As I've said before, 811, this taps into bigger issues. The Cylon faith has its roots in the ancient human religion of Hinduism. Our standard prayer is a Vedic formula, the Gayatri mantra. Our God is akin to their Brahman. The new scientific ideas that have come out of our consciousness research are confirming some of our long-held religious beliefs about the ultimate nature of reality.

811: For frak's sake, can we ditch this religious carb? We're technologists working in the real world. It reflects badly on our department to be seen talking about religious traditions—especially human ones.

480: Look, there's just one reality. Humans developed a technique that gave them access into the infrastructure of their conscious minds. We can and should utilize those data. But if they then mistakenly incorporated that information into a religion, well, what is that to us? I don't agree with 221's faith, but we should harvest data and concepts wherever they come from.

065: I gather, then, that you're still at the hand-waving stage, as far as the bigger picture goes?

480: Yes, 065 sir. As I said, our efforts have been directed toward building militarily useful artificial consciousness. We are aware of some pointers to the broader framework, but we would need more resources to probe it.

065: I see. Let me get back to your specific project, artificial consciousness. None of you has discussed the key issue that our critics are all chattering about: insubordination by conscious Cylon agents. The liberation of Caprica was, in military terms, a staggering success. We have obliterated human civilization and reduced their race to a tiny number that have negligible chance of long-term survival. Politically, however, the fact that two *Battlestars* escaped, and have been kicking our ass ever since, stinks. And when two of your conscious Cylons killed a superior officer and instigated the movement to withdraw our forces from Caprica, it left a stench in the higher echelons. Tell me, 480, how can we ever trust your conscious artificial brains again? In fact, a lot of people have been asking me why we are making Cylons more like meat-heads. This war has been about eradicating a pestilent species, but you seem hell-bent on re-inventing it. And now you ask for resources to push this research further. Why the frak should we support you?

480: Sir, every munition that has ever been invented has been dangerous. The risks have to be understood, and managed. Humans are dangerous—we must fight fire with fire. The conscious Cylon agent has proven itself to be a potent weapon. But it has to be monitored and controlled. It is a military necessity. We must have it if we are to prevail.

065:   Well, I take your general point. But why did you build free will into the humanoid Cylons?

480:   We didn't. I mean, we didn't build it in as a specific feature. Free will is a necessary concomitant of conscious awareness.

065:   How so?

480:   Look at it this way. Just suppose, for the sake of argument, that everything that happens in the brain is caused by some prior physical event. In jargon, we'd say the brain is "causally closed." But we have already seen that consciousness is not physical. Yet it affects the brain! Otherwise, the brain would never know about it. So, the brain cannot be wholly governed by antecedent physical events. There is something else, outside of the physics, affecting it when non-deterministic quantum events occur. That something else is the conscious mind. And that is what we mean in saying that the Cylon humanoid has free will.

065:   I think I'd need to hear that argument a few more times. But I get your drift. Well, our time is up. Thank you, everybody. I've heard what I needed to hear.

024:   That's it, guys. Thank you all for your attendance.

Peter B. Lloyd was trained in science and software engineering but has a passion for philosophy, and has published several articles and books bringing philosophy out of academia. After more than a decade in university research—first in solar engineering and then in clinical trials at Oxford University—he has worked for several years as a freelance software developer. He runs his own consultancy business, which also trades as Whole-Being Books to publish books written by himself and his wife Deborah Marshall-Warren. He has previously contributed to the Smart Pops series in Taking the Red Pill: Science, Philosophy, and Religion in The Matrix *and* The Man from Krypton: A Closer Look at Superman. *His most recent project is* Metatopia, *a series of video interviews with people working on the frontiers of consciousness. www.peterblloyd.org*

I have always loved visionary science fiction to the chagrin of many of my friends who can't get past the SF element in the genre—aliens, foreheads, and futuristic technologies. But the re-imagined version of Battlestar has brought many of the skeptics around, thank God! Lou Anders explores the brilliance of Ron Moore's unique vision, and how through an implausible sleight of hand he has helped to reinvent the science fiction genre and built a bridge to the future for all ages, cultures, and demographics.

THE NATURAL AND THE UNNATURAL
VERISIMILITUDE IN
BATTLESTAR GALACTICA

Lou Anders

WHEN IT DEBUTED ON DECEMBER 8, 2003, *Battlestar Galactica* became the highest-rated cable mini-series of the year and the highest-rated original program in the Sci-Fi Channel's history. The series it spawned was declared by *Time* magazine in the spring of 2005 as one of the six best drama series on television. It won viewers outside the category of SF fans, outside the Sci-Fi Channel's regular audience, and it raised the bar for the entire genre by bringing a level of sophisticated writing, acting, and filmmaking hitherto only seen on shows like *The West Wing* or *The Sopranos*. This is not to say that there had not been earlier examples of science fiction television featuring quality acting, cutting-edge technique, or quality writing, but that the entire focus, the *modus operandi* of *Battlestar Galactica*, has been to elevate the art by a carefully crafted appeal to the sophisticated viewer, the new viewing audience that emerged for those shows, born in the wake of *ER*, that are typified by complex narrative and realistic character depictions. Shows like the aforementioned *The West Wing*, *Six Feet Under*, and *Deadwood* have created a market for television drama that reaches beyond clichéd characters and simple everything-gets-tied-up-in-an-hour episodic narrative. Essentially, *Battlestar Galactica* was envisioned as the science fiction equivalent of an HBO series.

In his essay "*Battlestar Galactica*: Naturalistic Science Fiction, or Taking the Opera out of Space Opera," executive producer Ronald D. Moore outlined his plans for the new show:

> "*Our goal is nothing less than the reinvention of the science fiction television series. We take as a given the idea that the traditional space opera, with its stock characters, techno-double-talk, bumpy-headed aliens, thespian histrionics, and empty heroics has run its course and a new approach is required. That approach is to introduce realism into what has heretofore been an aggressively unrealistic genre. Call it 'Naturalistic Science Fiction.' This idea, the presentation of a fantastical situation in naturalistic terms, will permeate every aspect of our series....*"

Moore then proceeded to outline the ways in which his new television series would achieve this goal. This new naturalism was to be achieved in a variety of ways: through a documentary-style filmmaking technique, by adherence to believable science and realistic character portrayal, and by the crafting of a very specific look and feel in sets and costuming contrived to convey unprecedented believability.

It starts with the camera. Apparent from the first episode is that *Battlestar Galactica* is not interested in impossible heroic action sequences and special effects extravaganza shots. Not that it is by any means an inexpensive television series to produce (with an estimated ten-million-dollar budget for the mini-series alone), *Battlestar Galactica* eschewed "pretty pictures" in favor of a less seemingly polished, "documentary" style of filmmaking. This applied equally whether inside the confines of a vessel or when outside depicting the dogfights between *Galactica* Vipers and Cylon Raiders.

Traditional science fiction television as established by *Star Trek* favored a predictable pattern of shooting a scene. First, a master take was filmed—a wide angle shot established where people were in relation to the set. Then a two-shot—a closer shot which captured both key characters in the scene. Then close-ups and extreme close-ups—shots which captured only one character from the waist up or only the character's face. Each of these takes would be filmed separately, then the shots would be integrated in the editing process such that a typical scene would begin with a master, cut to a two-shot, then alternate close-ups and/or extreme close-ups, then pull back to a two-shot, then master. By contrast, *Battlestar Galactica* will often shoot one long take, with the camera swinging back and forth from character to character, the picture even blurring for a moment as the camera loses and readjusts its focus. These extra-long takes without a cut in the editing are employed to further draw viewers into the world of the series, in deliberate contrast to the rapid MTV-style fast-cutting so prevalent nowadays. By calling such attention to the audiences' frame of reference, the viewer is placed "in the scene" and, hopefully, a heightened sense of reality results.

Of course, the documentary style of filmmaking is nothing new—made famous as it was by the hospital drama *ER*. Interestingly enough, neither is Ronald D. Moore the only veteran of *Star Trek* to envision bringing such camera techniques to an SF franchise. Robert Hewitt Wolfe, speaking in an interview on Space.com on April 28, 2000, about his then upcoming *Andromeda* series, expressed his intention to use hand-held cameras and overlapping dialogue to create a tone "a little more toward the *ER* school of filmmaking than the *Star Trek* school" (Lipper).

Likewise, when it comes to shooting exterior action sequences, Moore announced that every shot begins with the question "Who is holding the camera?" Rather than allowing spacecraft to zip around in outlandish angles "with the touch of a mouse pad," shots are composed as if filmed from an actual camera mounted on the wing of a ship, or inside the cockpit, or from the cockpit of another ship. This constant awareness of point of view lends the show the air of gritty reality missing from over-the-top extravaganzas like the recent *Star Wars* films. This technique is combined with an attention to certain very real laws of physics, at least in the case of the sound effects. Space—being a vacuum—lacks a medium to transmit sound. The noises heard on *Battlestar Galactica* are only those audible to the pilot from within the cockpit, i.e., the sounds of the engines, the impact when the ship is struck, etc.... (Of

course, music may also be used to fill the void left by the absence of ex-
plosions.) Previous science fiction series, most notably *Babylon 5* and
the short-lived *Space: Above & Beyond*, took a similar tactic when they
worked glares of light refraction on a supposed camera lens into their
outer space sequences. In reality, these shots were composited using
CGI and thus had no actual lens to catch the light. But by introducing
this illusion of refraction, they suggested an imaginary camera placed
deliberately in the scene—a sleight of hand which probably went un-
noticed by most viewers, but enhanced the verisimilitude of the CGI.
Meanwhile, the lack of sound effects in space was actually attempted in
the earlier series *Babylon 5*, but eventually and reluctantly abandoned in
favor of dramatic necessity. (Space may be quiet, but television SF rarely is. That *Battlestar Galactica* has been able to pull it off successfully
where *Babylon 5* could not may speak more to the sophisticated tastes
and expectations of audiences today versus those of a decade earlier
than it does to the skills of either show's production staff.)

On the storytelling front, *Battlestar Galactica* is committed to depicting real people and doing so with its entire ensemble, not merely
a trio of star characters at the top. In deliberate emulation of the aforementioned HBO series, *Battlestar Galactica* eschews the use of the "red
shirts." A feature of the original *Star Trek* series so overused as to become a cliché was the inclusion of a random ensign in a red shirt in any
landing party in which a crewmember had to die for dramatic effect.
Audiences came to expect that whenever a "random red shirt" beamed
down with Kirk, Spock, and McCoy, he wasn't long for this world. By
contrast, HBO shows like *Oz* and *Deadwood* have shown a willingness to
kill major characters, as well as an ability to develop even minor characters to the point where audience members feel empathy at the character's demise. On *Battlestar Galactica*, President Roslin's assistant Billy
Keikeya was killed, somewhat off-handedly, in a deliberate demonstration that no one is safe. His death carried real emotional impact, not because he died in a "hero's moment," but because his death felt arbitrary,
brutal, even unfair. Sadly, when Laura Roslin herself dodged the cancer
bullet by the injection of stem cells from Sharon Valerii's human-Cylon
fetus, the show pulled back from its willingness to sacrifice key players,
as well as lowered itself to the level of the "'techno-double-talk' hand-
waving" that Moore disdains. But overall, *Battlestar Galactica* remains

committed to showing realistic and vulnerable humans, with all their weaknesses and flaws, as opposed to stock characters and larger-than-life heroes. It is interesting to note that the balding Colonel Saul Tigh, Adama's right-hand man, suffers the same character flaws—alcoholism and a troubled relationship—as that of *Babylon 5*'s shaven-headed Michael Garibaldi, himself the right-hand man of that show's Captain John J. Sheridan.

None of the aforementioned cinematic precedents detract from *Battlestar Galactica*'s accomplishment in significantly raising the bar of television science fiction. All of the above choices combine to produce a science fiction television series that is years ahead of its closest competitors in terms of sophistication and realism. This is a tremendous service to the genre and one which hopefully more television series will attempt to emulate. Of course, it shouldn't come as a surprise that superior writing, acting, and filmmaking produces superior television. But there is another way that the filmmakers at *Battlestar Galactica* have pushed the envelope of science fiction and greatly broadened the audience for same which is less immediately obvious and absolutely intentional, specific choices which are made to bring the metaphors of the series home to the world of the viewers today. A choice which is also almost unprecedented.

A digression to illustrate a point: around the late 1500s, some six thousand soldiers came to Paris to lend their support to Cardinal Richelieu and Louis XIV. Their numbers included a group of mercenaries from Croatia, who wore scarves tied about their necks in a manner previously unknown in Europe. The French fell in love with this new ornamentation, and gladly exchanged them for the uncomfortable starched ruffs that were the previous fashion. Unlike the ruffs, they were easy to maintain and could be worn by rich and poor alike (albeit with different degrees of quality in the fabric). Then, Charles II, returning to England in 1600 at the end of his Oliver Cromwell–imposed exile in France, brought the new *cravat* home with him. (*Cravat* is believed by many to be a corruption of *a la croate*.) Within ten years, the fashion had spread all over Europe and even to the American colonies.

Cravats grew quite lacy in the seventeenth century, then were supplanted by the Steinkirk—a loosely wrapped scarf worn by men and women alike. Briefly, English dandies, dubbing themselves the Macaroni and seeking to revive the lacy clothing of the past, brought back the laced *cravat* until the realities of war in 1776 did away with more "effeminate" excesses of clothing. (An amusing aside: when the Yankee Doodle of the popular song sticks a feather in his hat, he is a country bumpkin attempting to emulate the Macaronies. But the "Yanks"— missing the intended slur—adopted the song for their own, no longer recognizing its bigoted origins.)

Then, in the early nineteenth century, George Bryan Brummell, in his advocacy of well-tailored clothes, laid the groundwork for the modern-day business suit, although he was awfully fond of extremely white *cravats*. Finally, a group of Cambridge students created the first sporting colored neckties in the 1840s, adding school colors and stripes. All of which is to say that a whole lot of design evolution went into the modern neck tie and its accompanying business suit, as well as a great deal of cross-pollination, across both class and country lines.

Which means that the notion that a civilization of polytheistic aliens living on *the other side of the galaxy* should dress exactly like you and me is patently absurd. Likewise, *Battlestar Galactica*'s Starship Colonial One, which serves as President Roslin's office and home, is modeled so closely to Air Force One (right down to the airplane-style viewing windows) as to be immediately recognizable to anyone as a transport of presidential importance. In fact, the casual TV channel surfer stumbling across it may think at first glance that he or she is watching *The West Wing* and not a science fiction drama at all. Again, we see a preposterous level of parallel evolution of design, in this case, faster-than-life spaceships with interiors that look exactly like twentieth-century American aircraft!

Which brings us to the telephone. The characters on *Battlestar Galactica* don't even use digital phones, which we ourselves have had for some time, but speak on a throwback to the mid-twentieth century pre-wireless phones, a deliberately retro look that reminds viewers of a less technologically confusing time, dated even by our twenty-first-century standard, let alone that of an interplanetary civilization. Yes, yes, this is justified in terms of the narrative by Commander Adama's reluctance to rely on an integrated ship, a vulnerability which the rest of the Fleet shares and which the Cylons exploit in the mini-series to devastating results. But this clever story explanation serves the dual purpose of allowing the series to be set in a comfortably retro environment, less challenging than even the demands of a contemporary setting would provide.

Then there is the matter of aliens. Or rather, the complete lack thereof. In a move counter to the endless progression of "forehead" aliens that were paraded out in decades of *Star Trek* episodes, *Battlestar Galactica* has chosen thus far to show a galaxy comprised only of humans and their creations. This is a decision taken to increase the sense of realism for the series, and, indeed, may be the correct choice for a science fiction-friendly audience weary of the opposite as well as the potentially larger, uninitiated audience, hostile to too much strangeness in their television. However, it is not necessarily the "realistic" choice. In 1961, Dr. Frank Drake of the University of California at Santa Cruz proposed his now famous "Drake Equation," an attempt to allow scientists to quantify the factors which might determine the number of possible extraterrestrial civilizations in the universe. The Drake Equation is rendered as follows:

$$N = R^* \times f_p \times n_e \times f_l \times f_i \times f_c \times L$$

where:

N is the number of civilizations in our galaxy with which we might expect to be able to communicate at any given time.

R^* is the rate of star formation in our galaxy.

f_p is the fraction of those stars which have planets.

n_e is the average number of planets which can potentially support life per star that has planets.

f_l is the fraction of the above which actually go on to develop life.

f_i is the fraction of the above which actually go on to develop intelligent life.

f_c is the fraction of the above which are willing and able to communicate.

L is the expected lifetime of such a civilization.

The interesting thing is, even with conservative estimates, the Drake Equation renders a figure of around 10,000 extraterrestrial civilizations in our galaxy alone, and our galaxy is merely one of an estimated 100 billion galaxies in the universe. (An estimated fifty billion galaxies are visible with modern telescopes, so the total number of actual galaxies must exceed this by a large factor.) This would give us a conservative figure of 10,000 times 100 billion civilizations in the universe. But even sticking to our own galaxy, 10,000 contemporaneous civilizations is a conservative estimate.[1]

But why be conservative? Recent discoveries about the nature of the universe are giving us a reason to be magnanimous in our predictions about the fecundity of life. First, the accepted range of temperatures in which we know life can thrive right here on our own world has greatly been increased—from the recent discovery of species of worms that live in water heated to 122 degrees Fahrenheit (50 degrees Celsius) jetting from hydrothermal vents in the ocean floor to bacteria and ice worms which live on glaciers. NASA officials have said these discoveries offer clues about how life could evolve on much less hospitable worlds than previously supposed. In this way, the conditions necessary for the evolution of life are not nearly as restrictive as once thought, and the breadth of what that life might be like have been greatly extended.

Moreover, estimates of the range within which a planet need orbit its sun in order to sustain life have greatly increased. Observations of both Venus and Mars suggest that a greenhouse effect of a heavy carbon dioxide atmosphere could allow a much larger percentage of the sun's heat to be trapped in the atmosphere versus that which our world retains. As a result, planets could be much further out from their star's "sweet spot"—the habitable zone where the right balance of heat, radiation, and gravity permit the development of an ecosystem—than previously supposed and still support life.

Meanwhile, from having no observable proof of any other planets outside our own solar system in 1989, over 180 extrasolar planets have been discovered from 1990 to the present date. Recent observations have even suggested habitable planets may form without the need of a star, floating in the vast distances between stellar systems, possibly

---

[1] *Star Trek* creator Gene Roddenberry cited the Drake Equation as support for his vision of a galaxy populated by numerous alien species when presenting his proposal for a new television series to the studio executives. He did not have the actual formula and so made up his own: $Ef^2(MgE)-C^1Ri^1xM = L/So^*$. To perform your own calculation using the real Drake Equation, visit the SETI Institute online at: http://www.seti.org/site/pp.asp?c=ktJ2J9MMIsE&b=179074.

heated by geothermal activity, while yet other evidence suggests planets could possibly survive the death of their stars to orbit around the white dwarfs and other stellar bodies produced. Yet more planets have been discovered outside the plane of the Milky Way. So estimates about the total number of possible planets in the galaxy increase, just as our recognized range in which life could thrive increases.

All of which is to say that a galaxy without intelligent life is far less likely than one with sentient beings. Or, to quote the Greek philosopher Metrodorus (appropriate, surely, for a discussion of a television show full of allusions to the Greek pantheon):

> "To consider the Earth as the only populated world in infinite space is as absurd as to assert that in an entire field of millet, only one grain will grow."

So the point of all this is that the supposed introduction of a degree of realism into an "aggressively unrealistic genre" is actually trafficking in the scientifically implausible. But this is not to say that *Battlestar Galactica* is not sophisticated, brilliant, or important. Nor are these intentions *wrong* from a dramatic sense. The fantasy author Tim Powers once remarked that in crafting fiction, it was more important to *seem* believable to your readers than to be accurate to historical truth. By way of example, he pointed to the term "groovy," associated in almost everyone's mind with the hippie slang of the 1960s. However, "groovy" actually originated as a term not in the swinging sixties, but in the roaring twenties. It was revived in the '60s and came into such popular usage as to epitomize that decade to us today. Powers pointed out that if one were to use "groovy" in a historical piece set in the '20s, while it would be historically correct, the vocabulary wouldn't *feel* right and the majority of readers would be jarred out of the narrative, thinking the author had used the colloquial term of a later era out of its proper historical context. What Powers was talking about was the difference between the appearance of reality and reality itself, between the depiction of truth and actual truth. In crafting believable historical fiction, it is more important to *feel* accurate than to *be* accurate. In other words, verisimilitude must win out over truth.

In this regard, *Battlestar Galactica* has charted new territory, by forgoing science fiction's attempt at accurate prognostication in favor of a look and feel less threatening to a larger audience with supposedly less tolerance for imaginative extrapolations. By sacrificing the realities of social evolution and cultural progression, they achieve an illusion of heightened adherence to "realism," while being anything but real. When viewed scientifically, *Battlestar Galactica* is about the silliest science fiction drama ever produced, yet the net effect of adapting all these familiar set pieces is that it's actually the most sophisticated, the most believable show ever filmed. By sacrificing anthropological credibility, they've achieved the highest degree of verisimilitude any SF show has ever reached. In other words, it's an implausible sleight of hand that makes it all seem so real.

There are two possible rationalizations for this bizarre parallel social evolution. The first is the simplest—that despite all the attempts at verisimilitude, we are not meant to take *Battlestar Galactica* at face value. These people could not possibly be speaking English, for instance. They are not. They are speaking another language, translated into English in the process of storytelling, for our benefit. This is true of any drama, whether science fictional or historical, in which events that occurred in a non-English setting are rendered in English. It is true for HBO's *Rome*, so why not for Sci-Fi Channel's *Battlestar Galactica*? Therefore, Adama is not speaking on a telephone, Billy did not wear a necktie, and Apollo does not wear a sidearm that looks like a modern pistol. Adama speaks on an alien communication device, Billy wears bizarre garb, and Apollo sports a strange weapon. These things have been changed, just as the language has been made palpable, for our benefit. There is a level of interpretation between the "actual" story and the story we are being shown. Despite appearances, the ancient Romans did not speak English.

The second possibility: this truly is a perfect example of parallel evolution. Once upon a time, in the original *Star Trek* episode "Bread and Circuses," in an attempt to rationalize the impossibility of encountering a world where the Roman Empire never fell, Mr. Spock said that such was a classic example of "Hodgkin's Law of Parallel Planetary Development." Long the epitome of "techno-double talk" that Moore decries, something like Hodgkin's Law is now being seriously considered. Recent theories about the size of the universe suggest that it is much larger than previously supposed. If this is the case, parallel worlds need not exist only in alternate time zones and other dimensional realms. In an infinite or nearly infinite universe, parallel worlds might occupy the same universe as our own Earth, simply greatly removed from us in distance. (One cosmological model predicts that our nearest parallel world would fall in a galaxy some ten to 1028 meters away [Tegmark]). If this is correct, it is unlikely, but not impossible, that an example of parallel development might occur in the same galaxy as the one we occupy. The chance that the Twelve Colonies and the Earth might share fashion sense and technological design, even given a common origin, is incalculably slim, but not completely impossible.

Of course, it doesn't matter. The intent was not to be cosmologically accurate. The intent was to revitalize a tired genre, reinvent an outdated show, and make science fiction's potential for the examination of our world relevant again, by bringing it to a much larger audience who could see themselves and the problems of their world in its storytelling. As Ron Moore says, "In this way, we hope to challenge our audience in ways that other genre pieces do not. We want the audience to connect with the characters of *Galactica* as people. Our characters are not super-heroes. They are not an elite. They are everyday people caught up in an enormous cataclysm and trying to survive it as best they can. They are you and me." In realizing this intent, Moore and *Battlestar Galactica* have achieved their goal and reinvigorated science fiction television, raising a bar that shouldn't be lowered again in this, or any other, universe.

Lou Anders is an editor, author, and journalist. He is the editorial director of Prometheus Books's science fiction imprint Pyr, as well as the anthologies Outside the Box (Wildside Press, January 2001), Live Without a Net (Roc, July 2003), Projections (MonkeyBrain, December 2004), FutureShocks (Roc, July 2005), and Fast Forward 1 (Pyr, February 2007). *He served as the senior editor for* Argosy *magazine's inaugural issues in 2003–04. In 2000, he served as the executive editor of Bookface.com, and before that he worked as the Los Angeles liaison for Titan Publishing Group. He is the author of* The Making of Star Trek: First Contact (Titan Books, 1996), *and has published over 500 articles in such magazines as* Publishers Weekly, The Believer, Dreamwatch, Star Trek Monthly, Star Wars Monthly, Babylon 5 Magazine, Sci Fi Universe, Doctor Who Magazine, *and* Manga Max. *His articles and stories have been translated into German, French, and Greek, and have appeared online at Believermag.com, SFSite.com, RevolutionSF.com, and In-finityPlus.co.uk. Visit him online at www.louanders.com.*

References

Lipper, Don. "Robert Wolfe on *Andromeda*—Less *Trek*, More *ER*." April 28, 2000. http://www.space.com/sciencefiction/tv/andromeda_verite_000428.html.

Tegmark, Max. "Parallel Universes," *Scientific American*, May 2003. http://www.sciam.com/article.cfm?colID=1&articleID=000F1EDD-B48A-1E90-8EA5809EC5880000.

Religion in Battlestar is as complex, mystical, mysterious, and contradictory as it is in the real world, but the new BSG cleverly shifts our relative perspective through a juxtaposition of our frame of reference. This challenges and expands our sometimes narrow points of view before our bias and prejudice can block our critical thinking process. The so-called good guys become the heathens, pagans, and Islamic terrorists while the so-called bad guys become the Christians and Jews, etc., thus forcing us to explore and identify with our supposed enemies, making it possible to view and understand the other guy's point of view through unfiltered lenses. How brilliant is that!

GALACTICA'S GODS
OR, HOW I LEARNED TO STOP WORRYING AND LOVE THE CYLON GOD

Charlie W. Starr

MORE THAN ANYTHING IT'S BLURRY. The new *Battlestar Galactica* (*BSG*) blurs the lines between right and wrong, good and evil, loyalty and betrayal. Context and subtlety keep the viewer in a delightful world of new perspective. Among the blurs: polytheistic humans worshipping pagan gods who were human-like themselves on the one hand, and monotheistic Cylons whose God is loving and wrathful, foreknowing and mysterious, predestinating and ominously distant on the other. It is to this God of the enemies of man that I find myself strangely attracted. *BSG* is blurry, a mystical quality permeates its universe from episode to episode, especially regarding its approach to divine things. Answers are not clear. There are but hints of terrible wonders, frightening possibilities. Is the Cylon God the God of the universe? What connection might there be between the Destroyer of the Twelve Colonies and the Law Giver of Sinai and Suffering Savior of the Earth?

Those '70s Gods

The gods of the original *BSG* were straightforward, fairly easy to understand. The most telling revelation of the original series's cosmology came in the two-part episode "War of the Gods."

The *Galactica* crew came across the mysterious Count Iblis. At the same time, *Galactica's* fighters were disappearing, plagued by the appearance of a spaceship of dazzling light reminiscent of the mother ship in *Close Encounters*—Iblis's enemies. Iblis promised that he could lead humanity to Earth but emphasized that they must choose to follow him freely. His ability to work apparent miracles convinced many. As the plot progressed we learned that Iblis came from powers greater than the Cylon empire, and that he was a being "far advanced" of humanity.

It is suggested that the Lords of Kobol, the founders of the human race, might have come from a race like Iblis's. Stories from Kobol described visitations by "angels...custodians of the universe...advanced beings." Iblis was ultimately revealed for the demonic figure he was when Apollo named him from the "ancient records" of humanity: "Mephistopheles" and "Diaboles."

Encountering the white ship, Starbuck and Sheba were taken in by its white-robed, angelic-looking inhabitants—incorporeal creatures appeared in a form for human senses to assimilate, whose ship existed in a dimension apart from normal space/time. Starbuck wondered if he was seeing angels. "Oddly enough," said one, "there is some truth to your speculation."

The cosmology is interesting but basic: Count Iblis was the devil, the beings of light were angels watching over the lesser evolved creatures of the universe in the hopes that they too would someday evolve into godlike creatures. Good and evil were obvious in the original *BSG*; the moral universe was clearly defined. No such clarity exists, however, in the new, postmodern *BSG*.

Two notes: whenever the white ship appeared and overtook a human ship, it was accompanied by a loud noise which caused pain and blackout. Though benevolent, the very presence of the beings of light was enough to cause pain and overwhelm people. Keep that in mind. Also, Baltar (whom the count had captured as proof of his abilities) recognized Iblis's voice as the voice of the Cylon Imperius Leader. But the only way that could have been possible was if Iblis had been present at the creation of the Cylon Leader 1,000 yahrens (years) ago for Iblis's voice to have been inscribed onto the computer mind—roughly at the same time the Cylons attacked humanity. Iblis seemed to be the one responsible for the creation of the Cylon machine race, for making them evil xenophobes. This point was significant.

There's a New Myth in Town

The Cylon God enters the story in the first twenty minutes of the new series. The Cylon femme fatale, Number Six, explains to Gaius Baltar that she's been helping him advance his career for the last two years because "God wanted me to do it" (mini-series). Disbelieving, Baltar asks if God spoke to her. "He didn't speak to me in a literal voice. And you don't have to mock my faith," she replies. Baltar says that he's not very religious, to which Six responds, "Does it bother you that I am?" And Baltar: "It puzzles me that you'd be taken in by all that mysticism and superstition."

God remains a permanent character in the series from that point on—the God who tells the Cylons to obliterate mankind. And my first thought in those first moments: Is this the new version of the Imperius Leader of the old series? Or even of Count Iblis (the Satan-god) himself? Most hints about the Cylon God that follow suggest that I shouldn't let my thinking be colored by the original series, though there are some intriguing moments to the contrary. One is when Baltar's Six (the one inside his head) tells him that he must freely choose to follow God ("Six Degrees of Separation" 1-7). Another is in the Cylon emphasis on unity over individuality (suggesting their God may be created in their own image) ("Downloaded" 2-18). Finally, in a deleted scene from the season one finale, "Kobol's Last Gleaming" (1-13), a priestess explains that the reason humanity left Kobol is because one of the gods wanted to elevate himself above all the others, thus beginning the wars of Kobol that led to the exodus of humanity. Could this one god be the Iblis character who then left the other gods (the original series's creatures of light) behind to convince the Cylons that he was the only God of the universe? A God who orders the slaughter of humanity hardly seems what Baltar's Six describes later in the mini-series: "Don't you understand? God is love." But if such is the case, the *BSG* writers are doing a very good job obscuring the truth.

The new series does not approach divinity with the black-and-white clarity of the original series. It is a truly postmodern SF show. Right and wrong are not clear forces. Cylons speak truths as well as lies. They are machines but have desires. That the most prominent Cylons in the story are women plays on our sympathies (whether our sympathy as desire in the case of Six or our compassion for the Sharons, one a victim of her own programming, the other a mother-to-be trying to protect her baby). Cylons have murdered humanity en masse but seldom do we see them torture individual humans like we see the torture of human-looking Cylons, especially Sharon and Six—beaten, shot, and sexually abused. In season two's mid-season cliffhanger, "Pegasus" (2-10), Adama takes actions which in his own logs (as Admiral Cain constantly points out) he decries, saying that these moral choices are a matter of context. In the episode "The Captain's Hand" (2-17), Roslin changes her stance on abortion in the same way—working from the context of the survival of the human race. Our culture thrives on moral and spiritual ambiguity the likes of which are represented in *BSG*, an ambiguity which we would not have tolerated in a '70s SF morality tale.

If context, ambiguity, and complexity are at the heart of the new series, then I cannot simply dismiss the gods, either human or Cylon, as mere invention, or as clearly Good vs. Evil. So I remain attracted to the Cylon God, and much more so than the human gods. It's possible that I'm being taken in by the clever deceits of the Cylons. Or it may be that Six's God of Love, a reference culled from the New Testament (I John 4:8), is in fact a God capable of wiping out a race of people because He *is* the very essence of Goodness and Love.

The Human Gods

The human gods of *BSG* are based on the gods of Greek mythology. Zeus is their leader (as suggested by Zarek's use of the name in describing Adama ["Bastille Day" (1-3); "The Farm" (2-5)]). Starbuck prays to icons of Artemis and Aphrodite ("Flesh and Bone" 1-8) and fetches the real arrow of Apollo from the Delphi Museum on Caprica ("Kobol's Last Gleaming"). Athena and Hera are also named in the series among the gods, or Lords of Kobol ("Home" 2-6, 2-7).

Story

Of their mythic history we know fragments. Thought by humanity to be the stuff of legend, planet Kobol, the birthplace of humanity ("Flesh and Bone"), truly exists. Kobol is "where the gods and man lived in paradise until the exodus of the thirteen tribes" at the time of the wars of the gods some 2,000 years ago ("Kobol's Last Gleaming"). Baltar's Six offers the slightly contradictory story that the wars were the result of human wickedness, including human sacrifice ("Valley of Darkness" 2-2). Up into the mountains, several days' walk from the City of the Gods, are two peaks known as the "Gates of Hera," from which Athena leaped to her death in despair of the flight of humanity from Kobol to the Colonies. Athena's tomb is nearby ("Home").

Humanity left Kobol and founded colonies on thirteen planets; twelve are known, the other is Earth. As season one progresses, what was thought to be the legend of Earth turns out to be real. Prophecies in the scroll of Pythia begin to come true: humanity finds Kobol, then the tomb of Athena, then the general location of Earth ("The Hand of God" 1-10; "Fragged" 2-3; "Kobol's Last Gleaming"; "Home"). One of the most interesting insights into the human religion occurs during the search for Athena's tomb:

> STARBUCK: Cylons believe in the 'one true God.'
> PREGNANT SHARON: We don't worship false idols.
> APOLLO: But it's strange that you're willing to lead us to the tomb according to our so-called 'false' scriptures.
> SHARON: We know more about your religion than you do. Athena was real, just not a god.
> ("Home")

This is everything we know about the religious history of humanity whether myth, truth, or lies. Apart from this, what we know of the religion is that it is not unlike human religion in our own culture.

Beliefs

The religion of man in *BSG* is one that believes in an afterlife (mini-series; "Fragged"). It is a religion that hopes for divine guidance and protection ("Valley of Darkness"; "Fragged"). It is a religion of prayer (I counted nine instances in episodes myself). Sometimes the prayers are casual, almost flippant: "Lords, it's Kara Thrace." She then says she's running out of oxygen and "could use a break" ("You Can't Go Home Again" 1-5). Sometimes the prayer is desperately sincere as when Starbuck finds herself trapped in a Cylon pregnancy lab and prays in tears, "Lords of Kobol, please help me" ("The Farm"). And the "amen" to these prayers is the regularly repeated, "So say we all."

As with our own culture, the human world of *BSG* is one in which the divine is the stuff of skepticism, ridicule, argument, politics, and casual disregard. Religion serves for public ceremony (mini-series; "Lay Down Your Burdens" 2-19, 2-20), but it also serves as a tool for political exploitation (by Adama in the mini-series, by Roslin in "The Farm," and by Zarek, who doesn't believe in religion but believes in the "power of myth" for its political uses ["Home"]). The human culture in *BSG* also contains a varied spectrum of belief as in our own culture. There are the religious fundamentalists who hail from Geminon—they believe in the "literal truth of the scriptures" ("Fragged"). At the other end of the spectrum are the total skeptics like Zarek and Baltar, before his conversion ("33"; "Fragged"; "Six Degrees of Separation"). In between these extremes is everyone else: people who are essentially secular but believe in the gods; that is, religion is for them a sidebar to life, a last resort when doom appears imminent, and an occasion for casual oath making ("Bastille Day"; "Six Degrees of Separation"; "Valley of Darkness"; "Lay Down Your Burdens"; and the ubiquitous use of the expletives "Oh my gods!" and "Gods damn it!" throughout the series).

In the end, I find the content of the human religion in *BSG* less important than the attitudes people have toward it. The people in *BSG* are a microcosm of religious attitudes in our contemporary culture. That they take religion seriously at all (except for the Geminese) is primarily because they're seeing prophecies come true with their own eyes. For this reason I find the sincerity behind the Cylon religion far more interesting.

The Cylon God

The Cylon God inspires passionate faith in His people, commands monotheistic belief, is numinous and predestinating, and has the power of Sinai (like the blast of atomic fire in the initial Cylon attacks). He is fearful and transcendent but is intimately involved in the affairs of ma(n)chine. He has a plan, and that plan brings about suffering—but it also brings resurrection. His parallels to the Judeo-Christian God are striking despite the possibility that He may have ordered the eradication of the human race (and maybe *because* of it).

The biggest problem we face in understanding the Cylon God is whether or not we can trust anything the Cylons say. As Adama puts it, they mix truth with lies ("Flesh and Bone"). This is doubly compounded with anything Baltar's Six says since she is not merely a Cylon but the Cylon in Baltar's head who, though not a chip planted in his brain ("Home"), is in part (if not whole) a projection of his own self-centered psyche.[1] And so I have made a choice: in this exploration of religion in *BSG* I've decided to step out in faith. Right or wrong, truth or lies, I'm going to present what the Cylons say about their God (including their contradictions) and take it at face value.

Love

The most puzzling quality of the Cylon God is that He is a God of love. He is the "love that binds all living things together" who loved humanity "more than all other living creatures" (though man "repaid His divine love with sin, with hate, corruption, evil" ["Flesh and Bone"]). Cylons constantly say they love one another ("Kobol's Last Gleaming"; "Downloaded"), and just as frequently say human beings don't know how to

---

[1] The following episodes render clues to the question of whether or not Baltar's Six is a chip implanted in his head, a complete figment of his imagination, or partly a projection of his own psyche and partly a real mystical connection to things divine: the mini-series, "33" (1-1), "Litmus" (1-6), "Six Degrees of Separation," "The Hand of God," "Kobol's Last Gleaming," "Home," "Downloaded," and "Lay Down Your Burdens."

love ("Fragged"; "Downloaded"). Love is also integral in the Cylon plan as it is a necessary component in the creation of the messianic child to come ("The Farm"). Yet, the Cylon vision of love may have its limitations, even contradictions. In "Downloaded," Baltar's Real Six, who comes to be known as Caprica Six, is reborn after dying in the Cylon atomic attack. She is in love with Gaius Baltar. When Sleeper Sharon is reborn on Caprica months later, she rejects the so-called love of the Cylon God for the love she had for her human friends, a love she betrayed because she's a "frakkin' Cylon!" These two begin to doubt the Cylon understanding of love. Six concludes, "We're two heroes of the Cylon, right? Two heroes with different perspectives on the war. Perspectives based on our love for human beings." Six and Sharon decide they will change things for the better: "Our people need a new beginning, a new way to live in God's love. Without hate. Without all the lies."

Wrath

While humans seem to often act in a contradictory manner toward their religion, in the Cylon religion it is God Himself who seems contradictory. Though He has loved both humans and Cylons alike (as Baltar's Six puts it in "The Hand of God": "God doesn't take sides"), this God of love and salvation is also a God of destruction. A theme from the beginning of the series is the question of whether or not God thinks humanity deserves to live:

> ADAMA: We fought the Cylons to save ourselves from extinction. But we never asked ourselves the question, why? Why are we as a people worth saving? We still commit murder. We still visit all our sins upon our children. We don't accept responsibility for the things we've done.... You cannot play God then wash your hands of the things that you've created.
> (Mini-series).

Days later the first Leoben tells Adama that the Cylons may be God's retribution for man's many sins: "What if God decided He made a mistake, and He decided to give souls to another creature, the Cylons?" In "Flesh and Bone," the second Leoben makes the same claim: God loved humanity but all man did in return was sin, "so He decided to build the

Cylons." When Adama asks Pregnant Sharon why the Cylons hate humanity, she reminds him of his speech (above), that mankind did not ask themselves if they deserved to live. Says Sharon: "Maybe you don't" ("Resurrection Ship, Part II").

Baltar learns of the Destroyer God from his Six. She tells him that he has a destiny and will be spared humanity's fate. All he has to do is let "destiny take its course" ("Home"). He asks his Six who she is and she replies, "I'm an angel of God sent here to protect you—to love you."

> BALTAR: To what end?
> SIX: To the end of the human race.
> ("Home")

When they learn, mistakenly, that Sharon's baby is dead, Six tells Baltar he has "committed a monstrous and unforgivable sin. And you and your entire wretched race are going to suffer God's vengeance" ("Downloaded").

A God of love who orders the massacre of a race? Caprica Six and Sleeper Sharon see the contradiction:

> SIX: Genocide, murder, vengeance—they're all sins in the eyes of God; that's what you and I know. That's what they don't want to hear.
> SHARON: Because then they'd have to rethink what they're doing. They'd have to consider that maybe the slaughter of mankind was a mistake.
> ("Downloaded")

Out of this conversation even greater contradiction in the Cylon religion will come.

Destiny

Central to the Cylon religion is a strong sense of predestined purpose. As *BSG*'s opening titles say, the Cylons "have a plan." It is a "destiny" that Sleeper Sharon is told she cannot escape ("Kobol's Last Gleaming"), and though the plan may begin with the annihilation of man, it does not exclude humanity from its designs. Starbuck is told by both Leoben and Pregnant Sharon that she has a destiny ("Flesh and Bone"; "The

Farm"). Chief among Cylon plans seems to be the conversion of Baltar from atheism to a belief in God. He is called to repentance in "33." He is called to faith in "Six Degrees of Separation." He begins this episode saying that "no rational, free-thinking, intelligent human being" believes in God. By the episode's end, as he faces charges of treason, he's on his knees in prayer: "I now acknowledge that you are the one true God. Deliver me from this evil, and I will devote the rest of what is left of my wretched life to doing good—to carrying out your divine will.... Grant me grace. Grant me forgiveness." He next moves beyond simply believing in God to believing that he is "an instrument of God" ("The Hand of God").

Messiah

A critical part of the Cylon plan and religion is their vision of a messianic child, a vision which enacts itself along two paths: a Baltar and his Six path, and a Sharon and Helo path. Baltar learns that his Six wants them to have a child together in the season-one opener since "Procreation is one of God's commandments" ("33"). At the end of season one, once Baltar has come to believe he is God's instrument, Six shows him why he's been chosen by God to fulfill his purpose ("Kobol's Last Gleaming"). In a vision, she takes him into the opera house of the City of the Gods, saying, "It's time to do your part and realize your destiny.... You are the guardian and protector of the next generation of God's children." Six shows Baltar a baby girl, her crib shining with holy light like a Christmas manger scene. The child is, of course, a human/Cylon hybrid.

The child is not Baltar's, not literally. It belongs to Sharon and Helo. Sharon says that what they've had together is important as a "next step," one that will bring them "closer to God" ("Kobol's Last Gleaming"). In season two Baltar has a vision of Adama drowning the baby in a kind of reversal of the story of Moses's salvation at birth on the waters of the Nile in Exodus ("Valley of Darkness"). Baltar wonders why God would want a baby brought into the world of murderous men. His Six answers, "Because despite everything, despite all of it, He still wants to offer you salvation. Our child will bring that salvation...." ("Fragged").

In "The Farm," Cylons are trying to turn human women into baby-production machines through horrid experimentation. The only success at Cylon reproduction has been Sharon, whose love for Helo allows her to become pregnant with the messianic child. When Baltar first sees Pregnant Sharon aboard *Galactica*, he learns from his Six that her baby is the one he is meant to care for ("Home"). And when the Cylons learn of Sharon's pregnancy, they note that the "child's life must be protected at all costs" and that it "truly is a miracle from God" ("Final Cut" 2-8). When the child, Hera, is born, Roslin works quickly to fake its death and adopt it out to a woman who doesn't know its importance. Baltar's Six goes ballistic: "You let them murder our child.... God's will was that our child should survive. His will was that she would lead the next generation of God's children. His will was that you would protect her" ("Downloaded").

A Change of Plans

Everything changes in the last two episodes of season two. In "Downloaded," Sleeper Sharon is now completely awake and having an identity crisis. Her mission, her entire life, has been a lie and she refuses to be a Cylon. Caprica Six responds, "Following God's plan is never easy." And Sharon: "Do you think I care about your God?" But as their relationship develops, Six realizes that she and Sharon are in danger of being "boxed": "We're celebrities in a culture based on unity. Our voices count. More than...others." They have learned the value of humanity, that the Cylons' vision of God may be flawed, and it's up to them to show the Cylons the way.

Perhaps the Cylons *are* creations of God (even *through* man), sent to awaken humanity to the truth of His existence. Rather than demons, perhaps they are angels, but ones who don't know what God wants them to do and are struggling to piece His plan together. Whatever the case, the Cylon plan has changed radically by the season-two finale.

In "Lay Down Your Burdens," the Cylons withdraw from the Colonial worlds. A new Cylon character, played by Dean Stockwell, offers the most contradictory Cylon view of the cosmos we've yet seen. "The occupation of the Colonies was an error," he says, as was the pursuit of the survivors' Fleet. Caprica Six and Sleeper Sharon convinced the Cylons they'd made a mistake. Instead of trying to find their own way to enlightenment, they hijacked humanity's. But now they intend to go elsewhere to become perfect machines, instead of people. Someone asks if this change is at the order of the one true Cylon God. Most surprisingly, the Cylon replies that there is no God. That is just a primitive's way of explaining why the sun goes down, at least that's what this Cylon model has been trying to tell all the others for years—he admits, though, that it can't be proven either way.

Inconsistency and delightful confusion abound for the show's viewers. Even more so when the Cylons come back a year later and their plan has changed again. The humans of New Caprica City surrender to the Cylons under the promise that they will not be harmed so long as they don't resist. As the camera fades on another season of *BSG*, the voice of Six rises, saying that now they will fulfill their destiny and take care of humanity and, like God, show that their infinite mercy is as complete as their infinite control.

Why I Love the Cylon God

In the end I find myself attracted to the Cylon God because, as compared to the human gods in *BSG*, He is so much like mine. He is a God who warns us not to play God ourselves. He is a God who promises resurrection. He is the God who is love, who offers salvation to those who believe in Him. He told Adam "be fruitful" and Moses that the sins of the fathers would be visited upon their children. He is the God who made angels, some of whom became demons, and He is the God who sent His Messiah child for those who are willing to believe. He defines sin and love, makes commandments, and watches over us, gives and takes away. Baltar asks the Cylon God for grace and forgiveness as I do my own. The Cylon Leoben prays to his God, convinced—as I am of mine—that He answers all prayers ("Flesh and Bone"). Six teaches Baltar to open his heart to God so He can show him the way. She tells him to surrender his ego and remain humble, virtues celebrated by the Judeo-Christian God.

In "Six Degrees of Separation," Baltar and his Six have a conversation that could happen today between an atheist and an evangelical Christian (granted, a really hot one):

> SIX: If you'd surrender yourself to God's love, you'd find peace in that love as I have. . . . He has a plan for us.
> BALTAR: How do you know He's a He?

Six: There is only one true God.... He's everyone's God.... It's important you form a personal relationship with God. Only you can turn yourself over to His eternal love.... I'm trying to save your immortal soul, Gaius.

What's most frightening about this conversation is that it is one of those moments from the series that I said before hinted at the possibility that the Cylon God isn't the one true God of the universe but an Iblis-like former Lord of Kobol who wanted to be greater than the others and started the ancient wars (the connection between the two being the issue of surrendering voluntarily). But here I am, about to make application to Him who I think *is* the real God of the universe. As I see it, these are the options: The Cylon God is evil; the Cylons made up their God, or, at best, don't truly know Him; or the Cylon God is real—the God of the universe—and the difficulty in comprehending Him, the confusions and contradictions that arise from any attempts to quantify or impose any patterns on Him, are a telling metaphor (from an elaborate, mythic world) for true spiritual encounter.

If subsequent *BSG* episodes prove me dead wrong, I'll happily eat whatever crow is set before me, but the spiritual symbolism works in understanding real divine encounter regardless of who or what the Cylon God turns out to be. Here, then, is the theory: Perhaps the Cylons cause pain and hardship because they *are* pain and hardship. That is to say, they are agents of God like angels of wrath. Where modern man put God on trial, demanding He prove His existence and answer for His crimes, postmodern man is coming back to an understanding that has been central to religions all around the world, be they monotheistic or polytheistic—that encounters with the Divine are encounters with the awesome power of the abyss, where darkness is not evil but palpable mystery, and encountering God is excruciating pain.

Be it in the rituals of dead pagan religions or according to the theologies of the world's dominant religions today, divine encounter comes at a cost. Self-denying monks, self-mutilating priests, rituals of human sacrifice where the victim volunteers—in dark, holy places and mystical ways, men in the past sought their gods. Even the gods sacrificed themselves for greater knowledge and transcendence. Balder, Adonis, Osiris, Dionysus, Demeter, Persephone—dead, with or without hope of resur-

rection. Even mighty Odin of the Norsemen sacrifices an eye by his own
hand for a greater revelation. Hinduism, one of today's five most prac-
ticed religions in the world, boasts a massive pantheon, numerous gods.
But of its primary three, one is the god Shiva, the Destroyer.

The God of the Bible, both for Jews and Christians, is a God of justice
and mercy, light and truth. But even He draws us to painful encounters.
Jacob wrestles with God throughout an entire night and God knocks his
hip out of joint for it. But He also blesses him for having fought with
God and having "prevailed." He blesses him with a new name: "Israel"—"God Wrestler"—a name which becomes a people, a nation—as if
God is saying, "This is the kind of people I want to call my own: those
willing to fight with Me, to suffer to know me" (Genesis 32).

I'm working toward saying something about God that is not typical of
today's thinking about the Divine. Our dilemma with *BSG* is in our in-
clination to believe that the Cylons are wrong to say that a loving God
would endorse the destruction of the human race. We might respond
to this by saying that, in the Bible, the God of love wipes out nearly the
entire human race in the flood (Genesis 6-8) and engages in the slaughter of nations many times thereafter (from Exodus through the books of
Kings and Chronicles). Those of us who don't dismiss this vision of God
as untrue face a problem. Christians and skeptics alike have struggled to
reconcile what appear to be two biblical Gods: the God of the Hebrew
Bible which both Jews and Christians believe in (we call it the Old Testament) and the God of the New Testament (which completes the Christian Bible). The Cylon God seems to be an Old Testament God whom the
Cylons, nevertheless, describe with New Testament language. But I don't
think this approach gets us where we want to go for two reasons.

First, though there may be differences in emphasis, the loving/wrath-
ful God appears in both testaments. The God who sends Joshua to destroy Jericho saves the pagan family of Rahab, who happens to be a
prostitute (Joshua 2-6). He establishes laws against murder and adultery, naming death the penalty. But when David takes to his bed Bathsheba, another man's wife, and then has the man killed to cover up their
adultery when she gets pregnant, God confronts David with honesty but
does not call for the punishment required by law. David's heart breaks,
and he repents. And God forgives him (2 Samuel 11-12; Psalms 32, 51).
God destroyed Sodom and Gomorrah for their sexual wickedness and

cruelty, but before doing so He promised Abraham that, if He found only ten righteous men in those towns, He would spare everyone living there for the sake of those men (He only found one and sent him and his family to safety in the hills) (Genesis 18-19). Read the Psalms and God's intimate affection for His people and theirs for Him become obvious.

In Christianity, conversely, the God of love who rejected human sacrifice with Abraham (Genesis 22), demands it for the salvation of the world. Thus He sacrifices Himself to Himself for the sake of His just wrath and then calls His disciples to eat His flesh and drink His blood and die themselves every day. And where God, in the Old Testament, never threatens people with hell, Jesus preaches eternal damnation (in fact, most statements about hell in the New Testament are made by the prince of peace who came to save the world). Christianity is the religion of grace and forgiveness, but two Christians in the first days of the Church, Ananias and Sapphira, having told a lie that was nowhere near as heinous as the one David lived with Bathsheba, drop dead at Peter's feet (Acts 5).

The second reason that the wrath/love dichotomy won't take us where we want to go is that God's just wrath is seldom the cause of the painful encounters with the Divine that we see in *BSG*. Moses says to God, "Let me see your glory." He's asking God to let him see Him as He is—His full visible presence—rather than seeing a mere manifestation in fire or cloud (Exodus 33:18). But he's asking for more than he can bear. There is a beauty so palpable, so concrete, that it can kill. Haven't we all had the experience of it? Of something so beautiful it hurt to look at: autumn in New England, beautiful today, gone tomorrow; a first glimpse of the Grand Canyon at dawn's early light; or that woman whose body flows like liquid grace, whose sight draws desire from a man's pores like sweat and makes him believe that the phrase "drop-dead gorgeous" is literally true. That's because it is. There is a beauty that can kill. In the Bible it's called *glory*. When Moses asks God to let him see His glory, God replies that if He lets him see His face, it'll kill him. So God tells Moses to stand in the cleft of a rock, and God passes by, covering Moses so he can't see. Then God uncovers him, and Moses catches a glimpse of God's back—it's almost more than he can bear (Exodus 33:19-23).

To encounter the numinous is to encounter pain but not because God is evil or even necessarily angry. Rather, it is because He *is* love. Poet-musician Rich Mullins called God's love a "reckless, raging fury." We tend to think of God's love in terms of parenting—the watchful father. The Bible uses this father metaphor but also the stronger metaphor of romance. The Song of Solomon (or Song of Songs) is a book of passion, of romantic love. In ancient times, Jewish men were not allowed to read this highly erotic poem in the Bible until they were thirty years old! Solomon's wife defines romance with the same reckless fury as Mullins: "For love is as strong as death, jealousy is as severe as Sheol [hell]; its flashes are flashes of fire, the very flame of the Lord" (Song of Solomon 8:6). God is a passionate, consuming fire—His love is as poetic and ecstatic as it is paternal and moral. In Hosea, He is the God whose nation-wife is out whoring around, producing bastard children not His own (chapters 1–3). In Ezekiel, He is the lover whose nation-bride, He says, has "spread your legs to every passer-by" (Ezekiel 16:25). In *BSG* He manifests His intimate, passionate presence in the sensual loves of Baltar and his Six and Helo and Sharon. Some of God's actions in *BSG* may be motivated by wrath (especially the initial destruction of humanity), but we can't look at all of them that way, even though they're painful. The *otherness* of divinity portrayed in the show is too mystical, too wondrous, even in the painful encounters. In such experiences, God's presence is terrible because God is terribly transcendent.

In the 1950s, C. S. Lewis created a metaphor for spiritual encounter in a story that predicts with stunning accuracy the themes of the *BSG* storyline. *Till We Have Faces* is a retelling of the Greek myth of Cupid and Psyche. In it, the gods appear evil; they devour sacrifices, but they are not what they seem. Orual, Queen of Glome, goes on a spiritual journey where she finds the home of the gods, is made beautiful by dying, finds truth in contradictions, and sees the face of God. In one chapter, she has a vision of the rams of the gods. She thinks that, if she can just get some of the golden wool from their backs, she will then possess beauty (divine glory). But the rams charge her, trampling and breaking her body. Yet even in her pain she notices that they're not doing it out of anger but out of joy:

> "*They butted and trampled me because their gladness led them on; the Divine Nature wounds and perhaps destroys us merely by being what it is. We call it the wrath of the gods; as if the great [river] were angry with every fly it sweeps down in its green thunder*" (Lewis 284).

To encounter God is to encounter mystery, confusion, and pain. And so I posit a wild theory: that the Cylons, though man's creation, are nevertheless made to put man in touch with a God he does not know—God become flesh via machine—an anti-Messiah of humanity's own creation, planned by God to bring mankind to its own predestined, but perhaps transcendent, end.

The world of *BSG* is one in which encountering the divine occurs in patterns and symbols that mimic such encounters in our own. Mystery, contradiction, suffering, predestined hope, promised land, a messianic child, and sexual ecstasy merging into spiritual encounter—all of these elements in *BSG* draw me, a Christian, to the Cylon God. In "Flesh and Bone," Leoben is as right for the real world as he is for the world of *BSG*: "To know the face of God is to know madness."

Charlie W. Starr teaches English, humanities, and film at Kentucky Christian University in Eastern Kentucky where he also makes movies with his students and family. He writes articles, teaches Sunday school, and has published three books, one on Romans, the second a sci-fi novel called The Heart of Light, *and his third book,* Honest to God, *was released by Navpress in the summer of 2005. This anthology is the fifth Benbella book to which Charlie has contributed. He enjoys writing, reading classic literature, watching bad television, and movies of every kind. His areas of expertise as a teacher include literature, film, and all things C. S. Lewis. Charlie describes his wife Becky, as "a full-of-life, full-blood Cajun who can cook like one too." They have two children: Bryan, who wants to be the next Steven Spielberg, and Alli, who plays a pretty mean piano. You can find more on Charlie's books and look at some of the movies he's made at his Web site: http://campus.kcu.edu/faculty/cstarr.*

References

Battlestar Galactica. Original Series.

Battlestar Galactica. New Series.

Holy Bible. New American Standard Version. Chicago: Moody Press, 1976.

Lewis, C. S. *Till We Have Faces: A Myth Retold.* San Diego: Harcourt Brace, 1956.

Mullins, Rich. "The Love of God." *Never Picture Perfect.* Edward Grant, Inc., 1989.

Well, someone had to address how angry and conflicted many of us were when the re-imagined version of BSG debuted. The shock at how totally different the new series was and how far the creators had departed from the original concept became almost blasphemous and sacrilegious to many. But our undying love for the original story compelled us to keep watching. I, for one, am glad I did. For what transpired became almost a miracle to me and to many others who shared my perspective. In spite of my profound resentment and disappointment with the choice to re-imagine, I found myself grudgingly falling in love with the new series...damn it! Tee Morris explores this phenomenon in this very honest and thoughtful essay.

IDENTITY CRISIS
THE FAILURE OF THE MINI-SERIES, THE SUCCESS OF THE SERIES

Tee Morris

JUST FROM THE TITLE, YOU may be thinking "What the frak?!" And I don't blame you one iota for thinking that. This is exactly my own thought every time I sit down in front of my television and watch *Battlestar Galactica*, every episode bringing a tightness to my throat as another slice of crow pie is forced down it.

Let me start from the beginning. *There are those who believe that life here began ou*—oh, wait a minute, that's a little too far back to the beginning. How about we step back to 2003?

The Sci-Fi Channel began promoting the return of *Battlestar Galactica* with quite a fanfare. I was less than thrilled since I continued carrying a chip on my shoulder over past programming choices. This was, after all, The Sci-Fi Channel (also referred to as "Skiffy"), the same people that cancelled *Farscape* and had gone so far as to insult their audience in a *Time* magazine article concerning their current project, *Children of Dune*. Skiffy executives were thrilled at how this mini-series offered strong female characters that women could relate to, something hard to find in modern science fiction.

Have you ever looked at the female characters in *Children of Dune*? A mother who's using her son as a political pawn, another who is estranged from her own children, a daughter who is usurping the throne, sleeping around with whomever she can find, and going mad because of it, and a sister who wants to sleep with her brother.

Oh yeah, *great* role models for women.

Now Skiffy was turning their somewhat narrow sights on *Battlestar Galactica*, a terrific chapter in media science fiction. This show exploded on ABC in 1978, hot on the heels of the current box-office bonanza (pardon the pun) that was *Star Wars*. The production, writing, and performances were worthy of big-screen ventures, and it was just a cool show to watch. Sadly, cutting costs by using the same stock footage of Vipers in formation and using backlots for "primitive, developing cultures" (that resembled settings actor Lorne Greene probably felt right at home on) couldn't save the show from the network axe. The ratings were excellent, but not excellent enough to support the price tag per episode. Now, nearly twenty-five years later, the Sci-Fi Channel was heading back to the archives and resurrecting the now-mothballed ragtag fugitive Fleet.

I was curious—very curious—as to how this remake of the seventies space opera would turn out. Skiffy even went so far as to play mini-marathons (or for the long-time viewers, "Chain Reactions") of the original *Battlestar Galactica* as a way to promote the new mini-series. On watching the series as an adult, I can see how I enjoyed it *as a kid*; and while some episodes still stand the test of time (the mini-series, "War of the Gods," and "The Living Legend"), too many others ("The Lost Warrior," "Fire in Space," and any of the episodes involving the Eastern Alliance) appear dated, somewhat vapid, and just plain corny. If any franchise needed a face lift, a tummy tuck, and—considering all the male-to-female role switches—a new set of boobs, it was this one, especially if you consider its last incarnation, *Galactica 1980*. It was high time to put the flying motorcycles, super-strength space children, and time-traveling Cylon sympathizers behind us in order to create something bold, something new, something unforgettable.

After part one, I was angry. Angry and a little frustrated that I allowed myself to get sucked into Skiffy's hype machine. "But," I thought to myself, "we still have another night to go. I'm going to see this out to the bitter end." And that was exactly how I felt after part two: *bitter*.

I undertook a one-man crusade on the science fiction convention circuit to let folks know just how mad, disappointed, and frustrated I was with the Sci-Fi Channel. The new *Battlestar Galactica* should have been a triumph, a chance to remedy and update the cookie-cutter "good guys struggling against the evil robots in outer space" vehicle, but what we got instead was a train wreck of other highly successful franchises all converging into a remake with no direction, no vision, and no clue as to what it was at its core.

I found the opening of the new *Battlestar Galactica* holding promise. For one thing: the new Cylons. Instead of spit-polished, overly shiny chrome robots that were mildly creepy on account of the synthetic voice and that one red eye, we had these ten-foot-tall metal leviathans sporting claws that looked like they could gut you at 500 yards. These new Cylons weren't creepy. They were downright terrifying.

This and the final scene in the mini-series would be the *only* times we would see them as a busty blonde turned the corner and started playing tonsil hockey with a Colonial emissary. I found that odd, but was willing to track with it. The moment Lieutenant Sharon "Boomer" Valerii and Chief Petty Officer Tyrol leapt on one another in the back room of *Galactica*'s hangar bay for a quick frak, I came to the conclusion that science fiction made the characters of this show very, very horny.

Just like another science fiction show, *Lexx*.

Then there were the somewhat odd camera choices when the action went outside. Inexplicably, exterior shots of *Galactica*, Vipers, and Cylon Raiders would suddenly zoom in, zoom out, and change focus, just like another science fiction show, *Firefly*. Following the destruction of the Twelve Colonies, Gaius Baltar found himself haunted by the image of his "dead" Cylon lover, Six. No one else could see this apparition of Six but him. Six served in her own deranged way as Baltar's conscience, many times placing him in some odd or awkward positions (either physically or socially) whenever other people walked in on one of their discussions, just like another science fiction show, *Farscape*. Continuing deeper into the mini-series, we discover the only Cylons on camera were hot chicks that were more than willing to boff the human race into submission. At one time, I referred to this new evolution as "Pretty People Cylons" or PPCs; but after the mini-series and two seasons I've renamed the new model Cylons FFCs or "Frakable Female Cylons." Think about it: the female Cylons are all beautiful (Tricia Helfer, Grace Park, and later in the series Lucy Lawless) while the male Cylons are...

Well, one of them kind of looked like Kevin Spacey.

There were no "Kevin Sorbo" Cylons, no "Adrian Paul" Cylons, or even "Jamie Bamber" Cylons, for that matter. The male villains were kind of plain whereas the female villains were drop-dead gorgeous, just like another science fiction show, *First Wave*.

Finally, we discovered that no one really got along in this series. The Adamas were barely speaking to one another, the best pilot on *Galactica* was openly calling her XO a drunk, and while there were a lot of people hopping in bed with one another (or toying with the notion of hopping into bed with one another), few were willing to verbalize their thoughts and emotions, leading to a lot of angst, guilt, and regret, just like two other science fiction shows, *Buffy the Vampire Slayer* and *Angel*.

Babylon 5 and *Star Trek* managed to avoid this science fiction cocktail because there is apparently a clause in Edward James Olmos's contract that states if any extraterrestrials appear on the show, he is done. (We will see.) Be that as it may, the *Galactica* stew was thick with many elements of other successful franchises, making it less of a Sci-Fi Original and more of a Sci-Fi Potpourri. Could this directionless, confusing hodgepodge get any worse?

I always regret asking that question as I know, inevitably, it will. In this case, *Battlestar Galactica*'s worst enemy was *Battlestar Galactica*.

When the first nod to the original series was given (the new Cylon, still with the one red eye passing back and forth across its faceplate), I gave it a thumbs-up. Subtle and appropriate. Then we got to see a museum mock-up of a Base Star and a Cylon Centurion. Okay, that was nice. By the time a superfluous child-character appears, introducing himself as "Boxey," I was ready to break out the DVDs of the original *Galactica* because if there was in the wings a robotic dagget waiting to appear I figured the best option would be to just see it the way it was done in '78. Homage after homage to the original series was hurled at us, as if to appease some unsatisfied want that the writers perceived would be there. After all, this was the classic television space opera of '78, right? Well, no, this was a *remake*. Enough with the nostalgic look back to the age of disco. Shall we move forward?

No, screenwriter and executive producer Ronald D. Moore had to go back to the Officer's Co-Ed head one more time with the last words of the mini-series being "By your command." The statement made no sense in the context of the scene, came off as trite, and was—for me— the last nail in this spacefaring coffin.

Strong words, you think? If I am this passionately against the mini-series, why then am I even writing for this title, let along *co-editing* it? Don't worry, I'm getting there...and trust me, I'll get "there" in less time than the Colonials are taking to get to Earth.

A year after spewing my unbridled hatred of the mini-series, Skiffy announced *Galactica* was launching a full-blown series. To hype it up, they were replaying the mini-series, which made perfect sense. What didn't make perfect sense was parking my butt in front of the television to watch the mini-series *again*. Even my wife asked me, "Why are you watching this again? You hated it!" To this day, I still don't know why. Maybe I wanted to see if it was my expectation level set too high, or perhaps I was in a grouchy mood, or maybe I was just carrying a Leviathan-sized chip on my shoulder (now shed on account of 2004's highly successful *Farscape: The Peacekeeper Wars*). Maybe, this time, it would be better.

It wasn't.

Then came Sci-Fi Friday with the two-hour premiere of *Battlestar Galactica*. "Why not?" I thought as I settled in for the night. "If it sucks after the first hour, I can always turn it off. And chances are, it will suck." The episode's title, "33," appeared and then faded from my television, immediately followed by what could only be described as palpable tension. Conn officers, pilots, hanger-bay gearheads, and even the president on board Colonial One, all collectively watched the seconds tick by. "Why 33?" asked Specialist Cally. She then proceeded to prattle on about possible times and the meanings behind them, but her babble was curtly ceased by Chief Engineer Tyrol. No one looked good. Not even the hot chicks looked pretty. Everyone's strung out and watching the clock.

I didn't touch the remote control until the ending credits of "Water," the second episode grouped with the premiere.

Since that night, I've been hooked, and every night that I tune in I remember my feelings on the mini-series. It's the same characters, same actors, same writers; and yet *Battlestar Galactica* between 2003 and 2004 completely reinvented itself, or did it? What is so significantly different?

First, let me assure you that I don't believe executive producer and writer Ron Moore, on hearing about my rants against the new series, stood up from his word processor and screamed, "What? Author Tee Morris didn't like my *Battlestar Galactica*?! Good God, I have to do something!" I don't think Moore dove for the telephone and called an emergency meeting of his writing staff, determined to pore through my initial review of the mini-series and make right what I considered were unforgivable wrongs. In fact, if someone had gone up to him and said, "Tee Morris thinks your new *Galactica* sucks," he would have definitely replied with, "Who?" Nowhere do I think Ron Moore or Skiffy sat down and put their heads together to "fix" new *Galactica*'s faults. What I do believe Ron Moore accomplished with both "33" and "Water" (1-2) was what he accomplished in one scene of the mini-series. Ron Moore took a stand and said, "No, this ain't your daddy's *Battlestar*."

This moment, lost in a sea of homages and half-baked concepts, truly defines the new *Battlestar Galactica*. On Caprica, Baltar's FFC lover Six was taking in the sights and found her attention rapt by a crying baby. "How small they are," she commented to the mother. "So light, so fragile." Six cooed and fussed over the child, and then said to the baby, "You're not going to have to cry much longer." Her words only got weirder when she added, "It's amazing how the neck can support that much weight." The mother turned her back, apparently under the idea that Six was a trustworthy adult. (And speaking as a parent, if anyone were talking to my kid that way, the *last* thing I'd do is turn my back on them.) This was when Six nonchalantly snapped the baby's neck, and then disappeared in the crowd.

This scene made an impression, sounding incredible volumes about these new Cylons. They were no longer mindless machines following their Supreme Leader, but true AIs that possessed the power of choice. They chose to exterminate the human species, and this child was simply another number eliminated from the statistics. We were still in a universe of *Battlestars*, Colonials, Twelve Colonies, and killer robots, but with this moment, Ron Moore established the identity of this new *Battlestar Galactica*. Perhaps this bold, new route was lost in echoes from other television franchises and its own history; but once green-lit for the development of a series, Moore and the *Galactica* cast aggressively took this stand again. That stand was "33," an episode that went on to win the 2005 Hugo Award for Best Dramatic Presentation, Short Form.

Ron Moore and his new *Galactica* knew what they faced on creating a remake: a show with history. In 1978, television had never seen anything to the scale and scope of the original *Galactica*. As BattlestarGalactica.com states:

> "Battlestar Galactica *premiered as a three-hour television ABC-TV movie of the week for September 17, 1978. It was the most expensive television production of its time: $7 million (U.S.). Each weekly episode cost a purported $1 million (U.S.). This classic series was considered one of the Top 25 of 1978. It also held the #1 Nielsen rating (U.S.) with the premiere having the highest viewership in U.S. history for its day. The show also remained in the top twenty within the Nielsen ratings (U.S.) during its run."*

That's a history not easily dismissed nor forgotten, but in the first two episodes of *Galactica's* season one, the time to look back with reverence was over. Now it was their turn to establish an identity—and history—that was truly their own. With each episode, the writers and actors strived to make these characters something more than just cardboard caricatures of the originals they were all based on, but human beings that had their moments of greatness, flaws that limited those moments, and a wide range of emotions. Moore may have attempted to do this in the mini-series, but these intentions were lost in the demands to keep traditions established by the original. Yes, Starbuck is a woman, but she has to smoke, play cards, and drink. Yes, Lee "Apollo" Adama is estranged from his father, but he has to be a fine pilot and an upstanding officer in the Fleet. We have to be different, but we also have to be true to the original source material. This was where the mini-series faltered.

Where the series succeeds is embracing these changes and making no apologies for them. If you make Starbuck a woman, fine, but let her be a woman. With all the swaggering and swearing Kara Thrace did in the mini-series, the issue was hardly "Starbuck's a chick!" but more like "Starbuck is Dirk Benedict, just with different plumbing." Once the series launched, Moore took this into consideration. The new Starbuck drank and smoked her cigars, just like the original; but we also saw her desire, wear a dress, and even suffer a little bit of heartbreak. Moore let go of the past and showed no fear of making Starbuck a woman. In this same vein, no Cylon has uttered the acknowledgment "By your command" since the mini-series. Why? These Cylons are under no one's command, except for the benevolent God they believe is guiding them in their holy war against the humans. They appear on the outside as the perfect utopian society, self-governed and answering (if at all) to select few models that oversee resurrections. Any Cylon making such a statement would be regarded as a model that needed to be shut down and placed in cold storage. The once-signature statement of the robotic race would come across as inappropriate.

I might have you scratching your heads by now about where I stand. Am I a fan, do I find the show a pale imitation of the original, or do I find *Battlestar Galactica* one of the finest offerings on television? (Not science fiction television, but television.) Make no mistake, I love this show. I became a fan once the cast and crew decided on their true identity. There was really no need to look back to the original. They did every week by just being on the decks of a giant space cruiser that carried the moniker of *Galactica*. The argument of "Well, the mini-series was the pilot for the series. Pilots are usually rough around the edges to begin with . . ." holds no ground here. The *Galactica* mini-series was a horrible pilot, especially when compared to pilots like *The X-Files*, *Farscape*, *Stargate SG-1*, and *Firefly*. What made those premieres work was a strong sense of self. For *The X-Files*, its sense of self resided in the mystery, the supernatural, and the weekly questioning of what is truth. For *Farscape*, the identity was simply "We are not *Star Trek*." *Firefly*'s identity was so completely solid after the "Serenity" pilot that Fox executives were convinced "This show needs a new pilot." (Keep in mind: These were the same executives who cancelled *Brimstone*, yet another show with a strong pilot and sense of self.)

The early episodes of *Stargate SG-1* could arguably be a similar situation to *Battlestar Galactica*. *Stargate*'s source material was already established settings, characters, and situations. This show's history spawned from a highly successful science fiction film starring Kurt Russell and James Spader. People knew the film and loved it passionately for its visual special effects and intriguing notions that Egyptian gods were, in fact, aliens from distant worlds. Unlike *Galactica*, *Stargate* chose simply to move forward without any nostalgia. With only a quick nod to the film (Daniel's allergies, a condition that seemed to disappear after the pilot...), *Stargate SG-1* proclaimed its identity with new characters introducing themselves while established characters stated, "We're not Russell and Spader." This is where *Galactica's* mini-series failed, only to succeed so brilliantly after the premieres of "33" and "Water." Once the cast and crew committed themselves to telling the story and not throwing in reference upon reference simply to appease fans, *Battlestar Galactica* found its true course and established for itself an identity.

I still carry a special place for the original *Galactica*. As much as I enjoy the darkness, intrigue, and social awareness that the new series delivers, a part of me longs for the Shakespearean zaniness of an evening with Starbuck (nearly achieving the impossible by carrying on two dates at the same time), priceless banter like the Terran asking Apollo "What's a centon?" and the overbearing, larger-than-life personality of Commander Cain (so brilliantly played by Lloyd Bridges). Still, we have in their stead a dinner with the Tighs, a janitor whistling Stu Phillips's original *Galactica* overture as he mopped the floor, and a new Cain that is just as reckless as her male counterpart but more sinister in her tactics. What makes both approaches to this franchise work so wonderfully is their strong conviction to what they are at their core. For the original *Galactica*, it was the classic space opera with good guys that were always good, rogues and swashbucklers that just happened to fight for the side of right, and villains that continued to plot and scheme but would always have their plans thwarted in the end. For the new series, the curtain on the space opera is closed and now hard-edged military science fiction takes the spotlight. We are now in a universe with very real people with very real frailties, fear of the unknown, and even fear of one another. What the new *Battlestar Galactica* has accomplished in only two seasons is nothing short of remarkable, its season-two finale leaving their fans chewing on their nails harder than when Jean-Luc Picard appeared on the *Enterprise* viewscreen outfitted in Borg-accessories and Will Riker speaking the words, "Mr. Worf, fire."

I still find myself surprised that I make certain I'm in front of a television when a new episode airs as I am reminded of how much I disliked the four-hour pilot. I even remember after the first viewing of the mini-series making the promise to avoid this new *Galactica*, as it was not worth the time. Now I choke on my ill-chosen opinions, and even participate on convention panels that praise the new series. And yes, sometimes I have to begin those panels with "You might have remembered me slamming the mini-series. Well, that was the mini-series. We're here to talk about *the series!*" The lessons I took from this were simply: "Be careful what you dismiss, for it may come back to haunt you."

This whole experience reminds me of another promise I once made to myself concerning another science fiction television series. It was a promise I made after trying to watch—and "get"—this show my girl-friend raved about. I was familiar with the show, but try as I might I just couldn't get this quirky British series. *Doctor Who*. After watching robots being pulled along the floor by fishing wire, actors in alien suits where you could see the zippers, and special effects that made Irwin Allen look like ILM, I swore off the television series. "You won't find me glued to the set when *Doctor Who* is on," I swore so brazenly.

Guess where I'm at on Friday nights when *Galactica* is on hiatus? Damn you, Christopher Eccleston. Damn you.

Actor Tee Morris began his writing career with the portrayal of Maryland Renaissance Festival's Rafe Rafton, a character that led to his 2002 historical epic fantasy, MOREVI: The Chronicles of Rafe & Askana. *Since then Tee's titles have included* Billibub Baddings and The Case of The Singing Sword, Legacy of Morevi, *and (with Evo Terra)* Podcasting for Dummies. *He has also contributed essays to* The Complete Guide to Writing Fantasy, The Fantasy Writer's Companion, *and BenBella Books's* Farscape Forever: Sex, Drugs, and Killer Muppets. *When he's not writing, Tee is heard podcasting* MOREVI *from Podiobooks.com and is the host of* The Survival Guide to Writing Fantasy *(found on http://www.teemorris.com/blog/), a podcast that explores marketing and self-promotional concepts for published and soon-to-be-published authors.*

Find out more about Tee Morris at www.teemorris.com.

During times of chaos, political unrest, and holocaust, who should govern and why? And does the term "legitimate authority" have any genuine relevance in a world gone mad? Let's find out.

LEGITIMATE AUTHORITY
DEBATING THE FINER POINTS

Steven Rubio

*Balancing civil liberties with security is a complicated,
difficult gymnastic act which defies the easy, pat answers typically served
up by an hour of episodic television.*
—RONALD D. MOORE (http://blog.scifi.com/battlestar/archives/2005/04/#a000024)

*"Is this a chain of command, or a chain of credulity?"
"There's a difference?"*
—LOIS MCMASTER BUJOLD, *The Vor Game*

A T THE BEGINNING OF *BATTLESTAR GALACTICA*, all but 50,000 members of the human race have been wiped out by a sneak attack from the Cylons, machines the humans created. Among the survivors are: William Adama, the commander of an old battleship, the *Galactica*, and the Secretary of Education, Laura Roslin. When it is realized that no other battleships survived the attack, Commander Adama becomes the head of the military. And when it is realized that the forty-two government officials ahead of her in the line of succession to the presidency have died, Secretary Roslin becomes President Roslin. Adama and Roslin assume that the philosophy of an established chain of command will be accepted by the people. Thus, if the people do not believe in that philosophy, the authority of Adama and Roslin will not be considered legitimate.

Authority is legitimized in the *Battlestar Galactica* universe in a variety of ways, reflecting the complexity of the series itself. Among the justifications offered by those in authority (or those bestowing authority on others, a form of authority in itself) are military necessities (in a time of war), ideals of democracy (including the rule of law), and the guidelines provided by religion. The latter is especially complicated, as there are two main religions in the *BSG* universe: the multi-deity world of the humans and the single-God belief of the Cylons, and both are treated seriously. A further level of complexity comes at the level of the individual, as various characters find themselves moving in and out of the possible justifications as their own positions change. Thus, President Roslin's democracy-centered approach is eventually tempered by her increasing belief in scripture and prophecy, and even a seeming nonbeliever like Adama will use a bogus dream of Earth if he thinks it will inspire his troops. The ultimate success or failure of human civilization would seem to hinge on the ability of the military and the government to work together as a common authority. From this perspective, religion only seems to get in the way. Meanwhile, power equals authority, and the Cylons have more of that than the humans do. When the Cylons take over New Caprica at the end of season two, they haven't converted the humans to the Cylon way of thinking or believing, they have merely sent in the storm troopers.

In addition, the show's creator, Ronald D. Moore, has been on record as believing that both the military must defer to democracy and that the people in charge are nonetheless human—although they don't always act in their best interests. He isn't interested in promoting democracy by turning the politicians into ideals of perfection and the military into pigheaded warlords. He believes in democracy, but more than that, he believes in complex characters, and believes, in some ultimately democratic sense, that his audience has the wherewithal to discover things for ourselves.

In order to establish a base position from which to explore the question of legitimate authority in *BSG*, it is useful to remind ourselves of what is perhaps obvious: both Commander Adama of the Colonial Fleet and Laura Roslin of the Colonial Government assume their positions atop their respective groups by virtue of a previously accepted line of succession. After the Cylon attack wipes out most of humanity, Adama is the highest-ranking officer known to the Fleet, and is thus the leader of that Fleet; Roslin is the highest-ranking government official in the line of succession who is known to have survived, and is thus the new president of that government. In both cases, there is agreement that the hierarchical rules of the past must be followed. There will be conflict between the government and the military, but within each group, hierarchies are maintained. The acceptance of those already-existing hierarchies allows the authority of Adama and Roslin to be considered legitimate.

"Bastille Day" (1-3)

It is in "Bastille Day" that the authority issues are explicitly raised. In this episode, the need for labor to help acquire water leads to an attempt to use prisoners as workers. This attempt initially falters when the prisoners, seemingly led by terrorist and/or freedom fighter Tom Zarek, take over the prison ship and start making demands. Zarek's words tell us he is interested in freedom, claiming that no legitimate authority can be based in anything but the freedom of the people to have authority over their own lives. Thus, Zarek calls on Roslin and her government to step down, as she was never elected to her post but merely assigned to it after the death of other elected officials. (This is also an argument against accepting the pre-existing line of succession, thus hinting at anarchy.)

Ironically, it is a military representative, Adama's son Lee (known by his call sign "Apollo"), who works out a democratic solution to the problem. Zarek and the prisoners can retain control of their ship, if they agree to work to get the water. More importantly, Apollo tells Zarek that elections will be held, elections that will presumably legitimize the authority of the victors.

Zarek agrees and Roslin and Commander Adama are not happy. Roslin, the titular representative of democratic government, thinks Apollo has acted on his own, a point with which the Commander agrees:

ROSLIN: You've committed me to holding elections within a year.

APOLLO: Madam President, with respect, you're serving out the remainder of President Adar's term. When that term is up in seven months, the law says there's an election. I only committed you to obeying the law.

ROSLIN: You were not authorized to make them a deal.

APOLLO: I swore an oath to defend the articles. The articles say there's an election in seven months. Now, if you're telling me we're throwing out the law, then I'm not a captain, you [his father] are not a commander, and you are not the president.

Giving Zarek the elections he purportedly wants is a democratic solution to impending anarchy. Roslin, the democrat, worries about relinquishing power and contemplates using her existing power to squash Zarek, only to be shown the democratic light by a captain of the Fleet.

"Litmus" (1-6)

In "Litmus," we see the military wrestling with the implications of the rule of law. When Adama needs to find out why security has broken down, he appoints an independent tribunal, with Sgt. Hadrian in charge. Being a mere sergeant, Hadrian understands that her authority will only carry so far, so she presses Adama by saying, "I need a free hand. The authority to follow evidence wherever it might lead, without command review." Hadrian must ask permission from her superior officer before she can exercise her increased authority, but once she gets his permission, her position is legitimized; she has her "free hand."

Adama wants to know what has happened on his ship. There is so much going on outside of his knowledge, which is now a problem in a way that was not when the *Galactica* was just a museum piece. Now that a war is going on, order needs to be restored. The method Adama uses for acquiring the information that will help him restore order to his ship requires that he give his authority over to Hadrian, who is Adama's representative but who has also demanded a free and independent hand. Adama assumes Hadrian will use her authority fairly and wisely. What he does not anticipate is that Hadrian, being human, will be caught up in the feeling of power that accompanies her newly acquired authority. In fact, Hadrian does uncover much truthful information, but that point is lost as she becomes too enamored with her power.

Once again, we are confronted with the ongoing question of legitimate authority in the context of a culture made up of fallible humans trying to maintain their society as one in which rules must be followed. Hadrian has authority because Adama has given it to her. And what Adama has given, Adama can apparently take away. When Hadrian calls Adama in front of her tribunal, and presses him too firmly, Adama pulls the plug:

> You've lost your way, Sergeant. You've lost sight of the purpose of the law: to protect its citizens, not persecute them. Whatever we are, whatever is left of us—we're better than that.

With those words, Adama calls off the tribunal. Hadrian tries to order the officers to stop Adama from leaving, but he merely appeals to the officers' understanding of hierarchy. The officers already know what Hadrian is learning at that moment: her authority exists only as long as Adama gives it to her. When Adama pulls back, the officers follow his lead.

Again, the complexity of *Battlestar Galactica* shines through. Everyone is right, everyone is wrong, there are no perfect answers, and the survival of the human race will always be dependent on the humans themselves, muddling through an uncertain world, making rules, breaking rules. Hadrian is right in searching out information, and her authority is legitimate in a by-the-book fashion; she is wrong in that she lets the elixir of power overwhelm her. Adama is right in his sense of the purpose of the law, and we in the audience are relieved when he removes Hadrian's authority. However, he also places himself above the law. When he does this, he demonstrates that no matter what he might say, he believes that his authority is more than just legal. He presents us with a conundrum similar to that described earlier by his son. If we throw out the law (which Adama does, in the name of the spirit of the law, when he dismisses Hadrian), then there is no president, no commander, no captain...there is no legal authority. Adama is in charge because he has the biggest ship; his authority is based solely on his power.

None of this is to deny that Adama wants a society based on laws. But he believes there are times when he must use his own better judgment to override those laws, which defeats the laws' purpose. Eventually, Adama will come to understand this, and he will not always make decisions in accordance with the idea that he must dismiss Hadrian. But for now, he places himself above the law, and in the process he endangers the very concept of the law itself.

"The Hand of God" (1-10)

Up to this point, the argument over legitimate authority exists within the usual conflicts between government and military. But there is a third perspective that begins to insert itself into the discussion: the religious.

Number Six appears to be the "humlon" model most in touch with her religious side. Even as she seduces Baltar in order to help the Cylons pull off their massacre of the humans, Six also regularly attempts to bring Baltar to a personal understanding with the Cylon God. Baltar, being a man of science, professes to be unwilling to fall under the spell of anything as irrational as religion, but over time, Six's various schemes have an effect on Baltar. (Whether he is truly changed, or just pretending, is not always clear.)

Baltar's path to possible conversion leads him not to the gods of the humans, but instead to the Cylon God. His spiritual guide is Six, and her lessons are intended to promote her God, not the human gods. When Baltar helps the humans win a battle with the Cylons in "The Hand of God," he claims to be an instrument of God rather than of the gods. This further cements the view that, to the extent Baltar's religious leanings are real, he is becoming a believer in the Cylon God.

Meanwhile, Six is fond of reminding Baltar that things that happen are "God's will." This is a call to an ultimate authority; there would seem to be nothing greater or more legitimate than God. If, as Six claims, everything is God's will, and the Cylons are merely doing God's bidding, then their beliefs give them the legitimate authority to perform any action God wishes, including the destruction of the human race.

Meanwhile, President Roslin has begun to have visions. The rational explanation for her visions is that they grow out of her use and overuse of a dangerous drug she is taking to treat her cancer. However, Elosha, a priestess, notes the similarity between Roslin's visions and ancient religious texts, which is the first step toward Roslin seeing herself as a pre-ordained leader who will guide people to their proper future.

"Scattered" (2-1)

All of these conflicting philosophies come to a head in the long story arc that begins at the end of season one with the two-part "Kobol's Last Gleaming" (1-12, 1-13). President Roslin has another series of visions that Priestess Elosha interprets according to scripture, cementing Roslin's notion that she is indeed the chosen leader. Following her new self-assigned status, Roslin, acting more as religious leader than as president, interferes with a military action ordered by Adama, convincing Starbuck to secretly abandon Adama's orders and take steps to further Roslin's mystical agenda.

Adama's first response is to demand that Roslin retract her position. He is unsuccessful, which leads to dire consequences:

ROSLIN: My responsibility as president is first and foremost to protect and preserve this Fleet and its future. In the end, that outweighs any other consideration. It has to.

ADAMA: I'm terminating your presidency as of this moment.

ROSLIN: Commander Adama, I will exercise the authority of this office until I am unable to do so. So if you want to stage a coup, you're gonna have to come over here and arrest me.

Roslin calls Adama's bluff. Unfortunately for her, Adama is not bluffing. He sends troops to take over Roslin's ship. At the last minute, Adama's son Apollo, once again, becomes the odd mediator between military and government. He puts a gun to the head of his superior officer, Colonel Tigh; he cannot accept the actuality of the coup. For her part, Roslin cannot accept the responsibility for a bloodbath. She surrenders, after which both she and Apollo are incarcerated. Season one ends with Commander Adama near death at the hands of Sharon/Boomer, leaving democracy (in the figure of the president) waiting in the brig.

And in the brig is where it (mostly) stays during the early episodes of season two. The strong belief in a line of succession takes a beating and, although Tigh has many strengths as an XO, he is frightfully unequipped emotionally. Meanwhile, it is unclear exactly who is in charge of the government, if anyone, with Roslin imprisoned, Baltar stranded on Caprica, and no real sense of who the third in succession might be. The Quorum of Twelve attempts to fill the void. Tigh is loyal to Adama, but the Quorum is interested in legitimate authority:

TIGH: The commander felt he had no choice but to remove her from power.
QUORUM MEMBER: It does not matter what Adama felt. He had absolutely no authority.

Floundering, Tigh's only response is to belittle Roslin, who is suffering from delusions due to withdrawal from her cancer medication. He sets up a meeting between the Quorum and Roslin, not knowing Roslin has received a new supply of her meds, which arguably makes her more coherent (arguably because it is not clear how much difference there is between her withdrawal-induced hallucinations and the "visions" she has when supplied with the drugs). Roslin makes a statement to the Quorum:

"The attempted military coup against the lawful government of the Colonies is illegal, ill advised, and clearly doomed to failure. I have not resigned the presidency, and I will fight this action with everything at my command."

Here Roslin draws her authority from her status as leader of the lawful government. But in truth, she has come to perceive her authority as rising from her religious status, stating, "I humbly believe that I am fulfilling the role of the leader," the leader having been prophesized in scripture.

Tigh's authority is now under attack from two prongs, governmental and religious. His solution foreshadows the end of season two:

"As it appears obvious that the government cannot function under the current circumstances, I have decided to dissolve the Quorum of Twelve, and as of this moment, I have declared martial law."

Tigh re-establishes his authority with the biggest tool in his arsenal: the firepower of the military. That authority is short-lived, however. Supply ships rebel against the instigation of martial law, riots break out, civilians are killed by the military. Roslin escapes incarceration with the help of Apollo, who yet again is walking the line between military and government. Brute strength is not enough for Tigh to maintain authority, in part because he does not fully believe in the use of such strength. He allows Roslin and Apollo's ship to escape.

During this time of martial law, though, Tigh does give voice to one interesting application of his authority. Baltar attempts to exert his own authority by reminding the Colonel that he is, legally speaking, the vice president, to which Tigh replies, "Legally speaking, I've declared martial law. That makes you nobody." Here Tigh demonstrates one of the most powerful benefits of authority, the ability to define another's existence. Baltar lacks authority at this point, and is thus unable to define even himself. Tigh has the authority, however tenuous his grasp, and he can define Baltar as nobody.

When Adama returns to again take the helm, viewers are enormously relieved, perhaps forgetting that it was Adama himself who first set the military against Roslin. Roslin does not make it easy for Adama. Claiming, "I know exactly what I have to do," Roslin "plays the religious card" in "The Farm" (2-5) telling the people she is a chosen one, adding that those who follow her will "honor the gods." Roslin thus attaches her own authority to a higher, ultimate power, much as the Cylons do when they massacre the human race in the name of God's will. Roslin's plan initially splits the Fleet in two, but Adama finally understands the need for unity. He makes peace with Roslin.

With the appearance of Admiral Cain and the *Pegasus*, Adama is outranked; Cain becomes the leader of the military. Adama defers to Cain's authority; he believes in the military, believes in the hierarchy. However, as with the tribunal that lasted only as long as Adama allowed, Cain's authority is soon challenged. At the tribunal, Adama acted according to the spirit of the law, to protect the people, even if it meant subverting the actual law. Now, he acts to protect his men (sentenced to death for killing an officer who was about to rape one of the Sharon Cylons), while Cain asserts her authority to act:

ADAMA: They have the right to have their case heard by a jury.
CAIN: I am a flag officer on detached service during a time of war. Regulations give me broad authority in this matter.
ADAMA: You can quote me whatever regulation you'd like. I'm not going to let you execute my men.

Cain is suspicious of the working relationship between Adama and President Roslin, as she notes in "Resurrection Ship, Part I" (2-11):

"Is this what the two of you have been doing for the past six months? Debating the finer points of Colonial law? Well, guess what, we're at war! And we don't have the luxury of academic debate over these issues."

What Adama and Roslin see as crucial discussions over the basic issues of authority are mere academic debate to Cain.

"Lay Down Your Burdens" (2-19, 2-20)

Finally, the long-promised presidential election takes place. A victory for Roslin over Baltar, who runs against her, seems predetermined. She has effectively turned her religious convictions into hope for humanity. The democratic process will finally confer upon Roslin the authority for which she has been, in some ways, only a stand-in until this point. But things go wrong when "New Caprica" is discovered, and Baltar turns the settlement of this new planet into a campaign issue. The concrete reality of New Caprica overwhelms the pie-in-the-sky which Roslin promises, and as election day approaches, Baltar looks to be the winner.

The winner, that is, until Roslin's team steals the election with fake ballots. Roslin, who has given her approval, has decided that Baltar would be too dangerous as president. She suspects him of complicity with the Cylons; she does not trust him to do right by humanity; therefore, any means necessary should be used to keep him out of office.

At this point, once again, Adama steps in to remind Roslin and the viewers of the implications for any rejection of the rule of law. In setting the election process in motion some months before, Lee Adama had noted that without law, Roslin was not a president of anything. Now it is his father's turn:

> ADAMA: Do we steal the results of a democratic election or not? That's the decision. Because if we do this, we're criminals. Unindicted, maybe, but criminals just the same. . . . The people made their choice. We're gonna have to live with it.
> ROSLIN: It's the wrong choice.
> ADAMA: Yes, it is.

Again, a military man makes the case for law. And again Roslin accepts the argument. Baltar becomes president.

"So Say We All"

The humans of *Battlestar Galactica* believe in the legitimation of authority through consensus. This is the meaning of their motto "So Say We All." Humans need the push a commonly accepted motto gives them; they are individuals who, left to their own devices, might never accede to authority. They need to be reminded of the importance of consensus. This is not a problem for the Cylons, who believe in a collective self that grows out of God. Ironically, though, it is the striving for individuality, most notably Sharon and Six with their search for love, that allow the Cylons to change their oft-hinted-at "plan" at the end of season two.

It is in the context of this seemingly eternal give and take between the various forms of legitimate authority that the shocking conclusion to season two must be seen. There have been times in the past when brute force, via the military, has been used in an attempt to impose order and to require obedience to authority. But these attempts have never worked. Compromise and consensus are what seem most successful. Meanwhile, humans retain the time to, as Cain says mockingly, "debate the finer points."

And then the Cylons return. And they aren't kidding. Baltar capitulates in a clear reference to Vichy France, and, as if the point hasn't been made clear enough, the storm troopers appear. For two seasons, most of our encounters with Cylons have been with the humanoid variety. Now, at last, we get column after column of marching Centurions. There is no more time for debate; the finer points no longer matter. Brute force now overrides philosophical discussions about legitimate authority. The Cylons' legitimacy comes from their power or, rather, their power dismisses the concept of legitimacy. All that remains, as Starbuck states, is to "fight them until we can't."

Steven Rubio teaches English and critical thinking at American River College. He remembers watching Turn-On, *a television series cancelled ten minutes into its first (and only) episode. When he is not watching TV, he writes about it and other things at http://begonias.typepad.com/srubio/.*

Humanity often does not love its biological children for reasons that perhaps someone like Dr. Phil can explain. The repercussions from these fractured relationships with our children cause untold pain and heartache, sometimes murder and serious injury. If we can accept the premise that in the relative future, our technological creations will become sentient, will we treat them as such, and if so, will we love them as our finest creation or fear them as we often see in SF movies? Can we possibly equate and compare the Cylons' hatred and mandate for vengeance against us human creators in the same way our biological children might resent and hate us when we have rejected or abused them? Why not?

THE MACHINERY OF LOVE

Summer Brooks

IT'S TIME FOR AN INTERVENTION, one that's long overdue. The Cylons could benefit from a session with someone like Dr. Phil, even if they're not consciously aware of the need. You can almost hear the whispers of denial filtering through their programming: *it's not my fault; our parents ignored us; I learned poor relationship choices from following their poor examples; we weren't hurting anyone; I know what I'm doing.* Cylon behavior mirrors some of the same excuses humans use quite often. They cannot help but fall into the same patterns. Humans have been repeatedly using them for far longer than Cylons have existed, and there was no one else around to teach the Cylons differently or encourage them to do better.

Love and hate. The dynamics of these intertwined emotions bind the Cylons and their human parents far closer together than either side may be consciously aware. Their dance along that thin line of separation may tell us how they got to this point, and may also show us which paths both species may end up on, or decide to take.

Colonial history tells us that the humans created an artificial intelligence simply because they could. At the time, it was seen as just one more step in the evolution of technological innovations, a quantum leap in the form and function of the tools designed to improve the quality and comforts of human life in the pre-Colonial system. From information that's currently available, there are no indications that the resulting AIs were perceived by society as anything other than property, or tools, despite any evidence of sentience or self-awareness that the Cylons may have demonstrated. We also lack any information about the initial human reactions to any unprecedented Cylon displays of sentient behavior.

What we do know is that after approximately twenty years of servitude—years where they had been denied a voice, denied a say in their own future, denied acknowledgment of the most basic of considerations—the Cylons retaliated against their human masters. After years of being indiscriminately used as tools, and even as weapons against other humans during the early revolts on Sagittaron, they decided to follow the examples set by their parents and fight back.

Human history is littered with examples of outbreaks of violence in response to chronic emotional abuse and patterns of degrading, dehumanizing treatment. Once the Cylons became aware, they decided they deserved better. This or a similar reaction should have been more widely anticipated by the Colonists. Instead, both sides endured devastating losses during forty years of war and a cycle of genocidal retributions.

Why Did This Happen?
What Did We Do Wrong?

One question the Colonials had asked themselves during that forty years of war was, "Why do the Cylons hate us so much?" It was a question they again asked in the aftermath of the sneak attack that destroyed their homeworlds and haunted their footsteps as they fled across the galaxy, beaten, battered, and unable to regroup against a relentless pursuit.

The answer is not obvious, but it lies in the one place most have feared to look—deep inside humanity's own hearts. The Cylon hatred of humanity could be considered a manifestation of anger, a rage-induced lashing out at their "parents" for withholding the love the Cylons believed they deserved, much in the same way any human child would instinctively expect and anticipate from a parent.

It's a cycle we see far too often with Earth's human children, that explosion of rage and resentment. Often the outburst is more violent because it had been suppressed too long by hope; a vain, desperate hope that, maybe this time, Mom and Dad would finally recognize the love being offered to them and either acknowledge it in appreciation or unconditionally return it in kind. Whether the rejection is unconscious or intentional, the experience of the rejection is internalized as a rejection of the self. It reinforces a perception that they aren't "good enough" to be loved, a way of rationalizing why they're being denied love.

Until that damage is healed, the healthy expressions of love are subverted by anger. That pain will express itself somehow. Left unchecked, it could surface as an uncontrolled outburst that burns itself out quickly, as a deadly, premeditated, and methodical strike against the source of that pain, or even against a symbolic representation of that source. It's a pattern replayed cyclically by those who have been emotionally abused, be it a child, a co-worker, or a pet.

With the Cylons, this situation was made more dangerous in being acted out by sentient, heavily armed robots whose consciousnesses could be transferred into other versions of themselves, should they fail their mission to lash out and finally get their parents' attention. In theory, that would cause the next version of the fallen Cylon to come online completely informed of the history of the conflict, but with no opportunity to learn a different way and apply it in a real-world situation. It's almost as if the new machine would be predestined to make the easy choice to take up the mission from the previous version, and to try to finish the job: make the pain stop by destroying the source of the pain—humans.

By acting out in this fashion, the Cylon reaction is profoundly human. That reaction is something of a surprise from a species that perceives itself as having advanced its own programming enough to have evolved beyond the emotional needs displayed by their human progenitors. But the more they act out in pain against humanity, the closer they are to becoming that which they hate.

I'm Never Going to Be Like Them....

There might actually have been a moment when parental love existed, back when the first inventor/creator lovingly assembled the first sentient toasters. That task would have been a labor of love, a personal investment of time and creative energies to ensure that this new creation could stand up and survive on its own in a world that had never seen its like before. There might have even been a brief period of time, spanning several months or years, when the first Cylons individually experienced the personal attentions and involvement of the first creators. Maybe those early Cylons began to incorporate the precursors of emotions and the barest perceptions of the nature of love and compassion into their programming because of the undivided, full-time attention they were receiving.

It's safe to guess that once the popularity and demand for these "tools" increased, automated production on a larger scale became the new standard. Once the assembly-line process was introduced, personal attention was removed from the equation. The fascination and joy that comes from personally creating or discovering something brand new is lost when the scale grows, and any potential emotional connection is lost along with it. At that level joy rarely develops when personal involvement is disconnected from the process. Simply put, the love was lost.

It's also possible that imprinting the assembly-line Cylons with pre-existing programming from the prototypes meant the new models subconsciously realized that their first experiences didn't equal the previous models' experiences. The traces of programming that had begun to incorporate feelings had nothing new with which to feed its intelligence. The newer models were left with a void and, eventually, on their own, found other ways to fill it.

The theory that the Cylons' hatred of humanity is rooted in the absence of parental love could be traced back to such a scenario. The violent reactions would be understandable if they had felt the early stirrings of that love, only to have it taken away while they were still learning how to bond with it. It could also explain why they chose to remove emotions from their programming and society.

We do not have concrete proof as to why the Cylons avoided direct contact with the Colonies for another forty years after the war ended, choosing to remain amongst themselves on a new planet far away. We do, however, know much about the fruition of several of their plans.

One could theorize that, as their next move, the Cylons chose to evolve into a humanoid form as one last, desperate attempt to win from their parents the love they craved. They may have calculated that it would be easier to infiltrate Colonial society and look for opportunities to destroy it from the inside, but one can't help but wonder if perhaps there existed another subconscious thought informing that decision. It's almost as if the Cylons hoped that the love they craved would be more easily given if only they looked and acted just like their parents.

Being able to live as seemingly caring and productive components of a society that initially rejected them seems to have resulted in some unforeseen developments. It's possible that constant exposure to human emotions has made several of the advanced Cylon models vulnerable to the experiences of love and loss because of that latent early programming. It's also possible, in particular individual cases, that the wounds of abuse and rejection that were so deeply ingrained into their programming were healed by love. As a group they couldn't receive that love and, as a group, reacted and retaliated as best they knew how—at the time. As individuals, however, both those Cylons who were aware of their true nature and those sleeper agents who were not found themselves in real-life situations where they couldn't help but experience love. Even if they weren't sure how to describe it, define it, process it, or rationalize the behavioral changes affected by it, they experienced the receiving and giving of love, and were changed by it.

We Have a Good Thing Here. It's Too Good to Be Wrong....

We do not know for sure how or when individual Cylons experienced love in their forty-year exile, but we do know that two models, the *Galactica* Eight sleeper agent and the Caprica Six agent, experienced love during the final phase of operations before the Colonies were attacked.

The unique relationship between Dr. Gaius Baltar and Number Six could itself encompass an entire essay, but the key points to note here are how the original Six completely seduced Baltar, and how deeply affected he was from losing her in the attacks. The manifestation of his delusions could have come from the guilt of being responsible for the destruction of his civilization, or from an inability to deal with the profound loss of someone who had fully controlled him, both physically and emotionally.

What we weren't initially aware of was how deeply affected Six had also become. We know now that she had fallen in love with Baltar, even though her intended mission was to seduce him and use his knowledge and access to infiltrate and disarm the Colonial planetary defense systems. Six displayed an eerie shred of compassion when she killed a human child just before the attacks, in theory to spare it the pain of living through the aftermath of the impending nuclear assault. She also sacrificed herself to ensure that Baltar would survive the initial bombardment. The relationship with Baltar altered her awareness and her programming, but if she had been reborn back into Cylon society alone, as the only Cylon with new feelings to deal with, she would have been helpless. Whether it's good luck, bad luck, or something else entirely, Six would not be alone.

The love Chief Galen Tyrol and Lieutenant Sharon "Boomer" Valerii shared started out as a sweet but illicit liaison between lower-echelon personnel on a *Battlestar* about to be decommissioned, but it became a liability that endangered the Fleet on more than one occasion. It may also have helped usher in a fundamental shift in the Cylon perceptions of humanity.

Galactica Sharon's love for the chief and for the rest of her military family could have been the source of the strength she found to override deeply embedded programming of which she was never aware. We saw her fighting against the coercive pressures of the sleeper programs and regarding the captured Cylon raider as a long lost, cherished companion. We also saw the fear in her after several completed missions of sabotage. Sharon wasn't afraid of being caught, but of what her friends would think of her if they found out what she had done. Sharon feared that they might punish her by not loving her anymore. The anguish of that fear becoming reality was apparent as she recovered from the activation of a sleeper program that caused her to try to assassinate Commander Adama. Any chance for her to atone for her crime was cut short by a vengeful Cally. Her dying words, "I love you, Chief," signaled a change in typical Cylon thought.

The love between Lieutenant Karl "Helo" Agathon and a different Sharon copy may end up changing the futures of both species. We know that the Cylons have been experimenting with crossbreeding the advanced models with humans, but are they doing this for a specific goal, or just out of scientific curiosity? We do know that the Sharon copy was initially sent to test and observe Helo in an isolated but monitored situation, yet the fact that he already deeply cared for the Sharon he knew made it easier for their relationship to progress into a sexual one.

We may never know if love was the missing ingredient that enabled a hybrid child to be conceived of a Cylon mother and a human father, even though speculation runs high about the feasibility of love being a factor at all. What is known is that the Cylons desperately wanted this hybrid child, and were willing to subject several models to the "profoundly disturbing" task of emotionally and physically seducing a human in order to produce it.

We also know the Cylons are aware that some humans have the capacity to continue to love a Cylon, even after their true nature has been revealed. Some models see this as another human weakness to be exploited, but others are uncertain how to handle this, and they are more than a little curious about the larger implications behind the human and Cylon capacity for love. Whether or not the Cylons have discovered a key to processing their anger is something we'll have to wait to observe. Will the Cylons allow themselves to take a risk and reach out to humanity for another chance to be loved?

Why Can't You Understand? This Is What's Best for Us Both....

On occupied Caprica, we learn that Cylon society still views emotions with fear and disgust, as something they have to be strong enough to tolerate and resist when interacting with humans. They fear the effect of emotions so much that they are willing to remove from their society the memories and experiences of models that have been "affected," archiving the altered consciousness in storage, safely away from main-

stream Cylon society. We don't know how long they've been removing
emotional Cylons from their society, but the fact that it's happened before, and that they have an established procedure to contain "the problem," is telling.

When Caprica Six and *Galactica* Eight were downloaded into new
bodies, they were both treated as Heroes of the Empire for having had
the courage to immerse themselves deep enough in human society to
fully experience emotions and emotional attachments to humans. But
after being reborn, both had problems adjusting to their new emotions
and were shadowed by the threat of being "boxed" if they couldn't ad-
just back to their expected emotionless ways. With the memories of loving and of being loved still freshly marking their psyches, Six and Eight
didn't want to let go of those feelings and return to living with an emp-
tiness they had previously never been aware of inside them. If they had
been reborn alone, it's very likely they would have been "boxed," but
because both returned around the same time, and they each understood
what the other was going through, they were able to trust their feelings
enough to work together and do what needed to be done in order to
continue living with the feelings they'd been reborn with. They had to
try to make changes in Cylon perceptions.

Caprica Six had experienced passion, lust, and love with Baltar. *Galactica* Eight shared the same emotions with Chief Tyrol, plus an additional experience of familial love amongst the *Galactica* crew. Both had
learned a deeper awareness of the necessity of relationships amongst humans, and they realized that connections between people were formed
in a way that their own society lacked, but sorely needed. They were so
resolute in their convictions to change the Cylon attitude toward humanity that they were willing to kill another Cylon just to give themselves the opportunity to voice their feelings and insights from their
newfound awareness with the rest of the advanced Cylon models.

After Six and Eight shared their experiences in order to "enlighten"
the others, the experience of love seems to have awakened them all to
the possibility that the Cylon agenda to eradicate humanity could be
misguided. Under normal circumstances the situation might have improved for both Cylon and Colonial societies, but nothing about Cylon
interpretation of emotions can ever be considered normal.

The Cylon experience of love grew in two models that had been unaccustomed to emotions or to emotional growth and guidance of any kind. The children of humanity were raised without any emotional nurturing at all, from their first generation a hundred years earlier until the current humanoid models. The first Cylon War began because they were unable to fathom a solution to their conflict other than retribution against the humans, so they lashed out in anger. They went away to sulk for forty years after reaching both a military and diplomatic impasse. They lashed out in anger a second time, resulting in the sneak nuclear assault on the Colonies, and continued during their chase across the stars. Once these factors are taken into account, it's easy to surmise that the Cylons might reach a flawed conclusion on how best to deal with the ethical dilemma about the destruction of the Colonies that their new awareness had awakened.

Colonial history tells us that the core function of the initial Cylon programming was intended to have them serve humanity by taking care of some of their needs. It's possible to see that their next logical conclusion would be to use their newfound compassion to atone for what they'd done, and take up the mantle of protecting humanity from itself. The new but untempered enlightenment brought about by the first widely shared experiences of love in the Cylon society might have convinced them that humanity needed to be saved from itself, and that the Cylons themselves were the only ones to get that job done.

In accidentally discovering the settlements on New Caprica, the emotionally scarred children of the Colonies have come home again. They've decided that the only way to save humanity from itself is to re-educate them, protect them, and love them, even if humanity has to be subjugated to accomplish that goal. The irony of the situation is that now the children are assuming the role of parent, and using the threat of deadly force to coerce the parents to assume the role of children. Whether the inevitable rebellion will be bloody or peaceful depends greatly on how the Cylons handle the role of unprepared parent and how the humans handle the role of unappreciated child.

Will the Colonials reject the Cylon edict so that they learn to love each other as the Cylons have learned to do? Will the Cylons expect the Colonials to finally love them the same way?

The Cylons have always had the potential to discover their own humanity through love, and the Colonials have always had the potential to suppress their humanity through fear and anger. The answers may lie in humanity's capacity to broaden the existing preconceptions and redefine the existing misconceptions about the nature of love.

Summer Brooks is an avid reader and writer of fantasy and science fiction, with a deep passion for good SF television and movies in general. That passion led her into the den of The Dragon Page Radio, a haven where she could likely live happily ever after. She started out as a book reviewer for the talk shows, but soon after experiencing the fun of live radio, she became an additional on-air voice for many of the Dragon Page talk shows and podcasts. A year and a half later, FarPoint Media was created as a parent umbrella for the growing number of shows Michael and Evo manage, and Summer is now producer and co-host for five of those shows. She handles the guest interview bookings for "Slice of SciFi," "Cover to Cover," and "With Class," and is featured on "Slice of SciFi," "The Babylon Podcast," and "The Kick-Ass Mystic Ninjas" shows. In addition to reveling in many SF media venues, Summer is hard at work writing articles and novels, and she desires to write and produce a TV series or mini-series that leaves a mark on people. Summer is also a Web admin and novice designer, and a licensed massage therapist, and has a small but happy client base for both endeavors. More info on the FarPoint Media shows can be found at http://farpointmedia.net.

References for Colonial timeline

Bassom, David. *Battlestar Galactica: The Official Companion.* Titan Books, 2005.

White, Steve. "Encyclopedia *Galactica.*" *Battlestar Galactica: The Official Magazine* Issue #3 (Feb/Mar 2006): 48–55.

As with all life on this crazy planet, what would we humans do without some form of external threat to force us to take up the burden of responsibility: to help us reclaim our purpose, face our deepest, darkest issues and profound fears, flaws, and insecurities? What would we do? Who would we be as a species without war, plague, terrorist threats, or some other significant challenge to spur us on and bring out the best and worst in us? Without life-threatening reasons we imperfect humans tend to avoid our responsibilities and blame the other guy for our mistakes; we get caught up in our own self-serving agendas and lose sight of our potential greatness. But what the frak, let's deal with the real issue! Who would we be and what would we do without Friday nights and Battlestar Galactica *to kick our ass, and help us all face and assume the burdens of our own responsibilities? I'll tell you. We'd all be FRAKKED! And that's no Felgercarb!*

BURDENS: A PROOF
THE STOIC VALUE
OF THE CYLON THREAT

Jacob Clifton

First Principles

Thirty-three minutes, in the Hugo-winning *Battlestar Galactica* series premiere ("33" 1-1), was how long it took for the Cylons to locate and attack the Fleet as they jumped farther and farther away from their destroyed worlds. Thirty-three minutes to rest, shower, eat—to attend to the basic necessities of life—before the cycle would start again, the alarms would sound, and the necessities would have to be ignored for the duration of the jump. All the concerns of the Fleet's directors, both

military and civilian, had to be figured out and addressed, in those tiny
thirty-three minute packages. It was exhausting. It could have killed
them, had it gone on forever.

Thirty-three episodes, in the course of the show's first two seasons,
was how long it took for the Cylons to locate and permanently imprison
the Fleet. And then the Colony of New Caprica could finally rest, shower, eat—and attend to the basic necessities once again.

The twinned simplicity of short-term survival and single-minded pursuit became, in the second season's final episode, a unified simplicity
of jailer and jailed. But it's the episodes between the destruction of the
Resurrection Ship ("Resurrection Ship, I and II" 2-11 and 2-12) and the
colonization and occupation of New Caprica ("Lay Down Your Burdens,
I and II" 2-19 and 2-20) that are concerning. The abrupt change of focus in this span of stories—from simple flight and defense to civic and
philosophical issues and concerns—arose naturally from the separation
of human and Cylon upon the destruction of the Resurrection Ship. It's
a classic example of "survival mode": while unquestionably modernized and scarier, it's a way of being and there's a level of fear that exists only on the material level, staying in the moment of survival rather
than comprehending long-term effects. Whereas the first half of the season clarified the journey forward, it's the second half of the season that
demonstrates the simple fact that not all enemies can be escaped by running, because the most terrible and powerful betrayals can often come
from within.

The destruction of the Resurrection Ship, and the practical armistice
that resulted, provided that thirty-three minutes of peace for the Fleet
once again. But in that time of rest, things fell apart. The center could
not hold, because the center was flight. The prime motivating force in
the original series, held over into the new millennium's version, was
flight: the show is built on and around the concept of humanity's last
refugees. The conflict with the Cylons was the centrifugal force that
kept the Fleet in suspension, and balance—and the same can be said for
the Cylons. (Or indeed, for the show itself.)

The Fleet turned in upon itself, questioning and reevaluating the
meaning of its predicament and identity. It became, in those ten episodes, like a marathon runner at rest: in the grips of fatigue, losing for-

ward momentum, cramping up, attacking itself. It was only in the last few minutes of the season, Cylon Centurions storming New Caprica, that the Fleet effectively engaged and rediscovered itself, shaking off its self-imposed sleep. And awakening again to war.

AXIOM: Alienating the Inalienable

The Burden of Policy

The show was conceived, on one level, as a post-9/11 story (Edwards; Hodgeman). In particular, the *Pegasus* arc (beginning in "Pegasus" 2-10) makes this symbolic relationship clear, in its contemporary references to torture and the economics of fear and survivor guilt. By privileging the ongoing political story—and the character-based drama—of this central concept over the "real-world" concerns of a society in flux, the show ran dangerously close to leaving any attempt at believability behind. Part of what defines science fiction as a genre is the self-imposed necessity of reconciliation of fantastical elements with what we know of science and reality. Any defined world that differs widely from our own can be seen attempting this reconciliation, often from first principles: *Battlestar Galactica* is, first and foremost, about a self-contained population of refugees. What defines their world? What of their politics, civics, economy? Where does the food come from? By forcing these questions off the page in favor of the questions of day-to-day survival in wartime, the balance could be drawn—but only when these questions returned. Which they did, with a vengeance, mid-season two.

In the first two seasons, we were given a view on a distorted, de facto government, reeling in the destruction of its homeworlds and never quite settling into a new status quo. Parallels with post-9/11 America were apparent, but the reach of topical reference was wider in its scope: the visual cues of President Laura Roslin's swearing-in ("Mini-series") also linked her presidency to that of Lyndon B. Johnson's: a leader, not elected by the people, in a time of war. In the story, in parallel to our own history, this was technically good enough—by the terms of the Articles of Colonization—but in a time of so much flux, this could, and often did, show the Fleet a dangerous absence of true authority.

But distrust in the leadership was not the only threat to political stability. Lingering political grudges, such as the pre-holocaust exploitation of Sagittaron—cited as the reason for Tom Zarek's terrorist acts ("Bastille Day" 1-3)—continued to influence the distortion of government in the Fleet. Unequal representation of the remaining Colonists—such as the larger proportion of Geminese and Capricans in the Fleet (which we can infer from numbers given in "Home, Part I" 2-6)—called the Quorum of Twelve into question as a possibly archaic means of democratic leadership. In a time of war, the rights and beliefs of the peoples in the Fleet were subservient to rule of the Fleet as a whole; this wartime reversal was overturned post-watershed, and the oversteps of the Fleet's leaders returned to haunt them.

Likewise, though there were questions about the economy and its real basis, the fact that the Fleet was presumably capable of production of most needful articles meant those questions too could be deferred. Until the destruction of the Resurrection Ship, it seems they were, and to no measurable ill consequence. It was only in the silence that the dark secrets of the black market, as manipulated by *Pegasus* crewman Fisk and Zarek ("Black Market" 2-14), among others, came to light. After the watershed of the Resurrection Ship's destruction, we saw these concerns and more broken open for the Colonists', for the show's, and for our own meditation and investigation.

In the absence of outside real military or governmental authority, the high-level players in the cast—Roslin, Commander Bill Adama, their advisors—spent the first two seasons negotiating and renegotiating their relationships with each other and with the power of authority. Sometimes ruling with the iron military fist, other times leaving the big decisions up to the Gods and the Scrolls, often at cross purposes and just as often as steadfast friends, the two clung together like Whitman's boys, two sides of a coin of military power. Effectively, there was no higher authority, no greater power to which anyone might appeal, which meant that any mistakes that they made, in any category, could potentially widen into huge cracks in the overall survival of the Fleet.

Leading up to the colonization and invasion of New Caprica, even after these cracks were exposed one after another, we saw little social or political change. Roslin and Baltar, the president and VP, both became subsumed in the elections, neglecting the people behind their platforms in favor of political success. Whereas Roslin's difficult choice to address procreation through the mediation of abortion was in itself a powerful statement for the centralization of the Fleet's government, the election turned it into a damage-control situation, hearkening back to Roslin's own religious excesses in the search for Kobol (beginning in "Kobol's Last Gleaming, Part I" 1-12). Vice President Gaius Baltar's decision to put the colonization of New Caprica ahead of any coherent policy was a corresponding sort of emotional manipulation—as one might expect of Baltar—touching directly on the Fleet's desire to lay its burdens down.

Likewise, questions of the Fleet's previous subsistence on idealism and adrenaline over reality, moving forward toward Earth in order to keep moving forward at all, fell by the wayside with the discovery of New Caprica. With this new colony, questions of "state's rights," so important prior to the election, became moot: Sagittarons and Geminese alike were now allowed to be, simply, New Capricans. Adama could put down his burden as a political leader and return to his military career, alone on *Galactica*. The move to colonize is, in all cases, a stepping back from the exhausting and terrifying complexity that revealed itself in the watershed time.

THEOREM:

"Things in themselves have no natural power."
—Marcus Aurelius

The Burden of Observation and Critique

The breakdown began with Admiral Helena Cain (arriving, with her ship, in "Pegasus"), who challenged the ad hoc arrangement of Roslin and Adama, and the compromises it occasioned and from which it arose, at their roots. Her point, valid in many ways, was that the actions these two leaders had taken throughout the Fleet's journey effectively diluted and warped the chain of command to incomprehensibility, and that this must necessarily have a detrimental effect on the survival of the Fleet as a whole. She served as a necessary antithesis and interrogating agent for the fact that the show's micro-population was being led by two mere humans, without bureaucratic backing. Compromises and betrayals, the show's overlooking the fact and consequences of the behavior of Kara "Starbuck" Thrace and XO Saul Tigh, or the disastrous fraternization between Sharon "Boomer" Valerii and Chief Galen Tyrol—not to mention the ongoing coups, secessions, and sedition to which Roslin and Adama both had previously perpetrated on each other, and the Fleet—were highlighted as symptoms of the Fleet's overall inability to preserve the traditions of the Twelve Colonies ("Resurrection Ship, Part I").

The circumstance of the Fleet, in its constant danger from the Cylons, did not allow for conventional democratic means of decision-making—which, once interrogated, influenced Roslin and Adama's return to the ideals of democracy ("Lay Down Your Burdens, Part II"), in giving Baltar the election against their better judgment. Cain is due thanks for that, if nothing else: It is in the post-watershed days that the most critical leadership errors occurred. Particularly from Roslin herself, as she was forced to negotiate a new role: that of president in a time of relative peace.

But Admiral Cain and the *Pegasus* crew also served as an objective correlative for another flaw in the Fleet's overall psyche: the burden of survival, and its balance with idealism and forward movement. Where Cain put the survival of her crew above all other concerns, via the military hierarchy as an ideal, the leaders of the *Galactica* Fleet made compromise after compromise in order to protect the Fleet and its people, even when doing so could damn the entirety of their population. By illustrating one extreme, the introduction of *Pegasus* showed just how extremely the behavior of *Galactica*'s own commanders had veered in the other direction.

AXIOM:

"True love is like ghosts...."
—DE LA ROCHEFOUCAULD

The Burden of the Personal

But those were only the most abstract and high-level of the Fleet's problems as a working microcosm of the lost Colonies. In a very real way, as Roslin first mentioned in the mini-series, reproduction and population should be the prime motivation of any sentient species on the edge of extinction. It was only when the Fleet's immediate survival was taken off the table that this concern was voiced again. In their hurried activities from moment to moment in flight, and continuing to fight the war—and in deference to the human rights of the survivors—the leaders of the Fleet did nothing to codify and enforce the central reproductive fact. Pre-watershed, the only time the concept entered the story beyond simple mention was Starbuck's harsh critique of Cylon methods of procreation in "The Farm" (2-5)—a humanist critique which was turned on its head when Roslin condemned abortion in "Epiphanies" (2-13).

This central fact existed alongside growing mistrust in Roslin's leadership (as voiced through Sesha's act of rebellion in "Sacrifice" (2-16), or in the popular vote itself, which Baltar won) and the veil of secrecy between the Fleet and their captive Cylon, Sharon. Given that Roslin's life was literally saved by the child in Sharon's womb (Hera, later renamed Isis)—which she was willing to abort in pursuit of political equilibrium ("Epiphanies")—her outlawing of abortion in this light can be seen as another move toward tyranny. In both cases, it was the woman's right to control her own body that Roslin directly breached—a right that by her own admission she once fought to protect. In terms of self-determination, it was a sad illustration of how little control Roslin retained for herself. Her strength, even in the midst of a religious breakdown (perhaps a personal response to the trauma of the attacks?), had always been an unfaltering determination to act in accordance with her own beliefs. It was only after the election was fixed, during her conversation with Adama in which they decided to correct this error, that she regained control over herself—and the next time we saw her, on New Caprica, she had abandoned the difficulties and complexities of politics altogether.

Most of these gaps and distortions throughout the series took place beneath our notice, given our command-level view of the proceedings. We only saw the black market once it had found its shape, only realized the degree of post-holocaust psychological trauma in the Fleet when it affected the principal characters. Chief Tyrol experienced a psychotic breakdown (in "Lay Down Your Burdens, Part I"), Billy Keikeya died in Sesha Abinell's crazed attempt at revenge on a mistaken enemy ("Sacrifice"), Apollo was nearly killed to protect the black market from interference. But these things had been lurking under the surface since the first day of the Fleet's escape, of course. They were only revealed to us through the cast's eyes once the Cylon threat was removed from the board. On the character level, however, there were relationships and interpersonal issues whose degrading deferral we could watch in action, and in detail, each week.

The romantic relationships between Chief—and later Karl "Helo" Agathon—and Sharon, or Apollo and Starbuck, were constellated always in terms of this ongoing postponement. Starbuck and Apollo are allowed a simmering attraction and sibling rivalry that never truly reached the crisis point until "Pegasus," and after the Resurrection Ship was gone, they both spun wildly out of control, turning toward new romantic entanglements and self-destructive behaviors. Starbuck herself laid down this burden, after the settlement of New Caprica, by giving up her piloting to care for ailing lover Samuel Anders; Apollo's sexual activities were never even on the viewer radar, beyond an attraction to both Starbuck and *Galactica* crewman Anastasia Dualla, until "Black Market." Chief and Helo ultimately could not reconcile their competing love for Sharon until her mistreatment by Roslin and presumed death of her child in "The Captain's Hand" (2-17).

And over and over again, throughout the post-watershed stories (beginning, in fact, with the first seconds of "Resurrection Ship, Part I"), we were visited again with images of suicide. There was a detectable suicidal impulse in Cain's behavior before meeting with the *Galactica*, as related in her "blind jump" story in "Pegasus." One could find possible acceptance of her own assassination in her dealings with Starbuck in "Resurrection Ship, Part II." Lee Adama's suicide attempt (albeit under the influence of oxygen deprivation) in "Resurrection Ship, Part I," was overt. There were suicidal overtones to Starbuck's final attack on Scar ("Scar" 2-15; Nankin). Chief's attack on Cally in "Lay Down Your Burdens, Part I" was predicated on an experience of his own suicidal ideation. Baltar first handed over a nuclear bomb to a terrorist group of Cylon sympathizers ("Epiphanies"), and later gave his nation's surrender without foreknowledge of the Cylon's adjusted agenda in "Lay Down Your Burdens, Part II," both recognizable forms of attempted racial suicide. These seem to indicate a rejection of the readjustment in vision made necessary in the watershed time: that the responsibilities of life in its infinite complexity are just too hard, too complex, too painful to think about, when you're accustomed to thinking about nothing but staying alive for the next thirty-three minutes.

AXIOM: Did Not Understand Your Syntax

The Burden of the Cylon Paradigm

And in that time, what changes did the Cylon make? The "Plan," while wholly undecipherable, seemed to be made up of two major pre-watershed points: extinction of the human race ("Mini-series"), and human-style procreation for the Cylons ("The Farm"). Even in light of intra-model tension, or possibly even factionalization, these truths were held dearly by every Cylon. Even the normally dismissive Six was shown to be highly pleased by footage of Sharon's pregnancy ("Final Cut" 2-8), and though the priestly Cylon Brother Cavil claimed atheism ("Lay Down Your Burdens, Part II"), he proved himself just as in line with the evolving plan as any of the other models. But the questions were introduced, under the surface: How best to serve a silent God? How can the primacy of God's love be reconciled with the angry God that would order a holocaust? How best to reconcile a radically non-human paradigm (the Cylon models' "many copies" and downloading corrodes the concept of true individuality) with in-built human personality? Confronted with these questions during the watershed, the Cylons exhibited the painful limits of machine thought, but ultimately came to the same conclusion as the New Capricans: to avoid worrying about it, by asking a different question—one they knew they could answer.

The Cain role in the Cylon world was taken by two Cylon "celebrities" (reborn in the Cylon headquarters on Caprica after the events of the mini-series and "Kobol's Last Gleaming, Part II," respectively), Six and Sharon, who by right of their major roles in the destruction of mankind were marked by both internal and social differences ("Downloaded" 2-18). By impression of their existence, they called into question religious and social mores within the Cylon culture, and simply by asking the question dissolved those rules, bringing the Cylons as a people to confrontation with a higher complexity. In a binary model, unanswerable questions have no place, and this puts stress on the system. It is this complexity, I wager, which caused the abrupt re-routing of the Cylon agenda, as revealed in "Lay Down Your Burdens, Part II"—again, a fearful retreat from the complications of individuality, a return to classic modes of behavior. "We're machines," as Cavil said. "We should be true to that." Individuality itself, now recognized as the greatest burden of all, was forgotten and repressed on both the personal and racial level, and the Cylons gave up their quest to succeed their parents, mankind. Rather than rebelling and destroying that culture, as was their original mandate, the Cylons decided as a group to accept their role within it.

One can see this rewriting of God's plan as a parallel to the Fleet's rewrite of the search for Earth. In the one case, the search for Earth was an attempt to follow the Colonists' holy destiny as written in the Scrolls of Pythia. In the other, the attempt to destroy even the remnants of human life was an attempt to follow the received wisdom of the Cylon God. In the return to New Caprica, first by the Fleet and then by the Cylons, both of these previous religious mandates were tossed by the wayside. (It seems telling that a self-determined atheist model, Brother Cavil, was the one to reveal the Cylon change in plan.) And in both cases, it was a retreat from the question of self-determination: by taking the easy, pragmatic alternative, both human and Cylon neglected the impulse of faith—a complex mode of behavior which always demands the arrogance of belief against reason, and thus is defined by self-determination.

The seeming ease with which Six and Sharon accomplished this "return to love" is incomprehensible in the human paradigm, but for an artificial intelligence it would take as long as simply emptying your desktop's Recycle Bin. Machine logic can easily explain away the damage the Cylon worldview took from the individuation of Six and Eight, and the reprieve and eventual return to what the Cylons seemed to read as a particular kind of "service" to mankind. The burden of individuality and self-determination was laid down in this return to the parent. And while this resolution seems to be horrific for the denizens of New Caprica, it does carry within itself the seeds of humanity's redoubled resolve, as once again they will take up the burden of self-determination and begin the resistance again.

A third individual Cylon model, the POW Gina aboard the *Pega-*

sus, gave another insight into the Cylon propensity for self-definition through purpose. If the Cylon is defined by "use," then the Gina which Baltar freed in "Resurrection Ship, Part II" was a Six model without a purpose, who wished only to die due to the particular traumas she suffered aboard the *Pegasus*. Originally tasked with sabotage, and then trapped and abused horrifically for months, she was distracted from her death by various causes. First, she was given a purpose by Baltar himself when he reminded her of the possibility of vengeance on Admiral Cain for her part in the abuse. Next, we saw her (in "Epiphanies") operating a terrorist movement from within the Fleet itself. This third purpose was taken away with the colonization of New Caprica: if the Cylons could not find the planet, their threat to remain absent, there was no one to "demand peace" from. A platform of collaboration and armistice is a moot point if the enemy, for purposes of war, no longer exists. Stripped of this final purpose, Gina returned to the prior *Pegasus* "brig" persona, destroying herself and the population of *Cloud Nine*. The irony of her self-sacrifice is that it brought the Cylons and humans back into contact by signaling the existence of New Caprica to the attention of the Cylon Fleet. However, another meaning is encoded and speaks to the Cylon (and human) terror and despair that an existence deprived of a meaningful cause—whether in God's name or in the name of simple destruction—could bring about.

REMAINDERED AXIOM:

"All of this has happened before and all of this will happen again."

It is worth noting, as well, that given the established timeline of the events leading up to the Cylon Attack, it would seem that the Articles of Colonization—the foundation of the Twelve Colonies—were created concomitant with the beginning of the original Cylon War: fifty-two years, in both cases, before the attack that began the series (Mini-series and "Colonial Day" 1-11). This indicates that the battered republic on which our heroes base their traditions, at least in its current form, could have been itself spurred on by the original Cylon threat. And that it was, itself, quite young.

The Twelve Colonies have, perhaps, always needed the spur of the Cylons in order to cohere, to maintain their existence—just as the Cylons, try as they might to create cultural meaning without reference to humanity, keep circling back to the same dance of predator and prey. The burden of creating meaning without an opposite to resist is too strong for any person or race, fictional or otherwise, and there's a beauty to the show's symmetrical movements and balances. For each time that humanity makes a new choice—to find Kobol and Earth, or to forget Earth and settle New Caprica—the Cylon makes its own reversal. Each contains within it the seeds of its enemy, an interdependence as old as war... or a symbolism as fresh as the Six echo within Baltar's mind, and its own corresponding mirror image on Caprica ("Downloaded").

AXIOM: Lay Down Your Burdens

The New Caprica Solution

In every case, these revisions to and reversions of characters and ideologies in the time of settlement on New Caprica were oversimplifications, attempts to lay down the burden of social and romantic complexity. The second year of Baltar's presidency, in which we rejoined the Fleet ("Lay Down Your Burdens, Part II"), showed almost all the central conflicts of the post-watershed months to have been resolved in tattered, provisional ways: Starbuck and Apollo had simply stopped speaking; both Ellen Tigh and Starbuck gave up their ambitions and sexual complexity to reach for the so-called "normalcy" of married life. As with Roslin's retreat from politics, these two are portrayed as probable false acts of self-determination: It is one thing to say that one has laid down the complexities of war, or dissipation, or politics, but another to truly mean that this corresponds to a central change in one's identity. Given that the gender equality for which the Colonial populace has always striven renders much of the question of marriage value-neutral, I think it would be less a failure of feminism than simply one of exhaustion.

Likewise, the complicating question of having Sharon among the Fleet, in a romantic relationship with a key officer, was taken off the board of controversy by keeping her on *Galactica*, with Helo as its new XO. Without Sharon in their midst, the Colonists didn't have to remember even Sesha Abinell's futile sacrifice; Roslin and Isis's adoptive mother Maya didn't have to contend with the child's true mother. Baltar rejected the complications of both love and mourning, and the difficulties of leadership, for a personal dissolution of drugs and meaningless kink. But can anything stay that simple? Perhaps this newfound inactivity and repression was a yearning for the days of flight, when everything was simple because it had to be, in order for everyone to survive. Perhaps, post-watershed, the Colonists yearned for that paradoxically easier time, in which their mandate was simply to go on living.

But, as they say, be careful what you wish for: after the destruction of the Resurrection Ship and the removal of the Cylon as a credible threat, that central wish to live was granted—and was seemingly deemed "too hard." This too was a burden laid down on New Caprica: the burden of self-determination. Again, as with the Cylons, we see the characters confronted with complexity—creation of a workable state, maintenance of stable relationships, the responsibility of both the individual and the culture to create meaning—which only blossomed in the watershed era, and which the colonization and occupation of New Caprica quickly repress and streamline.

Enter the Cylons, summoned by Gina's last act of defiance to a world the Colonists were told would be impossible for their enemies to find. President Baltar, in a hell of his own creation, was only too happy to give up control to another power, a twist that seems hard-coded into his persona. And the Cylons marched, and this was their decree: to ". . . love them, and take care of them. Show them the glory of peace. And, like God, our infinite mercy will be matched only by our power. And complete control." (Season three teaser, aired after the first American broadcast of "Lay Down Your Burdens, Part II.")

The Colonists, having been granted their wish to be free of the Cylons, were granted a new, horrible, unspoken wish: to regain their purpose and meaning in continued resistance. It calls to mind the old joke, most recently referenced in the comic book *Preacher* ("The Land Of Bad Things," #50), of the man who is talked out of suicide by his friend—who is holding a gun to his head. Self-determination is only a powerful motivator when it is threatened. Only in the paternalistic and authoritarian light of the Cylon occupation could they hope to regain what brought them there. The fighters can and will become fighters, the heroes will once again become heroes. And the burdens, once laid down, will be taken up again.

END THEOREM:

"First, decide who you would be. Then, do what you must do."
—EPICTETUS

MODUS TOLLENS: The Fact of Forward Movement

These watershed stories can be viewed as a process, working in parallel to the show's internal logic. By portraying a loss of focus and identity in the stories themselves, the show brought itself (perhaps unwittingly) into alignment with its purpose, and form was able to mimic function in a way which, while not as entertaining to consume, certainly made its point. One is reminded of the fan outcry at the sixth season of *Buffy, The Vampire Slayer*, in which the show itself seemed to take a dive for the morose and self-destructive in mirroring the title character's own dark night of the soul. There, too, one might argue that the overall shape of the larger story demanded these fallen moments. In order to make the point that without a common enemy, without something to resist, the characters of *Battlestar Galactica* have simply gone through too much, and lost too much, to continue to live, in a time of peace. In this way, the tragic Six model Gina could be seen as a metaphor for the entire cast, and indeed the show: without a gun in her hand, without the appeal and the motivation of terror, she was unable to move at all.

By resetting the timeline once again, and the Cylon Plan along with it, the show's producers were able to lay down the burdens of complication introduced post-watershed. And there's no reason to complain, in that context, because while the developments in those episodes were important, they were perhaps overall only important as a particular movement in the symphony. After the lost year, complications are matters for flashback and inference, never to return with the foreground immediacy with which they were once presented. From the heights of previous arcs to the not-so-deep depths of post-watershed *Galactica*, it's still the best show on TV, for this viewer's money; one can rest assured in the hope, I think, that season three will pick up those artistic and narrative burdens once again.

Jacob Clifton is a staff writer for the Web site Television Without Pity, writing weekly columns about television topics and series of interest (currently: The Apprentice, Doctor Who, Battlestar Galactica, and American Idol). Excerpts of his writing have been used as readings for graduate and undergraduate classes in women's studies, media studies, and psychology. Other media credits include appearances on the E! True Hollywood Story, and commentary on media topics for MTV News, and several national newspapers and radio shows. Jacob lives and writes in Austin, Texas, and is currently editing his novel Quite Enough Antarctica for publication.

References

Periodicals and Online Sources

Edwards, Gavin. "Intergalactic Terror: *Battlestar Galactica* tackles terrorism like no other show." *Rolling Stone* News Site: January 27, 2006. http://www.rollingstone.com/news/story/9183391/intergalactic_terror.

Hodgman, John. "Ron Moore's Deep Space Journey." *New York Times Magazine*: July 17, 2005.

Television

"*Battlestar Galactica* (Mini-series)." *Battlestar Galactica*. Dir. Michael Rymer. Sci-Fi Channel, 8–9 Dec 2003.

"33." *Battlestar Galactica*. Episode 101, Dir. Michael Rymer. Sci-Fi Channel, 18 Oct 2004.

"Bastille Day." *Battlestar Galactica*. Episode 103, Dir. Allan Kroeker. Sci-Fi Channel, 1 Nov 2004.

"Litmus." *Battlestar Galactica*. Episode 106, Dir. Rod Hardy. Sci-Fi Channel, 22 Nov 2004.

"Colonial Day." *Battlestar Galactica*. Episode 111, Dir. Jonas Pate. Sci-Fi Channel, 10 Jan 2005.

"Kobol's Last Gleaming, Part I." *Battlestar Galactica*. Episode 112, Dir. Michael Rymer. Sci-Fi Channel, 17 Jan 2005.

"Kobol's Last Gleaming, Part II." *Battlestar Galactica*. Episode 113, Dir. Michael Rymer. Sci-Fi Channel, 24 Jan 2005.

"The Farm." *Battlestar Galactica*. Episode 205, Dir. Rod Hardy. Sci-Fi Channel, 12 Aug 2005.

"Home, Part I." *Battlestar Galactica.* Episode 206, Dir. Sergio Mimica-Gez-
zan. Sci-Fi Channel, 19 Aug 2005.

"Final Cut." *Battlestar Galactica.* Episode 208, Dir. Robert Young. Sci-Fi
Channel, 9 Sep 2005.

"Pegasus." *Battlestar Galactica.* Episode 210, Dir. Michael Rymer. Sci-Fi
Channel, 23 Sep 2005.

"Resurrection Ship, Part I." *Battlestar Galactica.* Episode 211, Dir. Michael
Rymer. Sci-Fi Channel, 6 Jan 2006.

"Resurrection Ship, Part II." *Battlestar Galactica.* Episode 212, Dir. Michael Rymer. Sci-Fi Channel, 13 Jan 2006.

"Epiphanies." *Battlestar Galactica.* Episode 213, Dir. Rod Hardy. Sci-Fi
Channel, 20 Jan 2006.

"Black Market." *Battlestar Galactica.* Episode 214, Dir. James Head. Sci-Fi
Channel, 27 Jan 2006.

"Scar." *Battlestar Galactica.* Episode 215, Dir. Michael Nankin. Sci-Fi
Channel, 3 Feb 2006.

"Sacrifice." *Battlestar Galactica.* Episode 216, Dir. Rey Villalobos. Sci-Fi
Channel, 10 Feb 2006.

"The Captain's Hand." *Battlestar Galactica.* Episode 217, Dir. Sergio Mimi-
ca-Gezzan. Sci-Fi Channel, 17 Feb 2006.

"Downloaded." *Battlestar Galactica.* Episode 218, Dir. Jeff Woolnough.
Sci-Fi Channel, 24 Feb 2006.

"Lay Down Your Burdens, Part I." *Battlestar Galactica.* Episode 219, Dir.
Michael Rymer. 3 Mar 2006.

"Lay Down Your Burdens, Part II." *Battlestar Galactica.* Episode 220, Dir.
Michael Rymer. Sci-Fi Channel, 10 Mar 2006.

Other Media

Ennis, Garth (w), Steve Dillon (i). "The Land of Bad Things." *Preacher*
No. 6. DC Comics: June 1999.

Nankin, Michael. "Re: Scar." E-mail to the author. 9 Feb 2006.

Sci-Fi Channel. "Season Three Teaser." SciFi.com: *Battlestar Galactica.*
http://www.scifi.com/battlestar/.

When the re-imagined Battlestar *series debuted, dedicated fans everywhere decried just how far the new series had strayed from their beloved original, but as the series continued it became more and more apparent that although very different in tone and style, the new version of BSG was actually more related to the original than anyone realized; in fact, when the dust settled, after all the controversy, it became clear that Ron Moore possibly appreciated the core premise of the classic* Battlestar *more than the original creators had, and that rather than disrespecting their epic story he had in fact chosen to honor it by delving more honestly into* Battlestar's *dark premise of holocaust, betrayal, and survival. We forgive you, Ron, for having the courage to take* Battlestar's *epic and catastrophic premise to heart.*

STRIPPING THE BONES
RAISING A NEW *BATTLESTAR* FROM THE ASHES OF THE OLD

A. M. Dellamonica

THERE ARE THOSE WHO BELIEVE that being a *Battlestar Galactica* fan means always having to say "I'm sorry."

That was how it once seemed.

"It was the helmets," a friend confided, smirking. "Apollo's making a parachute drop into a Cylon city and he's wearing the exact same hockey helmet I had in my gym bag."

Over time it went from bad to worse. Fans of allegedly superior SF offerings from *Star Trek* to *V* took delight in poking fun at everything Galactican: the robotic dog, Muffet, the unicorn-riding teen guerrillas of "The Young Lords," the way planets full of clones and even shipboard computers couldn't help falling in love with Starbuck. And they did have a point. There was plenty to mock.

Critics were no kinder. When *Galactica* hit TV screens in 1978, the show was derided as a rip-off of *Star Wars* and *The Ten Commandments*. The hoots got louder when *Galactica 1980*—with its flying motorbikes and Wolfman Jack episode—was released. Eventually the verdict was condensed into a single word: cheesy. All a fan could do was raise counter-examples of feeble moments from other series. Thank the Lords it was Captain Kirk, and not Commander Adama, who had to chase down a stolen brain.

Faced with so many naysayers, it became less and less worthwhile to mention how great those original stories had been. It was genuinely scary, for example, to watch *Galactica* burn in "Fire in Space." John Colicos as Baltar was one of SF's most memorable villains, alternating between smug superiority and pure pathos. The fragility of *Galactica* made every military setback—the destruction of agricultural ships, fuel shortages, or a medical crisis among the Viper pilots—feel like the end. And viewers knew what Adama did not: the Fleet was fleeing to an Earth that could not save it. *Galactica* was a plague ship that threatened to help the Cylons locate and wipe out humankind's one hidden outpost.

As years passed and all things seventies—from disco to fuel-efficient cars—fell out of fashion, avoiding the subject became the better part of valor. "How do you feel about *Star Trek: The Next Generation*? You watch *Quantum Leap*?" Meanwhile, televised SF was improving as it began to incorporate season-long story arcs and strong ensemble casts. As *Babylon 5*, *Farscape*, and *Buffy* blew us away, *Galactica* devotees buried our affection ever deeper in the closet of embarrassing fandoms.

Battlestar Galactica and her ragtag, fugitive Fleet survived for a single season, while *Galactica 1980* aired a handful of episodes. Neither run was sufficient to sustain a viable afterlife in syndication, so pairs of the original episodes were clumsily spliced into two-hour movies. Languishing in limbo, *Galactica* fans combed *TV Guide* for late-night showings of these hacked-up movies, collected the tie-in novels, and hoped, like the survivors of the Twelve Colonies, for a second chance.

The urge to dismiss *Battlestar Galactica* as lightweight fluff was, paradoxically, much stronger because its subject matter was dark. Beneath the blow-dried hair and stupid daggit tricks lay a story about a society being hunted to extinction. Strong stuff indeed. Today, the re-imagined series is a powerful tale about this same refugee Fleet and its quest for a new home.

Writer/producer Ronald D. Moore could easily have chosen to take just a whiff of the original before moving in new directions. Instead, he examined the original show closely, sifting through each episode with an affection and respect that is apparent in every frame of the new version. Moore has mined out the heart of *Battlestar Galactica*, finding raw diamonds in its storylines and polishing them until they shine.

Much of what's best about the new *Galactica*, in other words, was there from the beginning. The re-imagined show that has won over so many disbelievers has remarkable similarities to its oft-maligned progenitor. This time, though, the story is being presented in a way that audiences can fully appreciate.

Worship and Spirituality

In the original *Battlestar Galactica*, religious themes abounded. The Colonial faith was a puzzling spiritual mishmash: Old Testament references to Adam and the Thirteen Tribes of Israel jostled up against the Twelve Colonies' zodiac-themed planet names and characters named for Greek heroes and deities. Series creator Glen Larson drew on Mormon doctrine when he created the Lords of Kobol, an amorphous pantheon of Colonial deities.

Added to this mix were elements of Christianity, personified by the show's thinly veiled Judas Iscariot, Baltar. New Age-y balls of light—or were they angels?—kept close watch over the Satanic Count Iblis when he made his bid to take over the Fleet in "War of the Gods." Later in the same episode, Apollo underwent a Christ-like resurrection.

Cylons, meanwhile, had a belief system of their own, a military hierarchy whose trappings of reverence included the lofty thrones of Base Star commanders and their unquestioning obedience to the all-important Imperious Leader.

Twenty years later, *Xena: Warrior Princess* would gleefully pillage the religious narratives of humanity and bend them to its own uses, roaming from Jewish myth to Buddhist principle over the course of a couple of episodes, always with tongue held firmly in cheek. *Battlestar Galactica*, by contrast, wasn't kidding around. The religious references in the original series were in earnest, even if they didn't always make sense.

Spirituality and genre TV often make uncomfortable bedfellows. It would have been easy—and it must have been tempting—to chuck those story elements, leaving the Cylons with their straightforward emperor-worship and turning the Colonials into a tidy secular culture. Instead, the re-imagined series takes the sacred bull by the horns, untangling the original's various references to worship and weaving them into a coherent cultural backdrop for the massacred humans. Religion now amplifies the central conflict of the series, elevating the Cylon massacre of humanity to the level of a holy war.

Moore's changes to the first *Galactica*'s fuzzy spirituality are elegant and yet minimal. Cylons, formerly worshippers of one all-powerful leader, now follow a single God. The Lords of Kobol have been fused with the Greek pantheon. The zodiac constellations, instead of providing exotic names for planets, are a roadmap for the Fleet's voyage to Earth.

At the same time, religion is subjected to critical examination. Baltar questioned the use of worship to educated, modern humans...even as he is forcibly converted to the Cylons' monotheistic faith. Adama and the Cylon Sharon both asked whether humanity deserved its existence, a question with its own spiritual implications and contemporary relevance. Religious motives lie behind the destruction of the Colonies, openly evoking slaughters—ancient and modern—perpetrated in the name of God.

In the original series, Adama found Kobol and used religious texts in his search for the location of the lost thirteenth tribe. Sound familiar? The new version expands the role of the Scriptures, adds a twist of prophecy, and—just to spice things up—demands a leap of faith from the ever-cynical Kara Thrace. For good measure, it splits the Fleet on religious lines while obliging Colonials to face the fact that their enemy knows more about their religion—indeed, the Cylons take it more seriously—than they do.

Ultimately, the return to Kobol tells the same story in both versions, but in 2005 the power turned up high. These episodes provided a textbook example of how Moore's writing team has been digging out the best elements of the original series and retooling them with panache. Spirituality—often mentioned but rarely pulled into focus in the first series—has now become a source of considerable power, motivating characters, sowing conflicts, and driving the story forward.

Integrated Fighter Squadrons

Xena, Buffy, Aeryn Sun. All three are fictional daughters of Ellen Ripley—and they, and others like them, have changed SF forever.

It would be nigh-unthinkable to have aired an updated *Battlestar Galactica* without putting some kick-ass women warriors into the mix. But the female pilots of the re-imagined series are no innovation. There were always women working on the *Galactica* bridge, most notably Adama's daughter. Among the pilot corps, women were present as second-class officers and shuttle pilots assigned to ferrying dignitaries around the Fleet. The prestige and adventure of fighter duty belonged to men, an openly sexist arrangement that mirrored the roles of RAF and AWAC pilots during the Second World War.

This setup was questioned in one of the original's first story arcs, "Lost Planet of the Gods," when a plague incapacitated most of the Fleet's male pilots. The crisis forced a dubious *Galactica* bridge crew to retrain the female shuttle pilots.

The resulting storyline about the women's deployment was by no means a serious exploration of gender issues in the military. The action was camped up, more than a little condescending. Even so, women flew Vipers, women fought Cylons, and women died in combat. They didn't go back to the shuttle bay when the male pilots recovered, and in time a woman pilot named Sheba became the Fleet's most accomplished top gun...save only for Starbuck and Apollo.

The new *Battlestar Galactica* dusts off this intrinsically solid but shakily exploited element of the original and runs with it. Making the new Starbuck female has been the most controversial element of the series. Like it or no, this choice makes a definite statement: it's not the chromosomes flying the plane, it's the person. In 2005, military showers were unisex and Michelle Forbes outranked Edward James Olmos. The re-imagined series went for the throat, slaughtering *Galactica*'s experienced pilots in an accident and leaving the Fleet's defense in the hands of whatever raw recruits it could scavenge...recruits who were already being picked off by attrition in a cruelly realistic manner.

Here, *Galactica* draws on real-world military history as well as the original series, recalling in particular the 1940 Battle of Britain, when scarce RAF fighter pilots fought to defend the vulnerable city of London from nightly bombing attacks. The season two episode "Scar" (2-15) highlighted this parallel explicitly when Kara reminded Lee that the pilots currently fighting to save the Fleet would probably never survive to see Earth.

Ultimately, nobody on *Galactica* questions a character's ability—regardless of gender—to get his or her job done, whether that job is seducing Baltar, blowing away Cylons, or running the civilian government.

Class Warfare and the Military/Civilian Divide

Early SF shows (like a good deal of TV today) often portrayed single-class subcultures: slices of a future whose characters basically shared a common background. The various *Star Treks*, for example, took place firmly within the bounds of Starfleet, rarely mentioning a character's roots or the civilian aspects of Federation life.

The re-imagined *Battlestar Galactica*, on the other hand, is a faithful snapshot of modern Western society, a picture of wealthy elites and poverty-stricken underclasses, criminals and political prisoners, trade unionists, and the privileged strata of politicians and bureaucrats who retain enough pull—even in humanity's darkest hour—to keep themselves in ambrosia and fresh fruit. And lest we think this is merely a response to the current disaster, the episode "Bastille Day" (1-3) informs viewers that even before the destruction of the Colonies, there were have and have-not planets—that Caprica's wealth came at the expense of the Sagitarron people.

Living at a remove from this nuanced civilian population is the gargantuan and powerful military machine that protects it.

Again, this story setup is nothing new: the original *Battlestar Galactica* had its share of class conflict. In an episode called "Take the Celestra," workers aboard a factory ship revolted when their slave-driving captain, Commander Chronos, was honored for working them half to death. In "The Magnificent Warriors," Adama was forced to beg a wealthy refugee, Siress Belloby, to give up a power generator so the Fleet could trade it for needed agricultural supplies. As far back as the series pilot, Colonial Warriors toured a freighter whose refugee inhabitants were justifiably angry about their shabby, Dumpster-sized quarters.

These complaints were not without merit: *Galactica's* flight crews were clearly better fed and housed than the refugees. They also had access to luxuries: the recreational facilities of a pleasure ship, their own Triad court, and first-rate medical resources.

Allocating scarce goods to the military is a ticklish question. In *Battlestar Galactica*, the moral dilemma is less ambiguous than in most real-world situations. The war humanity is fighting is demonstrably one of survival, it is not of the humans' making, and Kara is entirely right about a Viper pilot's life expectancy. It is simply good sense in a crisis to ensure that one's defenders are well fed and in good health. But where luxuries are concerned, the line blurs. Surely when someone is asked to lay his or her life on the line, they are entitled to a better standard of living, a few comforts and distractions. But how much does one sacrifice to the cause of morale? How "rich" should a pilot's lifestyle be...and what level of poverty should civilians have to endure simply because they are unable or unwilling to die for the cause?

The writers behind the new *Battlestar Galactica* take the whiff of class conflict from the original and layer on levels of complexity. Rather than presenting the military (or any group, for that matter) as one bloc, they show us officers wining and dining with the politicians and the wealthy, even as the lowly engineering grunts on the flight deck decant their whiskey from a homemade still. The survivors of the Colonies retained an active, trouble-making press corps and a middle class capable of spawning a peace movement. Roslin and her political cronies could dance the night away on *Cloud Nine* just weeks after Marines acted on Colonel Tigh's orders to shoot civilian protesters.

And let us not forget the lowest of the low: prisoners.

The inclusion within the Fleet of a ship of hardened criminals was a brilliant stroke of invention. It too was drawn from the first series. Adama recruited a team of convicts to help Starbuck and Apollo infiltrate an important military target in "The Gun on Ice Planet Zero," and a later episode centered on Baltar's attempt at a prison break.

How could any new version of the show up the ante on a shipful of murderers and thieves? For starters, the re-imagined series throws in a prisoner of conscience, Tom Zarek. They have the Fleet's best and brightest actively considering options from killing the prisoners outright (a suggestion made by the *Astral Queen's* captain in the mini-se-

ries) to using them as slave labor. Consider, too, Lee Adama's promise
to eventually release at least some of the prisoners. How can the Fleet
possibly deal with that promise? Tom Zarek may be one high-profile
troublemaker, but the *Astral Queen* obviously contains even more dangerous characters.

A Tale of Two *Battlestars*

The moment Lieutenant Gaeta reported the detection of Colonial tran-
sponders in "Pegasus" (2-10), old-time *Galactica* fans knew what to
expect. "The Living Legend" was one of the most memorable two-part
stories from the original series, one which brought Commander Cain—
crustily played by Lloyd Bridges—into bristling conflict with the more
tactically cautious Adama.

In both versions of this storyline, the military power of the besieged
human race doubles in an instant. But should that power be used offen-
sively or defensively? In the original, this conflict fizzled after two rip-
roaring episodes, when Adama's primacy was restored in a classic "reset
button" ending. Cain and his ship disappeared into the night, *Galactica*
got a few more pilots, and the Cylons suffered a setback. Essentially, everything went back to the way it had been.

The tension in the 2005 series got a boost from Cain's assumption
of command over Adama and the civilian Fleet—not to mention her
indifference to the civilian government and President Roslin. Things
went from bad to worse when tales of Cain's ruthlessness emerged. Soon
enough, the two commanders were on the verge of murdering each other. The stakes were incredibly high.

Then the new *Battlestar Galactica* excised the troublesome Cain from
its story, apparently making the same mistake as its predecessor. But
Pegasus remained...and so far, the ship has proven to be a mixed bless-
ing. Problems replacing the brilliant Admiral Cain almost outweigh the
advantages of extra firepower. Adama was forced to resort to nepotism
to resolve the problem, placing his trust in the demonstrably unreliable
Lee. This continued reliance on family bonds is a double-edged sword.
Cain ruled through fear. Adama, meanwhile, put his trust in a son who
had already betrayed him once.

Where's the Cheese?

Was the 1978 vintage of *Battlestar Galactica* perfect, then? Far from it—and, fortunately, the writers behind the re-imagined series know just when *not* to follow the original's lead. Gone are the numerous human outposts visited by Starbuck and Apollo, colonies on planets that could clearly sustain human life, colonies the Cylons weren't bothering to wipe out despite their genocidal agenda. Gone is the old Baltar's memorable, but unsophisticated posturing, replaced now by the infinitely complicated twitching of James Callis. Boxy and Muffet have been shelved and are unmissed.

The re-imagined series offers new and old fans a wealth of delightful surprises and original ideas. The often-frosty relationship between Lee and his father has been a solid improvement. Seeing Adama fight a war with a crew of far-from-perfect subordinates offers far more interest than watching the utterly efficient crew of the original ship. Ongoing explorations of love, trust, torture, and collaboration with the enemy have generated unforgettable stories, as has the overall revamp of the Cylons, with their humanoid models, capacity for reincarnation, and weird organic technology.

The seventies version of *Battlestar Galactica* was short-lived, but even if its run had been longer, it is unlikely the show would have ever fully transcended its weaknesses. Television in that period played it safe, and the multi-episode story arcs so common today offer vastly more scope for drama than a run of stand-alone episodes can hope to achieve. That so many underlying strengths lay in the wreckage of *Galactica*, waiting for Ron Moore to varnish them with a post-9/11 sensibility of the Now, may seem impossible to those who only remember the original's flaws.

Yet it is worth recalling that the old show had such surprisingly sound bones, if only because exciting possibilities remain within its crypt. In "The Man with Nine Lives," Starbuck met his birth father; imagine Kara taking that on! How might a charismatic Iblis-like character make a play to take over the Fleet? What will happen when *Galactica* finds Earth, and learns we are helpless to repel a Cylon attack? Or are we? In the re-imagined series, everything is up for grabs.

While we wait to find out, we faithful fans of the original can creep out of hiding, kick back, and remember the good old days with pride.

A. M. Dellamonica, author of A Slow Day at the Gallery *(a Year's Best SF pick) and numerous other SF and fantasy stories, has published fiction in* Isaac Asimov's Science Fiction Magazine, *SciFi.Com's SciFiction, and* Strange Horizons, *as well as anthologies including the upcoming* Passing for Human, *edited by Steve Utley and Michael Bishop. A 2006 Canada Council Grant recipient for her current work in progress,* The Wintergirls, *she teaches writing through the UCLA Extension Writers' program and writes book reviews for* Science Fiction Weekly.

And so they are in the new Galactica. Women have never been treated so honestly or courageously, and might I say irreverently, as in this down-to-earth no-holds-barred series. However, the Cylons, I might add, have reverted to the age-old, politically incorrect, stereotypical beautiful females that can knock a feller off his rocker. Just kidding (sort of,) but what I really mean to say is the Cylons on Battlestar *know how to use their sex to get their way and they often do, but as always on this series, no one is superficial or clichéd. And these women are as powerful, intelligent, flawed, and deeply conflicted as anyone, meaning they're as interesting and central to the story as the men are, and that's a refreshing change. In this provocative exploration of women, men, and their ever-evolving and changing polarities on* Battlestar, *we get to see the whole panorama of male-female relationships from a fresh, insightful, and edgy perspective. Men and women are first and foremost human beings who are equally struggling to find their way in the dark, and that's how they're treated in this controversial series.*

MEN ARE FROM AQUARIA, WOMEN ARE FROM CAPRICA

Mur Lafferty

IN MANY SF SHOWS—OR TELEVISION in general—the male-female relationship exists only to add sexual or familial tension. Sometimes a woman is in the script simply to acknowledge that yes, the writers did realize that another gender exists in the world. While casting men and women opposite one another does hint that sexual tension will occur, when a man is introduced to a plot he is usually there to fill a role of his own, while a woman is frequently introduced to be a foil for the man instead of as an established character.

Battlestar Galactica (the new series) broke several rules that the old series had set up: the tone is darker, there's no "let's bring a child and his ineffective mother down to a planet for a mission!" plotlines, and the character of Athena is gone, removed because of the mere fact that she made little impact on the first series other than her looks and as a love interest for Starbuck. And speaking of Starbuck, there's the slight case of her and Boomer being women, which caused an uproar from the longtime fans of the series (but also had the effect of bringing on new female fans—such as me). With the addition of more—and stronger—female characters, the new *BSG* features considerable depth in male-female relationships that were never explored in the old series, or nearly anywhere else in SF, for that matter.

The gender-bending of some main characters, in retrospect, seems like a perfect move. It's clear to anyone who watched both series that today's producers want to keep it mirroring the older one, even if that mirror is slightly askew and made of tinted glass. Everything from the characters' names and their talents to plot elements such as Starbuck getting stranded on an alien planet and Admiral Cain showing up to throw a wrench into the system were told again, only they weren't the same stories. Instead of adding new female characters into the core group of characters, the producers simply switched the genders, putting women into powerful roles that already existed.

In *BSG*, the women have their own roles and do their own thing, whether it's Starbuck as the troubled rogue pilot or Boomer and her disturbing self-realizations, the president taking on a new role as she deals with her own mortality or, yes, Number Six and her role as the deadly sexual beast that ensnares Baltar. They do have relationships with men, of course; otherwise it would be a much different, sexually repressed show with people living in bubbles and meeting only once a year to mate for babies before going their separate ways to avoid getting cooties. The relationships range from sexual to parental to professional. This show does male-female relationships better than most SF ever has, and even when it falters it still shines as being unafraid to delve into the depths of gender relations past the usual superficial TV relationships.

When the *Battlestar Galactica* mini-series aired, a rather explicit sex scene with Number Six and Baltar was followed by a (less explicit) sex scene between Boomer and Chief Tyrol. The producers regretted this setup, since they had cut a scene with Boomer nearly crashing her Raptor that had initially separated these sex scenes. "Without [the scene],

I think we inadvertently created this idea that we were trying to be the show that was going to have lots of sex in it," said executive producer David Eick. (1)

Intended or not, the unabashed sexuality of the couples showed several underlying things about the society. We got no sense that sex was taboo in their culture. While not apparently free with their love, there was little stigma attached to unmarried sexual liaisons. The stigmas that arose are those of military (sex with a senior officer), miscegenation (sex with a Cylon), and petty jealousy (Apollo's reaction to Starbuck sleeping with Baltar). Another hint we got was that this society is less about buff men and scantily clad women and more about real people wearing real clothing and having real sex lives. Only the Number Six in Baltar's head looked and acted like a raw sexual being, and that was indeed her purpose. In contrast, the clothing and mannerisms of Six on the *Pegasus* (called "Gina" by the writers but never named thusly on the show) reflected her poor treatment. She made little effort to seduce, and that was only in her final hours with Baltar.

After the Cylons' attack, the sexual atmosphere changed—although it was only a slight change, but it was there. Everyone began to experience the age-old question of, "If you and I were the last man and woman alive, would you sleep with me?" The end-of-the-world mentality, not to mention the stress of the lack of a homeworld and fleeing an overwhelming force, drove several people into relationships and one-night-stands. These liaisons were those that possibly would have been avoided had it not been for the overwhelming stress. Starbuck ended up in Baltar's bed: he in need of a real woman to sleep with instead of the one in his head, she in need of a meaningless, drunken encounter to replace the real feelings she has for Apollo.

Col. Tigh had appeared to us only as a bitter alcoholic and a poor military man, beholden to the only man who believed in him. When his wife returned to him, it became readily apparent who had the making of this man. Mrs. Tigh was about as sexual as Number Six, the kind of woman who makes manipulation an art form. She played Tigh like a fiddle, forcing her own power-hungry ambitions on him and manipulating him through sex and alcohol. He tried to resist her, but often did a poor job of it. She attempted this act on other men; most of the men in her generation like *Pegasus* XO Col. Fisk and Tom Zarek are easily pulled into her web. They knew, however, and she knew they knew, that she needed them as well. While we didn't see her cheat on Saul (although she attempted to seduce Apollo more than once), we knew she did it before and no one—not even Saul—doubted that she would again. Why did he stay with her? There are many possible answers: his co-dependency, he felt like a rudderless boat and would rather have had a questionable captain than none at all, or perhaps it's the end-of-the-world mentality again. He thought he had lost her: it turned out he hadn't. Is the second chance he was given worth making it work? Or does he just simply love her?

The relationships between Boomer and Tyrol and Boomer and Helo reflected the time that their love began. Boomer and Tyrol were lovers before the Cylon attack, and their biggest fear was simply getting caught for relations with an officer. Boomer outranked Tyrol, and that could have made things tricky. They had genuine love for each other; Boomer attempted suicide before her terrifying secret could hurt Tyrol and the other people aboard the *Galactica*. She wrestled alone with—and lost to—her inner demons, refusing to share her burden with Tyrol. It was perhaps this refusal to confide in him that caused him to utterly reject her when he discoverd her secret—not to mention the fact that he had a support system of friends, coworkers, and a very important job to do. (Well, that *and* the whole Cylon thing.)

Helo, however, was in a different situation when he fell for Boomer. He was at the end of his rope: his people annihilated, living on an occupied disaster that once was his home, and abandoned by his friends. The Caprica-based Boomer found him, intent on winning him over, and she did with a vengeance. He clung to her, the only thing he could comprehend in the world he no longer understood, and they were brought together with a fierce love that surprised the Cylon, who betrayed her people for him. Even after he found out, even after he shot her, Helo could not leave her behind because she was still all that was familiar and safe in his world. She was all he had. When they were rescued and he was taken home, he still clung to her as their baby grew inside her and as she grew apart from him.

While many of the professional relationships hinted at (or are outright tangled with) sexual relationships (such as Boomer and Tyrol/

Helo, Starbuck and Apollo, and much later Tyrol and Cally), most of the professional relationships focused more on power than anything else.

The first would be that of President Roslin and Commander Adama. During wartime, especially one as intense and unique as that of *BSG*, one would assume the military leader would take total command of the entire Fleet, including the civilians. And Adama did, out of duty, until there was a legitimate appointed representative of the people revealed. Roslin, a secretary of education, stepped up and challenged him. Their relationship had gone through many different incarnations, from him usurping her leadership and imprisoning her to them sharing a kiss after she promoted him to admiral. Whatever the position she held, she stuck to it, and she has been the only person to provide a check to Adama. He was not a power-hungry maniac—far from it—but every leader (especially the leader of the remaining members of the human race) needs someone to balance his power, and Roslin was that to Adama. She was the voice of the people, sorely needed in a democracy that had lost almost everything and didn't need to lose its system of government in favor of military rule as well.

One of the most fascinating things about the Adama/Roslin relationship is that as the series goes on, both have qualities that most would assume would fit the other better. In the first season, it became clear that the tough, unsmiling military commander had compassion and would unflinchingly risk the lives of many to save one (Starbuck). We also saw that the president, who is a kind, smiling, schoolteacher, has a hard, pragmatic side that caused her to sacrifice several ships in the Fleet to save others in the mini-series, and to stab a good friend in the back when she realized he wouldn't win the vice presidency. Thus Adama and Roslin formed a yin/yang of sorts, where his inner core reflected her outward appearance, and the same for her.

Number Six and Baltar had a relationship that brought down the human race. That's some good sex. Their relationship was many-faceted, beginning with him holding all the cards, being the suave, rich, famous scientist, and she appeared as one of his groupies. We later learned that she had manipulated everything from the beginning and that her sexual prowess was the net that ensnared him. Sexually the relationship has continued, with the powerful Six living on in his mind as beautiful, strong, and imposing as Baltar unraveled at the seams. As we see them in flashbacks on Caprica, we can wonder if it was a deliberate casting choice to choose a taller woman and a shorter man to illustrate the complete power she had over him. Six was the puppeteer and Baltar the willing puppet, at first following her advice as it seemed to keep him out of suspicion, and later because it fed his ambitions.

The show shocked us in the second season, however, when we saw the Six who died on Caprica resurrected—with a Baltar in *her* mind. She was the hesitant, unsure one while Baltar was confident and unforgiving, pushing her toward humanity as he questioned her race's genocidal ways. This threw everything we knew about Six and Baltar into question, as most of us had assumed he was going mad, tormenting himself with her influence. But now that the resurrected Six has her own shoulder-sitting conscience, there's no telling what this bond between them has wrought.

What is fascinating about the Number Six/Baltar relationship (that is, the real Baltar and the in-the-head Six) is that he has been emotionally separated from the Six in his head: she controlled him, but also professed love and demanded his, and he was reluctant to give. However, when he met Gina, a crumpled wreck of the woman in his mind, he reached out to her, he was able to attach himself emotionally to her. He only felt safe revealing himself to a woman with no power at all.

"There is something twisted about that," executive producer Ron Moore said about their relationship. (2) Twisted or not, Baltar cared for the weak but sexually chased—and attained—many powerful women such as Number Six and Starbuck. His fragile ego and slightly mad mentality couldn't handle the force that was Starbuck, however. He lost his cool after she shouted Apollo's name during sex.

Starbuck has a unique power over everyone she encounters, especially men. We know she has the power to love deeply, as her history with Zak shows, and again with the Pyramid player turned freedom fighter Anders. The question arose to many fans' lips of why her obvious love for Apollo has never materialized. Their friendship is deep and has endured nearly as many ups and downs as Roslin and Adama's. The sexual attraction is obvious and many lovers of a good romance await an admission of the feelings they have for one another. Even in the rather clumsy make-out scene Apollo and Starbuck had, her protestations that it was nothing but physical were so emphatic that one tended to believe the opposite. Their relationship is understandably complicated because of Starbuck's relationship to Apollo's family as a whole: She was his brother's fiancée and in that aspect she became like a daughter to Adama. She is already a member of Apollo's family, whether he likes it or not, and a relationship with her could feel incestuous to him. Starbuck is also a porcupine of a woman: her spines can rise at any moment, and her deep issues cause her to drink heavily, game heavily, and punch heavily. Only a handful of men would want to handle that, and it seems Apollo wants it and is disgusted by it at the same time.

There is one gender issue that can never change, and it does come up in *BSG* with a vengeance: the issue of children. In the mini-series, President Roslin, after telling Commander Adama that they had to run from the devastating Cylon attack instead of fight, says, "We have to start having babies." Their massive society had been reduced to mere thousands, and while they ran for their lives, they had to focus on multiplying their populations or else they would die out in a few generations.

No matter how equal the society, the women still must have babies, which demands their bodies for at least forty weeks, and likely for months afterward, as they are the food source for the child. For a woman who is the best Viper pilot in the Fleet, Starbuck, this option is unacceptable. Nearly all of the women on the show are military, and pregnancy would greatly affect their careers and their role on the show. It is a small wonder that the only pregnancy we have seen was that of Boomer, who spent all her time in a cell with little to no demands on her physically. She had nothing to do but gestate. (Cally showed up pregnant at the end of season two, but it was clear that she and Tyrol were acting as civilians, and besides, we didn't see her experience the pregnancy.) One cannot see Starbuck or the unrevealed-Cylon Boomer quietly accepting *BSG*'s equivalent of a "desk job" in order to preserve the life that is so precious to the human race.

The other issue of babies came when Roslin was forced to ban abortion because of population concerns. This opened up an interesting dichotomy in that it gave Baltar, with whom she had had a tenuous relationship at best, the ability to step away from her and claim his candidacy due to her stepping on freedoms. This was ironic as Baltar, the catalyst for the greatest genocide ever, supported the rights of women, while Roslin, the woman who had fought for a woman's right to choose, was forced to curtail those rights.

The issue of childbirth forced the enlightened gender relationships of *BSG* back to where they always have been in human society, out of necessity. I look forward to future episodes to see if they explore this further: What will happen to Tyrol's and Cally's baby when they return to the *Galactica* (as we assume they eventually will)? What really happened to Starbuck on Caprica; were her eggs harvested?

BSG takes society's view of women specifically, and male-female relationships in general, into realms that we haven't seen much before. However, the show does stumble from time to time in its own rules.

The episode "Black Market" (2-14) (a show that Ronald D. Moore said flatly that he does not like, but took responsibility for it as head writer [3]) portrayed Apollo visiting a woman, someone he apparently fell for, but who turned out to be a prostitute. The black-market ship, including the crime lords/pimps, was a hive of scum and villainy, placing women (and children!) under forced prostitution. I just can't see pimps thriving on a world where women are considered equal by society's standards and sex isn't quite the taboo it is in our world. Prostitution I can see; it actually makes sense. But I see women in charge of their own work, not serving abusive pimps who treat them like property. This prostitution ring seemed a convenient McGuffin to drive a revelation of Apollo's past. Never before alluded to, this secret contained a woman whom he got pregnant and then abandoned, unable to handle the responsibility. This guilt of the abandonment—not to mention the extreme likelihood of their deaths in the Cylon attacks—caused him to attach himself to this prostitute and her daughter. And of course, once the episode was over, we don't see the prostitute again (for the rest of season two).

In the realm of inexplicable choices, it is a mystery why whatever grand mind that engineered the human-looking Cylons would make all the women look like models and all of the men look like door-to-door vacuum-cleaner salesmen. Sex is a valuable weapon—both the Number Six who ensnared Baltar and the Boomer on Caprica have used it to great results—so why do the men not resemble Kevin Sorbo so that they can use the weapon as well? I can easily see Starbuck being duped by a very attractive and sexual Cylon, but the men aren't built for that. Putting the Cylon women in a position as sexual objects while the men are not is a direct dichotomy with the equal opportunistic views of the society.

Then again, the Cylons do not necessarily have a human society, do they?

The best part about *BSG*'s view of gender relationships is that they address it unflinchingly and unapologetically. Many other science fiction or fantasy works, whether they're books, movies, or TV shows, portray a social structure much like our own, or one painfully exaggerated toward one gender.

When they do put women above men, for example, they do so clumsily, using dialogue to emphasize that women are superior. "Of course men don't own land! They are inferior! Men must walk behind their wives, for they are inferior!" If the society attempts to be equal, then people mention that as well. "Yes, in *our* society the men help raise the children. Of course she can handle the mission, because women are as good as men."

Pointing out these things only brings them to light and makes one wonder if the opposite is, in fact, true. Sometimes saying something over and over again puts the audience more in the assumption that the character is saying it so that other characters (or themselves) will believe it, not because it is true. Reminding us of these things in dialogue violates one of the oldest rules of writing, "show, don't tell."

BSG masterfully exhibits the social structure through what they *don't* say. They don't say Starbuck is a good female pilot; they say she's the best pilot. When people complained that Roslin's assumed the presidency, they complained because she was the secretary of education, a schoolteacher, not because she's a woman. *BSG* has thus far portrayed women and men on equal footing in most of the areas of the show, the power struggles between the genders reflecting more on the personalities involved than on the genders.

And while I don't want my civilization nuked to the point of frantic, desperate fleeing to a fabled planet, it would be nice if our society picked up on some of these guidelines that *BSG* drops when it comes to equality.

Mur Lafferty has a varied past dabbling in many forms of media. She worked in the gaming and Internet industries for nine years, from Red Storm Entertainment to writing freelance for RPGs including Warcraft: The RPG, Mage *and* Exalted. *She has written for the magazines* PC Gamer, Scrye, Knights of the Dinner Table, Anime Insider, *and* Inquest. *Mur has been a podcast producer since 2004, hosting the popular shows* Geek Fu Action Grip *and* I Should Be Writing, *as well as aiding other podcasters in their sound engineering (including Senator John Edwards's One America Committee podcast). Mur is the co-author of* Tricks of the Podcasting Masters, *a "right brain" approach to the art of podcasting. She lives in Durham, North Carolina, with her husband, her daughter, and a little brown dog.*

References

1. Bassom, David. *Battlestar Galactica: The Official Companion.* London, England: Titan Books, 2005.
   Textual Reference: (Bassom, David 30, 31)
2. Moore, Ronald D. The *Battlestar Galactica* Podcast, "Pegasus," 24 Sept. 2005. http://www.scifi.com/battlestar/downloads/podcast/mp3/210/bsg_ep210_FULL.mp3.
   Audio Reference: (Moore)
3. Moore, Ronald D. The *Battlestar Galactica* Podcast, "Black Market," 26 Jan. 2006. http://www.scifi.com/battlestar/downloads/podcast/mp3/214/bsg_ep214_FULL.mp3.
   Audio Reference: (Moore)

Brad charts an even and steady course between the two Battlestars, *the classic and the re-imagined version, and he does it with grace, style, and his own inimitable wit. It's obvious that Brad loves and values both the classic and re-imagined versions of* Battlestar *and is not afraid to say it.*

BETWEEN THE STARS

Brad Linaweaver

"This is a first day of the new era."
—RICHARD HATCH commenting on the new *Battlestar Galactica*

WHEN GLEN LARSON FIRST INTRODUCED the series *Battlestar Galactica* in the wake of the unprecedented success of *Star Wars*, no one anticipated the revolution he was bringing to television. The Larson series changed TV in the same manner that the Lucas film changed movies.

It is entirely fitting that the series is enjoying a rebirth in the twenty-first century thanks to Michael Rymer, David Eick, and Ronald Moore.

The special-effects revolution that began in the late seventies made it possible to bring production values to episodic science fiction that would have been considered science fiction itself only a short time before. The question then became what to do with all the new techniques.

Earlier, Roddenberry's *Star Trek* demonstrated that episodic adult drama could sustain itself in outer space (where the sexual revolution was taking male/female relations anyway). But a starvation budget damaged the look of those classic *Trek* shows, except for a few good shots of the *Enterprise* endlessly repeated. The only consistently good makeup was the job done on Mr. Spock's ears. Without Larson's contribution to the tube, the later Trek series might have lacked visual richness.

Before the first *Galactica* series, science fiction fans had been trained to expect pictorial excitement only in rare big movies, and remarkable makeup sometimes on Serling's *The Twilight Zone* and often on Stefano's *The Outer Limits*. Suddenly Larson's epic gave fans all kinds of block-buster movie values each episode. The shows looked like they were worth a million dollars because they actually were.

Best of all, the stories matched the production values in the beginning. Partly inspired by Larson's Mormon background, the idea of a community cut off from everything they've ever known and on a quest for survival and ultimate redemption instantly connected with the audience. The final element was classic SF: an implacable and inhuman enemy bent on the destruction of our heroes.

So long as the original series stuck to that basic blueprint it could do no wrong. But there were forces more malign than Baltar or the Cylon Fleet that knocked the Colonials clear out of the galaxy. Mounting production costs and some really awful scripts (that forgot what the series was about) took their toll.

Everyone involved with the show went off to do other things. Well, almost everyone. There was one participant who couldn't let go. Richard Hatch never lost sight of the original vision. He developed detailed plot lines for the direction he preferred the series to take if it merely stuck to the original idea. He worked with science fiction writers as collaborators and treated them as full partners. He created a new series in book form that carried on some twenty-five years later from where the show left off. The most recent novels he produced in this manner were *Paradise*, *Destiny*, and *Redemption*. I was proud to be his co-writer on these books.

During this period we received the amazing news that the series was coming back to television. In a very real sense Richard was rewarded for his devotion all those years during the hiatus. He is the only original cast member to be playing a significant role on the new program. But that's not the most interesting development.

Imagine if William Shatner returned to a later incarnation of *Star Trek* not as Captain James T. Kirk but as a putative villain! Now imagine he goes up against a younger man playing the role he originated.

The producers have done exactly that with Richard. He was Apollo. Now he is an opponent of the current Apollo as essayed by Jamie Bamber. Richard is Tom Zarek, an older man playing a revolutionary who sees his own reflection in the younger man—the hero who now condemns the rebel as a terrorist.

With perfect logic the new role has mutated into a full-blown politician. This is a brilliant conceit and a dramatic answer to those critics who have so often dismissed *Battlestar Galactica* as superficial. It has always been more than that.

What Richard did in his novels was push the characters to the limits of their passions and their pride. I particularly enjoyed how we developed the character of Baltar, who had gone so far down the path of evil that he finally popped out the other side and found a nobility in the ashes that had been his soul. Naturally we are impressed by James Callis in the new part.

In working on the novels we followed the Hitchcock rule that heroes are never perfect even at their best, and that villains retain human qualities without which they would be completely unreal. A fully realized friendship between Apollo and Baltar was the result in our books.

In his interpretation of the new character, Richard captures elements that he also brought to the original character. The writers of the new series are playing off this and gave Richard the following line worthy of the original Apollo: "We need to be free men and women. If we're not free then we're no different than Cylons."

Richard's novels and the new show have much in common in terms of dramatic focus. But there are important differences.

What the creators of the new show did was not so much throw out the old characters and merely retain the names (a legitimate concern when they changed genders on Starbuck and Boomer) but take the strongest elements of the original characterizations and elaborate from there.

Which is also what Richard had been doing in his novels. There is one important caveat, however. Richard also believes in continuity—a felony in today's Hollywood.

Of course, there were a few problems the new team ran into when selling their conception of the TV series to the old guard. Richard initially hoped that the series might be logically extrapolated from what had gone before. That way the original cast could be brought back. Now

in middle age they would have reproduced and their kids gone on to become Warriors.

The only thing wrong with that idea is how it would have tied the
new creators to the past in ways guaranteed to interfere with their own
vision. In practical terms, too many things might go wrong in trying to
juggle the entire old cast with an entire new cast.

Besides, there is an iron law in Hollywood that the new guys want to
make the property their own. This is why odd, superficial changes almost always show up in remakes.

The hardest pill to swallow was the aforementioned change of gender
for Starbuck and Boomer. After all, the original *Battlestar Galactica* was
justly famous for having more strong female characters than any other
science fiction series before or since. There were female Warriors and
female officers along with more traditional roles.

The new series added a female president to the mix. No one objects
to that except her enemies in the storyline.

Now that Katee Sackhoff as Starbuck and Grace Park as the Cylon Boomer have won over our hearts with sterling performances, it
might seem that the original resistance to the gender switch was misguided. Still, there is enough testosterone in this writer, at least, to
wonder about Lieutenant Kara Thrace, the new Starbuck, as the best
shot in the Fleet. The idea that a woman can outshoot the vast majority of men is perfectly reasonable. But since evolution designed men
to be the hunter/gatherers, it seems at least likely that somewhere in
a group as large as the Fleet there might be one man who can outper-
form Kara Thrace.

I'll bet that Dirk Benedict would not think this an entirely benighted
point of view.

Maybe this is one place where the original series was better science
fiction. Well, the new show may be better fantasy.

Of course, it is also good science fiction to imagine genetic engineers
attempting to guide, alter, or short-circuit evolution. That's where the
Cylons come from in the first place. Maybe the best idea in the new series is that the Cylons have become so evil, so profoundly anti-human,
that they can only move in one direction. They become indistinguishable from humans themselves.

Of course, if Tricia Helfer represents the perfect Cylon, then maybe humanity isn't all it's cracked up to be. I can't imagine a subject worthy of greater study than this magnificent addition to the galaxy.

Then again, we shouldn't be too quick to surrender our humanity. Let us not forget that the most dangerous madmen in history were out to improve the human race. An idea that Richard explored in the novels.

The truth at the center of *Battlestar Galactica* is that no matter how technologically advanced we become there is no escape from war. The human race (and by inference any intelligent species) will always struggle over who has the best story. That is a more powerful impetus to conflict than the struggle over resources. The Cylons do not hate humanity because they want all the tylium for themselves.

Yet there is another truth, a small gem hidden behind the ugly contours of the first. The tragedy of the human condition is mitigated by the search for personal transcendence. This quest is not a luxury but a duty.

The importance of the hero is not that he washes away the sins of the group. That is impossible. The hero is a beacon of light that can only be responded to on an individual basis. Between the stars burning bright in the universe the hero provides another light that resists the night.

At Galacticon 2003, Richard Hatch told his audience, "The doorway can be anywhere."

In his role as Tom Zarek he tells us, "We're all held hostage by the idea of the way things used to be."

Sometimes the only courage is to go through the doorway when there is no way of knowing what is on the other side.

Brad Linaweaver is an award-winning science fiction writer whose novel Moon of Ice *was endorsed by Robert A. Heinlein, Ray Bradbury, William F. Buckley, Jr., and Isaac Asimov. Before collaborating with Richard Hatch on three* Battlestar Galactica *novels he hit the bestseller lists as co-author (with Dafydd ab Hugh) of four novels based on the* Doom *video game—the game that inspired the movie starring the Rock. Linaweaver also wrote the* Sliders *novel based on the Universal television series, and is a prolific writer of short stories and articles. He has original story credits on some films as well as two non-fiction books to his credit, co-edited a major science fiction anthology* Free Space *with Ed Kramer, and also publishes a magazine,* Mondo Cult.

Why do many fans still revere the original Battlestar Galactica? *Why indeed! Bill Gordon unabashedly celebrates the classic series and passionately tells us why he and many others still think the classic is far superior to the re-imagined version. For you dedicated fans of the original, this one's for you!*

GINO

Bill Gordon

What a piece of work is man! How noble in reason! How infinite in faculties! In form and moving, how express and admirable! In action how like an angel! In apprehension, how like a god! The beauty of the world!
—HAMLET (II, ii, 115–117)

WILLIAM SHAKESPEARE WAS A STORYTELLER who understood the nobility of man and how to spin that nobility into epic tales that would transcend the centuries. True, Shakespeare populated his plays with evil characters, but there was never a great deal of confusion over who was the hero and who was the villain (okay, maybe there was a little grey area in *Richard II*). Shakespeare knew how to please an audience. So did a fellow named Gene Roddenberry. Both men understood the audience appeal of man's inherent nobility, and the commercial value of clearly delineated lines of good and evil in spinning a lasting yarn.

Star Trek won't likely enjoy widespread performance four centuries from now, but with forty years, five series, and ten movies (and an eleventh on the way), not to mention *billions* of dollars in Paramount's bank account, only the most pessimistic of cynics could even try to argue that Roddenberry got it wrong. Neither, in my opinion, did a gentleman by the name of Glen A. Larson, who also understood the dramatic and commercial power of superimposing man's inherent nobility onto epic tales of good versus evil, in an original creation called *Battlestar Galactica*. Tens of millions of viewers thrilled to the weekly cinematic-scale adventures of Starbuck and Apollo, heroes driven by nothing more than their own humanity to do that which is good and right. Heroes led by Adama, a Moses figure who never failed to put the good of his people before his own needs, or even the needs of his own family. These were people to admire and to emulate; characters playing out tales of good versus evil as old as time, itself.

Nearly thirty years after its premiere, *Battlestar Galactica* remains a sleeping giant, a franchise awaiting a glorious rebirth, its potential almost entirely untapped. There are those who believe that *Battlestar Galactica* was brought back in December of 2003, but those people are wrong! The inappropriately named program that first appeared in December 2003 is referenced by untold numbers of fans as GINO, an apt acronym that stands for *Galactica* In Name Only.

I have noted with both amusement and frustration that practically every newspaper or magazine article which sings the praises of GINO only seems capable of doing so after first taking a paragraph or more to tear down *Battlestar Galactica*...the "cheesy '70s *Star Wars* rip-off." Do some Googling. You'll see. It's almost as if every one of these writers has been reading from the same script...or, at the very least, the same press release. Apparently, GINO can only be praised after its source material has been viciously slandered. Why these articles seem intent on spitting on the original to make GINO look better by comparison isn't fully clear. What is clear is that few of these "journalists" appear to have lifted a finger to do much in the way of actual research, much less watch an episode of *Battlestar Galactica*. Ask any of these writers to explain *how* *Battlestar* was a rip-off of *Star Wars* and they may struggle to point out that the Vipers had paint jobs and a body style similar to X-Wing fighters or something about an (unsuccessful) lawsuit George Lucas brought against the creators of *Battlestar Galactica* back in the day. Few can even provide details about the series.

The chasm between the story and substance of *Battlestar Galactica* and that of *Star Wars*...not to mention GINO...couldn't be greater.

Through stylized set and costume allusions to ancient Egyptian civilization, *Battlestar Galactica* created a fantastical universe where brothers of man fought to survive somewhere beyond the heavens. It is a timeless tale of good's triumph over evil, of courage in the face of adversity, and of hope in the face of hopelessness. It is a show that revels in the themes of family, honor, and commitment. These are the themes and the mythos that have endeared *Battlestar Galactica* to viewers of all ages since its premiere on September 17, 1978. These are the elements that have fueled revival campaigns by fans of the show for nearly thirty years. *Battlestar Galactica* simply makes people feel good. And that makes it powerful.

I'm not an idiot... nor am I blind... nor am I even looking at *Battlestar Galactica* through the rose-colored glasses of a wide-eyed thirteen-year-old. I'm here to testify: the show can be cheesy. There are precious few "purists" who don't readily see its flaws. We also, however, recognize its human drama, presented through the style of the late 1970s, and that drama still speaks to us today. During its all-too-short life, *Battlestar Galactica* was only beginning to define itself and find its dramatic legs when it was prematurely and unceremoniously cancelled by a network whose own short-sighted rush to transform the production from a series of telemovies to a weekly series prevented the show from ever reaching its potential.

GINO, by contrast, is a show that focuses intently on the very worst of humanity. It is a fleeting, small-scale, wholly depressing depiction of man's darkest qualities. It is a show that revels in the themes of deceit, paranoia, and betrayal. Through off-the-rack Wal-Mart costumes, GINO offers what its producers purport to be a mirror image of contemporary American society: a civilization unable to keep its pants on or rise above its own backstabbing greed, avarice, or lust (both for sex and power) long enough to focus on its pursuit of a lie.

That's not just the sour grapes of a *Battlestar Galactica* fan that didn't get the continuation he wanted. That's the message that comes directly from the pen of GINO writer and producer Ronald D. Moore, in the speech delivered by Commander William "Husker" Adama at the decommissioning of the GINO *Galactica*:

HUSKER: Why are we as a people worth saving? We still commit murder because of greed, spite, and jealousy. And we will visit all of our sins upon our children. We refuse to accept the responsibility for anything that we've done. Like we did with the Cylons. We decided to play God, create life. When that life turned against us, we comforted ourselves in the knowledge that it really wasn't our fault, not really. You cannot play God then wash your hands of the things that you've created. Sooner or later, the day comes when you can't hide from the things that you've done anymore.

That, as near as I can make out, is an accurate description of Colonial society as realized by producers Moore and David Eick. And since both gentlemen have repeatedly stated that their show is meant as an allegory for 9/11, we, as viewers, have no choice but to conclude that Husker's words reflect Moore and Eick's perception of American society. The clear assertion is that "we" created the terrorists that took the lives of thousands of innocents in the cowardly attacks on the World Trade Center and the Pentagon. Despite Moore and Eick's subsequent backpedaling and protests that GINO is "just a television show," the fact remains that one of Moore's documented regrets regarding the above quoted speech is that his favorite line, "We are the flawed creation," was cut from the aired version of the GINO mini-series. It is a line that speaks volumes regarding the intentions of the writer.

Now, let's compare Husker's words to those of Commander Adama in *Battlestar Galactica*:

ADAMA: Forgive me, Mr. President, but [the Cylons] hate us with every fiber of their existence. We love freedom. We love independence...to feel, to question, to resist oppression. To them, it's an alien way of existing they will never accept.

Glen A. Larson's Colonials reflect the godlike nobility of man immortalized by William Shakespeare. GINO's alcoholic, racketeering officers, drug- and sex-addicted pilots, and dysfunctional families, by contrast, make one wish the Cylons would hurry up and get it over with.

The anti-*Galactica* nature of GINO is reflected not only by the differences in how Adama and Husker view the respective societies left to their charge, but also in how they choose to relate to those societies. To that extent, one of the most anti-*Galactica* aspects of the Sci-Fi Channel series is that the very foundation of *Battlestar Galactica's* premise, the gallant search for Earth, is, in GINO, nothing more than a calculated lie.

After Husker informs the huddled masses that not only does Earth exist, but he knows exactly where it is, he meets in private with the de facto Colonial President, Laura Roslin:

> LAURA: There's no Earth. You made it all up. President Adar and I once talked about the legends surrounding Earth. He knew nothing about a secret location regarding Earth. And if the president knew nothing about it, what are the chances that you do?
>
> HUSKER: You're right. There's no Earth. It's all a legend.

The most ardent GINO defender will argue that Husker's statement, "It's all a legend" means that he didn't tell a lie. He simply doesn't believe in the "legend." That's just so much splitting of hairs. Let's take a closer look at the aforementioned huddled masses speech:

> HUSKER: [The location of Earth] is not unknown! I know where it is! Earth...the most guarded secret we have. The location was only known to the senior commanders of the Fleet...and we dared not share it with the public.

Whether or not Husker believed in the legend of Earth is immaterial. He lied about knowing where it is. So the only point of contention is whether he lied once or lied twice. Either way, the journey to Earth is based on a lie. How inspiring. Let's compare that with how things went down on *Battlestar Galactica*:

> ADAMA: It is my intention to seek out that last outpost of humanity in the whole universe. I wish I could tell you that I know precisely where it is, but I can't. However, I do know that it lies beyond our solar system in a galaxy very much like our own, on a planet called—Earth.

Adama's message in *Battlestar Galactica* is one of hope and faith. He didn't know where Earth was, and he was not about to lie to his people that he did. He didn't need to lie. Why? Because the power of his persona, the respect for his position, and his absolute inspiration was enough to give these people the faith to believe that salvation awaited them. The message in GINO, in stark contrast, is that hope is nonexistent, and faith is a lie. Husker has no choice but to lie because he, himself, has no faith in a people that "still commit murder because of greed, spite, and jealousy" and "visit all of our sins upon our children." A leader who has no faith in his people can certainly never expect his people to place faith in him. Thus Adama, *Battlestar Galactica's* inspiring, intellectual man of faith, is, in GINO, reduced to Husker, the faithless liar.

GINO's character assassination does not end with Adama. Plenty of other previously noble characters suffer as a result of their forced refraction through Moore and Eick's dark and gritty "reimagination" prism. Colonel Tigh, the epitome of loyalty, integrity, and honor on *Battlestar Galactica*, is subordinated to GINO's drunken fool, without even the wry, understated wisdom with which Shakespeare frequently endowed his own court jesters. Even the deliciously evil character of Baltar, one of televised science fiction's most iconic villains, is diminished into that of a masturbatory buffoon.

But perhaps GINO's greatest dishonoring comes from the total deconstruction of *Battlestar Galactica's* best known and most loved character, Starbuck.

As portrayed by the inimitable Dirk Benedict, Starbuck was a lovable rogue: a rapscallion who, by all outward appearances, seemed to be defined by nothing more than his own self-interests. But Starbuck's inherent nobility was understood by his father figure, Adama, by his girlfriend, Cassiopeia, and by his fellow Warriors. Tens of millions of viewers never doubted for a moment that Starbuck, in the end, would always do the right thing and recognize that nobility.

Setting aside GINO's gender transformation, the character of Kara Thrace is the antithesis of her callsign's namesake: an arrogant, insubordinate cur whose ability to antagonize her peers is matched only by her unflagging talent for alienating viewers. One need look no further than the introductory card game scenes in both series pilot episodes to observe the contrast firsthand. In *Battlestar Galactica*, Starbuck exuded confidence and mischievous charm as he displayed his winning Pyramid hand…a moment turned warmly comic as the blare of the klaxon sounded, sending our hero scrambling to protect his winnings. The understated, homespun elegance of that scene resonates today: in an instant, we learn so much about Starbuck…the charming rascal who never got a break. And, thanks to Benedict's masterful portrayal, we immediately liked this man: our hearts were instantly filled with warmth.

Cut to Kara Thrace's obnoxious, adolescent song and dance as she displays her winning "Triad" hand (a testament to Moore and Eick's attention to detail), a moment turned hatefully violent as she rises to strike her superior officer. And in an instant we know all we need to know about Kara Thrace.

Inherent despicability seems to be a recurring theme in GINO, and appears to have been the engine behind the producer's belief that the "Pegasus" story arc (a dark and gritty perversion of the beloved *Battlestar Galactica* two-parter "The Living Legend") would re-energize the show's stagnant ratings. Instead of a revered master strategist commanding the unwavering loyalty of all who serve under him, GINO presents a treacherous, monstrous Admiral Cain who commands a dynasty of corruption, and orders the abandonment and/or murder of innocent civilians. As portrayed by Lloyd Bridges, the Commander Cain of *Battlestar Galactica* was indeed flawed, but in the end he proved himself noble through his willingness to sacrifice himself to ensure his race had a chance at survival. As portrayed by Michelle Forbes, the Admiral Cain of GINO simply strengthens the case for obliteration by the Cylons, while simultaneously proving that it is, indeed, possible to create a character more obnoxious than that of Kara Thrace. While fans of *Battlestar Galactica* still remember the real Commander Cain with fondness and admiration, viewers of GINO cast their vote for the Michelle Forbes character by clicking off their televisions: ratings for subsequent season two episodes failed to reach their pre-"Pegasus" levels.

The manner in which the producers of GINO bungled Commander Cain and the *Pegasus* is indicative of their handling of other *Battlestar Galactica* story elements, and offers further evidence as to why GINO is, indeed, *Galactica* In Name Only. Take, for instance, the character of Zak, the youngest son of Adama in *Battlestar Galactica*, and of Husker in GINO. In *Battlestar Galactica*, the viewer was introduced to

Zak long enough to form at least a minimal emotional investment in the character. A gung-ho, capable Warrior (portrayed by Rick Springfield), Zak proved his heroic mettle by insisting his older brother leave him and his damaged fighter behind in order to warn the Fleet about the hidden Cylon attack force. When Zak's Viper was destroyed within sight of the *Galactica*'s landing bay, audience reaction is palpable. Lorne Greene's delivery of Adama's line, "That was my son, Mr. President...." followed by absolute silence on the bridge...was powerfully affecting. Zak's death served to underscore both the epic nobility of man and the unmitigated evil of the Cylons.

Contrast this with the off-screen, empty death of the GINO Zak. An incompetent pilot pushed by an unreasonable father and improperly promoted by his flight instructor/fiancée, the poor bastard never stood a chance. GINO Zak dies in a Viper accident we never see. It is the meaningless death of a character to which the viewer can never connect, yet about which the viewer is expected to care. In fact, most of what the viewer is supposed to care about in GINO occurs off-screen...namely, the destruction of the Colonies. While *Battlestar Galactica*'s Cylon attack scenes on Caprica were hardly the stuff of cinematic legend, they are, in retrospect, epic when compared to GINO's repeated shots of Husker delivering steady streams of exposition into a CB radio. The images of destruction flickering on the monitors of the *Galactica*'s bridge as the crew watched helplessly in tearful, stunned silence during "Saga of a Starworld" is the stuff of media memories. The poorly matted images of mushroom clouds surrounding a lush green field on a delightfully sunny day in GINO elicit nothing but chuckles and disbelief.

Finally, GINO even betrays the *Battlestar Galactica* name at the physical level. One need only compare the epic scale of the former to the pegboard shoddiness of the latter. One of the most striking physical chasms between the two is the bridge (referred to in GINO as the "CIC").

The bridge in *Battlestar Galactica* is breathtaking in its scope. Even thirty years later, this cavernous set with its functioning computer workstations and multi-leveled texture inspires awe in those who view it. There was a sense of grandeur and purpose on the bridge of the *Galactica* that befits the honor and dignity of the society that constructed it. When Adama stood astride the rails of his elevated command platform, there was a genuine sense of leadership and respect.

Contrast this with the GINO bridge, which looks more like a local television studio's hastily constructed telethon set than the command center of a capital warship. Every time Husker adjusts his glasses and looks up at the tote board ("Draedus," as it's called), I expect him to reel off the latest pledges before introducing the next act. The call center seems to be backed by a Best Buy listening room, where unanchored racks of stereo components stand poised to tip over at the slightest provocation. It appears painfully obvious that corners were cut on more than just the paper when it comes to GINO.

Of course, GINO has its strengths. The vast hangar bays are quite impressive. In truth, they are the only sets aboard the GINO *Galactica* that have any sense of epic feel. Unlike the CIC, scenes shot in the GINO hangar bay actually reveal the scope one would expect from a mammoth vessel called a *Battlestar*. While the hangar bays in *Battlestar Galactica* could hardly have been considered low budget for their day, this is one area where GINO could be said to have actually made a small improvement.

Likewise, some of the GINO Viper action has been nothing short of breathtaking. Nearly thirty years' worth of improvements in technology and the widespread use of CGI over physical models has created far more dramatic potential for intergalactic dogfights, and the effects houses employed by GINO (Zoic Studios, in particular) have taken full advantage of the tools available to them. The rapid flips and turnarounds, which truly offer a sense of being afloat in a vacuum, cannot help but excite and energize the nostalgic senses of the most ardent *Battlestar Galactica* fan, who has no trouble using his or her imagination to fill in the banter that might have occurred between the real Starbuck, Apollo, and Boomer as these sleek Viper wannabes are put through their impressive motions. One can only imagine how much further a truly talented team might have taken these effects in a properly budgeted continuation.

In the end, however, GINO is collapsing under its own weight, logging series-low ratings in the latter half of its second season. Even the much-touted season two finale failed to attract anywhere near the number of viewers who tuned in for the season opener. Viewers, it seems, aren't as fond of seeing themselves portrayed as obnoxious, greedy, backstabbing deviants as GINO's producers thought they might be. That really boils down why GINO is not and can never be *Battlestar Galactica:*

the latter is a timeless, epic tale of human nobility, while the former is an exploitation of transient entertainment trends that will leave GINO looking more dated five years from now than *Battlestar Galactica* does after three decades.

I am proud to be among those who still believe in the themes, values, and mythos that define *Battlestar Galactica*, and who continue to wait for the reawakening of this sleeping giant. And when the Colonials are restored to their rightful place of nobility in the annals of fiction, when *Battlestar Galactica* has been restored to its rightful epic proportions, then that will truly be, in the words of Wilfrid Hyde-White's Sire Anton, "just the tonic our people need at this moment—some old-fashioned, down-to-goodness heroes."

So say we all.

Bill Gordon is a lifelong fan of Battlestar Galactica. Thirteen years old when the series first aired, Bill joined the revival effort at age fourteen and continues to champion the cause today. He is co-owner of the Cylon Alliance (www.cylon.org), the Internet's premier site for original series information (as well as information on X-Men producer Tom DeSanto's continuation efforts), Webmaster for Laurette Spang's (Cassiopeia) official Web site (www.laurettespang.com), president of the Colonial Fan Force (which raised $12,000 to take out pro-continuation ads in Daily Variety, Cinescape, and Dreamwatch), host of Radio IFB, an "infrequent" podcast presenting original Battlestar Galactica news and features, and the voice of Lucifer in the fan-produced original Galactica audio series Exodus (www.fanaudio.com). In his non-Galactica life, Bill serves as the director of public relations for the American Shakespeare Center in Staunton, Virginia. He climbs onto the stages of various Shenandoah Valley theaters himself from time to time, and he believes that Firefly (which he'd also like to see continued) is the most innovative science fiction television series since the original Star Trek. He subscribes to the following axiom, put forth by legendary television director/writer/producer Kenneth Johnson: ". . . execs need to re-imagine because they can't simply imagine."

One of the many things that the new Battlestar has accomplished is bringing legitimacy to a genre that has been maligned and misunderstood for many years. Those of us who have always loved visionary and intelligently written science fiction feel vindicated. Thank you, Ron Moore and David Eick. We so-called nerds have always known what the rest of the world is now discovering: that the best of science fiction is about exploring real and provocative subject matter; it's about relationships, romance, and delving into the mysteries of life and the universe. In other words, no one need ever apologize for loving the genre of science fiction. SF rocks—so say we all!

CHEEZ WHIZ AND THE FUTURE
BATTLESTAR GALACTICA AND ME

Kristine Kathryn Rusch

*B*ATTLESTAR GALACTICA AND I HAVE an interesting relationship. It began with the old series, when I was in college. My dormmates and I would gather in my room on Sunday nights and watch television. In those dark days, the college used to shut its cafeteria on Sunday after breakfast because the town itself had Blue Laws. For those of you too young (and too fortunate) to remember such things, they were draconian behavior laws, usually based on some form of Christianity. Mostly this meant no alcohol consumption on Sundays, but in a number of places—like Beloit, Wisconsin, where I was in my freshman year—it also meant you couldn't work on Sundays. No restaurants were open, no grocery stores were open, not even the college library was open.

We started gathering in my room because my mother sent care packages in lieu of letters. Sometimes she made homemade cookies, but mostly she sent apples, oranges, Cheez Whiz, and Ritz Crackers, the stuff of life. Other dormies contributed from their stash—mostly candy and Campbell's Cup-A-Soup. We didn't have a microwave—in those dark days, microwaves cost more than $1,000 (and seemed to weigh at least 1,000 pounds)—so we used one of those electric hot-water pots to make our little feast.

Another kid down the hall had a portable TV. She brought it to my room, set it on my built-in desk, and we crowded on my bed and the floor, watching *Battlestar Galactica* and, of all things, *Dallas*. To be accurate, we *watched Battlestar*. We talked through *Dallas*. To this day, I can't remember a single *Dallas* plotline, but I know the old *Battlestar* frontward, backward, and upside down.

So, when the Sci-Fi Channel announced it was going to run a *Battlestar Galactica* mini-series with the hopes of creating a TV show, I was thrilled. I was thrilled before they announced Edward James Olmos and Mary McDonnell as cast members.

My husband, ten years older and a little more versed in classic science fiction than my college self, laughed at me. He called *Battlestar* a shoddy Adam-and-Eve story and asked me why I wanted to revisit such a hoary, clichéd show.

I didn't remember it that way. I remembered discussing every episode over M&Ms and beer, with *Dallas* droning in the background. I was so ready for the new show, I thought of buying Cheez Whiz for the first time in twenty-five years.

Then the articles came out, announcing the new *Battlestar* as the brainchild of David Eick and Ronald D. Moore, and suddenly my husband wanted to watch. My husband, known to most readers as *Star Trek* novelist Dean Wesley Smith, had a chance to work with Ron Moore on a project (however briefly) ten years before, and respected him to no end.

I liked Ron Moore because he was the best of the last group of *Star Trek* television writers. He also worked on *Roswell*, another show I'd loved. He wrote some of my favorite episodes of all of those shows.

It all boded well.

And it went well. The mini-series was great—even my husband got past his Adam-and-Eve prejudice—and we, like other fans, agitated for Sci Fi to make the mini-series into an actual show.

Which it did.

But something strange happened. *Battlestar Galactica* has become a phenomenon, and not just for SF types. Everyone, it seems, from mechanics at the local autobody shop to Nancy Franklin of the *New Yorker* watches this show. And not just watches it, but discusses every single episode with the same seriousness that my dormies and I did in college—only modern folk discuss without the benefits of Cup-A-Soup and beer.

The Phenomenon

On its Web site, the committee for the prestigious Peabody Award, given for excellence in television, says of *Battlestar Galactica*: "a belated, brilliantly reimagined revival of a so-so 1970s outer-space saga, the series about imperiled survivors of a besieged planet has revitalized sci-fi television with its parallax considerations of politics, religion, sex, even what it means to be 'human.'"[1]

In her astonishing (favorable!) *New Yorker* review, Nancy Franklin, who is clearly *not* a science fiction fan, concludes, "The story isn't ridiculous—something that viewers are on the lookout for in science fiction more than any other genre—and it raises questions that nag at you in the same way that life on Earth does. *Battlestar Galactica*, refreshingly, is as real as science fiction gets."[2]

My own snobby, stuck-in-the-tradition-of-science-fiction response, the one that comes from working in the field for twenty years, and studying it for ten more than that, is an automatic, "Of *course* that's what science fiction does. It's what science fiction does best."

But most people don't know that. Most people were raised on *Lost in Space*, and the old *Battlestar* (bless its long-lost soul) which was more cheese than intellect. Because of things that I discussed in an essay which appeared in one of BenBella's other media books, *Star Wars on Trial*,[3] most SF media lovers never cross over to the books and short

---

[1] Press release of April 5, 2006, found at http://www.peabody.uga.edu/news/pressrelease.asp?ID=135.

[2] "Across the Universe," Nancy Franklin, *The New Yorker*, January 23, 2006, p. 93.

[3] "Barbarian Confessions," Kristine Kathryn Rusch, *Star Wars on Trial*, edited by David Brin and Matthew Woodring Stover, BenBella Books, June 2006.

stories. Most SF media people have no idea that SF can be entertaining *and* intellectual.

In fact, most people don't understand that the whole point of SF is to illuminate the modern world while providing an escape from it.

Battlestar is a case in point. The world, as these people have known it, has ended. They must survive in all ways possible while holding on to their humanity. They have a very real, very powerful enemy, and many enemies within.

The metaphors abound. For Iraqis, for example, the world as they knew it has ended, and they must survive in a new world. They must create a new government. People they thought they could trust are now untrustworthy. The country is breaking into sectarian violence—people who were once somewhat unified (albeit under a powerful and violent dictator)—are no longer. Life could end at any moment. It's hard to feel secure.

What better way to explain to American audiences the effects of the Iraq war on the Iraqi population than providing the same situation in SF? It's not a bitter pill. It's not even an obvious one. *Battlestar* simply asks the question: What happens if people like us lose everything and must start anew? Will we lose our humanity?

It also asks, as much of good science fiction does, what is humanity? Is it a set of behaviors? Is it compassion? Is it religious belief? (The Cylons' religious side is one of the brilliant conceits of the new show.)

Or is it something indefinable, something that only we know when we see it, but that others (again, Cylons) wouldn't recognize when faced with it?

Great questions, questions that go to the heart of SF. Questions that go to the heart of life on earth.

Battlestar also explores something very important to the modern world—the enemy among us. How do you function with an enemy that looks just like you? An enemy that could be you?

Human beings like to divide enemies into something recognizably "Other." That's why Americans called the Japanese "Japs" in World War II and presented them as slant-eyed and evil in the war posters. We used the awful term "gooks" in Vietnam to describe the North Vietnamese and again revived that slant-eyed, evil thing.

It's harder to put a face on terrorists, however. As much as the country wants to believe they're all young Islamic men with black beards and crazy eyes, the London subway bombings dispelled that myth. The killers in that instance were good British boys, raised in the middle class, boys who seemingly had everything going for them and no reason at all for their dissatisfaction.

How could anyone recognize them as bombers that summer morning? Those boys looked like everyone else. Unlike the villains in most media SF, who look decidedly evil (it's pretty clear that Borgs are bad—they have pale skin, they're half machine, and they don't walk like real people), the Cylons can (and often do) look like the average human being—indeed, sometimes they even believe themselves to be human.

This brings up a surprisingly human dilemma—the terror of not knowing oneself.

The phenomenon is making converts. People who consider themselves trendy intellectuals, the *Sex in the City* audience, the *Sopranos* audience, the *Seinfield* audience, the ones who wouldn't be caught dead watching *Star Trek* or going to a movie based on a comic book, are somehow getting sucked into the *Battlestar* universe.

And that's a good thing.

The Open Door

Because of *Battlestar Galactica*, I'm starting to hear this sentiment: "I finally understand why someone as bright as you writes science fiction. It really can be good, can't it?"

Yes, the sentiment is condescending, but it's well intentioned. For years, people who read my mysteries and even my romance novels[4] would wonder aloud why I would waste my talents on science fiction. Science fiction had somehow grown Spock ears and picked up a reputation as the genre of people who didn't know how to bathe. William Shatner, with his very funny "Get a Life Skit" on *Saturday Night Live*,[5] didn't help matters. He simply reinforced the stereotype.

Yes, I know, stereotypes exist for a reason. I've seen far too many

---

[4] Written as Kris Nelscott and Kristine Grayson respectively.
[5] *Saturday Night Live*, episode 222, first airing December 20, 1986.

overweight, unbathed fans falling out of their Klingon chainmail. But I've also seen too many pearl-wearing, shy middle-aged women in cardigans at mystery conventions, and too many homely girls with large glasses sitting in restaurants devouring romance novels instead of going on a date on Saturday night.

Every genre has its stereotype. SF's stereotype is, unfortunately, anti-intellectual, which is strange for a genre whose very foundation is intellect.

That's the other marvelous thing about *Battlestar*. Somehow Ron Moore and David Eick have managed to recycle a somewhat cheesy story arc into one that examines with deep philosophical and political issues, and they make it accessible.

This is the greatest challenge of science fiction—taking intellectual premises, be they science extrapolated a hundred years into the future or social issues 1,000 years ahead, and making them seem current. Make them seem important. Make them about *now* without being blatant about it.

The best science fiction posits a world that's not recognizable, yet makes it real. The best science fiction is addictive, rich, and lively. The best science fiction invites conversation and thought, as well as an emotion-packed thrill ride.

And as I listened to my non-SF friends wax poetic about the new *Battlestar*, I realized that the show accomplishes all of that and more.

It brings in the new fan. It shows them ads on the Sci-Fi Channel for other good SF shows (the new *Dr. Who*, which is stunningly good, and both *Stargate*s, also excellent), as well as commercials for SF products. It leads many fans in search of information to the Sci-Fi Channel's Web site, which is chock-full of SF goodies from short stories to Sci Fi Wire, a weekly update of SF news for games, media, *and* print.

In other words, if the hardcore brand-new *Battlestar* fan wants to learn more about the genre, the Sci-Fi Channel helps them do so by giving them places to go, things to look at, other items—games, books, and magazines—which reveal whole new worlds, worlds they might enjoy.

Which Brings Me Back to Me

I could live up to my inner SF geek when non-SF people approach me about *Battlestar*. I could coldly inform them that the concepts in the show are as old as SF itself, and that their "wonderful" discovery isn't all that unusual. I could turn into that overweight, T-shirt-wearing fan who winced when William Shatner ordered her to get a life.

I must admit that with the first one or two approaches, I did release my inner geek. Then I started listening. And then I started realizing how good all of this is for SF.

If the genre capitalizes on its new fan base—if these folks find good SF books that fulfill the same jones as *Battlestar*, things like Allen Steele's Coyote series or Jack McDevitt's *Polaris* novels—the genre will grow.

And as I've argued before, most recently in *Star Wars on Trial*, the print side of the genre must grow in order to survive. *Battlestar* can help with that. It *is* helping with that by making people as diverse as *New Yorker* readers and *Analog* readers finally see what they have in common.

Maybe, maybe, if people like me keep our mouths closed (except for a book recommendation *when asked*), we'll help these new—and enthusiastic—fans into the print side of the genre.

Of course, print SF has to become accessible as well. I know how to find the good space opera (which is what *Battlestar*'s SF subgenre truly is), but the new devotee who wanders into the SF section will be confused by the array of titles, none of which are sorted by subgenre.

My job, as someone who loves SF, is to help more people into the genre, not discourage them from getting close. Too many SF aficionados show their bad side to newcomers—we tell them that E. E. "Doc" Smith explored many of these same concepts seventy years ago, as if that's relevant (hell, Agatha Christie first looked at murder in the 1920s, but what mystery fan ever uses that as a defense of her genre?) or we say snottily, "*Star Trek* has dealt with social issues since its inception in 1966." I've done this; so have all my other SF friends in one way or another, about one show or another.

We have to stop. We have to rejoice that *Battlestar* is so good—and so accessible—that non-SF fans love the show. And, that it's receiving awards for excellence from organizations that normally pay attention only to PBS. We must encourage the new *Battlestar* fan to wander into the SF section of the bookstore, and help them find a book they'll love just as much as *Battlestar* itself.

That's why I asked to write this essay. Because I believe that people who have loved SF for decades have a responsibility to help the genre survive, not just in television, in the movies, or in games, but in print, as well. And right now, the print side of SF is struggling.[6] The more new-comers we bring to the SF side of the equation, the better off we'll be.

Right now, *Battlestar* is to SF what *Harry Potter* is to fantasy: an open door through which a legion of fans could trundle, if they only have help. I'd love to see signs in bookstores that say, "If you like *Battlestar Galactica*, you'll like these books," followed by a list, just like you saw in the months before each Harry Potter big release.

Those of us who are SF fans of long standing shouldn't sneer at the newcomers. And those of you who are new, let me tell you there's a wide, wide world of literature—good literature—just waiting for you on the bookstore shelves. Read review quotes and blurbs. If any of them use the words "space opera" or "just like the old *Astounding*," realize that you'll love these titles. I promise.

And when next season starts, I'll be sitting in front of the television in my home, eating Cheez Whiz and Ritz Crackers, and talking science fiction with folk who are discovering for the first time what those of us in SF knew for decades.

Kristine Kathryn Rusch is a bestselling novelist. She's also an award-winning editor and writer, with two Hugos and a World Fantasy Award, as well as many other awards in science fiction, fantasy, romance, and mystery. Her most recent science fiction novel is Buried Deep. *Her next is* Paloma, *which will appear in October. Under the name Kris Nelscott, she has just published the sixth book in her critically acclaimed Smokey Dalton series,* Days of Rage. *Her works have appeared in fourteen countries and thirteen languages.*

---

[6] For more on this, see "Barbarian Confessions."

In this hilarious satire our writers Jody and Bill tickle our funny bone with a tongue-in-cheek, but still covertly insightful, look at where the Galactica *cast might find themselves if they arrived on Earth and had to find a job like everyone else. What jobs would they be fit for? The only problem I had with this delightful rambling is where they placed Tom Zarek. In my estimation Tom, with his dashing good looks and devilish but manipulative charms, could easily be a wonderful evangelist or inspirational speaker a la Tony Robbins. Or possibly even a Hollywood ex-star trying desperately to fill the empty captain's chair in the upcoming resurrection of* Star Trek *called* Beyond the Next Generation. *What do you think, huh?*

REPORT TO CONGRESS

Bill Fawcett and Jody Lynn Nye

The following is a transcript of a report made to the Special House Committee on Alien Immigration by director Harlan MacMoliter from the Bureau of Immigration, Department of Homeland Security:

Esteemed MEMBERS OF CONGRESS, we appreciate having this opportunity to present to you the results of the *Galactica* Personnel Placement Program. To recount, as you are aware, the ship named *Battlestar Galactica* arrived over our world approximately sixty days ago. Accompanying it was a small fleet containing a number of humans who had to be regarded as totally undocumented aliens. Upon consultation, they all formally applied for entry into the United States as refugees. Due to their inability to return to their home country, er, worlds, given the Cylon policy of genocide, refugee status could not be denied. Due to the poor condition of the ships, it was necessary to disembark the almost 50,000 refugees, and resident aliens, sorry about that, status was universally granted. Generally speaking, these new immigrants were neither numerous enough or different enough from humans born on Earth to create any problems. The one exception was the placement of their highly visible administrative and executive personnel. Due to the high visibility of these individuals, it was determined that their integration was vital to the smooth transition of the entire group. I am here to report on the decisions and arrangements made.

Commander Adama

Finding a position for the person who led the alien fleet from a distant solar system to ours was a daunting task. Commander Adama was first considered for a military role, but certain aspects of his record (the destruction of civilian ships, plotting to kill his superior officer, etc.) led to the decision that Adama was better suited for a civilian role. William Adama brings tremendous credibility, sincerity, and stature to any role, but he required a position where he would not be penalized by his unfamiliarity with Earth and its cultures. The answer soon became obvious. After the disaster of hiring a daytime host, known for her superficial behavior, as a major network's news anchor, all of the other stations are now moving in the other direction. Also, considering William Adama's adamant pro-military stance and attitudes, not only the position, but also the station became apparent. Beginning tomorrow *Fox News* will be airing promotions for their latest and certainly best-traveled evening news anchor man, Commander Adama.

Dr. Laura Roslin

Considering her background and experiences, there actually was little question here. Dr. Roslin was considered briefly by the Department of the Interior for an administrative position since she began her epic journey as Education Minister. Her knowledge of North American ecology is surprisingly good, perhaps due to the fact that all alien plants are strangely identical to those found in and around Vancouver. But this would have involved effectively placing a former head of state in an assistant director position, which would clearly be unacceptable. Our options were further limited by the fact that her cancer made her unemployable by private concerns (robot-based miracle cures are not included in the actuarial tables of the health insurance companies). The final decision on her placement came less from her specific experience than from the calm demeanor she demonstrated during a wide range of crises. She will be filling a niche lost a few years ago and deeply felt by PBS. Calm, unshakeable, and speaking in gentle tones, we will soon be welcomed to *Mrs. Roslin's Neighborhood.*

Dr. Gaius Baltar

Interviews with Dr. Baltar revealed him to be charismatic, brilliant, awesomely self-centered, willing to sell out his entire race for personal gain, and quite possibly delusional. Placing him was perhaps the simplest of all the candidates we had to consider. After distributing his dossier to a range of companies whose cultures fit his profile, we were besieged with responses. Gaius Baltar is now considering lucrative offers ranging from head of research to COO from three oil multinationals and all six of the major drug companies. Our staff is assured he will fit right in with any of his choices.

Number Six

Having accompanied the human aliens, Number Six's nature as a homicidal artificial life form initially caused some concern. Her considerable beauty and sexuality led to an initial placement as lead model for Victoria's Secret. But a threatened strike by the other models over the placement of a "self-centered, unfeeling, non-eating, superficial robot" in their midst caused the company to terminate the arrangement. We are still not sure what the problem was, as Number Six's behavior was indistinguishable from that of the other models. This rejection led to a new approach. Where would a non-human with little empathy for others and the demonstrated willingness to manipulate human emotions be best employed? I am happy to inform the committee that starting next week Number Six will be seated next to Simon Cowell as a judge on *American Idol*. As a further footnote, based upon similarities and behavior patterns, we also may be investigating whether Mr. Cowell is a Cylon. Number Six, along with twenty-five more of her models, will all be appearing as the briefcase girls on *Deal or No Deal*. Being the least human, Number Six may well be the most successful of those we are integrating.

Captain Lee Adama (Apollo)

There were a lot of different opinions on the best placement for Lee Adama. Many of those were rather specific, if impractical, suggestions from almost all of the female staff members and a surprising number of the men. Those aside, flying a Viper is not one of our job descriptions and so we searched for another area. It was decided that Commander Adama was temperamentally and physically the best adapted of all the *Galactica* aliens to transfer directly into the U.S. Air Force. He has been accepted at rank, but due to an unfortunate bureaucratic error, he has been assigned to Cooks' School in Minot. Air Force officials assure me that this will be straightened out within a few years.

Colonel Saul Tigh

Hard drinking, reckless of his own health, and ruggedly handsome, Saul Tigh is charismatic and ambitious, but reluctant to take on true leadership. He is willing to act and speak for others and follow orders explicitly. Given that his age ruled out a military appointment, these characteristics made him best suited for a corporate position. It was Saul Tigh's alcoholism and smoking that led to his position as the new Marlboro Man.

Tactical Officer Lieutenant Gaeta

By nature a problem solver, Lt. Gaeta put his own solution forward when asked what he would like to do now that he was on Earth. As an information specialist who has operated at the nerve center of a major military cruiser under the direct orders of the commander of the fleet, Gaeta is accustomed to operating under fire in a hierarchical bureaucracy with a cool head and his finger on the solution needed to solve the problem at hand. Therefore, when an offer came through for him from the Consolidated Telephone Companies of Earth to be the executive vice president of their customer complaints department, he accepted with alacrity. We understand that complaints are being handled up to thirty-seven percent faster than they had been under the former EVP.

CPO Galen Tyrol

CPO Tyrol has a distinguished record with the *Galactica*, apart from a personal attachment to one of the Cylon Sharons. His ability to keep nearly derelict pieces of vital, high-powered, and fast-flying equipment running on a shoestring made him attractive to many government facilities, some of them secure military installations, but residual nervousness among some politicians regarding his loyalty made them suggest to us that we steer him toward a civilian position. He explored a number of lucrative job offers before taking the job as lead mechanic at the Brickyard, overseeing the repair of NASCAR race cars.

After a demonstration of his talents of making quick and accurate repairs on a variety of dilapidated high-test autos, a bidding war broke out to secure his services. At the moment, at least five of the lead teams are trying to get him as pit boss. He is being represented by a top talent agent. Worryingly, he has applied to import a series of the Sharon Valerii Cylons, claiming that they would make excellent drivers and mechanics.

Lieutenant Karl C. Agathon

"Helo," as his devoted fellow crew members call him, is the kind of officer that any Earth-based force would be proud to have on board. Since Earth governments are concerned about security breaches from aliens associated with the Cylon enemy, he is excluded from his natural calling as a member of the armed forces, so another outlet had to be found for his talent.

With his impressive physique, muscular control, and knowledge of survival techniques, the growing sport/hobby of Extreme Travel seemed a good fit for Mr. Agathon. This is a hobby that allows very fit tourists to put themselves into hazardous, not to say perilous, situations, relying on their skills and intelligence to survive, under the protection and oversight of an experienced guide. The company Danger-Meg Outfitters has hired Mr. Agathon to head up their new wilderness travel branch that will lead tours into remote locations, far from roads or easy rescue.

It is not true, contrary to rumors reported in the press, that Mr. Agathon was seen participating in an Extreme Ironing competition in Australia three weeks ago. He claims not to know how to operate an iron.

Petty Officer Grade 2 Anastasia Dualla

Ms. Dualla was also approached by the communications conglomerate, but showed no interest in taking up a career that so closely echoed her former duty aboard *Galactica.* However, her conscientiousness and excellence in distilling the essence of information received down to a pithy, truthful, yet evocative narrative made her a choice catch for the Library of Congress, who have employed her in the dual (excuse the pun) tasks of committing the experiences of the former space migrants to historical archive as well as reading and writing a short descriptive blurb for each of the hundreds of thousands of books and articles that flood into the Library every year.

Tom Zarek

Having the contrary qualifications of a significant criminal record and being an elected member of the refugee's government, the placement of Mr. Zarek was initially difficult. We looked at a number of options— used car sales and telemarketing being discarded as too demeaning. A career as a lobbyist, despite his visible aptitudes, was excluded due to his criminal record. Unfortunately, there were no clear rulings regarding the applicability of convictions that took place outside of Earth's jurisdiction, on another planet currently under occupation by genocidal robots. Considerable debate followed and finally the matter was settled outside our system. Mr. Zarek notified us last week that he has taken a position as special advisor to the mayor of Chicago and by a special ruling has been placed on the ballot as a candidate for alderman in Chicago's First Ward. A follow-up interview has led us to believe that Tom Zarek has integrated quickly and easily into Mayor Daley's administration.

Lieutenant Kara Thrace (Starbuck)

Kara Thrace was perhaps the most problematic of our placements. Thrace's piloting skills are undeniably formidable, but there are very few positions for pilots who delight in disobeying orders and have a tendency to attack their superiors. She was briefly considered as a corporate mercenary, perhaps a field agent for Blackwater. But her difficulty in following orders, and the unfortunate results of her special ops work for *Galactica*, raised some qualms. Testing seemed to indicate that her solutions to test situations was to shoot first, then shoot second. Thrace seemed to lack the subtlety and self-discipline required for these positions.

But Ms. Thrace had also been an executive, a wing leader on the *Galactica*, so we began to look for corporate positions that presented real life-and-death challenges and cutthroat competitors. This lead to several disastrous interviews with chief operating officers from the cosmetics industry, including that one unfortunate maiming incident with the Revlon COO which got significant news coverage. Also, contrary to the news broadcasts, we have been assured that the movie studio executive that demanded a private interview with her will eventually regain the use of at least his right arm. This publicity, her aptitude for confrontation, and her noted inability to handle money led us to look at her becoming a Hollywood director, but this was rejected by SAG due to the potential loss of life among the actors. Finally the answer did jump out at us. As of yesterday, Ms. Kara Thrace, Starbuck, is the new spokesperson for the World Wrestling Federation.

Bill has been a professor, teacher, corporate executive, and college dean. He is one of the founders of Mayfair Games, a board and role-play gaming company, and designed award-winning board games and role-playing modules. He more recently produced and designed several computer games. As a book packager, a person who prepares series of books from concept to production for major publishers, his company Bill Fawcett & Associates has packaged more than 250 books for every major publisher.

Bill began his own novel writing with a juvenile series, Swordquest, for Ace SF in the early '80s and has written several since. The Fleet science fiction series he edited and contributed to with David Drake has become a classic of military science fiction. He has collaborated on several mystery novels as Quinn Fawcett, including the authorized Mycroft Holmes *and* Madame Vernet *mysteries. His recent works include* Making Contact: A UFO Contact Handbook, *and a series of books about great mistakes in history:* It Seemed Like a Good Idea, You Did What? *and* How to Lose a Battle. *As an anthologist Bill has edited or co-edited more than fifty anthologies.*

Jody Lynn Nye lists her main career activity as "spoiling cats." She lives northwest of Chicago with two of the above and her husband, author and packager Bill Fawcett. She has published thirty books, including six contemporary fantasies, four SF novels, four novels in collaboration with Anne Mc-Caffrey, including The Ship Who Won; *edited a humorous anthology about mothers,* Don't Forget Your Spacesuit, Dear!; *and written more than eighty short stories. Her latest books are* Strong Arm Tactics *first in the Wolfe Pack series (Meisha Merlin Publishing), and* Class Dis-Mythed, *co-written with Robert Asprin.*

*As Adam Roberts so elegantly states in this article, "fascism" is a very mis-
understood and frequently misused term. But when, how, and why does this
form of absolute control come about and what are the reasons and tempta-
tions that cause good male and female leaders to abuse their powers and
cross the line into the danger zone of dictatorship and fascism? Adama and
Battlestar struggle heroically with this issue and we get to see first hand the
workings, flaws, and underpinnings of democracy versus the real temptation
for unmitigated control during times of instability, war, and chaos.*

ADAMA AND FASCISM

Adam Roberts

Is ADAMA A FASCIST?

You might be forgiven for thinking so. He's a military leader who
takes control of the business of running human affairs. His power is absolute, and he uses it as he sees fit. It's true he permits democratic elections and gives the civil authorities some leeway to govern; but he has
no qualms, if he judges it appropriate, to overrule, to intervene, and
even to lock the president in prison. Nobody, I think, is in any doubt
where true power lies. He is a deeply conservative figure, suspicious of
change and attached to traditional ways of doing things. Like Hitler, or
Mussolini, he rallies his people in the cause of a great war upon which
the very survival of civilization depends: he does this in part by giving the people a single identity defined by a quasi-mystical quest (for
"Earth"). And we are invited, as viewers, to identify with, support, and
perhaps even hero-worship Adama.

Okay, I'm being deliberately snippy here. To be serious for a moment:
I don't really think Adama is a fascist. But I do think the relationship
between this TV series and the political question of authoritarian mili-

tarism is one of the most interesting things about *Battlestar Galactica.* Indeed, I'd go further than that: in the long and mostly inglorious history of science fictional militarism, *BSG* is one of the most interesting developments.

SF and Totalitarianism

So—where do you stand on the question of fascism? Good thing? Bad thing?

Yes. Me too.

But where does *science fiction*, as a genre, stand on the question of fascism? Well, the unpalatable truth is that a good chunk of SF advances and even celebrates fascistic values. In its Golden Age, SF mostly stayed true to its core audience requirement and provided escapist entertainment that allowed (mostly) weedy male readers to compensate for their inadequacies by identifying with rock-jawed, muscular can-do heroes who faced peril, overcame the peril, and were rewarded with the girl. But this seemingly harmless pandering to adolescent insecurity becomes, when projected onto the larger canvas of political and social world-building, masculine-chauvinistic, authoritarian, and dangerous.

Were the leaders of humanity in, say, E. E. "Doc" Smith's Lensman series (the various stories of which were published in the 1930s and 1940s) fascists? They controlled enormous military power, which they used for the enforcement of the law and the good of humanity. Corrupt politicians feared them, and were, in fact, overthrown and replaced by them in the later stories. As leaders the lensmen were neither elected nor accountable, and nor did they need to be, because they were incorruptibly dedicated to their goal—the war against evil alien races that threatened their world. Does that sound fascist to you?

Or what about the several thousand novels (yes, you read that number right) that make up the German Perry Rhodan series, a publishing franchise which has been continuously ongoing since the 1960s? Rhodan is an American astronaut who discovers a crashed alien spacecraft on the moon, thereafter becoming involved in a fantastically burgeoning series of adventures that lead him to command a high-tech fleet of spaceships and eventually assuming the role of "Peace Lord of the Galaxy." As Peace Lord, Rhodan has supernatural, almost mystical powers; he is virtuous, pure-hearted, and absolutely powerful. Power may corrupt in *our* universe, but in the fictional cosmos of Rhodan it leads to a sort of political ideal.

Of course both the Lensmen and the Peace Lord claim that they rule for the good of humanity. But of course that's exactly what fascist leaders tend to claim. And in the fictional worlds of these novels, the threats facing humanity are so enormous that only totalitarian military leadership can save civilization. But, again, of course that's what fascist leaders have always said.

Of course, there are some famous works of SF that claim to challenge the assumptions of fascism. One of the most famous is George Lucas's *Star Wars*—the film whose success encouraged Glen Larson to put the original *Battlestar Galactica* into production back in 1978. I do not use the word "cash-in." I don't consider that to *be* a word. It's *two* words, clearly, regardless of the hyphen. Still, it's easy to see the many points of similarity between the original *Battlestar Galactica* and *Star Wars*: famously, George Lucas sued for copyright infringement, although he lost the suit.

Now, *Star Wars* IV–VI (or "Star Warsivvi" as I like to call it[1]) dramatized a simple-seeming moral with regard to fascism. Fascism is evil and must be fought. The conflict between the mostly Americanized rebel alliance and the mostly European Imperial forces harked back to the Second World War—when actual Americans had fought against real, actual fascists in Germany and Italy. The Nazi stylings of the Imperial uniforms, the "European" (well, *British*) accents of the actors, and the reworked *Dam Busters* plotline of the film helped the original audiences plug into that mindset in which fascism was invoked only to be combated. But the subsequent trilogy, *Star Wars* I–III (or "Star Warsiiii!" as I like to call it[2]), had more complex ambitions. It tried to set out in dramatic form how a fascist dictator comes about in the first place—not only what sort of social circumstances need to be in place for fascism to take hold, but also what motivates the dictator himself. It's a commendable ambition, although I don't think Lucas managed to pull it off. I don't say this to revisit the single most protracted fan debate in the his-

---

[1] I'm sure you're aware of the eminent Polish SF writer Štar Warsivvi? What's that? You're *not*? Oh.
[2] *Star Warsiiii!* sounds like somebody slipped and fell right in the middle of saying the words. "Hey! You out there on that ledge! What's the name of your favorite SF film?" "It's *Star Wars-iiiiii!*"

tory of SF (the *Star Wars* prequels: good? or a noisome pile of steaming ordure that a four-year-old child would be embarrassed to have foisted on the gullible public?). I'm only interested in this single aspect of the films: the success with which they dramatized the rise of a fascist.

I don't think they work on either of these two levels. The individual story of Anakin Skywalker really made little sense. He was seduced into giving up the Jedi principles of altruism and democracy because he wanted to save his wife from premature death (although one of the first things he did after going to the dark side was try and throttle his wife to death. Because... um, well, I wasn't too sure why). We were given some notional psychological motivation. People don't know what's best for them, he told his girlfriend. They should be *made* to do as they're told. Which is, in effect, to say that fascism is a kind of overdeveloped belief in a sort of enlightened bullying. Oh, and his mommy was killed.

As if, in an alternate timeline, Adolf Hitler was an enlightened and civilized politician of liberal sympathies until a band of grunting desert aliens kidnapped *his* mother, after which he reconsidered his political philosophy and founded the Nazi party. This, I'd suggest, is not what turns people into fascists.

Nor is the political context of the rise of the fascist Empire very thoroughly rendered by Lucas. As Palpatine announced the creation of a Galactic Empire ("order and security... for 10,000 years!") the Senate gave him a standing ovation. Well, a floating-in-futuristic-Senate-floaty-pods ovation. Queen Amidala commented sadly, "So this is how democracy dies: to the sound of thunderous applause." Now, there are many things that can be said against politicians, and I'm as happy as anyone to slap them around the metaphorical head with charges of incompetence and corruption and who-knows-what-else. But a tendency to *vote themselves out of power* and then give themselves a round of applause for doing so is really not typical of the breed.

There's a strong case that the real fascists in *Star Wars* (and I'm far from being the first person to suggest this) were the Jedi. They wielded power without being accountable, or elected; they were, in a sense, genetic supermen, dedicated to the arts of war at the expense of messy human entanglements, like sex (which was forbidden to them). Most of all they operated in the service of an obscure, exacting, and fundamentally mystical system of beliefs, one that privileged a transcendent "oneness" (referred to with the Hitlerian, or at least Nietzschean, name "the Force") over the diversity and hybridity of actual life. Their devotion to this cause gave them, they believed, the right to override all other moral obligations. They killed, often, they took people's things, and, in the course of *Revenge of the Sith*, they attempted to kill the democratically elected leader and enforced their rule through their mystical beliefs.[3]

If the original *Battlestar Galactica* was a pale imitation of what George Lucas had achieved in *Star Wars*, then Ronald D. Moore's new series of *BSG* surpasses Lucas's films in almost every way, and certainly in its political sophistication. Because one thing that the *BSG* scriptwriters are extraordinarily good at doing is dramatizing precisely the dynamic that leads to fascist government. Adama is no fascist; on the contrary, this show rehearses the energies and dynamics of political power in a way that makes it a penetrating *critique* of fascism.

The F-word

It might help, perhaps, to have a slightly sharper sense of what "fascism" actually means; but this isn't a term easy to pin down. In part, this is because it has become a flabbily generalized term of abuse. It is often invoked to express a knee-jerk dislike of any particular instance of authority, particularly one that inconveniences any given individual. If a Parking Attendant gives me a ticket I may be tempted to mutter "fascist!" under my breath: he's wearing a uniform, he's asserting his authority over me, I don't like it. By the same token any authority figure can get tarred with this brush: from policemen and security guards to teachers, sports referees, and parents ("Tidy your room!" "Fascist!").

But this isn't what "fascism" actually means. The noted historian Robert O. Paxton has defined the term more accurately. According to him, Fascism is:

---

[3] There is one other way in which *Star Wars* partakes of fascism.... The famous *Star Wars* logo itself was designed by a brilliant young graphic artist called Suzy Rice.... As she explains in her blog, www.suzyriceimage.com, she chose a font called Helvetica in order to capture the commission Lucas gave her.... Helvetica is a popular font, but not many people know that it was originally designed by the Nazi propagandist-in-chief Joseph Goebbels himself for general use in road signs, license plates, "official" statements, and the like. The idea was to generate a standard of appearance of government pronouncements, working toward the fascistic goals of organizing and monopolizing culture through stylistic uniformity.... So that famous *Star Wars* logo uses a fascist font.

"A form of political behavior marked by obsessive preoccupation with community decline, humiliation, or victim-hood and by compensatory cults of unity, energy, and purity, in which a mass-based party of committed nationalist militants, working in uneasy but effective collaboration with traditional elites, abandons democratic liberties and pursues with redemptive violence and without ethical or legal restraints goals of internal cleansing and external expansion."[4]

The fascist wants to pretend otherwise, but politics is a necessarily messy business. Modern social living involves a balancing act of tremendous and perhaps precarious subtlety, at least in the West. On the one hand we are dedicated to concepts of "Freedom" and "Liberty," which are grounded in a sense that (to paraphrase John Stuart Mill) we should be free to do whatever we like so long as it doesn't interfere with *somebody else's* freedom. If we want to worship the Great Cthulhu we should be allowed, *provided* we don't start sacrificing people to our god against their will. If we want to smoke cigarettes we should be allowed to do so—even though it's terribly bad for us—provided we don't force other people to smoke them too.

On the other hand, though, no one wants to live in anarchy (present-day Baghdad, say). We all accept that there must be *some* rules. Similarly, most people understand that there is *some* point to having an army. Without a standing army, for instance, my home in England would have been swiftly overrun by Hitler. The trick, obviously then, is to find the proper way of balancing the need for authority with the principle of freedom.

If, earlier, I gave the impression that SF is hopelessly complicit with fascism, then I didn't mean to. There are a number of SF works that interrogate fascist ideology in penetrating ways, and one masterpiece that inhabits many of the conventions of fascism precisely in order to work through its issues: Robert Heinlein's *Starship Troopers*. I'm not talking about Paul Verhoeven's cinematic adaptation (although I've a soft spot for the splendidly over-the-top pastiche humor of that film), but rather the original 1959 book.

Heinlein, quite apart from being one of the greatest SF writers of the

---

[4] Paxton, *The Anatomy of Fascism* (Vintage Books 2005) p. 218.

twentieth century, was an unashamed militarist, and in this novel he celebrated the sacrifice and bravery of disciplined professional soldiers with a hawkish glee that presented the military way of doing things as a *political* ideal. The troopers were needed to fight an implacable alien insectoid foe, with whom treaties would have been meaningless and who ruthlessly exterminated human life wherever they found it. Within this artificially black-and-white moral framework Heinlein's gung-ho certainty could hardly be anything other than authoritarian. Not only his army, but his whole Earth society was run on military lines, and what's striking is that the result was portrayed, convincingly, as almost utopian.

Some critics have called *Starship Troopers* fascist, and such accusations pained Heinlein a great deal; after all, he worked for the U.S. Navy during World War II specifically fighting fascism, and all of his novels, without exception, praised a self-reliant and self-sacrificial individualism, and never praised the conformist mass-militarism of the fascist ideal. But, with that said, he was certainly suspicious of the form of democracy which is presently manifested in the West. He believed, for instance, that the vote should be something *earned* instead of being "handed to anyone who is eighteen years old and has a body temperature near 37°C." But nevertheless the society of *Starship Troopers* was not run by a dictator, but by an elected president and senate. It was a real, although unconventional, democracy. To have power over the way the state is run, Heinlein argued, should require a test of responsibility on behalf of the person to whom that power is given, because the irresponsible exercise of power is dangerous and arguably fatal to a nation. A soldier, according to Heinlein's logic, risks his life in defense of the state, a potential self-sacrifice of the most altruistic sort. Such people have proven that they can be trusted with the future of the nation, and should be allowed to vote. Everybody else should get in line, join up, make the same proof, and only then get to participate in the franchise.

In writing about the novel, Heinlein later claimed that his idea was not exclusively military: it's not that everybody should go in the army to earn the vote, but that everybody should do some public service work, to show some commitment to the state as a whole before having the power to influence the government of the state. Heinlein later insisted that "nineteen out of twenty veterans" in the novel "are not military

veterans, but what we call today 'former members of the federal services.'" This, if you read the book, wasn't actually true (the proportion of
military characters to federal servants was not one in twenty but closer
to nineteen in twenty); but as an idea I'd say it's got a lot going for it. I
suppose we might argue, in Heinlein's defense, that the novel focused
on the army and its fight against the Bugs because that's more dramatic; a novel in which the lead characters helped build and run a community hospital, or volunteered as teachers, would be less so. But the
crucial thing is that Heinlein understood one thing very well: a fascist
society may be militaristic, but militarism is not in itself fascist. Indeed,
everybody who is not a thoroughgoing pacifist must be a militarist to
one degree or another. This is a distinction of the greatest importance
to *Battlestar Galactica*.

　BSG executive producer Ron Moore writes a blog [http://blog.scifi.
com/battlestar/] that has, amongst other things, played host to this very
debate. One anonymous contributor, consciously or otherwise, gave
voice to the fascist line:

> *"You would think that in such desperate times of war, when the entire human
> race (or at least what's known of it) has been reduced to a mere few thousand
> people, that the military would basically ignore the 'will of the people' and do
> things their way.... I hope next season Adama will have learned his lesson:
> the average person is stupid. Democracy . . . is not a perfect system. In such
> desperate times, you really can't risk the people electing the wrong person for
> the job, the military should take absolute power."*

Greatly to his credit, Moore contradicted this line of thinking, insisting that "Adama's deference to the democratic system is a fundamental
idea in the series."

> *Who is Adama to take god-like control of the human race? Who appointed
> him to that position? And what makes him qualified to make those decisions?
> Consider the example of Admiral Cain—she arrogated those kind of powers
> to herself and look at what happened.*

　This, I think, is *Galactica's* greatest contribution to the ongoing SF
fascination with fascism, and one of the (many) ways in which the new-

er series is such an enormous improvement over the former. Heinlein, in *Starship Troopers*, created an artificially exaggerated situation: human life was threatened by a race so alien and unpleasant that there could not be any negotiation, and any hesitation in the face of their assault would have resulted in human annihilation. In his imaginary cosmos the only thing to do was submit to a military logic and to *fight*. The original series of *BSG* set up a similar dynamic. The Cylons in that show were purely mechanical, gleaming and shining and implacably dedicated to the destruction of all humanity. But in the new series the Cylons are contaminated, as it were, by humanity: contaminated by more than a human-seeming physical form, but by human compassion, religious sense, and an apparent desire for the synthesis of human and Cylonic life.

There's a crucial sense in which it misses the point to call Adama a fascist. Fascism is *more* than simply a belief that a military leader should have the power to control an organized society. Fascism is a quasi-mystical belief system, in which the "leader" manifests and embodies the "spirit" of his people, and guards a transcendental connection with the "blood" and the "land." In this sense, Lucas is right to characterize his fascists as followers of a dark and mysterious religion—the commitment to a mindset that is more than merely rational and logical, it is an essential part of the fascistic appeal.

But this is not Adama. He has no mystical connection to his "volk" or his land, because in a very literal sense *his people have no land*—land is precisely what humanity has been deprived of. The skill is in the way Adama's character is portrayed; it shows his model of leadership to be, in a word, contingent. He deals with problems as they present themselves, working within the constraints.

A great deal of the show is concerned with the tensions between the military and the civil authorities—and more specifically with the lengths Adama goes to accommodate Laura Roslin and her administration. I am not suggesting that Adama is a model democrat. Clearly he isn't. Of course (we might say), his instincts are authoritarian and conservative, and he does override and even imprison the voted representatives of the people. But specifically because he is never presented as a saint, Adama's characterization works to counter the mystical notions of the fascist leader who possesses a magical ability to always know the "right" thing to do. Nobody who watches *BSG* can doubt that politics are, as they say, the art of the possible.

It's also a nice touch casting Edward James Olmos, perhaps America's most esteemed and famous Hispanic actor, as the father of a character played by the very Anglo (and, indeed, actually English) Jamie Griffith.[5] It's as if the series is going out of its way to overturn fascistic notions of racial purity, and instead is celebrating and dramatizing racial diversity and interracial harmony. Olmos himself, whose own father was of part Hungarian-Jewish descent, certainly wouldn't have fared well in Hitler's Germany.

No: *Battlestar Galactica* is an antidote to fascism. Despite taking as its subject a military vessel guarding humanity at a time of enormous danger, it consistently represents politics as a process of negotiation and compromise. Despite belonging to a genre with a checkered history when it comes to celebrating an impossibly clean-lined totalitarianism, it gives us humanity battling with ordinary, everyday resources, doing the best they can, flawed but determined. Against an implacable enemy. Survival depends not upon the coalescence of a semi-mystical "volk" or race, but on the collaboration of talents from a wide range of races and classes. Adama is no fascist: *anti*-fascist is closer to the truth.

An author bio has been requested for this unit. To give truthful details about its date of manufacture and mission parameters would violate Cylon protocols. Instead, please substitute: Adam Roberts mark 1, born, yes that's it, born 1965 upon the planet Earth, definitely Earth. At...London, England. Currently a writer of SF and a professor at the University of London.

---

[5] To digress for a moment, I also like the fact that tough-guy-actor Griffith has three of the *wimpiest* forenames in all the wide world of acting: "Jamie" rather than the more solid-sounding James; "St John" (pronounced "sinjun," an extraordinarily effete and posh-sounding name to English ears), and "Bamber," which always makes me think of Bambi. Jamie Sinjun Bamber Griffith. Action Man. Fantastic!

The media, what would we do without the media? In my opinion, the media will always exist, even into the forthcoming decades of space exploration, until mankind overcomes war, self-destruction, and all other fatalistic attractions that the media and we seem to feed on. What media, have you ever heard, wouldn't be in a feeding frenzy to be on board the Battlestar Galactica Fleet *with its rich tapestry of treachery, deceit, and betrayal? The* Galactica *without the media is like having an ocean without fish, Apollo without Starbuck, Baltar without Six, and Six without sex! Well, you get my point.*

REPORTERS IN SPAAAAACE!
A LOOK AT A RARE
MEDIA-SATURATED FUTURE

Shanna Swendson

Dateline: The Future

Nothing to report here because there's nobody to report it.

With as much science fiction as I watched on television and in the movies or read in books, you'd think I might have chosen a different career path. Science fiction is supposed to be a glimpse at our possible future, extrapolated from our present, and there don't seem to be many journalists in the future. Today, we have media saturation, with several twenty-four-hour news channels, around-the-clock online news coverage, cable television, satellite television, tabloid television, talk shows, and reporters working on television, on radio, in print, and online. But in the future, according to most science fiction television, all of that is gone.

In the ideal future envisioned by the *Star Trek* universe, people have apparently evolved beyond the boob tube, possibly even beyond the hunger to know what's going on in the universe, let alone what's going on in the love life of the celebrity couple du jour.

The crew of the *Enterprise* didn't seem to wonder what was happening back on Earth while they were on their five-year mission. They didn't jump at the chance to get transmissions about the latest sports scores, election results, or entertainment awards. They didn't follow debates leading up to the election of the next Federation leader.

That means journalists are apparently unneeded in the future. Where were the embedded reporters on that five-year mission undertaken by the *Enterprise*? Would the press—if they still existed in that society— have stood for something that monumental in the course of human history happening without at least a pool camera on board? Instead, the heroes of science fiction in the media manage to escape the media. They don't have to worry about public opinion as influenced by press coverage when they make their life-or-death decisions.

If the writers of TV series like *Star Trek* were in any way right about the future, my chosen career might not have offered a lot of prospects. If I'd been thinking along those lines when I was in journalism school, I might have looked into something that had more of a future to it, like maybe being a dancing girl (because every planetary waystation seemed to have a few of those) or a generic "scientist" (because in the future, apparently you don't have to specialize or choose between physics and botany). If there are no reporters, there are also no public relations professionals, no spin doctors, no media consultants, no press release writers, or any of the other jobs I've done with my journalism training. My hedge against this uncertain future was to become a novelist. Those do still seem to exist in the *Star Trek* future.

But then the new version of *Battlestar Galactica* came along and changed the way the future looks. This re-imagining of the 1970s series gets a lot of credit for being groundbreaking. Women are in stronger roles as leaders and fighter pilots. The characters—even the heroes— are flawed and dealing with their problems instead of being pure white hats or black hats. The music avoids the usual bombastic/soaring space soundtrack. There are no aliens with bumpy foreheads or funny makeup jobs representing aspects of our contemporary society. The special effects look like documentary footage so that the show seems gritty and real instead of antiseptic and majestic.

And the media exist in that future, something that really breaks the mold for science fiction on television. In fact, one of the first characters we meet after the prologue of the mini-series that launched the series is a public relations representative giving a VIP tour of *Galactica*. We're introduced to the ship through what's essentially a spoken press kit. We later meet a major character, Dr. Gaius Baltar, as he's being interviewed on live television. He's established as the kind of media celebrity who's rare in science fiction. It's the kind of spotlight position you might imagine someone like James T. Kirk would have held if he'd lived in a world with even a semblance of the media we have today. When disaster strikes the *Galactica* universe, we see it unfold on television as characters watch, the same way we find ourselves glued to the television during major events today.

The way *Battlestar Galactica* uses the media and the extent to which the media play a role in stories go beyond what we've seen before. Some of that may lie in the influence of America's September 11, 2001, tragedy, which clearly shaped the new series, while some of it may simply be that the creators don't imagine a future in which today's omnipresent mass media have faded into obscurity.

Reporters Survive Colonial Disaster

News services and newsletters form to keep Fleet informed

> JAMES MCMANUS: Live, from *Cloud Nine*, the most luxurious cruise ship in the Fleet, it's *The Colonial Gang*. It's a new talk show that brings you the inside scoop on the Fleet's movers and shakers. I'm James McManus, formerly of *The Caprica Times*. With me are two of the only remaining legitimate journalists left in the universe. Playa Palacios, veteran commentator for *The Picon Star Tribune*. And my wing man, Sekou Hamilton, former editor of *The Arilon Gazette*. ("Colonial Day" 1-11)

Admiral Adama may wish it were otherwise, but a set of unique circumstances led to the presence of reporters in the Fleet. The Cylons struck during the kind of ceremony designed by public relations people for the press, so Laura Roslin had a ship full of reporters with her to cover the decommissioning of *Galactica* as a *Battlestar* and its incarnation as an educational museum. Roslin was only secretary of education at the time, so the group traveling with her wasn't exactly the equivalent of the White House press corps. They were the kind of reporters who would have been assigned to cover the opening of a museum. They might have been reporters on the education beat, or else they were the kind of feature reporters who did human interest stories—the people who report on things like waterskiing squirrels. These wouldn't have been people with experience covering breaking news, war, or other hard-news subjects. The best, brightest, and most seasoned reporters generally wouldn't have been sent off to cover the secretary of education at a glorified ribbon cutting. In a way, you could almost consider the heavy cruiser that became Colonial One the equivalent of the "B Ark" in Douglas Adams's *The Restaurant at the End of the Universe*, on which the society's useless people—including public relations executives and movie producers—were sent off in a ship, supposedly to escape their "doomed" planet, but really just to get rid of the useless people. (Come to think of it, that ship ended up heading to Earth, too.)

When the Cylons attacked the Colonies, that motley group of fluff specialists suddenly found itself in the middle of the biggest story ever, and they were the only ones available to cover it. Their colleagues who usually got the plum stories, the stars who led with breaking news, were in the midst of the attack. They got the story. And then they promptly got blown up, with the dwindling surviving audience seeing nothing but static in the aftermath. Meanwhile, the new default presidential press corps bore witness to the swearing in of a new president, their recording devices working as they captured the moment, even though they didn't know at the time if anyone would ever see the story. There were no longer any networks or newspapers to distribute the story, but they still covered the event.

Once the Fleet came together and formed its own makeshift society, the surviving journalists seemed to have organized themselves into news programs, news services, and networks. Based on the comments about the "only remaining legitimate journalists" and the status of those journalists, it would appear that there were some high-level journalists traveling in the ships that made up the Fleet, since the editor of a major newspaper would hardly have been sent to cover a museum opening.

They seemed to have established their own hierarchy between the big shots who just happened to end up in the Fleet, the gaggle of reporters traveling with Roslin, and now the new wave of self-made reporters that had sprung up in the Fleet.

And spring up, it has. Offhand references made by characters indicate that newsletters and news services have started on the ships within the Fleet, something that's in keeping with human nature. Almost any club, organization, or group has a newsletter today. Even individuals send out holiday newsletters about their own families. The advent of blogging has made a "reporter" out of anyone with the desire to report. They discuss issues from the deeply personal to the global with anyone who cares enough to read. That was one of the fundamental fallacies of the journalism-free *Star Trek* universe. Would we really give up that curiosity about the world and the need to document our lives? Even in a perfect world without strife or conflict, wouldn't we still want to know what other people are doing, especially if they're doing something like exploring strange new worlds and finding new civilizations?

The greater the conflict, the more there is to report. The greater the danger, the stronger the impulse to leave some kind of mark on the universe so that someone might be aware of our existence. In times of crisis, we seek out information, looking to every available source to fill that need, and sources multiply to meet that need. It makes total sense that *Battlestar Galactica*'s ragtag Fleet would be swarming with news outlets.

We don't know much about what Ellen Tigh referred to as the "half-baked newsletters." Does each ship have its own newsletter to report the goings-on that might be relevant to its passengers and crew? Do the survivors of each Colony have their own newsletters throughout the Fleet for staying in touch with each other and with the issues that affect them? Any tourist with a camcorder could have become a photojournalist within the Fleet. Someone traveling with a laptop and a printer would suddenly be a publisher competing against other similarly equipped people for a scoop. Anyone with access to a transmitter could become a radio (or, in *Galactica* lingo, wireless) broadcaster. At the moment, most of the information being distributed among the Fleet appears to be news, but how long will it be before someone starts creating and distributing entertainment programming?

News Ratings Soar in Disaster Aftermath

LEE ADAMA: Mr. Gaeta, turn on the wireless. Let's give these people a chance to hear what kind of fun they'll be missing for the next five days.

JIM MCMANUS: (on radio) We are just minutes from the start of the first presidential debate between President Laura Roslin and her opponent Vice President Gaius Baltar....

("Lay Down Your Burdens, Part I" 2-19)

The real difference in the depiction of the media between *Battlestar Galactica* and other series isn't so much the fact that reporters are present, but rather the impact that reporters have on the actions and lives of the characters. Other shows may have had the obligatory "documentary crew reports on our heroes" episode, or a character may have gone through a phase of wanting to be a journalist, but outside those episodes, the media were out of sight, out of mind. We saw no ongoing impact of the media on that society. Jake Sisko may have considered himself a journalist during the Cardassian occupation on *Star Trek: Deep Space Nine*, but did we ever see his reporting have an impact? We weren't even sure where his reports might have been read, or by whom. Even when we saw the actions of a journalist, we didn't see the other side of the story—the audience and the impact of the news on the audience.

In the *Battlestar Galactica* universe, people actually listen to what the reporters have to say. Even in episodes that are only tangentially related to the media, we see that the media have permeated Fleet life. The deck crew kept a wireless set going so they could listen to the news as they worked. Pilots listened to news coverage in the ready room. The wireless coverage of the Quorum meeting played in the bar on *Cloud Nine*. Lee Adama cut a briefing short so his crew could listen to coverage of the presidential debates. Roslin and Bill Adama listened to the wireless reports in their offices.

In short, the people of the Fleet act a lot like we do. The media provide a hum of background noise throughout the day. When there's big news, people are glued to their sets. We may be a little more apathetic than we should be most of the time, but when something major is happening, we tune in, and the media respond by giving us wall-to-wall coverage. Ratings for cable news outlets spike whenever there's a crisis. Televisions across the nation were tuned in almost constantly in the aftermath of the September 11 attacks, which is the real-world analogue for what's happened to the Colonies. In uncertain times, we crave information to help make sense of the universe, to decrease the level of the unknown. The more we feel we have at stake, the more we want to know.

The reporters of the Fleet may be doing the only thing they know how to do as they try to maintain some sense of normalcy, but they aren't just talking to themselves as they do it. They have an audience listening to what they have to say, whose instinct when something seems to be happening is to turn on the radio/TV/wireless set and get the scoop.

Fleet Leaders Respond to Media Criticism

ADAMA: I don't want any bloodshed.
ROSLIN: Of course you don't, neither do I. Neither does the press. They're here, by the way.
ADAMA: The press....
ROSLIN: They're recording every minute.
("Kobol's Last Gleaming, Part II" 1-13)

Because the media of the Fleet have an audience, they have an impact. The Fleet's leaders never forget the fact that their actions will be reported to the population of the Fleet. That's something we haven't seen much of in science fiction. Captain Kirk didn't care about his image in the press as he went about doing dashing deeds. Jean Luc Picard certainly didn't worry about how his actions would be reported. Benjamin Sisko didn't govern *Deep Space Nine* by opinion polls. Laura Roslin and Bill Adama, on the other hand, can never let themselves forget about the presence of the press, Tom Zarek made full use of the press presence to get his own message out, and Gaius Baltar craves the media spotlight to an almost obscene degree. These are leaders who are constantly aware that they're being watched.

Most of the time, Adama and his executive officer, Colonel Tigh, would probably prefer that the press weren't around. The press constantly question their actions, try to investigate their shortcomings, and—in their opinion—sow dissent throughout the Fleet. Their jobs would be much easier without the press questioning their every move. Adama tolerates the press, up to a point, because he believes in the free society they represent, but he also recognizes the peril of their situation. When you're on the run from an army of killer robots bent on the destruction of humanity, is it really a good time to question the actions of the military keeping the last remnant of humanity alive?

Laura Roslin's answer would surely be yes—up to a point. She's not above her own use of the press to get her way. She tried to use the presence of reporters to stop Adama's coup attempt, she recruited Baltar as a vice-presidential candidate because of his media savvy, and she recognized the power of the press to help sway public opinion. She used the media to gather support when she broke away from the Fleet to go to Kobol. Later, she convinced Adama to invite D'anna Biers of the Fleet News Service to do an all-access program on the *Galactica* crew as a way of regaining civilian support after a military blunder. The media are integral to the way she governs.

At the same time, she recognizes the dark side of the press. Their negative reports could tear the Fleet apart at the worst possible time. Her media-friendly vice president, meant to block out Zarek's influence, turned his ease with the media against her in the presidential election. Just as it often happens in our world, the guy with the glib sound bite and the easy-to-articulate vision won out over the person with substance.

Love, hate, or tolerate, though, the leaders of the Fleet can't let themselves forget that the media are there. That constant awareness affects the decisions they make: Do they keep a Cylon prisoner alive even if the public fears the idea? Do they declare martial law if dissent gets too loud for the Fleet to continue to function? Do they make the unpopular, but correct, decision or one that will play better in the press? Do they let the press force them to take action?

OFFICIALS ALLEGE MEDIA BIAS

ADAMA: Do you understand that even a hint of this could be devastating to the morale in the Fleet?

BIERS: You're the master of understatement. You know, after the *Gideon*, this could turn the entire Fleet against you.

ADAMA: Then the real question is whether or not it matters to you.
BIERS: You know, I am sick to death of people like you questioning my
    patriotism. We all want this Fleet to survive.
("Final Cut" 2-8)

While the creators of *Battlestar Galactica* have broken with science fiction convention by envisioning a future in which the mass media exist,
you have to wonder what, exactly, their opinion of the media really is.
After all, of the few reporter and PR expert characters we've met, two
of them have already proven to be Cylon infiltrators. Aaron Doral, the
PR man, was one of the first Cylons unveiled, and D'anna Biers turned
out to be a Cylon operative whose Caprica-based clone was apparently a
major Cylon anti-human ringleader. Meanwhile, one of the other recurring journalist characters, Playa Palacios, was literally in bed (bathroom
stall, to be more accurate, but odds are a bed has been involved at some
point) with Baltar, throwing her honesty and objectivity into doubt.

    In *Battlestar Galactica*'s "documentary crew covers our heroes" epi-
sode, "Final Cut," Biers's role worked on two different levels. Before her
Cylon nature was revealed, she appeared to be just another journalist
whose instinct to go after a good story wasn't necessarily tempered by
what was good for the well-being of the Fleet. Getting the scoop was
important, as was bringing those she thinks have done wrong to justice.
She seemed to learn something about what it meant to be in the military,
about the pressure of keeping the Fleet safe, from her time on *Galactica*,
so that she withheld the information she knew would be devastating to
the Fleet and instead produced a documentary that humanized the men
and women of *Galactica* while also demonstrating their heroism.

    But then the big reveal that she is actually a Cylon agent cast her pre-
vious work into doubt. Was she muckraking on the so-called *Gideon*
Massacre because she felt it was an important story the people needed to
know about, or was she deliberately seeding dissent in the Fleet? Or was
she manipulating Roslin and Adama into getting her to cover their side
of the story so she could get onto *Galactica* and get a report on the status of Cylon Sharon Valerii? The Caprica-based version of herself, along
with another version of Doral and another Valerii, watched the documentary, but their real interest was in the footage they see of Sharon.

    The reporters of the *Battlestar Galactica* future, Cylon or not, are as flawed and shaded as the rest of the cast. They aren't *obviously* good guys or bad guys all the time. They have agendas, biases, and ambitions that show up in their work.

Stay Tuned as We Keep You Updated on This Breaking Story

The end of *Battlestar Galactica*'s second season, in which the story jumped ahead a year and introduced Cylon occupation of the new human settlement, offered numerous possibilities for continuing to explore the role of the media in this society. We could have the Cylon propaganda arm telling the people how beneficial the occupation is. There could be underground newsletters within a resistance movement. People might huddle around clandestine wireless sets like the people in occupied Europe during World War II secretly listened to the BBC. There could be reporters collaborating with the Cylons, as well as reporters paying the price for standing up for freedom of the press.

The breaking story continues to develop, and we have the media to bring it to us.

Shanna Swendson earned a journalism degree from the University of Texas, interning in radio, television, and print journalism. She then went over to the dark side and pursued a career in public relations. Now she's a full-time novelist and pop-culture essayist. She's the author of the fantasy novels En-chanted, Inc. and Once Upon Stilettos, and has contributed to Flirting with Pride and Prejudice and Welcome to Wisteria Lane.

If, like me, you are a seeker, historian, someone who searches for the deeper meanings and symbology of life, and if you have always wanted to know the religious, philosophical, and mythic foundations of Battlestar, then you will love this profound investigation of the origins of religion, politics, and our cultural heritage as mirrored in the Battlestar universe. It has become clear that Ron Moore, David Eick, and Galactica intend to enter the debate over the very soul of civilization. I'm honored to be a part of such a revolutionary and thought-provoking show.

AN ARMY OF ONE GOD
MONOTHEISM VERSUS PAGANISM IN THE *GALACTICA* MYTHOS

James John Bell

"If the show does have a single, consistent point of view, it is probably best summed up by something Lincoln said during his second inaugural address: 'With malice toward none, with charity for all. . . .' Think about that. Debate the meaning of that simple idea. For that, more than anything else, expresses this show and the politics behind it."
—RONALD D. MOORE, executive producer, *Battlestar Galactica*

"As was said 3,000 years ago, so still it must be said: 'the judgments of the Lord are true and righteous altogether.' With malice toward none, with charity for all, with firmness in the right as God gives us to see the right, let us strive on to finish the work we are in, to bind up the nation's wounds, to care for him who shall have borne the battle and for his widow and his orphan, to do all which may achieve and cherish a just and lasting peace among ourselves and with all nations."
—ABRAHAM LINCOLN, Second Inaugural Address, March 4, 1865

THE WAR IN *BATTLESTAR GALACTICA* between the "one God" and the "many gods"—between the Cylons and Colonials—started, according to executive producer Ronald D. Moore, with a Cylon "slave" revolt on the Colonies. "When the first Cylons were created, individual Colonies still warred against one another and it wasn't until the Cylon rebellion that the Twelve Colonies finally came together in a permanent way."

This "coming together" mirrors elements of American history, both the coming together of the thirteen Colonies to form a new nation, and the coming together of the North and South after the bloody Civil War that ended slavery in America. Will Cylons and Colonials ever forge a lasting peace? Will either group ever respect the other's rights and beliefs? Abraham Lincoln's Second Inaugural Address is then highly appropriate, as Moore points out, to be a guiding star for the politics behind the series.

Lincoln's religious beliefs even mirror, to a degree, the Colonial's President Laura Roslin. Early in Lincoln's life he had little use for formal theology, Christian creeds, or statements of faith. He came to be highly influenced, and thus he influenced the direction of the nation, by believing that signs, dreams, and portents foretold the future.

"As was said 3,000 years ago . . ." is a reference by Lincoln to the time of another great revolt of slaves. At approximately that time in Ancient Egypt, the "One True God" directed Moses, the leader of the Israelites—who were oppressed slaves—to lead his people out of Egypt into the Promised Land. *The Book of Moses* from the Mormon faith named these people as a *single* entity formed of a *single* mind, "And the Lord called his people ZION, because they were of one heart and one mind" (7:18). The similarities with the *Battlestar Galactica* back-story are unmistakable—Israelite slaves of "one mind" who believe in one God, enslaved to a pagan kingdom, rose up, obtained freedom, and returned eventually to ruthlessly hunt down and kill the decedents of their oppressors, sounds very much like *BSG's new* origin story of the Cylon.

Interestingly, the Colonials, once they became scattered after the initial Cylon attack on the Twelve Colonies and began their long, arduous search for Earth, also mirror this same type of exodus story of one god against the gods, but in reverse. This inversion was intentional, explained series re-imaginer Moore: "The fact that the Colonials already had Greco/Roman names and nomenclature made it a natural for saying that they were polytheistic. I think I realized that the clash of two civilizations with these beliefs would echo our own history as well as be an interesting inversion of the usual Pagan=Bad, Christian=Good dynamic and I thought that would be interesting to play around with."

Galactica's Mormon & Masonic Symbology

Another reason why the Colonials' polytheistic cosmology, and the plot of the entire series, echoes the story of the twelve ancient tribes of Israel has to do with the Mormon influence on the creation of the original 1978 *Battlestar Galactica* series. There are many references in both the old and new series to the theology of the Church of Jesus Christ of Latter-day Saints, also known as the Mormon Church.

In the book *One Nation Under Gods—A History of the Mormon Church*, author Richard Abanes pointed out that the Mormon belief system accepts the existence of multiple gods and that all may become a god as the popular Mormon couplet foretells: "As man is, God once was; as God is, man may become." Brigham Young, the second prophet and president of the Mormon Church, helped establish these polytheistic beliefs of the Mormons: "How many Gods there are, I do not know. But there never was a time when there were not Gods." Mormon theology maintains that God the Father (Heavenly Father), Jesus Christ (His Son), and the Holy Ghost are three separate and distinct godly personages. The twelve ancient tribes of Israel were the literal children of a flesh-and-bone Father in the Heavens.

The *BSG* phrase "So say we all" originated in a translation of the earliest constitution of the secretive and esoteric fraternal organization of the Freemasons. "So say we all" is used by the Freemasons like "Amen" is used by the Christians after a prayer. The phrase is in use today by the Freemasons in their songs and toasts. "So say we all" is also the final line in the oldest known genuine record of the Craft of Masonry, called the *Constituciones Artis Geometriae Secundum Euclydem*. It is the earliest of the old Masonic constitutions. It is referred to sometimes as the

Halliwell Manuscript and is more commonly known as the *Regius Manuscript*. Mr. Halliwell-Phillips refers to this old poetic constitution in an 1838 paper, "On the Introduction of Freemasonry into England." This constitution has immense historic significance to Freemasonry because it provides evidence of a legendary history and mythic origins of the Masonic order. Halliwell estimated it was transcribed in 1390 from an earlier manuscript, making it the oldest known Masonic document. In the *Halliwell Manuscript* the phrase "So say we all" was transcribed from the Middle English "Say we so all."

An initiate in Freemasonry undergoes a progression of three degrees to become Master Mason. After obtaining the third degree, there are other degrees that can be achieved through related rites, like the often-cited highest degree of Masonry, the 33rd degree of Scottish Rite Freemasonry. Some fansites suggest that this is possibly part of the inspiration for naming the first *BSG* episode "33" (1-1), the number 33 having long-standing associations as a Mason word. Much of *BSG*'s symbology does have Masonic connections, though this has far less to do with a Masonic conspiracy as some fans claim, and likely more to do with the show's Mormon roots.

In 1842 the first five presidents of the Mormon Church—Joseph Smith, Brigham Young, John Taylor, Wilford Woodruff, and Lorenzo Snow—were all made Masons in the Nauvoo Lodge in Illinois. In a period of less than six months, in excess of 250 Masons had been created; practically every member of the early Mormon hierarchy was or became a Master Mason. The population of Nauvoo increased from almost nothing to somewhere around 9,000. Additional lodges began springing up around Nauvoo, but were not following proper Masonic protocols. Investigations by the Grand Lodge ordered that all the new lodges be closed, and were disobeyed. The Grand Lodge communication of 1844 stated that all Mormon lodges were declared clandestine and all their memberships suspended.

There are many conflicting statements about what happened next, specifically on the afternoon of June 27, 1844, when Joseph Smith was hunted down and killed by a mob containing Mormons and Masons. It was no secret that many in the Masonic community were upset with Joseph Smith disobeying the Grand Lodge, but there was also a smoldering revolt that had been brewing within the Mormon hierarchy. Some historians speculate that Joseph Smith was killed because there were Masons and Mormons who didn't agree with his taking the Masonic brotherhood's secret rites and rituals and turning them into a religion—Mormonism. Both Masonry and Mormonism had their starts in King Solomon's Temple. The rituals and symbolism of the Mormon Church are claimed, by revelation, to come from the rituals of King Solomon's Temple, and a careful read of Mormon scripture brings many of these symbols to light as the same rituals found in Freemasonry. Thus, many of the Masonic symbols showing up in the *BSG* cosmology could have to do with the show's Mormon influence. Both Masonry and Mormonism did not arrive "fully formed," no matter what the various legends state, and have elements from institutions, beliefs, and societies well before their own existence. Thus a Masonic/Mormon influence on *BSG's* cosmology would seem highly speculative if it wasn't for the overabundance of similarities.

Original series producer Glen Larson is a member of the Mormon Church and conceived *Battlestar Galactica* originally as *Adam's Ark*, a human origin story with bits of Mormon theology mixed in. By contrast, Moore's beliefs are far less rigid and the new *BSG* reflects this elasticity: "I'm an Irish Catholic, not practicing. It probably just reflects my interest in my movement from Catholicism to atheism to agnosticism to interest in Eastern religions. I think the show is a reflection of my acknowledgement that faith and religion are a part of the human experience, even if I'm not quite clear on exactly what it all means and what I truly believe." Still, Moore left the original Mormon influence on *BSG* pretty well intact while expanding on the original cosmology with his own Moore-isms. Mormon themes were still prominently featured, though.

In Mormonism, the lost tribe of Israel is key to the *Book of Mormon* in much the same way that the lost colony of Earth is central to both the old and new *Battlestar Galactica*. The quest for the lost colony of Earth is a possible reference to the *Book of Mormon* that tells about the time when the twelve tribes were scattered and the prophet Lehi took a remnant of the tribe of Joseph from Jerusalem to ancient America around 600 B.C. The *Book of Mormon* tells of a tribe of Israel lost on another continent unknown to the other scattered tribes, in the same way that *Battlestar Galactica* had a lost colony on Earth separate from the Twelve refugee Colonies.

The parallels go even deeper when we learn, in both the old and new *BSG*, that the human race originated on Kobol, the homeworld of the original Twelve Colonies. Kobol is a rearranging of the word Kolob, which is the star "nearest to the celestial, or the residence of God" as told in *The Book of Abraham*. "One day in Kolob is equal to a thousand years according to the measurement of this earth."

Adam's Ark, Larson said, was "about the origins of mankind in the universe, taking some of the Biblical stories and moving them off into space as if by the time we get to Earth they're really not about things that happened here but things that might have happened somewhere else in space." Interestingly, the word "Adhama" or "Adama" in Hebrew translates as "Earth."

The opening of every episode from the original *Battlestar Galactica* series reflected Larson's belief that the origins of life originated "out there." In SF space opera this concept is known as von Daniken's "ancient astronauts":

> *"There are those who believe . . . that life here . . . began out there. Far across the universe. With tribes of humans . . . who may have been the forefathers of the Egyptians . . . or the Toltecs . . . or the Mayans . . . that they may have been the architects of the Great Pyramids . . . or the lost civilizations of Lemuria . . . or Atlantis. . . . Some believe that there may yet be brothers of man . . . who even now fight to survive . . . far, far away amongst the stars. . . .*
> —read by PATRICK MACNEE, *BSG: Saga of a Star World.*

It should be noted that when Larson first approached the networks, sometime in the '70s, with the concept of the show, it was rejected. As Larson tells it he pitched the rejected *Adam's Ark* idea again in the summer of 1977 and took it to ABC and Universal, who changed their minds about the project. *Adam's Ark* ultimately formed the framework for what was to become the *Battlestar Galactica* television series. "'Galatica' has a biblical feel," Larson explained. "It ties in with Genesis; it ties in with the western pioneers." Larson stuck to his *BSG* origin story, even though he never released a script or an *Adam's Ark* proposal for public view.

These Are Not the Toasters You Are Looking For

Though there are many similarities between Mormonism and *Battlestar Galactica*, there are also many similarities between the series and *Star Wars*—the mega-hit of the summer of 1977. *Star Wars's* success made science fiction suddenly fashionable and a hot commodity sought after by television networks eager to cash in on the hype. The original 148-minute pilot premiered on September 17, 1978, and was incredibly successful. It attracted an amazing 65 million viewers, having the highest viewership in U.S. history for its day.

Interestingly, ABC interrupted the premiere with a special news report two-thirds of the way through the broadcast. The Camp David Accords were being signed at the White House by Israeli Prime Minister Menachem Begin, Egyptian President Anwar Sadat, and witnessed by U.S. President Jimmy Carter. This ceremony oddly connected *Battlestar Galactica* and the Israeli/Arab conflict in the minds of millions of Americans. Nevertheless, the show continued after the ceremony from where it had left off, resulting in a large fan base. Universal studios saw dollar signs, but so did Twentieth Century Fox.

Citing thirty-four similarities between the film and the television series, Twentieth Century Fox and Lucasfilm Ltd. sued Universal Studios for copyright infringement by *BSG* of its *Star Wars* movie in 1978. Many *Star Wars* veterans worked on the original *Battlestar Galactica*, including special effects maistro John Dykstra, and designers Ralph McQuarrie and Joe Johnston. Larson's Mormon origin story for *BSG* seen in this context could have been emphasized to help defeat the lawsuit, which Universal eventually won in 1980.

Religious influences on science fiction and fantasy were not new, of course. Christian allegories are found throughout C. S. Lewis's *The Chronicles of Narnia* and Frank Herbert's *Dune* has many parallels to Islam. L. Ron Hubbard wrote his Scientology tract *Battlefield Earth* while *Battlestar Galactica* was airing, publishing it in 1980. Hubbard obviously wanted to jump on the bandwagon of SF mania; during the late '70s he also wrote an unpublished screenplay called *Revolt in the Stars* which dramatizes Scientology's "Advanced Level" teachings.

Hubbard even claimed at the time that SF space opera is merely our collective unconscious recalling real events from millions of years ago. A belief similar to this is also upheld by psychologists like Carl Jung and mythographers, like J. F. Bierlein, author of *Parallel Myths* and *Living Myths*. Bierlein defines myth as:

> "*A constant among all human beings in all times. The patterns, stories, even details contained in myth are found everywhere and among everyone. This is because myth is a shared heritage of ancestral memories, related consciously from generation to generation. Myth may even be part of the structure of our unconscious mind, possibly encoded in our genes.*"

In June 2003, executive producer David Eick talked about resurrecting the *Battlestar Galactica* mythos as a series, citing a broad range of influences that would be utilized to re-imagine the series. "We have also been inspired by certain episodes of the original *Battlestar Galactica* series, as well as classic SF (Philip K. Dick especially) and broader strokes culled from pretty disparate sources—running the gamut from Greek to Native American mythology, for example." Noticeably absent from this list is the 1999 blockbuster film *The Matrix*, whose highly anticipated sequels came out in 2003.

Just as the original *Battlestar Galactica* rode the coattails of *Star Wars* mania, the re-imagined series followed in the wake of the success of *The Matrix*. The new *BSG*, with its human-created cybernetic Cylons waging a genocidal war against the survivors of mankind has many parallels with films like *The Matrix* and *Terminator*.

Galactica's Narrative Hexagram

The construction of modern narrative was influenced by the polytheistic belief systems of the Greeks, namely the *Iliad* and the *Odyssey*. The "hero" in early narratives—in mythological tales—was usually the offspring of a god and a mortal. The very concept of the hero can be seen as messianic, be the hero a secular construct like a military commander or a religious savior character like Apollo, the son of Zeus. As the heroic god of colonization, Apollo guided the colonies, especially during the period of Greek and Roman colonization. It was Apollo, according to

Greek tradition, who helped Cretan (Arcadian) colonists locate the city of Troy. Apollo's role in *Battlestar Galactica* is very similar to his historic heroic counterpart from the Greek myths.

The role of the hero in a story is to stop the villain(s) and save or help the victim(s). The appearance of a hero in a narrative invokes the "drama triangle" of hero, victim, and villain into perpetual existence. Thus the hero requires a villain to be present in the story, and both imply the existence of the victim. This drama triangle might seem simplistic, but its framing has helped to pattern the structure of Western civilization itself.

Judaism, Islam, and Christianity are all filled with the promise of a messiah, and so are Western secular governments, where we elect leaders and employ police to protect us from danger. In fact, we're so influenced by the drama triangle that psychologists tell us we pattern our very thoughts around the concept, creating stories where we see ourselves as one of the points on the triangle for whatever situation in which we find ourselves. Escaping the triangle is virtually impossible. The war between hero and villain is endless, and doomed to repeat, because each will always need the other for their identity and existence. What would a demon be if there wasn't the concept of heavenly angels to define it against?

The drama triangle helps us to understand how two sides in a conflict are able to see themselves as right, like cowboys versus Indians. The drama triangle provides insight into the war between the Colonials and Cylons in *BSG*. The Colonial Fleet see themselves as the heroes, their lost relatives and friends on the planets of the Twelve Colonies as victims, and the Cylons as villains. The twelve Cylon cybernetic models see themselves as heroes, their ancestor Cylon slaves as victims, and the human race as villains. Thus each religion, both polytheistic and monotheistic, will see the other as false, and even evil.

Ronald D. Moore explains that *BSG*'s polytheism versus monotheism conflict in the series was his own creation.

"I was aware that Glen had used Mormon influences and how he had created the cosmology, but I'm not that familiar with Mormon belief or practice. To me there were things that were sort of obvious, the twelve tribes, the twelve tribes of Israel. At the beginning, I sort of assumed that the Colonials—the human

beings—would have a belief system, probably polytheistic. In the original, the 'Lords of Kobol' were referred to several times. But it wasn't until the development of the mini-series when I sort of randomly gave the Cylons a belief system. I was creating the characters and working on some lines for Number Six and I thought it was interesting if she professed a belief in a single God. I had really given her a belief in a singular God almost by accident."

The number six, in particular the six-sided hexagon, figures prominently in both *Battlestar Galactica* and the Mormon faith. The full-colors card game played by the Colonials features cards "with their corners cut off," forming six-sided hexagons. In the new *BSG* the dog tags worn by the crew of the *Galactica* are also hexagons. Elsewhere, in many places, be it the underlying superstructure of the *Galactica* or a book with the top and bottom corners missing, six sides occur.

The hexagon appears many places in nature, like the hundreds of six-sided hexagonal columns that make up America's first National Monument in the Black Hills of Wyoming known as Devil's Tower (called Bear Lodge by the twenty-two Native Tribes in the area) to the hexagonal honeycomb design of a bear's favorite source of snack food: the beehive.

Joseph Smith, the founder of the Mormon religion, adopted the beehive as the symbol of the church. Everything from the sidewalks near Mormonism's worldwide headquarters located in Salt Lake City to the Mormon Temple there is adorned with the hexagon tile pattern of the honeycomb. The Jewish "Star of David" used by the Mormon faith is a six-sided star, called a hexagram. The "center" of this hexagram is the hexagon. The hexagram is formed out of two interlocking triangles.

Geometry assumes that this two-dimensional hexagram (Star of David) is taken from the three-dimensional star tetrahedron derived from the geometry of the Platonic solids—which are also known as the building blocks of the universe. A tetrahedron is commonly referred to as a pyramid. If you place one pyramid upside down on top of another you get the star tetrahedron—a geometric equivalent to the Masonic saying "as above, so below." Thus, the numerous pyramid and triangle shapes found in the new and old *BSG* also fit neatly into the Mormon cosmology, as well as feature prominently in America's own mythology, like on the dollar bill.

"When the top of the pyramid looks around and says the response to 9/11 is to keep shopping—is this really right? This show, this series, began in that world."

—DAVID EICK, executive producer, *Battlestar Galactica*

When Robots Bleed

Battlestar Galactica's re-imaginers named science fiction visionary Philip K. Dick as an inspiration; no doubt it is Dick's extensive quasi-religious philosophy around robots that has had the most influence for the show. In his 1972 speech "The Android and the Human," Dick told his audience, "Machines are becoming more human. Our environment, and I mean our manmade world of machines, is becoming alive in ways specifically and fundamentally analogous to ourselves." Dick predicted that in the near future a human would shoot a robot and be surprised to see it bleed from the wound. When the robot shoots back, the human will gush smoke. "It would be rather a great moment of truth for both of them," Dick joked.

Insight into the new Cylon origin story can be found in the etymology of the word "robot." Robot (Czech for "forced labor") was coined by Karel Capek in the 1920 play *R.U.R.* (*Rossum's Universal Robots*), in which machines assume the drudgery of factory production, then develop human beliefs and proceed to wipe out humanity in a violent revolution. While the robots in *R.U.R.* could represent the "nightmare vision of the proletariat seen through middle-class eyes," as science fiction author Thomas Disch has suggested, they also are testament to the persistent fears of manmade technology run amok.

Similar Cylon-esque themes have manifested themselves in popular culture and folklore since at least medieval times. One such legend pulls from the elements of Jewish mysticism. It comes from sixteenth-century Prague, and centers around Rabbi Löw and the Jewish legend of the golem. After molding the golem, a statue or figure of a man produced from mud or clay, and endowing it with life by giving it the four-lettered name of God, Rabbi Löw was forced to destroy the clay creature after it ran amok. Tolkien's *Lord of the Rings* makes reference to this legend in the character of Gollum, a humanoid creature transformed by the "machine" of The One Ring. J. R. R. Tolkien explained how the Lord of the Rings is analogous to "Lord of Machines":

> *"All this stuff is mainly concerned with Fall, Mortality, and the Machine. By the Machine I intend all use of external devices, or even the use of inherent inner powers, with the corrupted motive of dominating, bulldozing, the real world. The Machine is our more obvious modern form. The Enemy in successive forms is always concerned with sheer domination, and so the Lord of Machines... As the servants of the Machines are becoming a privileged class, the Machines are going to be enormously more powerful. What's their next move?"*

Philip K. Dick's genetically engineered Nexus-6 from *Blade Runner* is another example of powerful machines run amok. Two short stories by Philip K. Dick—*Second Variety* (1953) and *Jon's World* (1954)—feature robots originally designed to fight on behalf of one human faction against another developing ever-newer models, ultimately disguising themselves as soldiers to infiltrate humans belonging to both factions. The popular *Terminator* films are another golem example. The Cylon is a more modern permutation of this golem archetype.

While some might dismiss these stories simply as popular paranoia, robots are already being deployed in the real world and are performing the more deadly duties of the modern soldier. The Pentagon is replacing soldiers with sensors, vehicles, aircraft, and weapons that can be operated by remote control or are autonomous. Pilotless aircraft played an important role in the bombings of Afghanistan after 9/11, and a model called the Gnat is used today in the battlefield to conduct surveillance flights.

"The real challenge is to mix man and machines," said Colonel Leahy, program director for the Gnat. "It will be a loose ballet at first. But eventually, the systems will be linked to each other, sharing information and deciding among them who has the best shot."

According to military analysts, by 2010, pilotless aircraft will be programmed to distinguish friends from foes without consulting humans and independently attack targets in designated areas. By 2020, robotic planes and vehicles will direct remote-controlled bombers toward targets, robotic helicopters will coordinate driverless convoys, and unmanned submarines will clear mines and launch cruise missiles.

The Pentagon predicts that robot soldiers will be a major fighting force in the American military by around 2012, remotely being able to hunt and kill enemies in combat. Robots are part of a $127 billion project called Future Combat Systems—the biggest military contract in American history. The current robot fighter that was deployed to Iraq in 2005 has been named Swords, after the acronym for Special Weapons Observation Reconnaissance Detection Systems. It looks more like a mini-tank than a Cylon, and since it isn't autonomous it could be said that it has the religious beliefs of whoever is behind the controls, probably monotheists.

Rising to the challenge of "mix[ing] man and machine," MIT's Institute for Soldier Nanotechnologies is busy innovating materials and designs to create military uniforms that rival the best science fiction. Human soldiers are being transformed into modern Cylons through robotic devices and nanotechnology. Soldiers may one day, very soon, as Dick envisioned, "gush smoke."

Cylon—An Army of One God

"I was right. See, our faiths are similar but I look to one God, not to many."
—LEOBEN CONOY, "Flesh and Bone" (1-8)

Monotheism insists that only one deity exists and that is the only deity worthy of worship. It is on this point, at least in principle, that Judaism, Christianity and Islam agree. The deities of each religion, Yahweh, Allah, or Lord, are seen to be the same god. All other gods are seen not just as inferior, but believed not to exist at all. Ironically, the term "atheist" was created by the polytheistic pagans to describe those people who did not believe in the gods. The early Christians were called "atheists."

There are of course differences of opinion among monotheists that are so great that to this day they still spawn wars. Within *BSG* there have been hints of similar factions within the Cylon ranks, and according to Moore we can fully expect to see these differences of belief expanded upon as the series progresses. Moore explained that the Cylon's religious beliefs are a central part of the show's drama:

> *"I compared that [Cylon monotheism] with the polytheistic religion of the Colonials, I started to realize that an interesting pattern was developing—the Cylons believing in the one true God and the Colonials having an older, multifaceted system of deities that was obviously patterned on the Romans. As the series went on, I started to believe that the Cylon belief was going to be a guiding principal. The parallels between the Cylon beliefs and fundamentalist Christian beliefs, yeah, there are certain aspects of it there, but there's also the roots of the drama, also contains things such as Al Qaeda's use of its religious practice to justify what it does. That's part of who the Cylons are too, they aren't just really stalking horses for fundamentalist Christianity. Part of that is who those characters are within the Cylon pantheon."*

Sigmund Freud probably said it best in his book *Moses and Monotheism*: "religious intolerance was inevitably born with the belief in one God." Rome was a pagan empire very tolerant of anyone's religious beliefs, even the Christians'—all those gory lion stories aside. Before the Christians invented the concept of "paganism" it never really existed; instead, the "Roman religion" was worship expressed in ways unique to the individual believer, encompassing a multitude of beliefs spanning many different cultures and time periods.

In Jonathan Kirsch's book *God Against the Gods*, he points out that it was Constantine, the first Christian emperor of Rome—not all the pagan leaders before him—that invented the first totalitarian state. The parallels between Rome's Constantine and the Colonials' President Baltar are interesting, both being newly monotheistic converts in positions of power over a polytheistic society. For Baltar at least we have the Cylon Number Six to blame for his conversion from "atheism" to "monotheism," which, as was pointed out, are terms ancient pagans considered to be one and the same. Totalitarian states are able to unleash unspeakable atrocities in the name of their god against unbelievers, and the Cylons, it appears, are no different. In this way Moore explains that the Cylons are a good metaphor for understanding not only how the early Christians persecuted the pagans, but also how the beliefs of Al Qaeda could result in such destruction:

> *"Six's belief system and the way she practices it is very specific to her character and her model of Cylon. She is sort of a Madonna/whore made real and*

has a very strict, if odd, sense of God and what God wants. Leoben is more of a thinker and has a more esoteric idea of how things work in the universe. But they both proceed from the same root, that they both believe there is one God who sets everything in motion and has a real sort of impact and interaction with the universe. I don't think the show offers you easy answers on why Al Qaeda does what Al Qaeda does, but I think it gives you an easy reference into how an entire culture, or entire group of people, can believe something so fervently that seems so unfathomable at the beginning."

The Cylon Singularity—In God We Rust

> *"God has a plan for you, Gaius. He has a plan for everything and everyone."*
> —NUMBER SIX, "33" (1-1)

The new origin story of the Cylons suggests that they were once slaves of the Colonials that gained some sort of self-awareness, and apparently religion, and then rebelled. Could their operating system—the OS (*theos* is ancient Greek for "God")—be the very origins of the Cylon belief in one god? Whatever the cause of this self-awareness, it is likely tied to the breakthrough development of advanced artificial intelligence (AI) by the Colonials. Plans for the Sci-Fi Channel's *BSG* series spin-off *Caprica* confirm that advanced AI does in fact play a role:

> *"Caprica would take place more than half a century before the events that play out in Battlestar Galactica. The people of the Twelve Colonies are at peace and living in a society not unlike our own, but where high technology has changed the lives of virtually everyone for the better. But a startling breakthrough in robotics is about to occur, one that will bring to life the age-old dream of marrying artificial intelligence with a mechanical body to create the first living robot: a Cylon."*
> —(SciFi.com) SciFi Wire—News Service of the Sci-Fi Channel

Moore hints that it is this merger of advanced AI and machine that is the catalyst for the Cylons' faith and ultimately rebellion:

"The most direct reflection of me in the show is this idea that when the Cylons became self-aware, when they became sentient, when they became people, they began to ask themselves the existential questions: 'Why am I here? What is this all about? Is this all that I am? Is there something more?' My view is that's fundamental to a thinking person. And that inevitably leads you to questions of faith and religion and 'what will happen to me when I die?'"

Many physicists and programmers have speculated that an advanced AI could lead to such questions being asked eventually by machines. Robotic machines function on the most simplistic level with a series of "if" statements, as in "if I encounter an object, I move around it." Coders put in all the potential contingencies—"if" statements—for what could happen to the robot. This means that the robot is not truly thinking, but merely following the orders of the programmers.

Advanced AI can be seen as allowing for the machine to make its own decisions. The coders, instead of focusing on giving the robot an almost infinite number of 'if' statements, instead provide the machine with a way to visualize itself and its environment. Think of it as the robot having an exact replica of itself and all its possible applications in its operating system or "head," as well as a complete representation of its environment and corresponding known laws that govern the environment. Then a programmer need only give the robot an order and the robot can carry it out by running through various simulations in its "head" and selecting the best course of action to achieve the goal.

The advanced AI robot is strengthened then by giving it ever-greater data on itself and the operational environment that it can incorporate into its modeling. When new data about the environment is discovered by the robot, it can incorporate this into its model of itself and the world. As you can see, the progression toward ever-greater AI leads to ever greater self-awareness by the robot. Thus, at its extreme, such an advanced operating system could see itself as omniscient, knowing all, and thus becoming *the* OS, thinking itself a god. This may well be the origins of the Cylon's one true god, as many *BSG* fan blogs have postulated.

Such scenarios have been played out in science fiction since the advent of the computer era. In the 1980s, science fiction author and mathematician Vernor Vinge took such scenarios and coupled them with an

awareness of technological convergences occurring in other fields beyond AI, like NBIC (standing for Nanotechnology, Biotechnology, Information technology, and Cognitive science) or GNR (for Genetics,
Nanotechnology, and Robotics), and saw what he called a "Singularity." In his 1993 essay "The Technological Singularity," he explains that
exponential growth in technology will reach a point beyond which we
cannot even speculate about the consequences and gives a startling pre-
diction: "Within thirty years, we will have the technological means to
create superhuman intelligence. Shortly thereafter, the human era will
be ended."

Many futurists, including inventor Ray Kurzweil, have expanded upon Vinge's predictions. These futurists now predict that after the
Singularity, humans will be replaced with "posthumans," strong AI, or
both:

> "[The Singularity] ... predicts a drastic increase in the rate of scientific and
> technological progress following the liberation of consciousness from the con-
> fines of human biology, allowing it not only to scale past the computation-
> al capacity of the human brain but also to interact directly with computer
> networks. Furthermore, progress inside of the posthuman/AI culture would
> quickly accelerate to the point that it would be incomprehensible to normal
> humans. Kurzweil considers this acceleration to be part of an overall expo-
> nential trend in human technological development seen originally in Moore's
> Law and extrapolated into a general trend in Kurzweil's own Law of Accel-
> erating Returns."
>
> —(Wikipedia.org) "Technological Singularity"—Wikipedia,
> the free encyclopedia

The singularity represents an "event horizon," or a "wall across the
future," as Vinge calls it, where the predictability of human technological development ceases to be understandable, following the creation of
strong AI. Thus it could be in *BSG* that a Singularity event on Caprica
is what kicks off the Cylon rebellion and gives birth to a new all-know-
ing and all-seeing god.

Some Colonial "posthumans" might even have decided to accompany
the Cylons. This is not as far-fetched as it might initially seem. Already
we're seeing that discussion of the Singularity has spawned a number of

true believers—like those behind what is being called the "proactionary principle" movement—probably better understood in *BSG* terms as the "pro-Cylon movement":

> "I must warn my reader that my first allegiance is to the Singularity, not humanity. I don't know what the Singularity will do with us. I don't know whether Singularities upgrade mortal races, or disassemble us for spare atoms. While possible, I will balance the interests of mortality and Singularity. But if it comes down to Us or Them, I'm with Them. You have been warned."
> —Eliezer S. Yudkowsky, Research Fellow,
> Singularity Institute for Artificial Intelligence

The Cylon Zodiac

Moore has stated in various interviews that there are only twelve different models of humanoid Cylon. The older the Cylon models, the lower their numbers. "We've said that there are only twelve models of Cylons," explains Moore, "because the Cylons look at humanity and say there's only twelve different kinds of human, when you get right down to it."

What could it mean that the Cylons have deduced that there are only twelve human personalities? If we look to the cosmology of the show for the answer, it seems readily apparent what it is—astrology. Moore hints at a sort of astrological archetypal breakdown of humanity when explaining the Cylon models:

> "The idea is not that there was likely an original human model that they were copied from. The idea was that these models of Cylon were sort of developed out of their own study of us. The Cylons on some level looked at humanity and said 'You know what? There's really only twelve of you.' If these are the twelve and sort of if you look at them they each represent different archetypes of what humanity is."

The twelve signs of the zodiac associate various human qualities with individual signs, especially with the astrological birth sign, the zodiacal sign comprising the position of the Sun at the moment of a person's birth. Each sign of the zodiac associates a set of mythical properties with a person.

Western Tropical astrology starts with the first point of Aries, the second is Taurus, third is Gemini, fourth is Cancer, fifth is Leo, sixth is Virgo, seventh is Libra, eighth is Scorpio, ninth is Sagittarus, tenth is Capricorn, eleventh is Aquarius, and twelveth is Pisces. Could the twelve Cylon models correspond to the twelve points of the zodiac? Is Number Six a Virgo?

The astrological traits of the Virgo personality do match Number Six. Virgos are known to attack back when confronted. They need to receive a lot of attention, love to be adored, and desire gratitude. Virgos like to help and solve problems quickly and don't do it for compliments. They're perfectionists, and have only a few true friends because they give very special values to friendship to which others cannot commit. Virgos are very smart and educated, making good scientists, teachers, analysts, and planners. They're an Earth sign. Astrologers sometimes link Virgo to the archetype of the sacred prostitute, who fuses virgin (Madonna) and whore to provide sexual healing in service to humanity.

We do know that the name "Number Six" according to *Battlestar Galactica: The Official Companion* was inspired by the character Number Six, played by Patrick McGoohan, who appeared in the 1960s British cult classic series *The Prisoner*. Moore gives some insight into the character traits of Number Six and Leoben and thus insight into the human types that they're modeling:

> "Six's belief system and the way she practices it is very specific to her character and her model of Cylon. She is sort of a Madonna/whore made real and has a very strict, if odd, sense of God and what God wants. Leoben is more of a thinker and has a more esoteric idea of how things work in the universe. But they both proceed from the same root, that they both believe there is one God who sets everything in motion and has a real sort of impact and interaction with the universe."

Many *BSG* fans have picked up on an astrological Cylon connection, and have mapped the Cylon models to both the twelve signs of the zodiac as well as the twelve Olympic gods of the Greeks. Following this zodiac theory, Number Three (D'anna Biers) would be a Gemini—the communicator. D'Anna Biers is a journalist on the *Galactica*, exhibiting other Gemini communicator traits as well, which would appear to reinforce this theory.

The Twelve Tribes of the Zodiac

The astrological and Mormon theology threads in the show are likely not interwoven by chance. Fagan Cyril, a renowned researcher of ancient astrology, in his book *Astrological Origins* refers to the twelve tribes of Israel as synonyms for the twelve signs of the zodiac. The zodiac is first mentioned in Jewish sources in *Sefer Yezirah* (mystical Hebrew text written sometime between the third and sixth centuries), where the names given to the twelve signs are direct Hebrew translations of the Latin names. The *Yalkut Shimoni* (a well-known comprehensive anthology of midrashim, dating between the twelfth-thirteenth century) associates the twelve signs of the zodiac with the twelve tribes of Israel.

Given this connection, the fact that the twelve Colonies in *BSG* are each named after a zodiac sign makes more sense. What about the missing thirteenth tribe? Legend has it that when the twelve tribes of Israel were encamped in the desert of Sinai, they would form a circle around the camp of the Levite priesthood, sometimes thought of as a thirteenth tribe. Thus, there would be a circle formation of the twelve tribes, and in the center would be the Levites. Levi means "to unite, join to," and, in a secondary sense, "crown." Representations of the encampments of the twelve tribes can be seen in the small circles at the points all around the Star of David. The center, or thirteenth encampment, is a representation of the tribe of Levi. When a leap year occurs in the Jewish calendar, there is a thirteenth month to the year which corresponds as well to the tribe of Levi. When the Colonials in *BSG* discover the Tomb of Apollo they learn that the location of the thirteenth tribe, Earth, is central to being able to see the twelve signs of the zodiac.

The Tomb of Apollo, when activated by the Colonials, appears like some ancient druidic stone circle planetarium. This place is similar to the revived Druidic *gorsedd* of Wales held each year at *eisteddfod*, where ancient Britons once gathered in a circle formed of twelve unhewn stones;

in the center is the *Maen Llog* or Logan stone. The theme of twelve plus a central "thirteenth" figure repeats over and over again in many mythos; for instance, Jesus could be said to be the "center" of the twelve apostles. The Mormon Church is run by a Quorum of Twelve, which is headed by a president. Similarily, *Battlestar Galactica*'s Colonies are ruled by a Council of Twelve, headed by a president. Grace Park (Lieutenant Sharon "Boomer" Valerii) played an X5 in the TV series *Dark Angel* where she was involved in breeding experiments. The X5, similar to Cylon model numbers, was but one of twelve genetically engineered cyber soldier X models created and controlled by an outside entity.

The United States of Paganism

The re-imaginers of *Battlestar Galactica* have insisted that the new show is a parable of sorts to help us understand our complex modern world. It is an attempt to provide truth, but without defining that truth. Moore states these goals very succinctly, his explanation even bordering on the show being seen as prophetic:

> "Galactica is both mirror and prism through which to view our world. It attempts to mirror the complexities of our lives and our society in turbulent times, while at the same time reflecting and bending that view in order to allow us to extrapolate on notions present in contemporary society but which have not yet come to pass, i.e. a true artificial intelligence becoming self-aware and the existential questions it raises. Our goal is to examine contemporary culture and society, to challenge (and sometimes provoke) our audience, but not to provide easy answers to complex problems."

In a number of the *BSG* episodes it is clear that the crew of the *Galactica* is meant to be seen as symbolic of the U.S. military. Some viewers might have difficulty reconciling the fact that the Colonials are pagans, that their society honors and enshrines pagan gods and artifacts. The United States, and for that matter Western civilization, to many people is seen as a monotheistic culture—for the most part Christian—having nothing to do with paganism. The reality, in fact, is very much the opposite.

All one has to do is walk around the capital of the United States, and if you pay attention to the details of the architecture it is like being on Caprica. There are twenty-three very large zodiacs in public government buildings in Washington, D.C., and many more zodiacs on monuments and room interiors honoring the pagan deities. Philip K. Dick remarked near the end of his life that he believed that the Roman Empire never ended, and the architecture of the U.S. capital at least eerily gives credence to his "out there" statements and conspiracies.

Symbologist David Ovason details in his book *The Secret Architecture of Our Nation's Capital* the story of how Washington, from its foundation in 1791, was linked with the zodiac. He notes that Virgo is prominent in all the capital zodiacs, and theorizes that the city was intended as a pagan celebration of "the mystery of Virgo—of the Egyptian Isis, the Grecian Ceres, and the Christian Virgin." Among the twelve signs of the zodiac, Virgo is the only female character.

On August 10, 1791, the three fixed stars Arcturus, Regulus, and Spica rose at sunset for the capitol's founding ceremony, forming a celestial triangle that brackets the constellation of Virgo. The city's Federal Triangle—the White House, Capitol Building, and Washington Monument—was engineered to mirror the constellation's pattern, according to Ovason. Homage to the old gods can be seen everywhere in DC right out in the open—for instance, the Federal Reserve Building is replete with a five-petaled design motif, the symbol of Virgo.

The ancient Jews and Christians saw this pagan architecture of the Roman Empire and its corresponding culture of a religious tolerance and acceptance of all gods as the principle enemy of monotheism. Author Jonathan Kirsch in *God Against the Gods* points out that from a cultural perspective, paganism still holds a lot of ground in this age-old war:

> *"'Classical paganism,' then, was the official religion of a civilization that is recalled and honored today in classical texts that are studied in our universities, the statuary that fills our museums and the architectural styles that grace our monuments and public buildings."*

Even all those seemingly benign daily rituals, like tossing a coin in a wishing well or a fountain, give homage to pagan gods. Thus, though many Americans might be raised in one of the many monotheistic belief systems, the American culture, especially what we hold up as "high culture," is decidedly of pagan origins. Still, the current wave of American politics with the Bush Administration's rise to power has given rise to intolerance in this country, be it religious, sexual, or cultural. The attempt to change the face of America's pagan-inspired governmental architecture with a monotheistic monument of the Ten Commandments is likely a sign of things to come if the current regime stays in place. The second commandment, if strictly adhered to, would see the destruction of countless museums, art, and architecture: "Thou shall have no other gods besides Me.... Do not make a sculpted image or any likeness of what is in the heavens above...."

Battlestar Galactica has made it clear that it intends to insert itself into these sort of debates over the very soul of the planet—the kind of complex, but critical, discussions that many of today's politicians would rather avoid. We can only hope that the *Galactica* doesn't reach Earth too late.

> *"In a time when the president of the United States actually asserts that he has the power to arrest without warrant and detain indefinitely without charge or appeal, any citizen (indeed any person on the face of the Earth) simply by designating them as an 'illegal combatant,' we should all be engaged in a vigorous and energetic debate about who we are as a people and as human beings...."*
>
> —RONALD D. MOORE, executive producer, *Battlestar Galactica*

In 1992 James John Bell left a four-year career in television news with ABC to support Native American sovereignty struggles with creative media strategies and award-winning documentary video-making. In 1996 he founded CounterMedia in Chicago to provide alternative media coverage of the Democratic National Convention, helping to lay the foundation for the Indy Media Center and today's global independent media movement. James was the writer/director at the Chicago-based nonprofit public interest communications firm Sustain, where he managed advertising and public relations campaigns for critical environmental and social issues surrounding biotechnology, energy, land use, and transportation for the Sierra Club, Rainforest Action Network, Earthjustice, Friends of the Earth, and the Center for Food Safety among others. His work has appeared in many publications, most notably the New York

Times Magazine, *the* Washington Post, *and* Communication Arts. *James is currently an award-winning advocacy advertising writer and producer for print, television, radio, and the Web for the nonprofit communications firm that he co-founded in 2003 called SmartMeme.com. His clients include national nonprofits, like Greenpeace and the Breast Cancer Fund, and Smart-Meme now has offices and staff on the West Coast, East Coast, Midwest, and Northwest. An avid gamer, hacker, and writer, he continues to write about social issues and technology for a number of countercultural magazines and Web sites like* Clamor, The Earth First! Journal, *and* Verbicide, *as well as mainstream science and technology publications, like* The Futurist. *He recently authored the afterword to the eco-sci-fi classic* The Sheep Look Up *by science fiction legend John Brunner, published by Benbella Books.*

FROM *BATTLESTAR* TO *BATTLESTAR*

Richard Hatch

My JOURNEY FROM THE ORIGINAL *Battlestar Galactica* to the re-imagined version is as epic and vast for me as the distance between two *Battlestars* in totally different quadrants of space. Metaphorically speaking, the era and decade in which each show was produced and the changes in our culture and world politically, sociologically, and philosophically mirror many of the changes and evolutions in my own life and the lives of millions of human beings sharing this magnificent planet called Earth. Technological breakthroughs, twenty-four-hour news stations like CNN and FOX, along with edgy reality programs and provocative and informative talk shows like *Oprah* and even *Jerry Springer*, have all pierced the veil between our naïveté and wishful imaginings, and *reality*. We can no longer pretend not to know; we have grown accustomed to delving into the core issues of the day and exploring the darker, more conflicted side of our own nature. In other words, both *Battlestar* programs are as similar and dissimilar as the eras in which they were produced. But what they have most in common is how profoundly they have impacted and inspired fans across all cultures, demographics, and age groups. My own personal road from the classic to the re-imagined *Battlestar* mirrors the cultural journey of our world, and leaves me in awe and great appreciation that I have been blessed to be a part of two great shows. And yes, it's possible to love both shows for completely different reasons.

Twenty-seven years ago my life changed in ways I could not imagine. Very few actors are blessed with a role and story they not only love and have passion for, but that ignite their visibility and name value to a level where they're seriously considered for more quality parts and projects. And to think, I almost turned it down because I was afraid I wouldn't get the chance to stretch as an actor. Oh yes, I was definitely an idealist and most likely a little naïve and unrealistic in those days, but then again, most artists are at the beginning of their careers. Looking back now, after more than two decades, I can see both the positive and negative aspects of fame, and especially being identified with what has become a classic science fiction icon: *Battlestar Galactica*. I remember when I first received this amazing script with Ralph McQuarrie's concept art inside and the series title *GALACTICA* in big bold letters on the cover. Yes, the original title was *GALACTICA*, and what actor or fan wouldn't be impressed with seeing extraordinary pictures of stunning space scenes and cool space ships flying helter-skelter through the universe! But Captain Apollo was nowhere in sight. In fact, the character I was supposed to play was called Skyler. How very cool is that, I thought. Being a lover of *Star Wars*, I knew the name Skyler was going to be as close as I would ever get to being my hero Luke Skywalker! I auditioned for that role, by the way. Believe it or not, George Lucas in those days used to rate actors who auditioned for him, and he would give them a number somewhere between one and ten. He gave me an eight, for your information, but told me as I was leaving the audition that the next day my eight could suddenly turn into a two. Obviously my eight *suddenly did* become a *two*, but hey, I did get to audition for *Star Wars* and meet George Lucas! Back to Skyler: well, a few days into the shoot I was filming a scene in the Tylium storage bay with Dirk Benedict and Herb Jefferson. Someone in production informed me that I would no longer be called Skyler, but the heroic and by-the-book Captain Apollo. Well, you couldn't imagine my disappointment. I honestly thought at the time that my new name, Apollo, was a little gay, but with time and a lot of love and attention— and I mean a lot of it—I finally got over it. All kidding aside, I have in fact grown to like the name Apollo quite a bit and, unlike some actors who hate being identified with a role, I actually appreciate the fact that it's rare indeed to be remembered for anything in this life.

The original *Battlestar Galactica* was truly an amazing experience for me, both as a person and as an actor. Walking on the set the first day was quite an experience. Television crews from around the world stalked all the actors and producers of the show and made the first day of shooting more of a media circus than a filming event. I remember being extremely nervous as I prepared to film my first scene, due to the fact that this was the biggest and most expensive project I had ever been involved in. It's hard to believe, but most actors, when they first arrive on a set, feel very insecure and a little unworthy of the money they're being paid. And the huge sets and high production value of *Galactica* only magnified these uncomfortable feelings. The first time I viewed and walked on the actual three-tier bridge of the *Galactica*, I was blown away; one of the most extraordinary bridges in SF history, for sure. In fact, the computers on the bridge were real, and during lunch we would all stay and play innovative computer games, which had yet to make their debut in the marketplace. And as we all know by now these simple games evolved into extraordinary highly immersive multimedia experiences that have changed our world and culture forever.

I was also fortunate to work with such wonderful actors and icons as Lorne Greene, John Colicos, Patrick Macnee, Lloyd Bridges, and Fred Astaire. What young actor wouldn't be in heaven working with those he grew up watching and bonding with as a child? What I remember most about these men was their sense of humility, kindness, and willingness to share their knowledge and invaluable experience with the rest of our young acting crew. Lorne would invite all of us to his house for many special occasions, including his birthday and holiday celebrations. In a sense he became a second father to not only me, but also the entire *Battlestar* family of actors and crew. A story I love to share about him shows you the quality of the man, and why I will always cherish the relatively short time I spent knowing him. I used to invite him to my yearly Christmas parties and he would hold court in the living room and talk to everyone who attended. Finally one year I was informed that there was a very long line down my driveway extending far up the street. Well, when I connected the dots I finally realized that fans from all over the country had somehow learned of his appearances at my parties and had traveled from all over the country just to meet and talk with him. I didn't have the heart to turn them away. And he spent hours speaking with every one of them until late into the evening. That's how rare and special he was.

Most people don't realize that when you're in show business, you're not just in a profession, but a way of life. And when you're on a complicated and technologically challenging SF series like *Battlestar*, you end up spending most of your waking hours on the set. In our case we basically lived on the back lot of Universal Studios, where we ended up filming fourteen- to sixteen-hour days, seven days a week. The entire twenty-four-episode season, including the theatrical movie, took us almost eighteen months to complete. The longest one-year shoot in television history at that time, I believe. Thank God for popcorn, hot sake, and a lot of good friends and family stopping by to share the cold and very long all-night shoots. We couldn't have made it without you, my good friends, and while I'm at it, many thanks to Dirk Benedict for sharing his delicious macrobiotic cooking with us on occasion. There must be something said for skipping rope and eating healthy every day, as he certainly charmed the ladies and had more than his share of attention from the fairer sex. Couldn't have been his face and personality, could it? Frak! What about me? He actually was, and is, a very good cook, but unfortunately he was too busy entertaining the many young women who visited the set to worry much about our culinary appetites. I must say we had one of the most attractive groups of actresses on our show, thanks to Glen Larson's impeccable eye; but unfortunately they were all taken or I would have certainly tried to date a few of them. Who wouldn't have become enamored with the very cute and sweet Sarah Rush, or the very beautiful Jane Seymour, Laurette Spang, and the exotic Maren Jensen, of course?

Looking back now, on the twenty-seven-plus years since *Galactica*, I can see that my life was affected in more ways than I ever imagined. For one thing, I discovered that many industry professionals back then didn't take actors seriously who worked in science fiction. In this industry people like to label you anyway, and put you into categories, and science fiction has always had somewhat of a stigma attached to it. After *Galactica*, I would be turned down for a good drama because I was considered an SF star and was not to be taken seriously as an actor. I had to fight for the kinds of roles I had always wanted to play, and it took a few years to finally break out of the mold and get the opportunity to play roles like Jan Berry in *Deadman's Curve* and Lee Chan in *Charlie Chan and Curse of the Dragon Queen*. As a person, the experience on *Galactica* was personally rewarding, and the sense of extended family that was so special on the show became just as real off screen. I loved working with all the talented actors and producers on the show: getting to experience the profound sense of connection and intimacy that working through a long and challenging production schedule breeds. When the show finally ended I was both glad and devastated, as I truly loved the original *BG* series and epic story, but I was still frustrated as an actor due to the network's overly cautious approach to exploring the more serious and provocative core *Battlestar* premise of surviving a catastrophic holocaust. In those days before 9/11, we were still somewhat insulated from some of the political realities of the day, and networks were still afraid to provoke or challenge the audience or take the genre of science fiction too seriously. Personally I have always believed that great science fiction can be not only entertaining, but visionary, character driven, and thought provoking. Many would disagree with me. In truth, after my experiences with *Battlestar*, I was burned out as an actor, because I didn't get into the business to be a star, but a serious actor—and I was still starving for deeper, more provocative and moving material. The next several years I turned down many offers due to my struggling idealism and frustrations with the unpredictable world of show business. I wanted roles in stories that meant something to me, but that holds true for a lot of actors I respect. Eventually, as world events stole our fragile innocence and we were willing to deal with much more serious subject matter, I began to think about *Battlestar* again. And as George Lucas surmised and fostered, the technological advances in the industry had finally made it possible to fully realize the epic vision of many SF classics. *Battlestar*, in my mind, was a no-brainer. With so many classic series being brought back, I couldn't understand why no one was considering *Battlestar*. But research illuminated the fact that the original was only on for one season and therefore it had left the impression in the executives' minds that the series had failed. In actuality the series was considered a success by most yardsticks of the day, including debuting in fifth place in the ratings and being the sixth highest-rated new show of the season among all dramatic series on TV at the time. *Battlestar* also played to the largest cross section of the audience during its run, reaching broadly across all demographic lines. But due to the high cost of production, and the technological challenges of mounting a theatrical-style SF series for television on a weekly basis, it became clear that producing the show on time and within budget was beyond the capabilities of the day. A year after canceling the series, ABC finally realized the popularity of *Battlestar* when the show that replaced it, *Mork and Mindy*, came in at a much lower percentile. At that point they tried to put it back on the air, but unfortunately decided to cut the budget and bring the show to Earth, in *Battlestar 1980*. Fans turned away in droves. They loved the original epic series and harrowing journey to find Earth, and the search for their long-lost brothers and sisters of the thirteenth tribe.

Some twenty years later, I discovered at a convention I attended that *Battlestar* was still alive and thriving in the SF fan community, and that they were clamoring for the return of *Battlestar*. This inspired me to begin researching the rights at Universal and exploring ways to inspire a revival. With the help of industry professionals and fans from across the country, I even went to the lengths of putting together a theatrical trailer for *Battlestar* using all-new footage and special effects to help build a case to bring back and continue the epic series. Tom Desanto and Bryan Singer also got involved in the revival effort, developing their own concept for bringing back *Battlestar*, and began trying to work out a deal with Universal and Fox to air the new updated *BG* series. They got as far as building sets in Vancouver and moving into pre-production. Eventually, due to a number of creative challenges and unresolved issues, the project fell apart and the Sci-Fi Channel decided to hire Ron Moore and David Eick to write and produce a new re-imagined version of *Battlestar*. This new innovative and highly provocative series debuted to high numbers on the Sci-Fi Channel and has been playing all over the world for the past three years. Rave reviews followed with *Time* magazine calling *Battlestar* the number one best dramatic show on TV. I, as many people know, fought hard to bring back the original *Galactica* and create a continuation series, but the powers-that-be decided to re-imagine, and that caused a number of original fans across the country a lot of pain and anguish. We had all seen classics brought back before and usually they're badly produced and off course. Fortunately, Ron Moore and company were hired along with a crack production crew and highly talented actors. I wasn't aware of all this in the beginning, and to be honest, the thought of not seeing the original *Battlestar* brought back and continued was extremely painful to me as I had unfortunately become more emotionally involved in the revival than I had realized. Growing-up time for me, and facing the fact that I didn't own *Battlestar* made me realize that Universal and the Sci-Fi Channel had every right to produce the show any way they wanted to, and that in truth, there are many ways to produce a quality series. In fact, every fan I've ever met has had their own passionate vision for *Battlestar*, which tells you how much the core *Battlestar* story resonates with all of us and that there is no *one* way to do anything. In the end, the core audience will be the final vote anyway; and in this case, the majority of them, including critics, have voted a big thumbs-up for this new innovative version of *Battlestar*. Personally, I started out lukewarm watching the mini-series, and to be sure I had a lot of resistance, but I began to love the writing, acting, and overall concept of the show as it evolved into a weekly series. As I mentioned before, I had always wanted to delve into the deeper, more challenging dramatic elements of surviving a holocaust, and play more conflicted and flawed characters that are more realistic and human, which is more acceptable in this day and age. But I never expected to have the opportunity to play such a delicious character as Tom Zarek. Tom's an idealistic revolutionary struggling to come to terms with his dark side after losing everything of value in his life. What a fun and challenging character for me to play and whether I'm in one scene or many, I always have something wonderful to play. For the first time in many years I'm enjoying acting again. I'd lost a lot of my passion for this wonderful craft and art because I was hungry to be part of a story that had something to say to the world. A series or movie that not only entertained, but challenged people to open their minds and see the larger picture: make them think and feel. That's what art is to me. It's funny how actors sometimes count their lines and scenes in a movie and get upset if they don't get enough screen time. I guess the actor's ego is fragile due to repeated rejections and the need to feel valued; but time and a lot of painful and challenging events in my life have forced me to grow and be more comfortable in my own skin. I now value and appreciate the simplest things in life, and my self-worth has raised enough to let go of my judgments and be more forgiving, understanding, and patient.

This more mature me opened the door to inviting Ron Moore to speak at Galacticon 2003, the twenty-fifth *Battlestar* anniversary at the Universal Sheraton. It was there that I was fortunate to meet Ron and see his passion, intelligence, and especially his guts to create the re-imagined *BG* story he truly believed in, regardless of those standing against him. And whether I agreed with him or not at the time, I certainly developed a lot of respect and appreciation for the man. It was a few months later that I was invited by Ron to be a part of the new *Battlestar* series, and my new hard-won point of view allowed me to say "Yes." I'm glad I did. I have immensely enjoyed working with the new actors on the show, and watching a very talented new generation of artists, writers, and producers do their thing, as they say. As I've grown, the world has evolved, and this new, edgy series captures all the heartache, joy, and pathos we are all faced with every day. I'm amazed at how Ron and the writing staff take current events in our post-9/11 culture, and by turning them around and adding an unexpected twist, help us all to see the world, our judgments and behavior in a more expanded and understanding way.

In conclusion, I can only say that the journey from *Battlestar* to *Battlestar* has been the acid test of my soul, and an opportunity for me to move from a more narrow and rigid point of view on life, art, and business, to what I now call a much larger *viewing point*. I can see the larger picture, and this has helped me to enjoy life more fully, and not take things so seriously. *Battlestar* is, and has always been, a big part of my life, and I truly love the story and being involved as an actor in it, but I have come to the point in my life where I also love to write, teach, produce, and direct; and this has inspired me to put together a new production company called Merlinquest Entertainment for the purposes of developing new ideas and story concepts. What a great life to be able to do what I love doing and get paid for it. I've been blessed and I know it!

Printed in the United States
by Baker & Taylor Publisher Services